'Newman's noir teams Boris Karloff with Raymond Chandler to solve gothic crimes in a 1930s Hollywood full of man-made monsters, dodgy movie studios, and ice-cold gimlets. Written in a James Ellroy rat-a-tat it's the perfect book for a summer afternoon by the pool with plenty of cocktails. If more mysteries were written like this, I'd read more mysteries.'

Grady Hendrix, author of *The Final Girl Support Group*

'Monsters and mobsters and movie sets, oh my! Only Kim Newman could have written this glorious, insane noir mash-up.'

M.R. Carey, author of *The Book of Koli*

'Kim Newman is the first to spot that between the worlds of Philip Marlowe and Frankenstein's monster is an LA-noir sweet spot where crime and horror overlap. His odd-couple pairing of Boris Karloff and Raymond Chandler is a genius crime-solving idea that pays off big time; hard-bitten, tender and a killer double bill for film lovers.'

Christopher Fowler, author of the Bryant & May Mysteries

'Movies, monsters and Kim Newman's sharp wit – what a treat!'

Sarah Pinborough, bestselling author of Netflix's *Behind Her Eyes*

'*Something More Than Night* is what happens when an encyclopaedic knowledge of film collides with pulp noir and turns Raymond Chandler's already mean streets into something altogether more eldritch and nasty. Classic Kim Newman.'

Jon Courtenay Grimwood

'Kim Newman is slowly making his way into the canon of English literary greats, where he'd be both entirely at home and deeply uncomfortable. He describes perfectly the way fiction has invaded our real lives, and he got there first.'

Paul Cornell, author of *Witches of Lychford*

SOMETHING MORE THAN NIGHT

KIM NEWMAN

TITAN BOOKS

Something More Than Night
Print edition ISBN: 9781789097719
E-book edition ISBN: 9781789097740

Published by Titan Books
A division of Titan Publishing Group Ltd.
144 Southwark Street, London SE1 0UP
www.titanbooks.com

First edition: November 2021
10 9 8 7 6 5 4 3 2 1

A CIP catalogue record for this title is available from
the British Library.

Printed and bound in the United States

For Robert Chandler and Billy Chainsaw

[The characters of hardboiled detective fiction] 'lived in a
world gone wrong, a world in which, long before the atom bomb,
civilization had created the machinery for its own destruction, and
was learning to use it with all the moronic delight of a gangster
trying out his first machine gun. The law was something to
be manipulated for profit and power. The streets were dark
with something more than night.'

Raymond Chandler, Introduction to *Trouble is My Business* (1950)

'Having gone through the greatest epic of struggle I have ever
heard in Hollywood, Boris Karloff is a mellow and sad man...
He has the appearance of a rajah. His eyes are dreamy, defeated,
tragic; the eyes of a man who has suffered much...
He does not seem to be in tune with the materialistic world. I would
hazard the guess that he may often find it hard to keep his dreamy
and poetical nature in rhythm with modern life.
Unfailingly polite, he is nevertheless aloof. There is a rose in his soul
which the searing wind of Hollywood has never touched.'

Jim Tully, 'Alias the Monster', *The New Movie Magazine* (1932)

PROLOGUE

THE STYX

1

Real drinkers make good murder suspects.

Amateur souses establish alibis wherever the bender takes them. The pie-eyed sot blundering into the floorshow has a club full of witnesses to testify he was across town from the alley where his former business partner got gunned. The loud, sozzled sister lodges in the memory of the waiter who has to mop up her vomitus on the evening when her husband was defenestrated in another state. Cops give such Saturday night lushes the lightest of grillings before turning the spotlight on the next most likely suspect.

Serious drunks slide through shadows.

Those ferociously intent on poisoning themselves body and soul do so alone. Their step quickens under street lights and slows in the darks between. Coat collars up, hat-brims low. They favour dim holes with short-sighted bartenders who know no names. They leave behind only moist circles.

They could be guilty of anything.

Sometimes – too often – that's the stripe of drinker I am. Fuzzy on dates and places, unclear about what I've done and with or to whom. Not sure whether the night's monsters were half-way unreal.

Oh, that's another thing.

There *are* monsters.

I have seen their faces and I know their names.

...

It was late 1931 or early '32. As I mentioned, dates get fuzzy.

I was in the habit of working conscientiously from nine till one, then drinking at (or for) lunch. A belt or two often turned into a bottle or more. Afternoons seldom found me returning to the twelfth-floor offices of the Dabney Oil Syndicate, above the Bank of Italy on South Olive Street. Secretaries covered for me, if they were so disposed... and didn't when they'd had enough. They always had enough in the long run.

The firm kept me on – at the rank of Vice-President – because they got a good morning's work. Paperwork was done, briskly and with precision. The hot thumbtacks behind my eyes didn't cloud my head for figures. My British accent lent their piratical concern an air of respectability. Not that I'm British – I was born in Chicago. But I am an English public school man. That means something, even at three or four sheets to the wind.

The title of Vice-President was misleading. I was a superior sort of bookkeeper, labouring under the handicap of being reasonably honest in a crooked business. No one in California oil – even in offices with rose-pink Tennessee marble floors – avoids getting their hands dirty as derrick wrenches. My manners convinced investors they weren't being robbed. Under me, lesser bookkeepers pumped adding machines as if they might pay out tokens. A percentage of our stenographers couldn't type above three words a minute but were eager to persuade out-of-town clients they'd had a fine old time in Los Angeles.

In most cities, dirty money smells like a newly printed slick magazine, so sharp you can cut your throat with a ten-spot. LA bills are soft, grubby with petroleum. Rolled between fingertips, they feel damp as orchid petals. Touch a lit match to one and it flares like magician's flash-paper. All that's left is ash and a stain. And a smell you stop noticing after a while.

In the dying days of the Herbert Hoover Administration, alcohol was illegal in these United States. The dedicated wine-bibber had to seek premises with no visible street address, knuckle-rap on a steel door, remember a foolish password and know a friend of Sam's. The government-approved stock of earlier and later years was not served. No federal snoopers checked for impurities, calculated alcohol percentages or ensured absence of rat-pellets. In actuarial terms, I was at less risk charging enemy machine guns in the Great War than I was downing paraffin gimlets in times of peace.

Drinking wasn't done in gay public places either – but in cellars, vacant lots and back-rooms. My preferred afternoon avenues to oblivion were second- or third-run movie theatres. Not the two-thousand-seater picture palaces on Broadway, with Versailles mirrors and plaster sphinxes, but concrete boxes called the Rex or the Lux – or perhaps the Styx. You were ushered to a row of bolted-together dentists' chairs and charged fifteen times the price of admission for a bottle in a brown paper bag with 'peanuts' written on it.

Smoke ghosts swirled in the projector beam, gold-digger legs dancing and cowboy guns puffing. Auditoria rattled with the tinny sounds movies made when they first started to talk. Characters set off firecrackers, tap-danced, honked car-horns and breathed husky songs. I did not patronise such places as a devotee of the cinematic arts. Or as an admirer of Miss Janet Gaynor or Strongheart the Wonder Dog.

I was only here for the peanuts.

That afternoon, the picture was *Frankenstein*.

Little of the original remained. My third form at Dulwich College scorned Mrs Shelley's novel as insufficiently terrifying fudge. Her Monster was as given to quoting Milton out of context and at length as our tedious house master. Schoolboy sophisticates with a yen for the horrors preferred the much-confiscated ghost stories of M.R. James. In a rare instance of American literary pride, I argued for Robert W. Chambers' *The King in Yellow*. Now, *that's* a frightening book.

My eye was occasionally drawn to the screen.

After murky doings in a graveyard, *Frankenstein* settled into drawing-room guff staged and played to the standard of a 1910 touring production of *Mrs Tanqueray's Past*. A soppy blonde and her second-string swain drew hoots from the back row.

A dwarf with a tiny cane scuttled around a laboratory. A brain in a jar was stolen. The *wrong* brain. This abnormal cerebellum was sewn into the skull of the bandaged giant. The subject was hoisted up to the eaves in a crackle of electric arcs while cabinets of machinery fizzed and flashed.

I was disturbed by Henry Frankenstein, maker of the Monster. His haggard cheeks reminded me of the haunted mask that floated in my shaving mirror. A fellow drinker, I figured. The actor's accent gave him away as another English public school man.

'It's alive, it's alive, it's moving… it's *al-i-eve!*'

The picture abandoned the drawing room for a stone-clad ruin, a cathedral filled with purposeless contraptions. I felt lightning strikes in my temples, my spine, my teeth.

I was on my second peanut bag when the Monster appeared.

Movies were getting clever with monsters. Before the Vitaphone, Lon Chaney would tear off a mask and stick his face – all eyes and teeth – into the camera. The orchestra (and the audience) provided the mute heroine's scream. At such moments, my friend Warren Lloyd and I would sit at opposite sides of the theatre and laugh out loud. Audiences can be infected with forced, inappropriate hilarity. The experiment was usually a roaring success. Two or three times, I got popped in the eye or kicked into the foyer. I lacked Warren's talent for defusing the wrath of those who resented being drafted as sociology specimens on their evenings out.

Lon Chaney had died, talkies were all the rage and Hollywood had a vacancy for a bogey man.

In the opening credits, the actor playing Frankenstein's Monster was billed as '?'. Question Mark. Had Mr Carl Laemmle of Universal Pictures scouted the freak shows of the world for a stitched-together face? Plenty of broken mugs were around. Broken minds too.

The audience at the Styx was sparse. Not a few had peanut bags. Some even munched peanuts. The film fostered apprehension. We were grown-ups, no longer scared of ghosties and goblins. A good percentage of us had been through the War. We lived in a country where cops could knock you down or lock you up for having a hip-flask. But I could *feel* the fear. I was a part of it. A *frisson* can be delicious, like the thrill of turning a page to find out what horrors lurk in *The King in Yellow*. Years on, the anticipation of fright wasn't a tingle but a knife to the throat. We grew sick as impatience blended with dread.

The actors not playing monsters were shrill. Was the film running fast?

The fug of drink usually slows time. Rat-tat-tat tommy guns in a gangster picture sound like the parp-parp-parp of a flatulent frog. Here, the doctor, the girl, the swain and even the dwarf hurried through their lines as if they wanted the curtain rung down before sunset, afraid to walk home in the dark.

After the spectacle of electric vivification came earnest talk of infinity and promethean ambition... and finally the entrance of the Monster.

A door opened. Did it creak? It ought to have.

Bulky shoulders in a workman's jacket. Big boots. That flat head.

No one breathed.

At that time, I was – in Hollywood terms – a civilian. I knew stars by name but had no idea what a director did. I had heard of Mary W. Shelley, but not James Whale. He was the madman who directed *Frankenstein*, the *real* maker of monsters. Whale didn't have Question Mark pop up like Lon Chaney-in-a-box or clutch like the Cat who clawed the Canary. Whale opened the door and had the Monster walk into the room *backwards*. The first we saw was the rear of his misshapen head, terminals on his neck, black hair lank.

I wanted to raise the wrapped bottle, but my hands didn't work. The world was out of focus, pictures wavering on dust motes, but the screen was clear and fifty yards across.

Question Mark turned to the audience.

Those eyes – heavy lids, inkblot irises, clear agony. That twist of a mouth. The black cheek sore, like potato blight. A gaunt martyr's face. A Monster, all right – assembled on a slab at Universal Pictures, shocked to life by stage lightning. But also... another English public school man.

The audience did not laugh. A small boy shrieked.

Cuts brought the Monster's face closer, made it bigger. A looming moon of hurt.

The horror was that I knew that face.

I knew what those eyes had seen.

'*Billy*,' I exclaimed involuntarily, '*Billy Pratt!*'

PART ONE

MALIBU PIER

2

A telephone call at 2.30 a.m. is never good news.

At the first ring, Taki's claws hooked through my pants, pricking the meat of my thighs. Our cat, mistress of the house, arched her back, fur rising like porcupine spines. I shooed her off my lap and picked up the phone.

'Raymond Chandler, speaking,' I said.

'R.T.,' came that insidious whisper, 'it's Billy.'

I knew who it was even before he gave his name. In this hemisphere, only Billy uses my initials. And, of course, his voice is famous.

At the muffled sound of him, Taki relaxed.

Cats love Billy. As do women. And small children he hasn't drowned.

William Pratt is now known as Boris Karloff.

Nine or so years previously, he gave me a shock in *Frankenstein*. Not like the shock he gave everyone else. My terror was more intimate – a shock of familiarity, of *remembering*...

Nearly thirty years before *Frankenstein*, in a cricket pavilion in England, Billy became my secret brother. So he remains, decades on at the far edge of the United States. The story that explains our association is one – as the fusty, careless Conan Doyle would have it – 'for which the world is not yet prepared'. Translated into language people might actually use, coughing up that yarn would be a one-way ticket to the booby-hatch.

Radio comedians who do 'Boris Karloff' pretend he has a lisp. But no little bird flutters in Billy's upper register. His susurrus never slurs to mush, just hints that it *might*. As the Mummy, he deftly sidestepped elephant trap phrases like 'the scroll of Thoth'. His real imitable tic is a slight elongation of the vowels, like the mid-word pause a vicar takes to suppress a nasty notion about a parishioner in the third pew.

An English public school voice, ostensibly mild rather than monstrous – yet with something sinister in it. His eye-gleam is simultaneously a twinkle of charm and a glint of malice.

Billy plays monsters because he understands them.

Monsters can sport an old school tie. Many do.

A ghost in blue pyjamas appeared at the door of my study.

'Raymio,' she whispered in reproach – more chilling than a call from the talking screen's reigning Demon King.

Taki padded over to the ghost and licked her lacquered toes.

'R.T.? Are you still there?'

'I'm sorry, Billy,' I said. 'It's Cissy.'

'Ah, your sweet white-haired mother. Give the old dear my best wishes.'

'It's Billy Pratt,' I said.

The ghost vanished, pulling shut my study door.

My wife closes doors on any part of me that disappoints or frightens her. She locks her own doors too. We share much, but not everything. She keeps the secret of her true age as *djinni* conceal the names that give sorcerers power over them. I do not expose her, too much, to the drinking – now it's legal, I am mostly dry – or the secretaries. Or the monsters.

Cissy sleeps through most nights. I do not.

We change addresses often, as if dodging bailiffs… or, as it would have been in the pulp magazines that butter my crusts, on the run from a remorseless, methodical killer who would eventually poke a gun-barrel through the door-crack of any hideout. Cissy and I hole up in rented apartments and small houses, moving out of the city and then back to its fringes. Monrovia, Arcadia, Pacific Palisades. No-places, mostly – a fair drive from anywhere people have heard of. The air heavy with sea salt, oil stink, desert wind and scents of flora nurtured with stolen water. Mimosa, manzanita, grevillea, yarrow, hummingbird sage.

I was eventually cashiered from Dabney Oil for bringing the profession of rapine and banditry into disrepute through spotty attendance, persistent drunkenness and misconduct with female office staff (secretaries). After that, I spent a long decade honing a new craft, equally inimical to polite company and far less remunerative.

I write mysteries. Not novels, not books – mysteries.

In outline, I have a non-mystery set to go. *English Summer*, subtitled *A Gothic Romance*. It has just one murder in it. P. Marlowe, Esq. wouldn't get out of bed for just one murder. After I shove Marlowe over a waterfall, I'll write about manners and morals rather than mugs and murders. Manners and morals are fit subjects for novels. Cissy, not a devoted *Black Mask* reader, says my stories are romances at bottom. My questing knights wear hats rather than helms and brandish automatics rather than lances.

'Is it *her*?' I asked Billy.

Cissy says all the she-cats in my stories – the blondes in need of rescue, the dark ladies with guns in handbags – are portraits of our Taki's moods. One reason I stay unfashionably married despite proximity to America's divorce resorts is that my wife is my most perceptive, imaginative critic. Alexander Woollcott wouldn't look half so good in blue pyjamas – and, besides, I doubt he's a natural redhead.

I don't disabuse Cissy about my *belles dames sans merci*.

My wife doesn't need to know about Ariadne.

Billy didn't breathe the name either… but I usually heard from him when her great wings beat and palms bent in the backwash.

'It's *not* her,' he said. 'Though she's in it, I'm sure.'

In horror movies, Frankenstein's Monster had a Bride and Dracula a daughter – ghosts of Ariadne, who retired from acting before those scripts were written. In her brief screen career, she might have been one of the spectre concubines in *Dracula*, the pale blonde with dark sisters.

Her face never changes – a girl's, with ancient eyes. Green eyes, threaded with red.

She hadn't followed us from Dulwich drizzle to Hollywood sunshine. If anything, we were drawn in her wake. After knocking about the world, Billy and I both ended up where dreams were made. The fountains of terror and wonder.

21

At the other end of the line, I heard rain and the crash of waves.

'Where are you?'

'Malibu Pier,' said Billy. 'You know the one.'

'I ought to. It's where I killed that bloody chauffeur.'

'Ah, so you *do* know who did it? Is that a confession?'

'Yes, I with my typewriter, I killed the chauffeur. Strictly, he killed himself – wedged the pedal and aimed the big black Buick at the ocean.'

'Did you also take off the unfortunate's face – and the greater part of his noggin – with a shotgun?'

'No,' I winced. 'I have *some* standards. I don't write *your* sort of story.'

'Someone does,' he said. 'Someone imagines your sort of story and my sort of story mixed together. Mystery and horror.'

'You didn't call in the middle of the night to discuss which pulp to sneak off the stands – *Dime Detective* or *Terror Tales?*'

'No, I'm with the police. You know the police. They aren't overly fond of you.'

'I shouldn't wonder.'

'Ah, but they love *me*. Murder children on the silver screen and everyone loves Uncle Boris. Sneer at coppers in a mucky book and you've enemies for life.'

I had a spasm. Did I have an alibi?

Even sober, I make a good murder suspect.

Taki side-eyed me as if she knew I was guilty. She'd rat me out in a second, for all that she was loved, fed and made obeisance to. The feline would land a new sugar daddy as easily as a showgirl gaffs her next monied scion.

'Have you been arrested?' I asked.

'Good Lord no. The bracelets slapped on an Uppinghamian! It would never do. I am, sad to say, merely called on to identify the corpse.'

'The fellow without a face?'

'Indeed. And not wearing a chauffeur's uniform.'

'The dead man went off the pier in a car?'

'A big black sedan. Does that sound familiar?'

It did and Billy knew it would. *The Big Sleep*, my first book-length mystery, features a similar incident. That corpse is Owen Taylor, chauffeur to the Sternwood family. P. Marlowe expresses only minor interest in a below-stairs fatality he has not been hired to investigate. Therefore, little thought is given to the question of whether Taylor ended his own life or was murdered. The loose end flaps.

If Chandler, R.T. had known so many readers, professional and amateur, would find the flunky's demise so fascinating a subject, he'd have clipped a coroner's report to the typescript. The world should have moved on but we were back to poor inconsistent Owen Taylor, who only appeared in *The Big Sleep* as a corpse. Someone invented only to be killed off. Mystery readers demand regular homicides, relevant or not, explicable or otherwise.

'Could this be the work of one of your demented fans, R.T.?'

A few years earlier, Billy and I tangled with 'Prospero Prince', a wealthy bibliophile whose hobby was recreating highlights of the tales of Edgar Allan Poe – pulling a party girl's teeth, bisecting a tennis pro with an Inquisition torture device, stuffing a gossip columnist up a chimney. Prince had to be tricked into a final homage – 'A Cask of Amontillado', played in the wine cellar of the Spanish mission he'd decorated as the House of Usher. We walled him up and walked away. He's almost certainly run out of air by now. The crimes were kept out of the papers, but at least two movies – one starring Billy – were inspired by whispers that went around about them.

'Not likely,' I said. 'Prince had the dough to get a giant pendulum razor custom-made to Poe's specifications. My demented fans can't afford big black Buicks. They ride the Red Cars. Or steal bicycles.'

'You have readers among the police. It was they who thought of you.'

'I'm happy to autograph flyleaves in office hours.'

'I shall relay the offer. It might give them cheer after a gruelling night shift. Fishing an automobile from the vasty deep is tricky. The operation involves a motor-tug, a diver with a foul disposition and chains and pulleys and braces.'

'Why are you in Malibu? It's a long way from Coldwater Canyon.'

'The police insisted I attend. In the glove compartment of the car they found a waterlogged motion picture script. *The Man They Could Not Hang.*

I played in that for Columbia a year or so ago. It is, in point of fact, *my* copy of the script of *The Man They Could Not Hang*.'

'How can they tell?'

'I mark my sides. In this script, Dr Savaard's lines are underscored by my distinctive flourish. Dr Savaard was the role I played. They couldn't hang him. He was brought back from the dead. By electric shock.'

'You speak in films? I've only heard you grunt.'

'Grrr… arrrh,' said the Monster.

It was always like that between us. English public school men joshing, Old Uppinghamian and Old Alleynian. Even when it was no joshing matter. *Especially* when it was no joshing matter.

'How did the Faceless Man come by your copy of a script?'

'I rather think I gave it to him. There's a dedication on the title page. I wrote that. But he wrote the script itself. I think it's *Joh*, R.T. Joh Devlin.'

Now I understood why he'd called.

'I'll be right over, Billy.'

'We'll still be here. The police are having a devil of a time finding a coroner at this hour.'

'The police generally have problems finding people.'

'Perhaps they should hire Philip Marrow.'

'Marlowe.'

'I said that.'

'Sure you did, Bela. Sure you did.'

3

Joh Devlin. Not John, not Joe. Formerly Johan Dieffenbach.

Everyone in this story changed their name. Cissy was born Pearl Eugénie Hurlburt. William Henry Pratt became famous as Boris Karloff. Ariadne was once known by an ululation of awe and terror emitted by knuckle-walkers whose general vocabulary was the Monster's 'grrr... arrrh'. Alone in this muddle, I kept the name I was given at birth. I showed my father what I thought of him when I put Chandler on lurid dust jackets.

My mysteries sold well enough to keep us out of the poorhouse. But not well enough for us to be too fussy about addresses. Or our car. It was not big, not black and not a Buick.

In my drinking days, there would have been a bottle in the Packard roadster's glove compartment. Now, there weren't even any gloves – just a sad street guide, useless three years after publication. Los Angeles continually knocks half of itself down to drill for oil or build restaurants shaped like the meals they serve.

The city spills out into the desert like a stain. White stucco palaces rise along the coast, permanent as chalk dentures. Studio heads have clifftop mansions made by their set construction departments.

Rain had been falling for a day and a half. Cacti were swollen like sponges. The downpour petered out as I got to the Pacific Coast Highway. Signs put out to warn of mudslides had been pushed into the road by sliding mud. Driving round them was like avoiding barbed wire in No Man's Land.

Billy's voice struck terror in me. Not the way it did to everybody else.

Our personal, shared fear was unique. It made us a couple, shutting out Cissy or whichever of his seven or eight wives Billy was presently married to. Universal kept trying to cast him as Bluebeard, but that story was too close to home.

Billy Pratt's greatest role wasn't the Monster. Billy shared *Frankenstein* with Mary Shelley, James Whale, a little Greek make-up man named Jack P. Pierce, and every child in a cardboard mask at Hallowe'en. No, Billy's best part, for which he could claim sole rights of authorship, was Boris Karloff.

Asked where the name came from, he would lie. 'A distant connection of my mother's had a name like Karloff.' *No one* has a name like Karloff. Not even in Russia. At Uppingham, being a Pratt was to invite kicks to the ankles on the stairs. 'Oh look, chums, Pratt's taken a prat-fall! What a prize prat is Pratt!' Kicks came often because young Billy looked more like a Patel than a Pratt. Dark-complected even before California sun, his family tree had roots in India. 'A touch of the tar-brush,' they used to say, 'but a useful bat.' Knowing Uppingham, I imagine they still say that. At Dulwich College too.

It's an open secret that some of the best English public school chaps are scarcely English at all, even if they play cricket with Sir C. Aubrey Smith, insist on tea breaks at eleven and four and perform music hall songs with freshly filthy lyrics to raise funds for blitzed blighters back home. Basil Rathbone is South African and George Sanders is Russian.

I am myself American and Irish Quaker and was in a Scots regiment of the Canadian army. But I broke my face playing rugby. I am a typical English public school man. To place stories with *Black Mask*, I had to study American idioms the way Joseph Conrad – a favourite author of Billy's, as it happens – learned English as a second language before turning to fiction. I write in a language I don't generally speak, though Philip Marlowe's vocabulary – and, more damagingly, his combative attitude – creeps in after the third gimlet.

Billy had taken a long route from Dulwich to Hollywood. Shedding the Pratt name, he'd shipped out like a remittance man to act in melodrama for Mounties and gold-panners. Joh knew Billy from Canada the way I know him from Dulwich. Not in an anecdote fit for a studio biography, but from an ungodly mess of the sort men like Joh Devlin were paid to keep out of the papers.

Perhaps Joh was Best Man at one of Billy's early weddings, where the bride was an understudy and the parson the company's senior character actor in a clergy costume from *The Importance of Being Earnest*. Maybe Billy saved Joh's life in a bar-room fight out of a Robert W. Service poem. That would be like Billy, especially if he ended the brawl not with a roundhouse right to the unshaven jaw of an angry fur trapper but a kiss on the lips of the lady known as Lou while wrestling the garter-holstered shiv out of her stevedore-sized hand.

Needing his life saving would be like Joh.

Until now.

In my mysteries, P. Marlowe drinks my brand of coffee (Huggins Young) and favours my cocktail (the gimlet). He smokes a pipe like I do – the only thing he has in common with Crockpot Holmes. The rest of Mr Marlowe is Joh Devlin. Fired from the DA's office for insubordination. Licensed private investigator. Twenty-five dollars a day and expenses – no divorce business. All Clients Distrusted Equally – plutocrat and plug-ugly. A good man to have on your side or in your debt. A bad man to cross. A hard man to know.

In a mystery, Joh would be the hero. In life, as it now turned out, he was the corpse.

Billy owed him and I owed him. Joh mixed the mortar in the cellar while Prospero Prince recited 'The Raven' to us at gunpoint. Joh shot Ape Ricotte… found Valda Darnay telling fortunes in Ensenada… told me the mystery writer whose far-fetched murder methods I'd poked fun at had spitefully smeared my typewriter keys with curare… spirited Billy out of a Mississippi blind pig when the Ku Klux Klan decided he was dark-skinned enough to be hunted by men with torches – not an unfamiliar situation for the Monster. We didn't even pay him his day rate. That meant we were on his side and in his debt and the two of us together weren't half the man he was. But we would do our best for him. Obligation was drummed into us at our schools.

Joh was another secret Billy and I shared. Another strand in the web that held our lives together – our worlds of crime and horror.

It didn't do in writing a mystery to fix on the culprit before doing the detective work. Only real cops decide on a killer when the call comes in, then beat a confession out of him to tidy up the story. Guilty parties are brought to book by that method – if only coincidentally. Big criminals remain out of reach – too well-connected to arrest, too venomous to kill.

It couldn't be Ariadne.

Or not *just* Ariadne. There was more to the web than its mistress.

Ariadne gave Prospero Prince an inscribed first edition of *Tales of the Grotesque and Arabesque*… was worshipped beyond reason by the formidable Mr Ricotte… and designed the fall wardrobe Valda Darnay wasn't wearing much of in the photographs Joh was hired to locate and destroy.

Still, it wasn't *always* her.

Inland, the black sky closest to the mountains frayed to blue.

The sun was up by the time I got to Malibu.

4

The entrance to the pier was an arch between stubby towers. The gates were off their hinges. The Knopf sub-editor who carped that an automobile couldn't get up enough speed in the approach to plough through the barrier was proved wrong. I considered composing a limerick to mark this belated vindication.

'Chandler?' asked the motorcycle cop.

Dawn light made oily rainbows on his black cape.

'I'm afraid so.'

'Go on through,' he said, standing aside as if ushering me into an exclusive area of the casino where I could be robbed more politely of much more money.

I stepped onto the boards and smelled yesterday's fish. That was enough to make me seasick.

'So, writer,' the cop called out to my back, 'who killed the chauffeur?'

'You're the policeman,' I said. 'It's most often a gypsy with a limp and a glass eye, I believe.'

'Yeah, or a Mex.'

Some accuse my mysteries of unfair depiction of the salaried police.

The cop chuckled, shaking water off his sou'wester.

The boards creaked. The further I walked from the shore, the louder the noise of the surf beneath.

In the near distance, a Coast Guard cutter passed. It was fitted with guns, grapples and mortars – for action against gambling ships moored beyond the three-mile limit rather than to counter any distant threat from Japan. It circled in search of anyone thrown out of the wreck. The likelihood that such a person would be living was diminishing.

A thin man stood at the end of the pier, next to a jagged break in the railings where something had crashed through, his back towards me. He wore white linen pants, a heavy black jacket padded at the shoulders and a wide-brimmed hat. His silhouette was unmistakably the Monster's.

Muddy tread marks showed the long, straight run a driver had taken, with – going by the not unquestionable reasoning I gave in *The Big Sleep* – a living hand on the wheel to make it suicide rather than murder. The pier wasn't supposed to be driven on and some boards had cracked under the weight of the car. If I'd seen this before I wrote that scene, I'd have used that detail.

The Monster turned to face me, supple of waist and slim at the hips, though bow-legged. His crooked smile was a practised cover for a wince that showed in his narrowed eyes.

I remembered that smile from when we were twelve. His dark hair was silver-streaked now, but the smile was the same.

He extended his arm to wave, then brought it over as if bowling at me.

From instinct, I sidestepped. A Pratt delivery could crack pads, shins or the wicket.

Despite all his injuries on and off film sets, Billy moved like a cat. No wonder Taki loved him.

'Where's the body?' I asked, nearing the end of the pier.

Billy pointed at a stretch of the railings, where a chain usually hung between white two-by-fours. The chain was unhooked, allowing access to rickety stairs.

A flatbed salvage barge was moored at a small jetty. A derrick had hauled a car out of the water. Cops and crew gathered around, examining the car's crumpled snout and smashed headlamps. Not a Buick, but a Studebaker Champion. Not black, but dark olive green. That squashed the demented Raymond Chandler devotee theory. Fans are sticklers for getting these things right. Prospero Prince didn't disembowel the tennis pro with a giant razor yo-yo.

Besides, I recognised the car.

It was Joh's.

'There are bullet-holes in the trunk,' said another caped cop.

'They were there before,' shouted Billy.

We both remembered that evening. Not fondly.

'Looks old,' admitted the cop. 'Wonder why he didn't get them fixed.'

'Sentiment,' said Billy.

'Whatever you say, Mr Karloff.'

A movie star, no matter how gruesome, gets instant respect – more so the further away from Hollywood they venture. Shackled by contracts, a star is but a pampered slave on his home backlot – as they learn if they try to toss a shoddy script back at Jack L. Warner or L.B. Mayer. But the magic glow pulses bright when they walk among real people. As a restless youth, Billy had slunk out of England in disgrace. On his return as a movie monster, he was greeted like prodigal royalty. Numerous Pratts who'd made respectable careers as diplomats or judges (one sent Gandhi to jail) must have felt they'd wasted their lives.

'Is that Chandler?' shouted a man with a misshapen hat and a cigar that cut through the fish smell. I knew a cop hat and a cop cigar when I saw them.

'It is he,' responded Billy.

'Come down,' said the policeman, flapping back a wet lapel to show a badge. He hadn't been issued bad weather gear and was soaked. The new-risen sun crinkle-dried his coat, tightening it around his upper arms. He had a moustache like a wipe of grease. His expression was rosier than mine would be if I worked a job where regular early morning calls involved messy, stupid death.

'This is Detective-Lefftenant William Corder,' said Billy.

'"Lefftenant",' echoed Corder. 'Cute.'

'My apologies,' said Billy. '*Loot*, not Leff. Detective-Lieutenant.'

I climbed down to the jetty, not gripping the rusty chain banisters too tightly. Cissy always warned me against tetanus. The plainclothesman stuck out a hand and helped me aboard the barge.

'Corder,' I said. 'That's a murderer's name.'

The cop looked at me as if I were screwy.

'He means the wicked squire who strangled Maria Marten in the Red Barn,' said Billy, who descended the stairs with confidence and ease. 'Happened in 1827 or so, in Suffolk.'

'Out of my jurisdiction,' said Corder.

'You'd think I'd have played the rascal,' said Billy. '*Murder in the Red Barn* was a warhorse when I stormed barns in the Great North West, but Actor-Managers copped the plum roles. In those days, I was a callow juvenile. Carlos the Gypsy, honest lover of poor murdered Maria. I hanged Corder at the curtain. A last act string-'em-up always gets a cheer in Saskatchewan. Up there, they applaud by shooting the ceiling.'

This close to the pier, there were eddies around the pilings. Brown kelp floated on brown froth. I tried to get my sea-legs. Billy stepped onto the unsteady deck, at ease on water like all true Britishers.

'This is Chet Stuckey,' said Corder, indicating a sun-bronzed lifeguard type in a wool cardigan. 'From the medical examiner's office.'

So the police had finally scared up a coroner. Stuckey bared perfect teeth in a grin. For a moment, I thought he was going to ask for an autograph. He had an open notebook.

'I have to warn you,' said Stuckey. 'It's not pretty.'

'I'm used to not pretty,' I said. 'I was in the War.'

'And I was in *Scarface*,' said Billy.

Stuckey stood aside. The cop crowd parted.

The driver's door was open, popped out of its frame. Sat at the wheel was the man without much of a head. A double-barrelled shotgun wired to the steering column aimed upwards where a soft underchin might have been, looped cord around the triggers. Had he set out to kill himself twice? A Jekyll and Hyde homicide-suicide. Another party might have rigged the gun, though the makeshift ingenuity was Joh Devlin all over. His wet white hand – smaller in death – flopped on the running board.

I was grateful for the fish stink and Corder's cigar.

The death-smell gets into your mouth. You taste it for months.

'Was a brick or block of wood wedged on the pedal?' Billy asked.

'Nothing was found,' said Corder.

'So he drove himself?' I asked.

The cop shrugged. 'Is that a *deduction*?'

'It's a question.'

'Which you've no business asking,' he said. 'You're here as… let's say, a material witness. That's a usefully elastic term.'

'Gentlemen, please,' said Billy, as if reprimanding players who were bad sports enough to argue with an umpire. 'We only wish to help.'

'We're grateful for the assistance,' said Corder.

Even the top cop on the scene deferred to Boris Karloff.

'Show him the wallet,' said Billy.

Corder handed me a sticky leather billfold.

In compartments were Joh's Screen Writers Guild membership card, private investigator's licence, business cards (in several names, misleadingly representing the bearer as several brands of licensed busybody) and about thirty dollars in bills. I didn't envy the cop who'd had to go through the dead man's pockets.

'Devlin's wallet,' said Corder. 'Which doesn't mean this is Devlin.'

I knew what he meant. I'd read enough mysteries.

'I shouldn't be the one to say this,' I said. 'But no one *really* dresses up a dead tramp in their clothes, stuffs his pockets with personal items, then trusts even this much mutilation to ensure misidentification. That only happens in Crime Club selections written by women with three names.'

'Books give people ideas,' said Billy.

'Are Joh's fingerprints on file?' I asked. 'With his licence application?'

'Search me,' said Corder. 'Shouldn't you know that?'

I'd always meant to ask Joh how exactly Marlowe would go about obtaining and keeping a licence and the rights and responsibilities entailed. Too late now. This was the first time I'd even seen a detective's licence. My mysteries skirt day-to-day detail. Erle Gardner knows enough law to pepper his Perry Masons with procedural guff. I rely on invention. As Cissy says, I prefer romance to research.

Stuckey looked at the dangling hand. Getting prints off it would be another prize job.

Billy examined the red mess spread in lumps and patches across the

33

car's rear seats, ceiling and windows. Some smeared when seawater washed in. Enough stuck where it had been blown to be disturbing.

'Joh Devlin has – had – a silver plate in his head,' said Billy. 'That's it there.'

A twist of metal was embedded in the upholstery. Stuckey went in with big tweezers and pulled it out.

'Is this the body or is this evidence?' he asked Corder. 'My envelope or yours.'

The cop shrugged. A finer point to be settled later.

'The War again?' Corder asked.

'Uh-huh,' I said. 'Prohibition. Police Sergeant with a nightstick.'

'Nice people in your circles.'

I shrugged, exasperated. 'Your circles too. Joh tried to bring his own bottle into a protected speakeasy. The cop was standing guard for a beer baron. Not exactly legal, not exactly surprising.'

Billy kept looking into the car. He couldn't help but seem ghoulish. It was in the lines of his face. His eyes caught light even in the bar of shade cast by his hat-brim. He contemplated the ingredients of a friend's head. The puzzle had too many pieces missing ever to make a picture you'd want to look at.

'Any idea why Devlin would ice himself?' asked Corder.

'Honestly, Detective, no,' I said. 'I don't understand suicide.'

'So I hear. I've not read that book of yours.'

'I expect you have little time to read in your profession.'

'I like a book on a stake-out,' said Corder, around his cigar. 'Non-fiction, for preference. In *Le Suicide*, Émile Durkheim says egoistic suicide is prompted by excessive individuation and estrangement from social norms, altruistic suicide by subsummation of the will to a group's goals and beliefs, anomic suicide by moral confusion and lack of social direction and fatalistic suicide by a sense that futures are pitilessly blocked and passions violently choked by excessive discipline. Into which category would you say Mr Devlin falls?'

'Egoistic, definitely, Professor,' I said.

'Who knows why a chump chumps?' commented the bullet-hole connoisseur cop.

'In this case, Wellbeck, the question is still *if* rather than *why*.'

Wellbeck was put in his place. As was I.

If Corder claimed he'd read Durkheim in the original French, I'd now believe him. Individuation. Subsummation. Anomic. He used words out loud I wouldn't put in print.

The cop turned back to me.

'When did you last see Devlin?'

'A month ago. He helped my wife and I move apartments. You can get a lot of luggage in this car. The trunk is surprisingly roomy.'

'Mr Karloff?'

'Not as recently in person, but we talked on the telephone only last week. He wished to discuss a story. Columbia need something for me.'

'A picture, huh. Have a title?'

'*The Man Who Lost His Head*.'

'Ouch.'

Billy bared his teeth.

'Know how people kill themselves in California?' asked Corder. 'Pills and booze… razor blade in the bath-tub… walks into the sea or off those cliffs up there… cars, well, yes, sometimes – though that's a better way to break your back or mess up your face than end it all… guns, by all means, and manners, all the time. We're still cowboys out here. But people don't, in my experience, combine cars and guns. It's baroque is what it is. Excessive and unnecessary. The Hays Code dislikes suicide as a plot device and so do I. Except this isn't *only* suicide. Not even the most egoistic *Selbstmord* ever catalogued by Dr Freud. Not with the scene setting from your book, Mr Chandler, and that script of yours, Mr Karloff, peeping out so we couldn't miss it. This death is a whopping smoke signal, designed to summon you two… which makes me wonder just what this is about. Why him? Why me? And, most of all, why you?'

I was squirming. Billy was calm.

Neither of us wanted to speak.

So, at this opportune moment, came a tapping – as of someone gently rapping – from the submersible Studebaker.

'Hear that?' said Officer Wellbeck.

'Fish in the trunk?' suggested Stuckey.

The sound definitely came from inside Devlin's car. More a scraping than a rapping now. A human sound. Fortunato's fingernails against the brickwork as the air gave out. I felt cold in the sunshine.

Without asking permission, Billy yanked open the trunk.

In a gush of water, out tumbled a very wet, very alive woman.

5

With an elongated sigh, she fainted or fell asleep. Her face glistened. We all knew she was a wrong thing. If, as I suspected, her swoon was a sham then she knew it too and didn't want to answer questions.

'How long was the car in the sea?' asked Stuckey.

'Two hours at least,' said Wellbeck. 'Nightwatchman called in from the phone in the kiosk around eleven thirty. Half an hour – maybe forty minutes – to scramble a crew for the barge. Then it was a mare fixing chains and working the winch.'

'Was it completely underwater?' asked Corder.

'Sea's not deep here, but the trunk was in the drink.'

'Air pocket?' suggested Stuckey.

'Bullet-holes,' Wellbeck reminded everyone.

We looked at the car and the woman in the big puddle. Her chest rose and fell, so she was breathing.

'How is she alive?' asked Corder.

'Search me,' said Wellbeck. 'She just is.'

Billy and I exchanged a look. We'd been here before.

People who know magic isn't real look straight at a ghost and see a flapping bed sheet. They deal with an irrefutable demonstration of how things really are the way an oyster deals with a speck of grit. The truth gets coated in a hard, shiny shell that can be worn proudly. A pearl is a lie you can roll between your teeth.

Corder, Stuckey and even Wellbeck weren't stupid or they wouldn't have their badges. Yes, there are stupid cops and officials. They get where they are through graft, nepotism or because a machine needs an oilable cog. Those boys are cushioned against having to do dirty jobs in the middle of a rainy night. You have to be clever and honest – and, therefore, unpopular – to rate duty like that.

So, these smart people were confronted with an impossible woman. It threw them, at least for a moment. They could not complete the course without jumping a high fence.

Which they would do, even if it gave them a headache.

Eventually, smart people just tell better lies to themselves.

'There *must* have been an air pocket,' said Billy, showing mercy. If a movie star – even Boris Karloff! – said something in a British accent it could be taken down in shorthand and typed up in the report.

'He's right,' said Wellbeck, not even realising he was going back on what he'd just stated. 'Air pressure or something.'

'Stands to reason,' said Stuckey – though it surely didn't.

Corder wiped his forehead with the back of his hand. His hat was still damp. He chewed the cigar and narrowed his eyes. Maybe he had an inkling of what Billy and I knew. A lot of cops do but school themselves to look away. It's how they stay sane – if they do.

The woman coughed in her sleep. A little water leaked out of her mouth.

She was not drowned. Not nearly.

So the bullet-holes must have been plugged. The Studebaker's roomy trunk perhaps had a sturdy rubber seal. That must be it. And enough air for an hour or two. Though, if the trunk were air-tight, why was the woman wet? We'd seen water pour out with her.

She coughed again and her eyes popped open.

The train of cop thought I'd followed – sure Corder was getting uncomfortably close to chewing on a bone that'd poison him – got blown off the tracks. There was a woman to be looked after. A lady from the sea.

In the early morning sunlight, she stirred to life.

'Mermaid,' said Billy, quietly.

That was ridiculous, of course. No gills.

But this woman had *something*.

If she'd worn make-up, it was washed off. Her black hair was short, except for an asymmetrical fringe. I couldn't imagine how it would look dry. She had a swan neck, a chin dimple and high cheekbones. One of her green-blue eyes was alarmingly bloodshot.

Stuckey, unused to living patients, touched the side of her head as if probing a fatal wound. He peered into her red right eye.

'Petechial haemorrhage,' said the Boy Coroner. 'You see this with strangulation. No ligature marks, though.'

The woman sat up and pushed Stuckey off.

It had probably never occurred to him that the dead might be sensitive about how they got that way.

The woman's wet silk dress was transparent, stuck like cellophane wrapping a bon-bon. Her figure would draw the eye in dry church clothes. Now she looked like the centrepiece of a *Spicy Mystery* cover, tethered to a hooded fiend's altar.

If suddenly aware they are essentially nude and surrounded by pop-eyed men, most women instinctively adopt the classical *pudica* pose, hand over the pubis, arm across the breasts. Instead, this woman's hands flew up like startled birds and fixed her hair. Our Aphrodite had no shame about her figure, but was bothered about something else.

Satisfied, she let her hair be. The longer side of her fringe was a raven's wing masking her red eye.

So that was the trick.

Stuckey leaned closer, still concerned.

'I've had this since school,' she said, waving him away. 'Nothing to be done about it. And it's a vitreous haemorrhage, *not* petechial.'

Stuckey backed off.

Her accent was English – neither cut-glass nor corner-house, with a slight, appealing nasality. I had an urge to ask her which school she meant. They played rough games, apparently.

Without asking, Billy slipped Wellbeck's rain-cape off him. Kneeling with an audible creak, he gallantly wrapped the cloak around the woman. She looked up to thank him and saw *Boris Karloff* smiling sweet reassurance.

The Monster, the Mummy, Fu Manchu. Her wrist covered her mouth as if she might scream. Billy patted her shoulder, understanding. She smiled tightly, without showing teeth.

'Miss?' said Corder.

'… Bostwick,' she replied. 'I'm Leila Bostwick. Where's Joh Devlin?'

Stuckey tried to position himself between her and the open car door, but she saw the headless body. She didn't stifle another scream, but her mouth set firm. A tell. This wasn't her first corpse-viewing.

'I don't understand,' she lied.

Then she pretended to faint again.

Everyone bought it, except me and Billy.

'You're not Leila Bostwick,' Billy told her. 'At least you weren't Leila Bostwick in the Home House case. You were Ives, then. Laurel Ives.'

'They called you "Witch-Eye",' I added.

She kept up the sham swoon.

But she heard us. Leila Bostwick. Laurel Ives. Witch-Eye.

Joh had hunted down other names she'd used. Carolyn Vedder. Philippa Zhan. Pamela Grayle. He'd shown us her head shot, from when she was in the movies.

We'd been told her original name was Stephen Swift.

British families get set in their ways when it comes to christening first-borns. A little thing like sex is no reason to break with tradition.

Not even Stephanie Swift. Stephen.

No wonder she'd taken to changing it every chance she got.

Billy and I knew the Home House case. Joh Devlin always insisted that story wasn't finished. We wanted that book shut, but he kept scratching at the cover. Here we were, in the next exciting chapter. A lid popped off a can and worms were loose.

The papers made out that Joh rescued Laurel Ives from the Home House Horror Man – also known as 'Frank N. Quine'. Good press didn't do much for Joh Devlin in the short – or, now, the long – run.

Having pulled the girl out of death's dark embrace, why would Joh try to send her back – and rush on ahead himself? I already knew three versions of the Home House story – the official announcements, the stuff in the scandal sheets and Joh's inside dope. Now, there was obviously a fourth. Onion layers around a heart of darkness. It would never stop.

Unless we stopped it. Billy and me. Corder was right about the smoke signal.

Joh had dropped this on our desk. We both had debts to him that – as English Public School Men – we were obliged to settle.

Billy picked the woman up. He got a good grip under her shoulders and knees but her arms flopped. Girls rescued by Clark Gable wrap their arms around his manly shoulders. Girls abducted by the Monster lie back in a faint. Their dangling arms get caught in the bushes.

A label inside her wet dress was legible in mirror-writing.

'By Ariadne'.

PART TWO

HOME HOUSE

6

Three years before Joh Devlin's Studebaker went off the pier, the Home House case was page one news for weeks.

No one could miss Home House itself. In a city where everything is new – plated with chrome and polished to shine, then replaced rather than cleaned – it takes fortunes to fake oldness. Designed and built inside six months in 1932, the exterior of Home House was in a mock Gothic colossal style that might have been imagined by Ann Radcliffe in a laudanum dream. The interior was metropolitan *moderne*.

Home House was a gift from Ward Home to his son, on the occasion of a wedding that didn't take place. Ward Home Senior was an oilman so glutted with wealth he could have left the Dabney Syndicate on the side of his plate as not worth the wear on his porcelain teeth. Ward Home Junior returned the presents his bride-never-to-be hadn't absconded with, but still moved into his new-old house on the day the final Welsh slate tile was fitted in the roof.

The fortress replaced a patch of Beverly Hills scrub Senior initially purchased as a buffer. The Old Man wanted to stop idlers on Sunset Boulevard gawking up at La Casa, his own mansion. Though the point of ostentatious displays of riches is that they should be highly visible, Senior had second thoughts after completing his own castle. Peasants shouldn't be reminded too forcefully of his eminence.

Home House was a cutting from a great tree, planted in its shadow. Its four-foot-thick Pennsylvania black granite walls could resist an artillery barrage. The only street-facing windows were arrowslits three storeys up. Perched in alcoves above Sunset were gargoyles with friable faces that, within a year, wore down to show skull-like steel understructures.

It was an open secret that a concealed door opened from the inside. Rumours circulated about late-night comings and goings of veiled ladies and slouch-hatted gents. When the bride ran off, columnists hinted at what was supposed to happen on the wedding night. And who besides the bridegroom might have been expected to be involved. Scandal sheets ran novelette illustrations of the ingenue fleeing Home House in her wedding dress, disembodied eyes glowing in the sky above.

As you'd expect, Ward Home had changed the family name. *His* father, who hailed from Thuringia, went by Sigurd Heim. Senior Senior came to California too late for a gold rush but early in the oil boom. Old Man Heim sunk the first wells, but Ward Home built an empire.

Senior was oil money. His bank account grew with each pulse of a derrick, swelling with every barrel sucked out of the ground. Junior Home was Hollywood money. His fortune sizzled like a nitrate print caught in a projector gate.

Senior gave orders to state governors and city officials and considered Home Estate a vest-pocket kingdom separate from the State of California. Junior flaunted luxury on a Babylonian scale but studio ledgers insisted he was penniless. He'd fill a pool with asses' milk for a screen star's publicity photographs, but make writers pay for the lightbulbs in offices where overseers cracked whips if their daily page rate fell.

Both were men of well-below-average stature, but only Junior got ribbed for it. He wore shoe lifts and signed five-foot starlets to personal contracts so his dates at premieres were shorter than him in photographs.

Pyramid Pictures boasted a logo to equal Paramount or Metro-Goldwyn-Mayer – a disembodied eye above a pyramid, the Masonic symbol on the dollar bill. But the lot, occupying a stretch of the Estate, was equivalent to the follies on which eighteenth-century English nobility squandered pocket money. The studio was a backyard train set for a grown boy who wanted to wear a driver's hat and toot a whistle.

Junior's house was the same – for playing with, not living in. Who really wants underfloor lighting? Or a third faucet on every sink, spewing carbonated water from a pressurised tank in the basement?

The man who made the machines for Universal's *Frankenstein* was Home House's gadgetry genius. Norman Quin, middle name Francis. The rags called him 'Frank N. Quine'.

The apparatus that adorned the battlements was Quin's work. Lightning-rods attached to cages, gauges and dials. They crackled on nights when there were no storms. Sparks rained on the sidewalk, setting small fires on hats and dogs.

One Thursday night, the rooftop electrics of Home House went wild. Alarming arcs played between the pylons and the streetlights. Tutankhamun trumpets blared from loudspeakers. The Pyramid Pictures fanfare.

The concealed door pushed open from the inside. Several witnesses – who presumably had good reason to be on Sunset at three in the morning – were startled. A man on fire stumbled through the door, screeching. He was bolted into an exo-skeletal frame like an all-over medical brace.

'It was Junior Home,' Devlin told Billy and me. 'It was as if the shrimp were *wearing* an electric chair. Batteries were wired to a leather belt and canvas vest. He staggered a couple of steps and someone tossed a pail of water over him, shorting out the whole kaboodle. The bucket thrower was Quin, who came out after Junior. I'd have stood still to be doused rather than blundered away, but maybe the shrimp was in a mad panic. The door slammed behind the both of them. When the flames were out, Junior was still alive... which shows he has more grit in him than his Pappy reckons. Quin scrabbled at the wall, trying to get his fingernails in the invisible crack. When the patrol car showed, the cops panicked and did something they shouldn't. They called Queen of Angels first, *then* Pyramid Security.'

When he woke to the news, Senior made a fuss about getting his only son out of poor people's hospital – for all that he was a donor to the Franciscan Sisters who built the place – into the Lamia Munro Clinic. The Old Man wanted the patient treated by doctors he could fire and blacklist if a medical outcome was not to his liking. The Clinic, another well-funded hobby-horse, was also situated on the Home Estate.

Joh had theories about the enterprise.

'Rich folk will go to great lengths to get out of things the rest of us put up with,' said Joh. 'Like dying, for instance. The Homes and their kind want death to be optional for the upper income tax bracket… not that they pay taxes if they can help it. But if they *have* to die, they want to come back. They see your movies, Billy – the Frankensteins and that Warners thing, *The Walking Dead* – and reckon those curtain speeches about not meddling in God's domain or there being some things man is not meant to know are for the rubes. To them, it's absurd that they *can't* replace the batteries, have the butler throw a switch and jump up off their death-beds frisky as pups. That's what the Lamia Munro is about. They say they're one breakthrough away – just one gassed dog shocked back to life – from perfecting a revivification process which will be exclusive to the Home Clan. What the rich want, what eats them up that they can't buy, is more *time* than you or I have… and *better-quality* time too, not more old age and infirmity but more prime of life. They talk a Frankenstein game, but what they really want – who they really want to *be* – is Dracula. Eternal wealth in evening dress. Drained-dry dollymops discreetly swept up after they're finished with them. The bastards are right about one thing – real monsters don't die. Not fire, not a wooden stake, not a squadron of planes… nothing kills money.'

'Junior Home might disagree,' said Billy.

Joh grinned at that. 'But, despite the hot seat vest, Junior Home is *al-i-eve!*'

7

The three of us sat in garden chairs, shaded under mismatched parasols. We were relaxed in the backyard of 2320 Bowmont Drive, Coldwater Canyon – *chez* Karloff. The property he'd bought from Katharine Hepburn, who said it was haunted. 'It is now,' he told Kate. 'By me. Boo.'

It was a weekday, mid-morning, routinely sunny.

Joh was telling us about the Home House case.

His latest gag was to call us, respectively, 'Invisible Ray' and 'Visible Ray'. In a picture called *The Invisible Ray*, Billy played a scientist who messes around with a new kind of radium. It makes him glow with unhealthy, pulsing light, which at least hides the black, curly wig Jack Pierce slapped on him for the role. The mad scientist develops a Death Touch, for use on his enemies – starting, of course, with Bela Lugosi. So, Joh called Billy 'Invisible Ray'. My name was Raymond and people could see me, so I got elected as the second part of the joke. 'Visible Ray'. Coming up short in the sense of humour game, I couldn't see what was funny about it. Joh chuckled at that most of all. It was more befuddling than irritating. If Joh rode a joke too hard, Billy held up his hand with the fingers splayed and looked at him with a mild smile – as if itching to use his Death Touch again. The heel of the hand jammed against chest or forehead… and it was all over for the victims of 'Invisible Ray'.

I didn't feel particularly visible, though I was working on it. *Black Mask* had dismissed the discerning editor who'd bought my first stories. Taking offence, I rode my high horse over to *Dime Detective*. My new market was even more déclassé but paid fractionally better. They were less likely to pencil through the nuggets of sly kidding that made me feel more warmly about churning hardboiled blood and guts. In the last year, I had sold as many stories as Cornell Woolrich places in any given month. It wasn't really a living.

Writing for periodicals scheduled to go in the trash thirty days after they hit newsstands had no future. I might as well work a treadmill. So I had committed a bigger crime. I gutted some previously published novellas and gummed scenes together to pass off as a book-length mystery. If Dashiell Hammett fit between hard covers, so could I.

The Big Sleep, the result of this cannibalism, was with the august New York house of Alfred A. Knopf. Mr Philip Marlowe, my newly named detective, would soon make his debut in polite society – or, at least, the lending libraries. If the book-length mystery racket didn't work out, I'd need another means of supporting myself, Cissy and Taki. Possibly prospecting for gold, if I could scrape together the purchase price of a mule and a pick-axe.

Billy was between pictures. A cabal of English public school men known as the British Board of Film Censors thought it a jolly wheeze to ban Hollywood horror. The lower orders in the cheap seats enjoyed being frightened a little too much. That couldn't be allowed. Half-way around the world, their airy edict was enforced by the lickspittles of Universal Pictures.

The spook business hit the rocks. Bela Lugosi was on unemployment. Jack Pierce scowled at starlets, dreaming of fitting fangs into their lipsticky mouths. Billy owed Warner several pictures. The studio was whipping up a Chinese warlord script to replace the *Dr X* shocker he'd been set for. There was something *personal* in the horror prohibition. Could some censorious chap still smart from the fiendish Billy Pratt bouncer that bowled him out for a duck?

Joh Devlin wasn't investigating for the DA because he'd been fired.

He'd broken the Home House case, but no one liked the solution.

Comments about rich people looking to buy off death weren't popular either.

I've had that with editors. They love everything about a mystery but the solution. It's been noted that I tend to pin any murders on the most prominent dame in the case. When that comes up, I cite Cissy (or Taki) as my primal *femme fatale* so I don't have to invoke She Who Must Not Be Defied. Hammett had the same quirk before he got too much money to bother writing any more. I have an idea where he picked it up.

Joh didn't hang Home House on the woman in the case. That would have played better with his audience. He didn't want applause. He wanted truth – and truth is seldom a box office winner.

Police reports aren't supposed to test out of town then get rewritten. Studios can change endings from sad to happy. Jimmy Whale killed Henry Frankenstein twice, then rescued him in reshoots. The DA shouldn't do business that way. When evidence suggests a handsome young fellow should go to the gas chamber, Joh Devlin didn't care whether the preview cards preferred he live and get the girl. So Joh was out of a job, if not off the case.

It took more than being canned to throw this bloodhound off the trail. That's a thing I owe Joh Devlin for – or, rather, *Philip Marlowe* owes him for. Joh stuck at it until he was satisfied justice or its nearest relation was done. To cover rent and food bills, he snatched a leaf out of my book and sold to detective magazines. He couldn't crack *Black Mask*, but *Dime Detective* overlooked his grammar and ran his yarns. They were thrilled to have an actual dick write for them and played up his experience with a cover by-line. 'J.D. Devlin – City Investigator!'

There is, of course, no such job as *city investigator*, but Joh lived in a city and investigated there. I thought the tag sounded as if he investigated cities for a living – determining whether Detroit had an alibi when Cleveland was set on fire... getting pictures to prove Kansas City, Kansas was cheating on Kansas City, Missouri, with the trampier of Minnesota's twin cities (that shameless slut, St Paul).

I stole something else from Joh – not for Marlowe, but for me. If asked why I was fired from Dabney Oil, I don't mention drunkenness, absenteeism or secretaries. Instead I own up to undue, inconvenient honesty. I adapt the tale of Joh Devlin being kicked out of the DA's office, casting myself as hero. After several gimlets, I even remember it that way.

So, there we were – three gentlemen of temporary leisure.

Billy lounged on a day-bed, wearing swimming trunks and a top hat. In *Frankenstein*, he was hobo-thin from under-eating. His jacket needed padding. After a few prosperous years, his leanness had become lithe. Walking across the patio, he couldn't hide the pain, but at rest he was comfortable as a cat. He idly tossed tidbits to Violet, the pig he kept to trim the lawns. Stuffed with treats, the sow turned up her snout at mere yellowing grass.

Joh wore an ice-cream suit with panama hat and sunglasses. He perched on the edge of a wicker chair, leaning forward. I was overdressed in tweeds. We had drinks – some devilish mix of wines, spirits and fruit concocted in the Karloff Kitchen by Gracia, the maid of all work.

Like all true Englishmen, Billy loved 'pottering about' in his garden. Smiling to himself – the same expression he showed while torturing people in films – he would patiently prod earth with a hand-fork, sprinkle water from a can and make calculated snips with his secateurs. He had a talent for cultivating plants he couldn't name.

His morning's pottering done in the relatively cool early hours before our arrival, Billy now fished ice-cubes from his tumbler and cracked them in his mouth like rock candies.

I verged on caution and tried to neglect the punch – taking gulps every twenty minutes rather than sips every ten seconds. I wasn't not drinking. I partook to be sociable – which is what they all said, even if there was no one else in the room.

A tiny brown girl played horsey on the lawn. Gracia's niece.

'Tell Beata she can swim if she likes,' said Billy as the maid sloshed another gallon of *brujeria* juice into the silver punchbowl.

Gracia nodded thanks. The pool reflected sunlight.

Billy smiled whenever the little girl galloped by.

He hadn't said so outright, but he and his current wife were hoping for a child. At his age too – near as dammit *my* age. Pushing fifty. Cissy and I could barely cope with Taki. Pratts are a family-minded tribe. Uncle Boris wanted to be Papa Boris.

'Tell the kid not to toss in any blossoms, *Tía* Gracia,' said Joh.

Billy frowned, wounded by the memory.

He'd protested about the Monster drowning the child in *Frankenstein*. Jimmy Whale said infanticide was 'part of the ritual' and insisted Billy chuck the little girl in the lake. When he told the story, Billy expected people to think the director an appalling sadist, but I knew what Whale meant. Billy was too tender-hearted to make up the scenarios he played in.

At the typewriter, we're all murdering devils. Carmen didn't shoot Rusty Regan and put him in the sump. I did. I killed the pornographer Geiger and the blackmailer Brody and poisoned that poor sap Harry Jones. I give voice to Marlowe, who sees justice done, but am the true author of any murders he avenges. Christians have to be thrown to the lions or Romans get bored.

Innocents have to die or there's no story. Bodies have to drop or detectives are out of work. Monsters too.

Beata hid behind a California lilac, aiming her pop-gun between purple flowers. She drew a bead on Billy. He gave her a genial 'rarr', the growl of the Monster, but without the pain or the fury. His purr was light-hearted let's-pretend, as opposed to the serious let's-pretend he (sometimes) did on sound stages. The girl squealed with delight. She popped her gun and Billy clutched his heart.

'You got me, pardner,' he gasped, fluttering his eyes closed.

He was always great in death scenes.

Beata whooped off across the lawn.

Billy peeped to see if his murderess was gone, then sat up smiling. He was as happy with an audience of one child as a full house at Grauman's Chinese Theatre. More than happy. Exultant. He *needed* to act, to keep acting. If he stopped being Boris Karloff, he wouldn't even go back to being a Pratt. He'd be a ghost, if that.

He held up his hand slyly, flexing as if summoning his Death Touch.

One gentle press from those deadly fingertips and the gunslinger girl would giggle no more.

For a moment, he scowled like Boris Karloff.

Then he shook out his fingers and was goodfellow Billy Pratt again.

53

The child rampaged through the rhododendrons – girl ranger turned jungle heroine. Billy wasn't concerned for his shrubbery, though Gracia muttered and crossed herself.

Joh stirred his drink with a stick of celery. Gracia put extra vegetables in everything.

Joh wanted to talk about Home House.

We had the bare puzzle pieces – Junior on fire, a life wavering at the Queen of Angels, Quin with the pail of water, a suspect in the wind… a science dungeon in the basement, a damsel in distress. Now we tried to make out the picture on the box.

My teeth sharpened when material came my way. Joh knew as much. Several of my stories grew out of dirt he'd dished – a circumstance he never mentioned except the one time he admitted that *True Detective* nixed his memoir of the Ricotte case as 'too Chandleresque'.

Joh was a big, handsome man – running a little to plump, with a roll under his strong chin. He had curly dark hair and a moustache with piratical twists at the ends.

His bio was a picaresque romp Hemingway would have loved to slap on a flyleaf. He shovelled enough coal on the Grand Trunk Railway one winter to heat hell for five years; earned a battlefield promotion during the Battle of Argonne by being alive when anyone else who could give orders was dead, but got busted to private for bayonetting a staff officer (who lived); spent a year in the sub-arctic with the Royal Canadian Mounted Police and served as Captain of the Guard at San Quentin prison during two riots and a typhus outbreak.

Cracked head aside, he generally did more damage to others than was done to him. He'd taken the silver shield in the interdepartmental rifle contest in 1931, kept out of first place by a cold-eyed vulture of a judge who'd ridden with Earp in Tombstone fifty years earlier. When anyone looked at Joh's life, they didn't believe half of it – though it was all true.

Eventually, they wouldn't believe his death either.

Until the day before our meeting at the Hacienda Karloff, Joh Devlin was Special Investigator under Los Angeles District Attorney Buron Fitts.

Joh tempted Violet away from Billy with his celery wand and chuckled when the pig nuzzled up to him.

Billy looked benevolently jealous.

'So, Boris, this Quin bird… you know him?'

Billy's face darkened again.

'Is this an interrogation, Joh?'

'I don't see how it could be. I'm an unemployed bum. I'm taking up Chandler's line now. Pulpsmith.'

I took a drink to cover my smile. Joh could type but didn't have the imp in his head that made me – when I began – spend half a year honing a novelette that brought in just about enough to cover an oilman's lunch.

'This is background,' said Joh.

'Ah, well, in that case… yes, I know – *knew* – Norman Quin. He tested for the Monster. After Bela was out and before I was in. Quin was a studio electrician. Not an actor, not even an extra. A big man – more your size than mine, Joh. He'd not need the lifts and shoulder pads. He'd have made the Monster a burly brute. He has hands so delicate they might have come from a dead girl. Jimmy Whale noticed his seamstress hands. All the better for fiddling with wires and tiny components. Then Jimmy looked up and saw half Jack Pierce's work already done by the War. Burn-scars. Jimmy was taken with the idea of casting Quin. He always liked to talk about his war…'

… the way Joh and I didn't like to. Whale spent most of the Great War doing amateur theatricals in a nice warm prison camp. Polished his accent, but not so it would fool anyone British. It passed with Americans. They couldn't tell he'd barely been to school at all.

Billy didn't like to talk about the War because he hadn't been in it.

'Jimmy cooled when he saw what Quin was like on film. Stiff, you know. Self-conscious. "Too horrible," he said, with Quin in the room. "Get that fellow from the gangster picture who always sneaks an extra helping in the commissary. He has a lean, hungry look about him." Quin was more interested in electrics anyway. To Jimmy, the Monster wasn't much of a part at all. It was Colin Clive's show. *Frankenstein* was the name of the picture and Colin played Frankenstein. When it came out, children thought Frankenstein must be the name of the Monster. Colin didn't take that well. Neither did Jimmy. Only Jack Pierce guessed the Monster was the star part.'

Billy had a faraway look as he reminisced. He still couldn't believe he'd ended up with his own swimming pool.

'They call what I did acting,' he said, 'but I defy anyone to have all that gunk on under arc lights and be poked and prodded all day without suffering showing in his eyes. Except Quin. Nothing showed in his eyes. No matter what pain he was in. Jack told me Quin's face still hurt. A few seconds on fire and he felt it thirteen years on. Bad bloody business. When Jack was putting the fright face on me for tests, I saw Quin out of the corner of my eye, hanging around, watching me disappear into the Monster. I don't know how he felt... whether that hurt him more, watching a ship sail off without him. Some people *want* to be monsters. Poor Bela scowled like he was digesting barbed wire when he learned Universal wanted me for the Mummy. Then I got to be Fu Manchu at Metro and Bela had to be *Imitation* Fu Manchu at Monogram. He has been most appallingly treated, you know.'

Billy was active in the founding of the Screen Actors Guild. He said actors were physical labourers like truck drivers and ditch diggers – he had the lasting injuries to prove it – and should be organised. Not a very Pratt cause, but very Billy. He was a proud holder of a union card.

'Later, at Metro, Tod Browning made *Freaks* with people from the carnival, rather than Jack Pierce make-up. People without limbs, dwarfs, pinheads. It did not go over. The Laemmles advised Jimmy against casting a mangled soldier as the Monster. Showmen know not to show too much. Pierce first sculpted his Monster on Quin. The flat head. The neck terminals. Pennyweights of putty on the eyelids. Jack said Quin disappeared under the make-up, but my fizzog shone through. That was my fortune. Just a cut of the cards.'

Billy always said that. It was luck.

Not Ariadne – no, never her... not running from her, nor her qualified, acid-edged mercy. She takes from us, as vampires take... but she gives back too. After our first meeting with her, Billy couldn't be a Pratt much longer. He tried everything else, including digging ditches and driving trucks, before becoming the Monster. What was in his eyes didn't come from a war. It came from her. Oh, the spark was there – but she was the flint that made it a flame.

Quin had a different sort of luck.

And so did Joh Devlin.

He told us the story.

8

THE HOME HOUSE HORROR: A SHUDDER PULP
STARRiNG J.D. DEVLiN — CiTY INVESTiGATOR!

IF BURON FITTS HADN'T BEEN SHOT, Devlin wouldn't have drawn the Home House case. If a killing was going to make the headlines, the District Attorney preferred Maxwell or Goldfarb. When it came to crimes of the rich, those investigators were registered blind.

Say a millionaire's frisky son ravishes a nun on stage at the Hollywood Bowl in front of a capacity crowd during the intermission of *Lohengrin*... Maxwell would hang a lewd conduct charge on the victim. Want prints smeared off a murder gun, a witness deposition lost behind a radiator or a complainant scared off? Goldfarb is your boy.

It wasn't a bright idea to cross the road when a motion picture director with a snootful was behind the wheel of a new roadster. Mart Maxwell couldn't even spell 'vehicular homicide'. Him and his old lady got invited to the Oscars for burying that one. She never shut up about meeting Wayne Morris.

Devlin typically worked cases the DA *wanted* to prosecute. Nice clean mob slayings and bozo–goes–nutso–with–a–knife–in–a–diner bloodbaths. Devlin's job was to tee up some unshaven, wild–eyed slob so his boss could get a hole in one. Fitts itched to fulminate against penniless guilty parties. Coloureds, for preference. Or talka–lika–dis gents whose last names ended in vowels.

Well-heeled guilty parties seldom came to trial.

Sure, any rap can be beat with smart lawyering – but Fitts hated to be a loser in court. Bad for re-election prospects. It was simplest if touchy cases evaporated. Poof! Prison doors open, perpetrator free, reputation unbesmirched, pocket book lighter. Plenty of guilty parties were walking around town with a spring in their step, eager to do again what they did before and got away with.

Devlin didn't blame Fitts personally. It was how the town worked. How any town worked.

All District Attorneys run on a reform ticket. By rights, the department should have wound up so reformed it'd pass for Sunday school. But, in office, the DA has to manage a high-wire act. Dust under the rug as usual but with the *appearance* of a new broom.

Fitts worked under former District Attorney Asa Keyes, then ratted him out for corruption. He was terrified some like-minded minion was building a case against him. That wouldn't be a challenge. The DA had barely scraped through the last Grand Jury hearing.

Besides investigators with more tact than guts, Fitts surrounded himself with unimaginative, unambitious pen-pushers. Little or no law enforcement experience was a recommendation.

Enter Justus Follard, career bureaucrat.

At the Department of Education, Follard was in charge of checking the teeth and hooves of schoolmarms. When he learned California children didn't recognise New Mexico and Arizona as states, he made damn sure every classroom got an atlas printed after 1912. That coup earned him a transfer to the District Attorney's office as Fitts' *Segundo*.

Then a volley of shots (all two of them) got fired through the DA's windshield.

Showing the interdepartmental co-operation for which the City of Angels was famous, Police Chief Davis posted an unofficial reward – not for the apprehension of the shooter, but to be claimed by any person who could prove they plugged the son of a bitch (with the proviso that they aim better next time). Sheriff Gene Biscailuz said it definitely wasn't a gangster job. A pro machine gunner would have riddled the car with bullets till Fitts was dead as Fatty Arbuckle's career.

With the DA laid up, his Number Two was Acting District Attorney. Fitts wheezed from his bed that Follard should go by the book. Of course, Fitts didn't mean the actual law book, but the unwritten code that kept greased wheels grinding. Follard wasn't one for linguistic subtleties. He blew dust off a law book and read it. Memos circulated about usage of pencils, pads and paper clips. Follard enforced regulations about ties, hats and jackets. And insisted on a strict duty roster.

A call came. Next man in the batting order came off the bench.

Devlin should have gone fishing till Fitts could play the violin again… but, no, he was dumb. Or bored. A city investigator could only spend so many hours in windowless rooms with morons who didn't understand beating wives to death with a wrench wasn't a legal right in the county of Los Angeles. He hungered for something off the menu. A tasty case with a possibility of eking extra shekels by changing the names and spilling the beans in *Dime Detective*…

… what he got was Home House.

At eight sharp on Friday morning, Devlin arrived at the office freshly shaved and full of coffee and vitamin E. He was handed a rundown of the previous night's incidents. Under the log line 'suspicious man on fire', he read a street address on Sunset Boulevard and the names of two responding officers.

He didn't realise the address was Home House until he got there.

The dimwit guarding the smear on the sidewalk had let people track footprints through it. He wasn't a cop, but a studio bull. Pyramid guards were mostly cowpokes who'd fallen off too many horses to work in pictures any more. Their uniforms were swipes from the fetching outfits modelled by Mussolini's praetorian gunsels. Devlin rolled down the window of his Studebaker and hollered his credentials at Cactus Slim.

The guard waved him towards the main gate, a mile and a half away.

He used the additional minutes' drive to rethink what he'd taken for a mop-up job. One man on fire and another with a bucket of water would be a funny story with principles of average to below-average income.

A Home House tie-in meant a headache wrapped in a nightmare. Was tipping gasoline over a chum and putting a match to the seat of his pants the latest craze among the smart set? Screwier things had caught on.

The main gates of the Home Estate looked like a portcullis. The clan liked the serfs to know feudalism was still in flower.

Dan Ysidro waited behind the bars.

'Howdy, pardner,' sang Devlin.

'J.D. Devlin – city investigator,' trilled Ysidro. 'What did I do to deserve this?'

Pyramid's Chief of Security was another hombre who'd been a miss in the movies. The studio snagged him off the rodeo circuit and signed him as yodelling pistolero 'Dan Starr'. He rode through three fifty-minute Westerns before the front office noticed he looked like a rabbit and sounded like a duck with a frog in its throat. Okay for a cartoon character, lousy for a matinee hero.

Ysidro's seven-year contract didn't specify employment as an actor. Pyramid gave him a black shirt and shiny cap and had him patrol the perimeter to see off real rustlers. He put a stop to night raids on the studio corral – poverty row companies weren't above securing nags for their own cowboy junk by means felonious – and dealt with the Estate's mountain lion problem. A fair hand at the job, he got promoted. His ex-sidekick Dry Bone Mullins and ex-horse Trooper went on to make forty-some oaters no one cared he wasn't in.

Failing to respect the Almighty Power of the DA's Office, Ysidro gave the gate guard no indication that the portcullis should be raised. Instead, he reached for a wall-mounted telephone… which inconveniently rang before he could call Follard and plead for Mart Maxwell to take over.

Ysidro answered the phone and straightened as if the person on the other end could see him. He sucked in his cowboy gut and puffed out his fascist chest. His shiny badge looked more cop-like than sheriff-like. Off the Estate, the shield was costume jewellery. Standing where he was, it gave him authority – but only at the sufferance of his master's (angry) voice.

Devlin gathered Ysidro had foolishly dared to be off-duty at three in the morning. Catastrophic mistakes were made while he was asleep. Sheriff Dan took a mighty dressing-down from the Sky Chief. He'd be saddle-sore come sundown.

Taking advantage, Devlin flashed his tarnished but wholly legitimate badge at the turnkey. The guard looked pleadingly at his boss. At his merest wave of consent, the portcullis rose.

As Ysidro turned to watch Devlin's car roll under the spikes, the phone cord wound round his neck. He still stood to attention and winced at the locust-shrill harangue in his ear.

Beyond the gate, it was as if Devlin had driven out of the city. La Casa perched on its promontory, white as a bleached skull picked clean by vultures. If the original Spanish settlers of these parts were twelve-foot giants, the Old Man's aerie was built to their scale.

The Estate was sub-divided, with demarcated grounds for La Casa and Home House. The Pyramid lot stretched out where the shadow of the mountain didn't spoil the light. Its office building was disguised as the studio logo – an Egyptian pyramid with an eye-shape blimp tethered above. Sunlight flashed off east-facing windows. A thousand secretaries signalling for help. Devlin wasn't here to rescue them.

A buzzing made him look up, expecting a swarm of hornets. A red Fokker triplane flew low over hills that – as he well knew – in no way resembled the muddy shambles of No Man's Land in 1918. Black smoke puffed from its guns. In pursuit was a bigger, slower plane with cameras mounted where its Maxim guns ought to be.

Ever since *Wings* and *All Quiet on the Western Front* made a mint and won a shelf of awards, Junior Home had been commissioning and throwing away German air ace scripts. So *Flight of the Red Eagle* was finally in production. Just in time to ride the wave of publicity provided by the next European War. He wouldn't put it past Pyramid Publicity to sabotage the Munich talks to boost ticket sales.

The gingerbread church where Sigurd Heim sang in the choir as a squirt nestled in its own forest grove. His son had ripped the fairy story illustration out by the roots and brought it over stone by stone, tree by tree. He even imported family graves. In Thuringia, a patch of bare rock remained where a giant hand had gouged a fistful of forest. Most of the congregation came with the church. Old country hangers-on padded the studio payroll. Bar-room brawls in Pyramid pix sounded like rowdy meetings of the German-American Bund.

The Homes were three-quarters German Catholic. Lamia Munro, Sigurd's frontier whore wife, brought in a sect of snake-handling Pentecostalists who clung to the shady side of the hill. Ysidro sometimes got orders to clear them out, rescinded as soon as shots were fired. The feud quieted at holidays when the clan got together to blame the ills of the world on the Jews. Married at fourteen and a mother six months later, Lamia was still alive – somewhere north of eighty – and shuffling around the halls of her son's castle, having outlived her husband – fifty-three on their wedding night – and seen off four daughters-in-law. The Lamia Munro Clinic was named after her – possibly, the place kept her alive with glands transplanted from chorus girls.

Devlin drove past the German woods and onto the grounds of Home House.

The dark stone mansion's driveway cut through unnaturally green, obscenely thirsty lawns. Sprinklers came on hourly round the clock to keep Junior's grass lush. The approach to Home House was lined with wrought iron gas-lamps – jets replaced by electric candles – that went with blind cockney knife-grinders and cries of 'orful murder' from street to street. Surplus from Pyramid's *The Fiend of Fog Lane*.

Devlin remembered the film.

A hypnotised gorilla in top hat and opera cape dismembered London bobbies at the bidding of an embittered fakir played by Mischa Auer because Lugosi threw a self-sabotaging fit when he learned Pyramid offered it to Karloff first. Knowing Boris had turned down the role, the back-up bogeyman hemmed and hawed in Hungarian. Before Desperate Dracula could cave and take Fortunate Frankenstein's leavings, Pyramid signed Available Auer. The ape in the cape was the name part anyway. The film was banned in England and booed everywhere else.

The Studebaker crunched onto the driveway. Devlin's gut knotted.

Sometimes he'd breeze into a triple homicide and find cops playing pinochle among corpses. Sometimes, a movie siren shoplifted a can of peas and it was like the *Hindenburg* crashed into an orphanage. In Los Angeles, it's not what the crime is, it's who's done it – or who it's been done to.

A crowd milled on the lawn. Uniforms, staff, guests. The evening dress at breakfast type. Extras from the war picture had wandered over in muddy grey battle-dress. One officer looked so much like Erich von Stroheim that Devlin used his detective brain to deduce von Stroheim was playing the Colonel in *Flight of the Red Eagle* and this shave-pate Prussian was his stand-in.

The looky-loos and bystanders all stood well away from a white-face clown with French loaf shoes, a red Einstein wig and tattooed tear-drops. Pinky Sparx. From Pyramid's trademark-infringing comedy trio, the Sparx Brothers. Pinky, Gecko and Screwball weren't related to each other or to anyone or anything funny. They had made a string of lawsuit-provoking cash-in comedies... *Monkey Tricks*, *Hockey Puckers*, *Bugs Soup*.

Junior kept one or more of the Brothers around to enliven social events by assaulting guests. Screwball Sparx was doing ninety days in county because an Indiana theatre owner's daughter didn't find having her party dress ripped off her back while she was being introduced to Douglas Fairbanks Jr as funny as everyone else at that reception did.

From the way everyone avoided looking at Pinky – it's *hard* to ignore a clown – Devlin could tell the ersatz funnyman was little-liked on the lot. Rumours about other work the Sparx Brothers did for Pyramid might explain why they were among the studio's highest-paid stars despite the so-so earnings of their films.

Devlin parked in the gravelled semi-circle in front of the big doors. He got out of the car. A flashgun popped, dazzling him like a starlet at a premiere.

The shutterbug was a pocket-sized blonde with a silver feather pinned to her beret.

Devlin sucked in his cheeks like Garbo and gazed into the far distance.

The photographer snapped off exposures until her subject grew weary of glamour. The blonde wasn't a stringer for the *Hollywood Citizen-News* but one of the flacks from Pyramid Publicity, Fritzie Minikus. If anyone got arrested here, their mug shots would be touched up to give eyebrows more definition and hide crow's feet.

He looked around for someone who knew where the bodies were buried. No one stepped forward. Not even the von Stroheim substitute, who had the stiff spine and bull neck of the original – but not the arrogance to assume command.

Then Sheriff Dan rode to the rescue.

A motorcycle tore up the driveway with Ysidro squashed into its sidecar. The rider's helmet was stamped with a variation of the Pyramid logo where the pyramid is tiny and the eye huge. Pinky and a footman helped the Chief of Security out of his buggy.

'Devlin,' said Ysidro, 'we've been waiting for you…' as if he hadn't just flat out admitted he personally didn't want him here. 'I've had the house sealed. I know the DA likes fresh snow. Nothing's been touched.'

Between deed-doers, blundering dolts and sticky-fingers cops, most crime scenes Devlin saw were as set-decorated as a bedroom interlude in a DeMille costume picture. Everyone tidies up after murder. Someone always said, 'nothing's been touched'.

It didn't pass his notice that Ysidro had been ordered to co-operate – or seem to co-operate – with the authorities.

The double doors of Home House were tethered with a skipping rope, tied in an elaborate bow around the door-handles. Ysidro had a cowboy undo the knot. The mansion could only have been sealed for a few hours, but the ritual played like a tomb opening. A woman – a maid, or a day-player dressed as a maid – whimpered.

'An eternal curse upon unbelievers who violate the resting place of Anck-es-en-Amon,' Devlin intoned in an imitation that always made Boris wince.

'That's a terrible Peter Lorre,' said Fritzie.

'Everybody's a critic,' said Devlin.

Ysidro had the cowboy throw open the doors. Cold air shushed out.

Devlin wasn't going to be shoved into Home House yet. He spotted a uniform in the crowd. 'You a real cop?' he asked.

'Trapnell, out of Rampart.'

Not one of the two names he'd been given. So Trapnell was new-ish on the scene. He must have sinned grievously in a past life to rate this detail.

'So, I've got a burning vic... identity as yet unknown?'

No one wanted to volunteer information but the massed intake of breath was a giveaway. Devlin should have asked how hot the potato was before catching it like a fly-ball.

'The man on fire was Ward Home,' said Officer Trapnell. 'Junior.'

Now no one even wanted to look at Devlin.

The Home Heir... someday, all this would be his.

Would have been his, if he croaked.

It wasn't too late to fake Spanish flu and hand the case off to Maxwell.

'I don't suppose Junior could have been smoking in bed?' he floated.

Ysidro pointedly ignored Devlin.

If this were just an accident, the DA needn't get involved. Insurance people could take over. It worried the city dick that no one bothered to suggest an innocent – or at least, non-actionable – explanation. Either a fix was already in or the cataclysm was so godawful even pro cover-up men wouldn't go near it.

Devlin looked up at La Casa as though he could hear the screams.

He was here because Junior had flamed onto Sunset through his well-known secret back door. He should have done his roman candle act on the Home House lawn, away from passing trade. Then, his incendiary indisposition would rate three lines under the classified ads. Pyramid Publicity would sell it as a tennis accident.

Devlin smelled dead smoke. And something like bacon.

He stepped into the vestibule. That *was* what they called the arched, glass-roofed space beyond the main doors? It could be a foyer. Or an antechamber. Ray Chandler would know straight off. He always had the right word for any occasion. The city investigator was just human. Thick vines swarmed up poles and entangled overhead.

A crowd crammed behind Devlin. He barred the way like Horatius at the Bridge. He couldn't let a mob swarm over the threshold. Still, he needed trusty companions.

As if picking up a sandlot scratch team, he assembled an expedition. Trapnell, of course. Ysidro, because lies should at least be heard before they were scorned. Someone who worked inside the house and knew his way around was a must. So... Devlin called for Steward, a butler – or maybe the man was Butler, a steward. The only thing about the servant that stuck in the memory was the little sting of contempt added to the word 'sir'.

Because pictures might be useful later, Devlin took along Fritzie Minikus. If Pyramid Security favoured mutts who flunked as movie tough guys, Pyramid Publicity ran to tolerably decorative gals who came third in beauty contests but screen-tested poorly. Fritzie's fingertips were yellow and scabbed from handling white-hot flashbulbs, as if she'd tried to burn off her prints.

Ysidro told Pinky to keep everyone else out.

Interesting – the rumours were solid. The comedian moonlit as muscle. Squeaky sheriffs, not-funny clowns, arthritic cowboys. Were there also two–left–feet hoofers, ugly glamour girls and creampuff tough guys on the payroll? If Pyramid needed a horror man who wasn't frightening, they had Mischa Auer.

Devlin stepped into a hall the size of the ballroom on a Cunard liner. Lights came on, one by one, all around. Glass Cupid statues lit up from the inside. Lamps glowed in the floor. He had depressed a trick tile that banished dark and brought the house to sparkling life.

Music poured from speaker grilles.

Devlin caught the butler's smirk at the sudden *son et lumière*. He was the fun-house barker who knew when the air jet was going to blow up girls' skirts.

The piped music came from the studio orchestra. Never underestimate the bone-bred cheapness of the rich. The session must have been written off against the budget of Pyramid's *Unfinished Symphony*. Young Schubert (middle-aged Fredric March) can't complete his magnum opus, because his composing arm gets skewered during a duel with Lord Byron (Franchot Tone). If the picture had been any bigger a bomb, the Luftwaffe would have dropped it on Guernica.

Devlin still smelled smoke – and followed his nose.

'Trapnell, the report mentioned a man with a bucket of water who doused Mr Home. Any identification on him?'

'Norman Quin,' said Ysidro, who hadn't been asked.

'Yes, a Mr Quin,' the cop admitted.

'He was trying to help the victim?'

No one confirmed or contradicted.

'Quin is responsible for all this,' said Ysidro. 'He made the electric straitjacket.'

'The doohickey that caught fire? Where is it now?'

'At the hospital, I guess,' said Trapnell. 'Bystanders tried to get Mr Home out of it, but got shocked. Only this Quin bird knows how it goes on and comes off, apparently. He's, ah, an inventor.'

'An *eccentric* inventor,' put in Fritzie – as if tweaking a press release.

'And he's absented himself? Run away?'

'I've men searching for him,' said Ysidro.

'A vigilante posse, eh, Sheriff? You're aware those are what we in the justice business technically term *against the law*?'

'There's a bulletin,' said Trapnell. 'We've a good description.'

'Quin is easy to describe,' said Fritzie. 'Once you've seen his pan, you'll know why.'

'He has scars,' said Trapnell. 'From the War.'

'The man's a menace,' said Ysidro, with feeling.

Devlin started to see the picture developing, like a publicity shot in a tray of chemicals. Fright Face Inventor Burns Boss. In Hollywood, pictures are stories. Electric Maniac on the Loose. Stories are stories, not necessarily the truth. Brave Philanthropist Foully Flambéed. Not even *a* truth, most of the time. No one believed publicity shots.

The cursory report that came to the DA had Quin trying to put out the fire. Everyone here preferred the version where he lit it in the first place. No reason both couldn't be true. But independent witnesses vouched for the soaking. So far, arson against the person was unattested conjecture.

'Make sure Mr Quin is not accidentally shot before he sits in the office of the Acting District Attorney and tells his side of the story,' Devlin told Trapnell.

It wasn't fair to rag a beat cop about it – but Devlin's mood was getting poorer.

'Show me the door Home and Quin went through,' he said to the butler. 'The secret exit everyone knows about.'

'That egress is from the basement. Home House is built on a slope. You would have to go downstairs.'

'If I must…'

'Staff are restricted to the first floor and above,' he said. 'Mr Home and Mr Quin insist on privacy for their researches.'

No one reacted as if that were out of the ordinary.

'Researches in the basement?' said Devlin. '*Private* researches?' The unmemorable servant's face was stony. Not a flicker of sardonic smile. No innuendo intended. 'What a man gets up to with another man and an apparatus involving straps, batteries and near-lethal voltage is best left in the basement, eh? You can let us down there? You being Keeper of the Keys.'

The butler led the little group to a padded red leather door. A lintel was carved with sigils and signs. Aztec, Egyptian, Celtic, Gnostic. The Pyramid logo was proudly in the centre of all the art direction.

It was a strange door. No handle. No keyhole.

'Interior doors have no keys,' said the servant. 'Locks are opened with numeric or letter combinations.'

'And you don't know the code? I find that *impossible* to believe. Mr Home and Mr Quin may conduct mysterious researches in the basement, but I'll bet they don't clean up after themselves. You must send the maids down to dust.'

Devlin had him and he knew it. The butler's glance swivelled, an actor drying and looking for a prompt.

'Ignore Sheriff Dan and his twitchy eye,' Devlin said. 'He'll be no help if you get hung with an obstruction beef. You probably think obstruction is a misdemeanour like littering or whistling on Sunday… but it can be a felony, hard to distinguish from *accessory after the fact*. Many have those words ringing in their ears as they start a ten-stretch in San Quentin. So make with the *open sesame*.'

The servant turned to a brass plate set in the wall beside the door. It had slits and tumblers like a Babylonian slot machine. The butler fiddled until the combination read ELECTRA13 then pressed a big metal button. Sparks shocked his thumb. He yelped a German word Devlin's uncle once told him didn't damn mean what he knew it damn meant. He flapped his hand, trying to shake away the pain.

'Has the code changed?' Devlin asked.

The servant recovered most of his composure and wiped tears with his good left hand. Then, as gingerly as possible, he made an adjustment – ELEKTRA13 – and stood back. No one wanted to press the button.

'Nightstick,' Devlin said. Trapnell unslung his club and handed it over.

Holding the baton brought back memories of a three-month headache. His skull was held together by a cap of unspendable silver. Cops kill more with their nightsticks than their guns, Devlin knew. They were handy implements, with many uses.

Devlin jammed the stick against the button, expecting lightning to strike his plated cranium… but, with a definite click, the door swung open. It didn't creak, but Fritzie – for a lark – made a creaky sound in the back of her throat. Then she giggled.

The city investigator hung on to the stick a moment longer than he should have and handed it back.

A staircase descended into darkness.

'After you, Devlin,' said Ysidro.

A wailing sounded – a mewling, like a cat partially flattened by a truck, pleading for tyre iron euthanasia. Devlin whip-turned to shush Fritzie, but she'd quit playing sound effects wizard. The noise came from below.

Uh and – indeed – oh!

Ysidro undid the button on his hip-holster. Devlin felt the weight of the .38 under his armpit. The city dick carried a Colt Super .38 Semi-Automatic, made for Transcontinental and Western Air as a reaction to the invention of airmail robbery. He wasn't as obvious about being strapped as Ysidro's black leather cowboys. His work jackets didn't button up – the holes were sewn shut, so he wouldn't fasten out of habit. He could fish out his gun without getting tangled. Pulling a roscoe like taking out a wallet to settle the cheque wouldn't raise matinee cheers, but fast-draw gunnies are often butterfingers who lose their grip and fling iron across the room. Those boys looked stupid and surprised in the morgue.

They listened to the whine.

'Is that an animal?' asked Fritzie.

Devlin would have liked to tell her it was but couldn't.

He led the party down. The staircase was enclosed, with a low, arched ceiling. Every step he trod on lit up. The uncarpeted steps were hard translucent bricks with lightbulbs inside. Each stair was stamped with a black Gothic number – not quite in descending order from twenty to zero, as if innumerate workmen laid the steps and put a few in the wrong slots.

'*Not the thirteen,*' shouted the butler.

Devlin's foot hovered over the unlucky number. He drew back as if it were a man-trap. The code was a warning. ELEKTRA13 meant Electric Thirteen.

The bribes Junior must have laid out to get his house passed as code!

'You can step over it,' the butler said. 'That's safe.'

'Thanks for the tip, pal. Lose many gentlemen callers this way?'

He trod on the next step – fifteen – and didn't plunge into an acid bath.

Instead, a door opened at the bottom of the stairs. Orchestral Schubert gave way to tinkling solo piano. Erik Satie's 'Rêverie de l'enfance de Pantagruel'. The smoke stink was worse down here. The mewling was shriller. Closer. More human. More in pain.

'Any more surprises?'

The factotum didn't say anything.

'Everyone,' Devlin said, 'tread carefully and don't touch anything you don't have to.'

For once, he reckoned people would follow crime scene protocol. Maybe electrification had its uses.

Devlin went through the doorway.

It struck him. The *wrongness*. Like being stabbed in the side but reaching down to feel unbroken skin and no blood.

He'd seen enough Karloff pictures to recognise a mad scientist's basement laboratory. Whitewashed stone walls. Antique torture implements. Gadgets and gizmos. Lights and sparks and crackles. Retorts bubbling like a gin still in Hades. A framed portrait of Otto von Bismarck with the eyes cut away – all the better for peering through from the next room. Chimera specimens in sturdy jars, hanging in brownish liquid. Unborn Siamese twin alligators, a fusion of octopus and platypus, a Shirley Temple doll with a cat's face.

Just as Junior Home had studio musicians underscore his house, he'd had the art department decorate his hidey-hole. Half Frankenstein, half Buck Rogers. And all Perverts' Playground.

Fixed to the far wall were four people. Devlin had been told about Junior's electric suit. These people were stuck in similar get-ups. Bulbous steel hoods with glass faceplates. Canvas coveralls pinned inside complicated wire-and-rod armatures. He thought of the constricting devices portrait photographers used when exposures took minutes and slight movements made a ghostly blur. Thick, stiff belts were ringed with holsters for blocky batteries, connected by wires to the armature's struts and the helmet's metal ruff. The gear might be protective like a diving suit or a form of fashionable iron maiden. Any scientific purpose wasn't obvious.

One of the four was a giant: seven and a half feet tall and broad at the shoulders, with arms and legs so spindly the sleeves and trouser-legs of the coveralls were loose as socks on a golf club. A wide face squashed against the glass plate, eyes popped like deepwater fish hauled to the surface. Alive, he could have auditioned for *Son of the Fiend of Fog Lane*.

The next two were regular-sized but just as dead. One was burned from the helmet-ring down, suit blackened and charred into flesh. That was the smell they'd had in their noses since setting foot in Home House. Fritzie didn't faint or get sick and took pictures without Devlin telling her to. Maybe she had angles figured. She might sell the negatives to the yellow press or charge Pyramid to lose the plates.

The last of the four was the one making the noise.

The helmet shook. The faceplate was cracked. The electric belt was cinched at the waist and buzzing. The other three suits had burned out. This one was live.

Inside was a woman.

Without getting too close, Devlin sized up her situation. Besides being trapped in an electrified apparatus, the woman was shackled to the cross-piece of a frame bolted to the wall. Multicoloured wires from her helmet and belt were attached to measuring devices. Yards of graph paper unrolled on the floor, with jagged red lines scratched down the middle. Some of the paper had caught fire and been stamped out.

A muzzle inside the woman's helmet worked like a scold's bridle. She couldn't talk – just make noise.

'Should we turn off the juice?' asked Trapnell.

Screwed to a wall panel were four copper and Bakelite knife switches. The type beloved of tinkerers like Dr Frankenstein. All closed and possibly live. The unvarnished wood of the panel was soot-blasted, so some might have burned out along with the suits. Wires fed from the switches, got in a spaghetti tangle on the floor and plugged into the bedsteads.

'Might not help,' said Ysidro. 'Mr Home wasn't wired up and he was still sparking.'

A bucket of sand stood in a corner under a 'for use in case of fire' sign – with a wet space next to it where there'd been a bucket of water.

The woman in the iron mask indicated with her head that they should stand back. The butler retreated towards the doorway. Devlin had a minor worry about the servant straying from the group but had bigger fish to fry just now. Satie still plinked and plunked through a grille above a glass oval Devlin took to be a fogged mirror. If the music was supposed to be calming, it wasn't.

Trapnell sorted through a selection of tools and implements on a work-bench.

'Give me those,' said Devlin, pointing at a set of heavy-duty wire cutters with rubber-sheathed handles. The cop tossed them over. Devlin flexed them a few times while considering where to cut. He saw alarm in the woman's single exposed eye. Half her face was hidden under plastered-down black hair.

'These any use?' asked Trapnell. He'd found a ring of shiny keys in a house where doors didn't have keyholes. They were clunky and simple: metal shapes, like parts of a child's toy.

Trapnell knelt to unfasten a bar that fixed across the woman's feet. The first key he tried worked. She kicked free, nearly booting the cop in the face, and shook her wrist-cuffs.

'Careful,' Devlin told Trapnell as he unlocked the restraints.

Fritzie took a shot of the heroic rescue. Her flash made everyone jump. The woman clutched at her helmet-ring with freed hands.

'Less spontaneity, Miss Minikus,' Devlin said.

The woman tapped a rope of wires attached to the helmet. Urgently. Then she made a scissors gesture.

Devlin got the blades round the rope and snipped. It was harder than cutting off a finger, but with a twist he got through.

The electrified woman stepped away from the wall and took the cutters from him. She extricated herself as if she knew the device well enough to be sure what she was doing. She cut armature joints and shucked the frame. It stood by itself like a wicker dressmaker's dummy. She undid a clasp and dropped the belt, which she kicked into a corner as if it were a rattlesnake she'd shot before it could kill her.

She took off her helmet and unwound the mesh gag. She squirted backed-up spit into the steel cowl.

Then she pulled a zipper and wriggled out of the coveralls, emerging in her scanties, bruises and burns on her legs and arms. She chose a laboratory coat from a selection hanging from hooks and belted it around a wasp waist. Oversized for her, the coat looked like a white, floor-length dress. It might have done for Devlin, who had to buy custom-made clothes from the Big and Wide Store. She rolled the sleeves up above her elbows.

Without looking at the useless mirror, she fixed her hair. It still covered half her face, now deliberately. A patch on her crown was singed.

She was a looker but not a pin-up. Casting would call her in for the lovelorn heroine's wiseacre gal pal or the princess's scheming lady-in-waiting. She wouldn't be an above-the-title cutie. He didn't think she was in pictures. She didn't have that slight vacant look actresses had when the cameras weren't rolling, as if they were waiting for direction. She got on with extricating herself from a trap without being told to.

'Sister...' Devlin began, but she held up a hand to quiet him.

He didn't expect a rescued maiden to melt into his arms... but Miss Manners would recommend a simple thank you.

This woman was distracted – not out of danger yet.

She checked the three corpses. She hadn't real hopes, but had to be sure they couldn't be helped.

She took the helmet off the burned body.

'So you weren't fireproof,' she said.

She spoke with an English accent.

'Is he at large?' she said. 'The bloody monster?'

'Quin?' asked Devlin. She just looked at him.

The Satie shut off. Three tuning fork tones sounded, like a temple bell. The oval glass unfogged to show a bearded man sitting at a desk. He fidgeted, unbending and twisting a paper clip. A smaller oval above glowed slightly – a camera. This was a visiphone – a two-way television. One of Home House's modernisms. Devlin had seen a similar marvel demonstrated at the Homes of Tomorrow Exhibition.

The bearded man had a widow's peak like Dracula's wig. Piggy little eyes. Not much of a mouth. His image was distorted like a portrait on a stretched sheet of rubber. If he was what's on offer, Devlin couldn't see television taking off. Any face that popped up in his magic mirror would have to look more like Ginger Rogers to get his subscription fee.

The paper clip escaped the man's fingers. He hunched forward, almost cross-eyed. He must be peering at an identical screen and camera set-up at his end.

'Chief Ysidro,' said a hollow voice from the grille, 'ensure no more damage is done to Mr Home's laboratory equipment. Qualified technicians will be with you soon. Please secure any documents. They could be invaluable to the progress of a course of vital experiments. Mr Devlin, kindly call your office. A statement has been delivered from the Lamia Munro Clinic which should settle any concerns the District Attorney might have. Miss Ives, you are entitled on top of your honorarium to a bonus of ten thousand dollars. A contract will be with you within half an hour. You of course remain bound by the agreement signed yesterday and should not discuss the work of Home House with outside parties.'

The words were slightly out of sync with the lip movements.

There was a beat after he'd finished speaking before the oval fogged over. The piano music resumed.

'Who was that?' Devlin asked. 'The family lawyer?'

The woman – Miss Ives – shook her head.

'Family *doctor*,' she said. 'Vaudois. Dr Lionel R. Vaudois. Doctor V, as in "I do not like thee, Doctor Vee…"'

'*Doctor Voodoo*,' said Fritzie, as if announcing next fall's horror picture.

'I've heard him called that,' said Miss Ives.

Ysidro and the butler kept schtumm. They had contracts and agreements too. Pyramid people knew to be close-mouthed with 'outside parties'.

Dr Vaudois had classified rescuing the woman as 'damage to Mr Home's laboratory equipment'. That raised more concerns than any statement would settle.

Ysidro didn't make any move to secure the documents mentioned. Too busy mulling over how badly the morning was turning out. Devlin suspected the material that interested the doctor was unrolled and partially burned on the floor. He didn't have a clue how to read the runes, but – given time – could find people who would.

'Enough with the wonders of science,' said the city investigator.

'Remarkable as the means of delivering the message was, it's still the bunk. I see three deceased persons. Fritzie, take a *lot* of pictures. Trapnell, is Sergeant Lockley still on the homicide desk at Rampart?'

The cop nodded.

'We'll need Lockley, and all the troops he can muster.'

'Hold your horse,' said Ysidro. 'You can't make a murder case of this.'

'Who said anything about murder? Dead persons fall under homicide. Nature to be determined. Do you want to sell me on "natural causes"?'

Miss Ives looked at Ysidro, who was sweating. She took mercy on him and spoke, very carefully. More carefully than Devlin would have after being near-killed in a mad science experiment.

'Dr Vaudois mentioned agreements,' she said. 'We accepted the risk and waived away certain rights. Technically, we committed suicide. Or abetted in our ends. Of course, we were assured we'd be alive come morning. But Mr Home and Engineer Quin were exonerated in advance in case of… precisely what's happened.'

Devlin would have told her someone had to answer for the deaths, but he'd worked for Buron Fitts long enough to know he'd be blowing hot air. Cemeteries are full of the unavenged.

'Who are *they*?' he asked, meaning the corpses.

'This fellow was from a circus,' said Miss Ives, indicating the giant. 'He had a bone condition. His head and hands and feet were enormous, but the rest of his body was stretched thin – like he'd been on the rack. He could scarcely stand. His stage name was Groto the Gargantuan. His real name was Herb Something. We weren't formally introduced.'

She reached up but didn't – or couldn't – touch the dead man's helmet.

'The man who caught fire was another carnival performer. Eustis Amthor, the Mystic Yogi. He bent coins and cutlery with a touch and swallowed or pierced himself with pins and nails. I saw him open his forearm with a straight razor, then press the wound shut like a zip fastener. When he wiped the blood away, there wasn't even a scar. Look at his face… you can see patches of new skin forming over burns. But whatever his trick was, it wasn't fast enough to beat the fire. The other chap was Chinese. I don't know his name. He didn't speak much

English. Double-jointed. Elastic bones. An acrobat or a contortionist.'

'And are you from a sideshow, Miss…?'

'Ives… Laurel Ives. No, I'm from Potters Bar. That's north of London. I'm not especially special. Not these days.'

'I wouldn't say that. You're alive. In this company, that makes you special and precious and a prize.'

She shrugged. 'If you say so, Officer…'

'Devlin. And Trapnell's the officer. I'm an investigator from the DA's office.'

'Yes,' she said. 'You would be.'

'You know what a District Attorney is?'

'I've seen them in motion pictures. He's the fellow who represents "the People" when the case is "the People vee-ess Bad Hats". In England, he'd be a KC. King's Counsel. Our bad hats don't fear the people, they're terrified of the King's Man. We have "the Crown versus Rascal Rotters" instead. Excuse me, I'm babbling…'

She flicked her frazzled fringe and Devlin glimpsed the eye she liked to cover. It was badly bloodshot.

Fritzie took more pictures. Ysidro was tight-lipped about that.

'You can always smash the camera later,' Devlin told Ysidro. 'Pyramid'll take it out of your wages.'

He looked back at Laurel Ives. She wasn't where she'd been when he'd been distracted. He opened his mouth to raise the alarm…

… then heard a toilet flushing. A small door opened and the rescued woman came out of a bathroom the size of a cupboard.

'I've been shackled to the wall for seven hours,' she explained. 'It was supposed to be for fifteen minutes. At first, being in a room with the dead and dying and plugged into a machine that might kill you at any moment is enough to worry about. Then, after an hour or two, all you can think of is how desperately you need the lavatory.'

'I wouldn't have held it,' said Fritzie.

'Urine is an annoyingly excellent conductor of electricity,' said Laurel Ives. 'Never pee on anything with a current running through it. I think that's what Eustis Amthor did. You can see what happened to him.'

'A handy hint, Miss Ives,' said Devlin. 'Now, if you're quite comfy, perhaps you could explain a few things. Weigh a flimsy paper you signed yesterday against well-established state laws on withholding evidence. What happened?'

The English woman looked at him, thought a moment... and said, 'I really don't remember.'

Ysidro had been holding his breath. He let it out.

Laurel Ives scratched her cheek, thumb stuck out strangely.

'Smaller question, then. Who fixed you into that thing and cuffed you to the wall? You couldn't have done it by yourself.'

'No. Indeed, I couldn't. I did put the suit on of my own free will. That's in the flimsy paper. The restraints were fixed by Norman Quin.'

'*Hijo de puta*,' spat Ysidro.

'Whose *idea* was the shackling? Did Quin act of his own accord or under direction or duress?'

'Is that legal language?'

'I have some law school. I know I look like I shovelled coal instead of going to college. I did that too. And other things which are murder on the manicure. Answer the question, please.'

'Mr Quin signed a paper too. It'll be with mine.'

'That's not an answer.'

'I think you'll find it is. I went to several very good schools.'

'Thrown out, eh?'

'Mr Devlin, you will have to accept that I am saying what I am empowered to say. I am not trying to make your job more difficult than it already is.'

She scratched her face again, twitching her mouth in the direction her thumb was stuck.

'You're not stalling till the ten grand gets here.'

'That had never crossed my mind...'

He followed the direction she was pointing... and looked at the visiphone.

The oval screen was fogged – but the camera above still glowed.

They could be seen and heard.

No wonder she was watching her language.

He looked at her and scratched his own face. She dropped her hand in some sort of relief and puffed air up at her fringe. She seemed sweet and reasonable, until you glimpsed that witch-eye.

'We could put you back in Old Sparky,' he said, deliberately, 'and chain you up again. Leave the scene as we found it. I'm sure you can entirely trust someone they call "Dr Voodoo".'

'I'm sure I entirely can't,' she said, wanting to be heard by the eavesdropper. 'And, genuinely, I am grateful for my release. You have saved my life. I shall write a testimonial to that effect and recommend you be awarded a lollipop for outstanding performance. I also trust you'll pursue this matter to the fullest of the law. But I'm not a star witness in anyone's trial. You wouldn't want me on the stand. My background is not of the best. My word on anything is likely to be set aside. I'm afraid I qualify, in your colourful argot, as a "shady lady".'

'Who says "colourful argot"?'

'Me, Investigator Devlin. I do. I say such things.'

Devlin knew he'd been talked around but couldn't see how. Seven hours in a death trap and this dame was still scary-sharp. Her witch-eye was doing the thinking while she ran off at the mouth.

In Ray's book – well, in his stories – she'd be guilty of it all.

Chandler always pinned the murders on the dame.

In real life – well, in *this* real life… who knew? 'Laurel Ives' was at the least a dubious, uncooperative witness. He believed her name about as much as he believed 'Screwball Sparx'.

'Sir,' said Trapnell, 'the butler's gone.'

Devlin looked around. This time, the disappearee didn't pop out of the john. The door they'd come through was open. Lights indicated someone was running up the trick stairs – presumably avoiding unlucky thirteen.

Ysidro's eyes were narrow with annoyance. He wasn't in on this.

A scream came – the highest-pitched, strangest sound Devlin had heard out of a human throat. Devlin went to the door and looked up the staircase. All the step-lights flashed. The servant stood on the seven stair – not the thirteen – and convulsed. Froth dripped from his mouth onto his stiff white shirt front.

Then he tumbled, face blackened, clothes smoking. The current kept him jittering where he lay, but he was cooked.

'That step wasn't live before,' said Fritzie.

Devlin tossed the ring of shackle-keys at the stairs, half-way up – further than the butler had got. A jagged lightning flash etched into his vision, persisting even when he shut his eyes and rubbed them. He blinked and smeared tears on his cheeks.

Laurel Ives made an another-damn-thing face.

'It's Home House,' she said. 'It doesn't want us to leave alive.'

'You're *loco*,' said Ysidro, offended.

'And you're expendable,' she said. 'If you'd read your contract, you'd know that.'

'I'm not blaming a house,' Devlin said. 'Someone has to throw switches. Murder from a distance is still murder.'

'What about the street door?' asked Trapnell. 'It was open last night.'

'You're welcome to try,' said Laurel Ives, 'but loopholes get plugged fast around here.'

Trapnell was close to an exit that must lead to the secret street door. He drew his hand away from a push-bar. No one in the room wanted to touch metal.

'What do you suggest?' Devlin asked Laurel Ives.

'So now I'm rescuing you?'

'Consider it a system of mutual benefit.'

She considered it.

Fritzie photographed the dead servant where he lay. Maybe she had a yen to get into crime scene camerawork. Ysidro didn't even tell her off. He'd been thrown out of the same boat as the rest of them.

Laurel Ives finished thinking.

'There'll be a secret passageway,' she said. 'Possibly several.'

'That's just in horror pictures,' said Trapnell. 'No one's built secret passageways since Prohibition.'

'This house was designed by people who make horror pictures,' said Devlin. 'Where might this secret passageway be, Miss Ives?'

'I said there must be one, not that I know where it is. Home wouldn't have left out secret passageways when building his sandcastle. Look for hidden switches and sliding panels. Pull sconces, if you can locate such beasts…'

'… that aren't electrified.'

'Good point, Mr Investigator.'

She handed him back the rubber-sheathed cutters.

'Did anyone see *The Fiend of Fog Lane?*' he asked.

'Pyramid don't pay me enough to *watch* their lousy pictures,' said Fritzie.

Ysidro shrugged. If he skipped homework, he wouldn't admit it out loud. He also knew walls had ears and eyes.

Devlin remembered the portrait with holes for eyes.

The picture wasn't the real Bismarck, but Emil Jannings under false whiskers in Pyramid's *Iron Chancellor*. When Berlin started banning films made by moguls with names like Mayer and Cohn, Pyramid – a rare Hollywood studio not owned by Jews – courted the German market with oompah musicals, mountain pictures where bandit heroes sported Hitler haircuts and costume dramas set in the Franco-Prussian War where the French were bad guys. In *Flight of the Red Eagle*, Roy Brown would miss von Richthofen and the Kaiser would win the War.

On closer examination of Jannings' face, Devlin realised the eyeholes were tinted glass. In *The Fiend of Fog Lane*, the secret passage was behind a double portrait of Mischa Auer and his gorilla dressed as Prince Albert and Queen Victoria. This basement dungeon might have been designed by the art director who decorated Auer's lair. That cat-faced doll prop was certainly recycled set dressing.

The picture wasn't hung, but screwed to the wall – which was plasterboard textured to look like stone blocks. It wasn't painted on canvas, but a tin sheet. Devlin rapped Jannings' chest with the cutters. The panel shook like stage thunder.

Mischa Auer opened his secret panel by pulling a fake book out of a case. There was no such arrangement here.

'Look at Fungus Face's medals,' said Trapnell. 'One sticks out.'

Devlin saw it. Not any order the real Bismarck would have worn, but a badge with the Pyramid Pictures logo. He pressed the point of the cutters against it.

The metal plate shushed upwards into a slot, like a raised guillotine blade.

In a dark room beyond the picture was a modern chair – black leather straps and chrome tubes, with a coaster built into one arm. Perfect for peeping.

'Okay, everyone through here,' said Devlin.

No one moved.

Someone had to go first. Devlin knew he'd look an ass if he ordered Trapnell – the one person here who had to do what the city investigator said – to be guinea pig, so he squeezed through the aperture himself. It was a tight fit.

No blade fell.

Lights came on in the small, spare room.

Laurel Ives followed him. Then the others.

The room was crowded. It was a spying station for one or two peepers. Devlin had to bow his head not to scrape it on the ceiling.

Ysidro was last through the hole. He looked back at the visiphone eye, as if hoping for orders. He was sweating.

'Remember the butler,' Devlin whispered. 'For all your bosses care, it could have been you on the shock stairs. What's one studio bull, more or less, to them?'

Sheriff Dan saw the point.

'New problem,' said Fritzie. 'There's no door apart from the hole we just came through. That makes this a big closet rather than a room *per se*… so we're not really closer to getting off the ghost train.'

The whole ceiling was a light fitting – a sheet of hard, milky non-glass, with glowing spots. Devlin pressed his fingertips to the stuff. It was warm, with a slight give like linoleum. The unilluminated walls were of the same material. No portraits, bookcases or cracks that might be secret doors. The chair arm had dials and switches. Within reach were a set of controls like gear levers.

'It's Flash Gordon's rocket ship,' said Fritzie. 'That's how we get out of here. Take off and zoom.'

Laurel Ives sat in the low chair and reached for the switches and levers.

'Are you sure you should be doing that…?' Devlin asked.

'No,' she said.

She flicked switches like a pilot readying for take-off. A hum started.

'If the walls slam together and pulp us like oranges, it'll be your fault,' Devlin told her.

'I don't think this is a room *or* a closet,' she said. 'Or a rocket ship. This is a lift… an elevator.'

She pulled the biggest of the levers. Devlin's stomach lurched.

The room was pulled upwards. Devlin saw brickwork through the hole that had been covered by the portrait.

Fritzie fell against Trapnell, who gallantly supported her – the sap.

Ysidro put his hands out and kept balance without touching anything.

After a minute or so, the capsule stopped rising. Instead of brickwork, the hole showed sheet metal – with holes at eye-height. They were on the first floor or above and behind another picture. Laurel Ives' hand went to the controls, searching for an open sesame button.

Devlin put his face to the holes.

Beyond was a corridor. No one in sight.

Laurel Ives threw the right switch. The panel slid up.

This time, a press of people wanted to get out first. Trapnell helped Fritzie through, then followed. The itchy, anxious Ysidro was close on their heels. Devlin let Laurel Ives go next – more because he wanted eyes on her than from gallantry. He didn't trust her not to spring another, more permanent disappearing act if he turned his back. He had to tuck in his head and arms turtle-fashion to get through the hole and still scraped against the sides.

Devlin sympathised with Groto the Gargantuan. Nothing here was to his scale. La Casa had high ceilings, panoramic windows and a ten-foot-deep swimming pool, as if built for the Goliath family. Home House was made for shrimps like Junior Home. If it had conventional light fittings, regular-sized people would bang their heads against them.

The tin sheet slid down again. Stuck on this concealed door was a poster for *Oktoberfest Hayride of 1935*, Pyramid's all-star musical revue – a cacophonous assembly of oompah and hillbilly acts, with unwelcome guest appearances from the Sparx Brothers, Dry Bone and Trooper, Chick Chang the Chinese Contortionist and Sir Guy Standing. The concealed button was the Pyramid logo beside the credits block.

'Chick Chang,' said Laurel Ives, pointing at a human pretzel with a pigtail. 'He was…'

Devlin knew exactly who he'd been.

The other wired-up corpse. Now he came to think of it, the Fiend of Fog Lane was more rubber-limbed than the common or garden variety gorilla-suit goon. That must have been the late Mr Chang too.

The roster was a giant, a fakir, a contortionist and… this English rose? Who said she wasn't 'especially special'.

No, she'd said she wasn't 'especially special… Not these days.'

Which meant she had been once. Now she was special again. The only survivor. The sole witness.

Except for Junior and Quin. The city investigator had them filed as suspects rather than witnesses.

Of course, Laurel Ives wavered on the edge of 'suspect' too.

She gave him a tight, formal smile and asked, 'Coming?'

The whole troupe were eager to move on.

This section of the house looked less likely to feature electric death traps. If Devlin were a mad mastermind, that's exactly where he'd place them. Where the unsuspecting would drop their guard and get zapped to smoking ashes.

'Watch your step,' he reminded, like a Scoutmaster. 'Touch nothing you don't have to.'

Lining the corridor were posters for bread-and-butter Pyramid pictures… *Unashamed Dame… The Bandit Baron of the Harz Mountains… Maisie and Minnie Go to Moscow… Say It With Tubas*. When he walked past the *Carnival Crackles!* poster, Pinky Sparx's google eyes wobbled. They were on springs and set off by a plate under the floor. That could as easily have dropped an anvil on an unwary head.

Here, the music was Russian – the selection from Act II of *Swan Lake* that played over the titles of horror pictures.

At the end of the corridor hung a full-length portrait of a slim, ageless woman. Her long dress was either very classical or very modern. Her hair was a fall of pure white. Her eyes were closed. The dress shimmered as they approached. The eyes opened like faceted emeralds. An optical illusion.

'Is that Garbo?' asked Fritzie. 'Metro would never let her go, and if they did she'd play burlesque houses before she'd sign with Pyramid.'

'Looks more like Carole Lombard,' said Trapnell. 'If she'd never laughed in her life.'

'The painting's not new,' said Ysidro. 'It came from Germany with Mr Home Senior's father.'

Devlin knew who it was. He could no more look straight at those trick eyes than stare into the sun. Along with the snatch of Tchaikovsky, her face threatened to take him away... out of this mystery into other, deeper puzzles he'd pulled at but got nowhere with.

He kept running into her.

Ariadne.

Rather, he kept stepping into rooms she'd just left and finding her leavings. Dissipating smoke phantoms. Husks of people, dead and alive. Works of genius as by-products of insanity. Whoever had painted this was probably one of her pets. So was poor Tchaikovsky.

Of course she was in this.

Ray and Boris revered her but were terrified of her wrath. Devlin didn't have his friends' connection with the creature but knew enough to stay away from her.

He saw a funny side to it. Muses fall on hard times too. There was a long drop-off between *Swan Lake* and *Say It With Tubas*.

Laurel Ives – who looked everyone square in the face, if only with one eye – turned her head so the picture was on her blind side.

The corridor jackknifed and opened out onto a landing.

They were at the top of the main stairs, looking down.

Some of the people they'd left behind less than an hour ago were still there. The real Pinky Sparx faded into the crowd, as much as a clown could. His mean little eyes weren't like the humorous poached eggs on the gimmick poster.

New faces had arrived. The three Ivy Leaguers with black briefcases must be the lawyers with statements, contracts and cheques – as promised by the man on the visiphone. A couple of day players in white coats – one even had a stethoscope around his neck – tried to look like doctors. They'd also be from the Lamia Munro Clinic.

Just barging in was Sergeant Burn Lockley. Who'd called homicide? Lockley had a couple of uniforms with him. He was reasonably straight for Rampart. Anyone he sent to the gas chamber had most likely earned it.

Lockley waved his notebook at Devlin.

The crowd stirred and parted for a late, important arrival. The awkward figure forced his way through, coat cloaked over an arm-cast, hat awry, white face furious. He had escaped from a concerned nurse.

Another miracle. Buron Fitts, raised from his bed like a graft-taking Lazarus, dragged to Home House.

Devlin could only imagine the pull it took to vault over Follard's acting head to force the recuperating DA back to work.

Fitts glared around and saw Devlin at the top of the stairs.

He'd looked less aggrieved with fresh bullets in him.

An axe was about to fall. Lockley closed his notebook.

One of Ysidro's goose-steppers followed the direction of Fitts' angry glance and did a Gecko Sparx double-take at the returnees from the basement expedition.

'Hey,' he said. 'Didn't you go downstairs? You're coming back from the wrong place.'

Devlin couldn't argue with that.

———

9

As he told us about Home House, Joh Devlin drank steadily. His face gleamed with perspiration, but his speech didn't slur. He could have been giving evidence in court, though credible witnesses tend not to ladle so much spiritous punch while testifying.

The DA wouldn't have him on the stand in this case. An official story was being cooked. Joh wouldn't parrot what they came up with. Which is why he was out of a job.

My mouth dried. In long pauses between draughts my tongue swelled like baked leather. When I swallowed, iciness trickled in my chest. Not intoxicated, I was drifting a little, rudderless, anchorless. I could blame the heat of the day as much as the punch.

Phantoms rose just out of view, at the far end of the extensive, well-cultivated Karloff gardens (as featured in fan magazines). If I looked straight at them, the ghosts weren't there. If I didn't, they gathered in gloom at the edge of sight. I doubted they were the same spooks that bothered Katharine Hepburn.

A sylph crouched in the shade of a weeping golden willow that trailed in the swimming pool. Gracia's niece was still playing hide-and-seek or peek-a-boo with imaginary monsters. The little girl pushed her face into fronds and shook her head, letting long leaves tickle her cheeks. Beata liked the sensation on her nose and shut eyes, and pushed harder – until the tree was almost scratching. Then she threw herself flat on her back and waved up at the agitated foliage, giggling as if the willow had whispered something wicked in her ear.

Billy lay in the sun like a salamander, eyes almost closed.

He had a capacity for stoic stillness. It took Jack Pierce upwards of five hours to turn Billy into the Monster or the Mummy, so he developed a trick of going inside himself. The daily ordeal recurred for the length of a shooting schedule, and must be endured. He could hold out under torture.

He lived with pain. As an actor, he used it. Possibly, he *needed* it. Monsters are always in agony, lashing out at the world to pay back inflicted hurts. Chaney put fishhooks in his cheeks, stretched wires around his eyes and strapped his limbs the way the Chinese once bound girls' feet. The silent star was his own make-up man; he did it all to himself. I could imagine what – or who – drove him to that.

Boris Karloff had it done to him by other people.

He submitted willingly in Jack Pierce's House of Pain.

He told me one way he coped with having a hundred yards of rotten linen wound around his body or layers of collodion shaped about his head was to mentally recite verse he learned at school. As the Monster, he growled and grunted. Inwardly, along with Mrs Shelley's Monster, he quoted Milton.

'Did I request thee, Maker, from my clay to mould me Man, did I solicit thee from darkness to promote me?'

It's always been a fair question. Makers have never answered to anyone's satisfaction. Jimmy Whale's 'part of the ritual, old boy' wouldn't send anyone home happy if their face still burned from acid dripped to melt away the Monster's mug at the end of a shooting day.

We both knew from the beginning how Joh's story ended.

With Joh fired. Justice not done. Innocents unavenged. The guilty free. I couldn't sell that to *Dime Detective*.

The movies wouldn't take it either. Unless it was Hemingway. Even then they'd change the finish to be happier… before fixing the beginning and middle to match up with the end. And putting in songs.

'Fitts asked for my report,' said Joh. 'I gave it to him. Straight. He asked what my next move would be. I told him I needed to interview Ward Home Junior. I played it smart – I said "interview", not "interrogate". Fitts saw through it, though. He's no dummy. In Home House, Junior called the shots. Quin only threw the switches. Just like in Billy's movies. Mad scientist and hunchbacked assistant. Yes, the shrimp caught fire, but the evidence was hard to ignore – even with all the mouths shut by signed contracts and accepted pay-offs. I didn't come out and say I pegged Junior for doer and Quin for maybe-unwitting accomplice but that was – and still is – my thinking. Fitts ordered me off the case. I pointed out that four people were dead – one of them right in front of me. The score didn't impress him. He looks dead himself. His nurse kept telling him he shouldn't be out of bed. Being angry got him on his feet. Being frightened kept him there. Someone with pull reached him overnight. Calls were made.'

'Home Senior,' I said.

'In the end. I doubt the Old Man would deign to talk with someone as lowly as a District Attorney. He'll have poured fire on the Governor, who'll have roasted three or four lesser pooh-bahs before the heat got under Fitts' sick bed. But the evidence is still there, lying in the morgue. After someone figured out how to turn off the juice to the cellar stairs – and how it got turned on is a whole other question no one wants answered – they brought the inarguable facts in the case out of the house on stretchers, under sheets.'

'With you off the picture, how's it playing out?'

Joh smiled bitterly.

'Fitts likes Quin for Sole Culprit and Junior for Wholly Innocent Victim. A lot of other mucky-mucks would happily give the thumbs up to that scenario, even if it is the bunk. Sergeant Lockley is running a dragnet, which is one of the LAPD's very favourite pastimes. Norman Quin can't easily blend into a crowd. I agreed he should be found and interviewed. He's obviously privy to germane information. His story about the night should be on record. Fitts choked at that. The DA sees no need for niceties like evidence and a confession when it comes to stamping "case closed" on this file. Bringing 'em back alive isn't a priority. Notice how many on the FBI's Most Wanted list get ventilated in one-sided shoot-outs. It'd be called assassination if the guy with all the holes in his chest were a European grand duke rather than a mid-west bank bandit. I reckon there's a bounty on Quin's pelt. Wanted – Dead or Deader! Lockley's a decent murder cop, but you know Rampart… they don't apply for arrest warrants, they take out hunting licences.'

Billy raised himself from his lounger, straddled it like a horse and leaned forward, eyes glittering darkly. He felt something – obligation, kinship – for the man who'd nearly been the Monster.

'That won't do, Joh,' he said. 'That won't do at all.'

'I said as much. The butler – Moritz Stewart, his name was – died well after Quin ran off in the night. No one wants to think too much about that. Nobody's that worked up about the others, really. The fried freaks. The only concern is with what happened on Sunset, in public. Not what happened in Home House, behind four-foot-thick walls. New information isn't wanted. It messes up the story. The business with Stewart is a case in point. In mysteries, nobody cares about a butler. Whether he's a corpse in a wardrobe or a killer in the last reel, he's only a cadaverous joke in a monkey suit. Rich people are trained to see servants as furniture. Smart alecks like me treat 'em as punchlines. Moritz Stewart has a family. A son in the Navy and a daughter in college. I didn't much warm to the guy, but it's on me that he went into the basement where he died… where he was killed. He wasn't there of his own free will. Better than any of us he knew it was dangerous. He died because someone threw a switch.'

'Dr Vaudois?' I asked.

'He needs looking at.'

'Did you share that with Sergeant Lockley?'

Joh shrugged. 'I would have. I'm generous that way. I walked Lockley through the mad science dungeon, pointing out features of interest. I told him Fritzie had a roll of film on the crime scene. Then things got heated with Fitts. When I gained the distinct impression my ten cents' worth was unwanted, I skipped a lot of the rundown. Ysidro and Trapnell may have filled some of it in by now. If Lockley wants to sift through evidence, I left plenty just lying there. Mart Maxwell rolled onto the Home Estate with his wife's autograph book in his coat pocket, ready to take over. He'll go at the case hard… in any way that doesn't inconvenience the Home family.'

I asked Joh whether he'd ceded authority with good grace.

'No sirree. I said this was my case and I was sticking on it. That's when Fitts yanked my badge. I tossed it at his feet like a showboating idiot. He spluttered so much his cast cracked. He'll be a candidate himself for Dr Voodoo's Revivificator if he doesn't watch out. So, I was off the job by midday… I went back to the office and all the stuff from my desk was in a box on the sidewalk. Pinned under my silver shield for rifle shooting was a severance cheque. When I got home, after time spent in a local hostelry, one of the Ivy Leaguers I'd seen at Home House was sitting on the stoop of my apartment house. I didn't catch his name, but he'll be "Chip" or "Tag" or something like it. He proffered one of Dr Vaudois' famous binding agreements and showed me the cheque I'd receive if I signed. Substantially more substantial than the city's pay-off.'

'You tore it up,' said Billy.

Joh toasted him with a wink. The juice had gone and the punch was just fruit pulp and alcohol.

'Hush-up paper and cheque both,' he said. 'Damn fool that I be.'

'Did you sock the shyster?' I asked.

Joh smiled. 'Swung and missed. I'd say it was the booze, but the Chipster or the Tag-Man is fast and clever and knows dirty scrapping. Pyramid feed their lawyers on spinach and give them practical lessons in pugilism. The boyo knew to leave me with my pretty face, but I've saucer-sized bruises under the corset.'

'What about the woman?' asked Billy.

'Ah, yes, the woman. Witch-Eye. I almost forgot her. While I was telling Fitts about my plans to shove plutocrats in front of a firing squad and establish a workers' soviet in City Hall, she mingled with the innocent bystanders and sneaked off when Maxwell had them shooed away. I suppose I could have yelled "halt" but I was off the payroll – so that was someone else's job. I imagine Lockley and Maxwell are trying to run her down about now. She's marginally less likely than Norman Quin to get shot by a cop but that doesn't mean she's not on several players' to-be-silenced lists. In some quarters, they'll ruminate on how much tidier the story would be if she'd fried with the rest of the sideshow acts. What were they – test subjects? That part of the story is blurry. I don't blame Witch-

Eye for taking it on the lam first chance she got. You'd enjoy Laurel Ives, Ray. She's your type. I know you like 'em with claws.'

'That's cats, Joh,' I said.

'You don't want to let this lie, do you?' said Billy.

'Not hardly. This is one for us. One only we can handle. Like the Mystery and Imagination Murders or the Ape Ricotte Abductions.'

I was dubious, as usual… but Billy was already in.

He stood up and put on a black silk robe with quilted lapels. Beata whistled and Billy did a girlish twirl that flared the robe's skirts. He'd be good casting for the dual role of Grandma and the Wolf – especially in the scene where the ravenous beast pretends to be the sweet little old lady.

'Your Laurel Ives is English?' Billy asked.

'She talks like you two do,' Joh replied. 'I knew that'd pique your interest.'

'We're looking for a mystery dame?' I asked.

'You say "dame" like it is a foreign word, Ray. I know you mean "lady". You're a whisper away from thinking "fair damsel". Yes, we're looking for her. She'll have to work hard on a disguise. I've never seen an eye like hers. Part of her hair was scorched off. She'll wear a beret or a wig or both. Probably dark glasses. Like Quin, she can't keep to shadows forever.'

'We're looking for a monster, too,' said Billy.

'Takes one to catch one,' said Joh. 'Laurel Ives and Norman Quin have stories that *need* to be told.'

That I understood. Stories are insistent sometimes.

'… and here's another funny thing,' Joh said, opening a document satchel and bringing out a slim folder. 'This was slid under my door this morning. I doubt it was left by Chip Chippington Tagsworth – Strongarm Shyster. It must be a gift from an interested party, though. Maybe the Ives frail. Maybe Fritzie. Hey, maybe Lockley. He could have enough of a conscience to want us picking at scabs he's been told to leave alone.'

The folder was an expensive piece of custom stationery, embossed with the initials LMC. Lamia Munro Clinic. I made do with the folders they sell in lots of ten at the Post Office. If I could only indulge in one luxury it would be stationery like this.

'Those English mysteries you hate but read all the time, the ones with the green covers… they treat murder as a puzzle. In every chapter, a piece is doled out. The dodge is to hide a clue so the reader doesn't realise in the front of his brain that the offhand mention that the vicar is left-handed in an extraneous brandy-pouring scene in chapter six scotches the suicide theory the slow-witted inspector sticks to in chapter nineteen. The bullet-hole is in his right temple. See, I *have* been working on construction and plotting in my yarns. In the last chapter, the sleuth puts all the pieces together and you get the whole picture – *voila!*'

'You use French words like a Canadian,' I said.

'There's a simple explanation for that,' he said. 'Anyway, as you have said on many occasions, real murder cases don't break like that. Most cops ain't slow-witted, but your average murder policeman isn't like the reader of a green-jacket mystery. He doesn't get enough puzzle pieces. Some are tossed in the trash or lost in the post. There's a temptation to use a nailfile on the pieces they do have to make a picture Fitts can exhibit to a jury and get an easy win.'

'Is this metaphor ever going to coalesce into a point?'

'Yes. Now. Sometimes by a miracle the cops get all the pieces to make a picture that matches the one on the box. But after "Monarch of the Glen" has been completed and smoothed out on the table, there's an extra piece or two left over. Part of the puzzle, undeniably. But with nowhere to fit it in. Know what a cop will do with pieces like that?'

Joh handed the LMC folder to me.

I ran my fingertips erotically over the smooth cardstock, then opened the folder and looked through the documents. First was a publicity still – not a staged scene from a film, but a candid shot of cast and director. At least, I pegged the guy with a beret and a moustache as a director. A megaphone would have sealed the deal. He was surrounded by odd characters who cosied up to him as if their jobs depended on it, which they did. Midgets, a bearded lady, a couple of microcephalics, a fellow in a maître d' tux whose body ended at his belt, a Hindu with no arms or legs (smoking a roll-up cigarette), a sad-faced clown and a spindle-legged giant.

I gave the still to Billy.

'The fellow in the middle is Tod Browning,' he said, tapping the guy with the moustache. 'This is from *Freaks*. The Metro horror that flopped. They sold it off to tent shows.'

The giant was at the back of the group of carnival people. So tall that his head wasn't in the picture.

'Is this…?'

'"Groto the Gargantuan"?' said Joh. 'The late "Herb Something". Yes, it is. Herbert Holloway, according to the folder.'

The next still was a solo of Holloway on the *Freaks* set – sawdust on the floor, striped canvas backdrop. The camera was angled up to get most of him in the picture – long, long legs and longer crutches. His swollen, almost-hairless head was tilted permanently to one side. His neck couldn't properly support his skull so his mouth was lost in wrinkles. A protruding ridge of cheekbone stretched his face. He wore stars and stripes britches and a tiny Uncle Sam hat that wouldn't be that tiny on a regular person. On the back of the publicity shot was gummed a piece of yellow paper with typewritten information.

'"Herbert Holloway… Groto the Gargantuan",' I read aloud. '"Represented by…" so-and-so and so-and-so, theatrical agents. List of circuses, not including any of the ones I've heard of. List of film credits… "*He Who Gets Slapped* (M-G-M), *The Unknown* (M-G-M), *Don Juan* (Warners), *The Call of the Circus* (Pickwick Pictures), *Island of Lost Souls* (Paramount), *The Freaks* (M-G-M)" – typical, his agency get the title wrong – "*Trooper's Terror Trail* (Pyramid)." A telephone number. Pencil notation – "special projects?".'

'He worked on Lon Chaney pictures,' said Billy, who always lowered his voice when the silent bogeyman came up.

If Chaney hadn't died, Universal would have made *Frankenstein* with him. And Billy would be a swarthy, English-accented cowboy or gangster henchman – gunned in the third reel. His credits would have been as sketchy as those of Herb Holloway, who was in big pictures as a prop and little ones as a stooge.

'Browning and Chaney collected carnies like this Holloway chap,' said Billy. 'Louis Mayer hated the idea, but Irving Thalberg – the only person

Mayer's afraid of – made him go along with it. The dwarfs and giants were grateful for the work. I know what that's like. I suppose Holloway was hard to use. It looks like he couldn't get around easily.'

In a posed still from *Trooper's Terror Trail*, Holloway towered over a whiskery comedian who was hiding behind a horse that was unquestionably the best actor in the scene. Trooper conveyed his desire to gallop off the backlot and bolt for the high country to run free with palominos. Holloway's deformed chin and cheek were covered by a spongey fake beard. He wore patched mountain man dungarees and sleeve-length gorilla gloves.

'It's an injustice that Junior Home has never won an Oscar for Best Picture,' I said.

'This is just a curiosity angle,' said Billy. 'Where's this extra piece of yours, Joh?'

Joh smiled. 'Keep reading.'

A thin, fragile sheet of paper almost came apart as I unfolded it. A handbill for a revivalist meeting. A crude pencil drawing represented an unmistakable Herbert Holloway standing next to a horse and cart (for scale), at eye-level with the driver. He wore an Old Testament robe and had hair down to his shoulders. Either he'd gone bald since or he wore a wig when hellfire preaching.

'Hark unto the Last of the Nephilim,' said the poster. 'God's truth from One who can bear witness to the Happenings of the Old Testament.'

'"There were giants in the earth in those days,"' I said, quoting a text on the poster. '"And also after that, when the sons of God came in unto the daughters of men, and they bare children to them, the same became mighty men which were of old, men of renown. – Genesis chapter six, verse four."'

'"And God saw that the wickedness of man was great in the earth, and that every imagination of the thoughts of his heart was only evil continually,"' intoned Billy, as if over the opening reel of a DeMille Biblical epic. 'If you got so much as a "begat" or an "abideth" wrong, the prefect dropped a cinder from the fire into your palm and told you to make a fist.'

Billy showed his hands. The marks were still there. A martyr's wounds.

'This looks like it's from the 1880s,' I said. 'Holloway must have been a teenage evangelist. The Aimee Semple McPherson of the day.'

Joh made a 'turn the page' gesture.

Next in the folder was a photostat copy of two pages of a magazine. The first page was a woodcut portrait of 'Lieu't H. T. Holloway, late of the United States Navy'. He was less crinkly around the chin and without the cheek protrusion. He wore an early nineteenth-century naval uniform with rows of buttons. The second page was headed *Analectic Magazine and Naval Chronicle*, September 1816, *A Repository of the Lives and Portraits of Distinguished Americans*. The article below wasted the first paragraph on guff like 'the poor Greeks, it is true (Prof.p.2), were not capable of subjoining a portraiture of the body to a delineation of the mind' before even mentioning Lieutenant Holloway, 'the famous giant of the Battle of Put-in-Bay', then rather disappointingly owning up to the fact that the early American hero of unusual size spent his time in the service as a land-based bureaucrat rather than tossing British sailors overboard like rag dolls in the War of 1812.

The final item was a sheaf of pages stapled together. They'd been clipped out of a recent edition of *The Ingoldsby Legends*. The entirety of the chapter entitled 'The Windmill-Man of Kent: A legend of Bertram Halleweigh'. The story came back to me as I skimmed the text.

'This is an old wives' tale,' I said. 'Rather, an old curate's tale. Thomas Ingoldsby was the pen name of a clergyman called Barham. We passed round this book at school. Some tales are stuffy but think they're amusing. Others are dull but think they're spooky. I'd forgotten this chapter, which is neither one nor t'other. It's about a fellow who was so prodigiously tall he could wave his arms and whip up a gale that made game break from cover. More like an electric fan than a windmill but they didn't have such things then. The Windmill-Man is supposed to have lived in the 1600s. King Charles II came to see the human wonder and had his wig blown off.'

The illustration of the Windmill-Man and the King, with Nell Gwynn laughing along with the jest, was a nineteenth-century fancy by Arthur Rackham. Not drawn from life, though something about the face was familiar.

'"Rather your wig than your head", quoth the beauteous wit, referring to the monarch's late father, Charles I. For Ingoldsby, that's a laugh line. Today's readers might prefer P.G. Wodehouse.'

Another Old Alleynian, by the way. Plum Wodehouse. As is Dennis Wheatley, who writes those silly black magic stories. So I'm neither the best nor the worst writer of my Dulwich College generation.

Joh tapped the Ingoldsby page.

'It doesn't take much to mangle Bertram Halleweigh into Herbert Holloway,' he said.

'It can't be the same man,' I said.

'Can't it? I had Genesis whipped into me, too, in a one-room schoolhouse up North. "And the LORD said, my spirit shall not always strive with man, for that he also is flesh: yet his days shall be an hundred and twenty years."'

'Holloway would have to have more days than that if he were the Windmill-Man. As many as Methuselah? *His* days were nine hundred and sixty-nine years. If so, this dossier should be fatter.'

'The file seems calculatedly thin to me. Just highlights. Not too much to stretch belief. It doesn't tell you something you wouldn't believe straight off… it lays out evidence and leads you down a path you might not take of your own accord.'

'When you say "you", you don't mean us, do you, Joh?' said Billy. 'A centuries-old giant isn't beyond what we might believe. Grouse-scarer, patriot, preacher, film extra. What a career for an immortal!'

'Not immortal. Long-lived, yes… but Holloway managed to die.'

'Like Bela in *Dracula*,' said Billy.

'And you in *The Mummy*,' said Joh. 'Centuries-old, crumbling to dust in daylight.'

'This could be a mock-up,' I said. 'Movie props. Studios have whole departments to rig up forgeries. The poster feels old, but that can be faked. The *Analectic Magazine* pages aren't even the originals. The *Ingoldsby* chapter is real, but the book was a deliberate farrago of nonsense. Herbert Holloway might have taken his stage name from *The Ingoldsby Legends*.'

'Then why not call himself Bertram Halleweigh?' said Billy.

'If it's a hoax, it's hard to figure the point,' said Joh. 'The Powers That Be don't want attention paid to what happened at Home House. This guarantees we'll stick on the case, even unofficially. My gut says it's not bunk. I *saw* Holloway… what was left of him. He didn't turn to ash and bone like Mr Mummy, but he was… *wrong*. Not just his physical condition, not just his ugly death. Everything about him. Same for her, Laurel Ives. How I wish the mystery benefactor had given us *her* folder. She's quite the creature. You know what I mean. *Wrongness*, like…'

She is wrong. Her. Our Queen of Air and Darkness.

Her unsaid name hung in the air.

'These are extra puzzle pieces,' he said. 'Ones Lockley and Fitts can't use in their jigsaws. But we're different, aren't we? Our box-fronts have stranger pictures. Hieronymus Bosch and Fuseli's *Nightmare* and the woman who does the covers for *Weird Tales*. That's why it's down to us to put it together.'

Billy and I were hooked. The mysterious deliverer of dossiers had roped us in too.

'What do you need us to do?' asked Billy.

'I'm going to stay on the runaways,' said Joh. 'Quin and Ives. I've still got informants on the street. Favours are owed. When they surface, I'll hear about it. You two should come at the mystery from another angle. One uniquely suited to your position in the industry.'

'How so?' asked Billy.

'I can see it on a marquee,' said Joh, hands up like a press agent selling a dream, 'Invisible Ray and Visible Ray Meet… Dr Voodoo!'

PART THREE

THE NIGHT OF
THE STORM

10

The Lamia Munro Clinic was all art deco curves, like the luxury decks of an ocean liner that had run aground on Los Feliz. Whitewashed concrete slabs of abstract art on the forecourt prevented mobs parking tumbrils too close.

Perched on a half-pyramid above revolving doors was a more representational, equally hideous statue. The Oscar's nymphomaniac sister, arms raised, udders out. A winged flagpole sprouted from her forehead. Snakes in her hands indicated she'd just torn apart a caduceus. The cheap gilt finish had flaked, giving her an overall mottled effect. It didn't exactly suggest radiant health.

'What is the artist *saying*?' asked Billy.

'"Meet me round the corner in a half an hour",' I guessed.

Billy chuckled.

We met in Papa Heim's *Gaststätte*, across the street from the Lamia Munro. I had coffee and bee sting cake. So did Billy, after a waitress with Brunhilde braids virtually spat at the mention of '*englische* tea'.

An anti-vivisection group once rented a shopfront opposite the Lamia Munro and put on a disturbing window display of photographs showing horrors inflicted on dogs and chimps by the Clinic's fiendish doctors. The store happened to burn down one night. The cops – this was also in the Rampart division, of course – said it was arson for sure, but named no suspects. They hinted that if the animal-loving busybodies complained, further investigation might conclude they torched their own premises.

To prevent future embarrassments, the Home Estate bought out the block. Now it was a gingerbread slice of the old country – a row of bakeries, lederhosen outfitters and beer halls run by Heim cousins and uncles. Some had Hitler pin-ups in their windows. If war came, this is where a battle-line would be drawn in Hollywood.

According to the city directory, the Lamia Munro Clinic was dedicated to advancing medical research.

Old rich people went in and came out younger and poorer.

Imagine Colin Clive sparking Billy to life in his laboratory, then presenting the Monster with a bill and attaching the poor slob's *Frankenstein* sequel earnings until the debt was worked off.

Mad medicine needn't be Socialist, you know.

After breakfast, we crossed the road, saluted the golden harlot and bravely entered. The cylinder door whirred like a giant vegetable slicer.

An acre of tile gleamed in the reception hall. Silver arrows embedded in the floor pointed from the doormat to a desk. A generously proportioned woman in a tight white uniform, which included an oversized wimple, was reading a recent issue of *Dime Detective*. Above her, huge sculptural fists were stuck to the walls, clutching disturbingly detailed, ruby-eyed gold snakes. That sundered staff of Hermes motif again.

A tall, broad youth in white pants and a singlet that showed off his well-defined chest and oiled, shaved arms stood casually where an armed guard would be stationed if the Clinic were a bank. Many keys hung on thongs fixed to his belt.

We followed the arrows and the receptionist looked up.

I could tell from her practised look of incipient sourness that she was about to tell us to scram. No one saw Dr Vaudois without an appointment, a Depression-proof stock portfolio and a letter of introduction from Eleanor Roosevelt.

Then the nurse saw a movie star… and smiled.

Okay, so Boris Karloff isn't Clark Gable or Robert Taylor…

Very few women – with or without wimples – dream of being dragged to the Mummy's desert tent for a night of dusty passion. More have nightmares of being torn limb from limb by the Monster.

… but Billy is still a movie star. In this town, a recognised face is a pass-key.

Next to him, I might as well have been the Invisible Man.

I realised why Joh had suggested Billy and I visit the Lamia Munro. Even if he'd kept his 'city investigator' badge, he wouldn't get past Nursie and her attendant Tarzan. The famous were universally welcome.

'My name is Boris Karloff,' he said, elongating his vowels deliberately. 'Dr Vaudois should be expecting me.'

That, of course, was a fib.

The woman looked at an appointment book. Very few names were inscribed on today's page and none of them were Boris Karloff or William Henry Pratt or the Monster (c/o Dr Frankenstein).

She looked up at Billy, unwilling to contradict him.

'Ward Home Junior made the arrangement,' he said. 'I'm doing a picture with him about the fine work done in the Lamia Munro Clinic. I'm here to get a feel for the place. First-hand research, you might say.'

Now she wanted to cry.

'Ah, Mr Home is here…'

Which was news. Senior *had* rescued him from 'poor people's hospital'.

'He's not in the best of health, Mr Karloff. He was in an accident the other night and badly burned. He's in a coma. That's a deep sleep that goes on for days. No one knows if he'll ever wake up. He may not have been able to tell Dr Vaudois you were coming.'

'I quite understand.'

His face was a mask of dignified disappointment. As if he were a long-lost explorer returned after ten years away to find the leading lady had given him up for dead and married a dimwit second cousin. He sighed, about to walk nobly off into the jungle – or onto the ice floes or into boiling lava – to an unknown but honourable fate.

The woman now *was* crying, if only a little.

'I'm sure it'll be all right. Dr Vaudois has no appointments this morning.'

Billy blessed her with a crooked smile.

'Splendid,' he said, beaming with the radiance of a dozen suns.

'I'm Angelica DiCenzo,' she said. 'Call me Nurse Anne.'

'It will be my pleasure,' he said, kissing her hand.

She squeaked with delight. Though seated, she wiggled. A thrill passed through her entire body.

I now believed she was a nurse, not a showgirl in costume. She'd told us what a coma was.

Then, finally, Nurse Anne noticed me.

For a moment, she thought she *might* recognise me. I wasn't Bela Lugosi, of course. Perhaps I was one of those other actors. Someone playing a junior medic who makes a wrong diagnosis the brilliant hero corrects? No, I was too nondescript in tweed and spectacles even for that, though not so long ago I was reckoned a 'catch' among secretaries.

I am married to a famous beauty whose nude portrait hangs above the bar of a New York hotel.

When the War ended I was training to be an air ace.

I can fly a plane. I have shot at wicked people.

I have dragged the wounded off the field of battle. I have remained calm under machine-gun fire.

But I am not a movie star.

'This is Mr R.T. Chandler,' said Billy. 'The famous writer. He's on the project.'

'Famous, eh,' said Nurse Anne, doing her best to appear interested. 'So, Artie, have you written anything I've read?'

This question, every writer gets used to. The usual answer is a huffy 'obviously not', whereupon the party who asked gets offended and vows never to read anything by the rude scribbler even if it is filleted in the *Reader's Digest*.

For the only time in my life, I could have told someone they *had* read something I'd written. At least partially.

From the way she'd flopped her magazine on the desktop, I could tell she was in the middle of 'Mandarin's Jade', by one Raymond Chandler.

'Good Lord, no,' I said, dying inside. 'I doubt you've come across anything of mine.'

'Shame,' she said. 'I read a dreadful lot. Not much else to do on this job.'

It wasn't a surprise that nursing took up little of her time.

'Bim,' she said, signalling the athletic young man. 'Take Mr Karloff and his writer to see Dr Vee. You understand?'

Bim clicked his heels and nodded smartly. He couldn't be more German if he wore a *Pickelhaube* and sang an aria from *Die Walküre*.

'Ja, Bim understand,' he said. 'You come mit me.'

He even talked like Tarzan – if Edgar Rice Burroughs let Karl May script the jungle man's dialogue.

Bim used one of his many keys to unlock a door we hadn't even noticed. It just looked like frosted glass.

'Say cheery-bye on your way out,' said Nurse Anne.

'But of course,' said Billy, making a gallant flourish as if waving a hat with a feather in it.

The nurse sighed.

I tell you – Clark Gable doesn't knock 'em down as smartly. Some say Errol Flynn is Hollywood's leading boudoir swordsman. John Barrymore's priapic exploits are legend. But those dime store Don Juans get stiff competition from your friendly neighbourhood Monster.

11

Trotting along a corridor after Bim was exhausting. His walking pace was a third faster than a normal person's. He used his keys deftly.

It was impossible to go ten yards inside the Lamia Munro Clinic and not run into a locked door. Getting in had proved easier than expected. Getting out might be more of a challenge.

Fewer would raise a protest if Dr Voodoo dissected a writer than if he cut up Cheetah's brain.

The Lamia Munro was light and airy. Frosted glass everywhere.

We passed several fellows who could have been Bim's doubles. When Bim met Bim, they had a peculiar single-shoulder-hunch reflex like a suppressed salute that served as a comradely greeting. Wimpled nurses also strolled with purpose, on white high heels. Dr Vaudois had published books on eugenics. Was he breeding Bims with Nursies to spawn superior physical specimens? Rich old people whose lives he prolonged might be in the market for slaves.

Bim took us to a central atrium. A silver spiral staircase led up to landings. A frosted-glass roof let sunlight filter down to a courtyard. Aglaonema Crete grew out of gravel-filled buckets set around a misfiring mechanical fountain that squirted beyond its bowl to spatter the floor.

'Wait here you,' said Bim, indicating a stone bench. '*Danke.*'

He marched through a door that locked behind him.

Billy sat, with his usual slight wince. I didn't want to. I was fascinated by the arrhythmic pulse of the fountain.

'See what Nurse Anne was reading?'

'One of yours, R.T.?'

'Uh-huh. So, we've located a Chandler reader in the wild. A Karloff fan, to boot.'

Billy waved that away with an instinctive modesty that was almost a tic.

A thing that scared the bogeyman was being thought too full of himself, too puffed-up about accomplishments, too dependent on praise or recognition. Not what you'd expect from a movie star. Exactly what you got from an English public school man. If a boy shows any symptoms of *headus biggus*, as they say, extra thrashings put him in his place. Official chastisement to be administered by masters and senior prefects. If that doesn't prove a curative, vigilante attention from stout chaps with pillowcase hoods and carriage whips will. *Be* better than lesser mortals, but don't make a bloody fuss about it, Pratt.

'Do you notice the spying lenses?' he said.

I hadn't until Billy aimed his eyebrows at them. Eye-like apertures in frosted glass. I remembered Joh talking about the two-way television set-up at Home House.

Trust a film star to know where the camera was.

A Bim came back. I presumed it was the same one.

'Dr Vee can see you not,' he said.

'I rather think he see us can,' I said, pointing to the nearest camera.

I could swear the lens irised in irritation.

Billy smiled and waved. He also set his jaw to show determination.

We would be seen. We would not be seen off.

'Dr Vee can see you not,' repeated Bim.

'A shame,' said Billy. 'But, since we're here, we must peep in on our dear friend Ward Home Junior. We have only just learned of his tragic situation. A fearful coma, we hear. He's a fine fellow, a credit to the motion picture industry.'

'Dr Vee can see you not.'

Bim had only been given one line and he was going to say it until it took.

'Kindly take us to Mr Home's room. I'm sure you know where he is.'

A minion with a better grasp of English would have denied all knowledge and lied to our faces. Bim wasn't that minion.

But he still wasn't caving in.

'Dr Vee can see you not.'

Billy uncrossed his legs and stretched. Only he could seem comfortable on a bench designed to dissuade loungers from slacking off.

I tried not to look at the camera. I didn't do that particularly well. There's a reason I went into writing rather than acting.

A door unlocked on one of the landings. A man spiralled down the staircase as slickly as if it were a helter-skelter. He had a detestable little pointed beard and wore a white doctor's coat over a suit suitable for a crooked banker in 1898 – starched wing-tip collar, cravat with stickpin, striped pants. A jarring Californian touch was white tennis shoes, worn without socks. From the ankles down, he was a beach bum.

'I am Dr Vaudois,' he announced.

'Lionel R. Vaudois?' said Billy, like a cop confirming identification before making an arrest.

'Yes, of course,' said the doctor, irritated.

'I am… Boris Karloff,' he intoned.

'I'm aware of your work.'

'And I of yours. A thousand pardons for this intrusion at a difficult time.'

Dr Vaudois peered at Billy… not sure who he was speaking with. He knew the Monster and the Mummy. This was a tanned Englishman without a stitched cleft in his forehead or bolts in his neck. But the eyes were the same. Moist, with an inner light.

The doctor also flicked a glance at me.

'Who is this?' he asked. 'Your lunch?'

Billy chuckled. 'A writer,' he said. 'R.T. Chandler. You'll know his essays from the *New Yorker* and *Atlantic Monthly*. And you'll have seen his pictures. *House of Rothschild*, *Mutiny on the Bounty*.'

Dr Vaudois looked at me again, unable to discern a speck of talent or celebrity.

I hadn't written either of the motion pictures Billy cited.

I had never written a screenplay – and planned not to in the future.

But claiming to have written any given film is an easy entrée in Los Angeles.

It's a bluff no one ever calls because – really – who would own up to being a writer for the picture business if they didn't have to?

No one knows who writes movies. The public reckon the stars make it all up – that Cary Grant, he's terribly witty, you know… throws away whatever rot he's handed and just comes up with the *funniest* things, right on the spot… and Katharine Hepburn, you don't think anyone could *learn* as many words as she spits out through those divine teeth when she's on one of her acting jags, do you? A few subscribers to modern journals believe the director – especially if he has a 'von' or an '-ovitch' in his name – paints in light, masters a thing called 'montage' and is the verifiable genius behind *Ants in Their Pants of 1934*. Writers just sweep up behind the elephants.

If, on a million-to-one-shot, you run into a freak with a photographic memory who *can* remember names listed in the opening credits, you claim the studio chief's nephew did you dirt. The pinhead waltzed on set on the first day of shooting, picked up the script, decided the leading lady ought to say 'I'll take vanilla' five times throughout the picture and insisted any other by-line be blotted out. Frankly, that does happen.

'You were in *House of Rothschild*,' Dr Vaudois said to Billy.

'Yes,' said Billy. 'Good part. A proper meanie. Wonderful lines, all courtesy of R.T. I have him work on all my pictures.'

'Grr… arrrgh… bread *good*… fire *bad*!' I grunted.

Billy flash-frowned at that. He hated that Jimmy Whale gave the Monster toddler speech in *The Bride of Frankenstein*.

'"You'll swing for this, Mr Christian!"' he said, making no attempt to imitate Charles Laughton. 'That was R.T.'s.'

'You said Pyramid Pictures intends to make a film about the Clinic,' said Dr Vaudois, who must eavesdrop on conversations in the foyer. 'I wasn't aware of such a project.'

'Perhaps Mr Home wanted it to be a surprise?' I said. 'He is a showman.'

'You do such valuable, admirable work,' said Billy. 'Yet the Lamia Munro is often misunderstood. I understand there was an unpleasant incident… a shop across the road… small-minded protests… a display of upsetting images… there was, I believe a fire…'

Dr Vaudois didn't want to hear about that.

'Dr Pasteur, too, was condemned by the ignorant,' said Billy. 'And the Scots fellow who discovered penicillin.'

'Alexander Fleming,' said Dr Vaudois, beard bristling.

He entertained the idea of his name being cited alongside the others… those fools! – they scorned Pasteur… Fleming… Galileo… they called them mad!

The fools scorned Dr Frankenstein, Dr Jekyll and Dr Fu Manchu too. They *were* mad.

'A thrilling motion picture could be of great value in getting the public – and funding bodies – on the side of the Lamia Munro,' said Billy.

'We have no problem with funding,' said Dr Vaudois, offhandedly.

Which made the Lamia Munro Clinic unique in the annals of American medicine – and, to the cynic, uniquely suspicious.

'The research done here has to be presented in, ah, the most *sympathetic* light possible,' said Billy. 'There's a risk those of limited intelligence will misunderstand, misconstrue…'

'Yes, that is the case. Those pictures…'

The doctor shuddered at the memory – not of the horrific photographs of vivisected animals, which the Lamia Munro incidentally never dismissed as fakes. No, the doctor shuddered as he recalled petitions, phone calls, newspaper articles and pickets.

A gleam came into his eye.

He pictured himself as Paul Muni, working into the night, with Olivia de Havilland in Nurse Anne's uniform mopping his fevered brow, teasing his adorable little beard. In the last reel, the miraculously cured orphan – who else but Shirley Temple! – bestows a brave simper on him as she wakes up on starched, glowing sheets with her new glass heart pumping like an oil well, curls frizzed out by electricity.

Then he looked at who was pitching him this dream.

And shuddered again. He now saw himself played by *Boris Karloff*.

That film didn't star Muni and de Havilland and inspire millions. It wouldn't get him a cover on the *Saturday Evening Post*. No, the Karloff flick was called *The Castle of Dr Voodoo* and ended with peasants setting the Clinic on fire and the doctor howling amid flames as decerebrated chimps took gruesome revenge.

'The Lamia Munro would have to have a voice in the writing of any film project,' he said. 'Mr Chandelier would have to submit his screenplay for approval. We would need to be empowered to make binding suggestions.'

This is why I plan not to write film scripts.

Even on a made-up movie no one intended to shoot, the writer had to take notes from idiots. If the imaginary film *were* completed, I'd be rewritten and screwed out of credit.

I imagined Bim smiling as he held up his Oscar for Best Original Screenplay before being hustled off stage so the Academy could get on with awards people care about.

'Mr Chandelier would be delighted,' I said. 'He is but a facilitator of the genius of others.'

I simpered like a contented eunuch.

'*The Story of Lionel Vaudois*,' stage-whispered Billy, pausing to allow rapturous opening night applause.

'Now, if we could look in on Mr Home…' said Billy.

'Yes, of course,' said Dr Vaudois.

Billy had mesmerised him.

Dr Voodoo pictured searchlights ranging across his name on the marquee at Grauman's Chinese… fans pressing at the barricade, held back by cops, shrieking as the limousine ambulance parked to allow him to make an entrance… natty in top hat, white tie, tails and tennis shoes (with no socks)… microphones shoved at his face, so he could modestly credit himself with great medical – and now *artistic* – advances… posing on the red carpet with Joan Blondell on one arm and Hedy Lamarr on the other.

Everyone loves a Happy Ending.

Except the writer.

12

Going up a spiral staircase after Dr Vaudois was more exercise than following Bim on the ground. For every pep pill prescribed, the nimble doctor must keep back two for himself. Few would have the wind to match him over a distance.

Joh said the Lamia Munro lawyer hit fast and hard, more like a night-club bouncer than a paper-shuffler. All the Clinic's staff, from the director down to the carry-and-fetch boys, were in tip-top shape. Fleet, strong, with excellent wind. Good advertising? Or was Dr Voodoo building an army of *Übermenschen*? A moustache-chewing house-painter had the licence for that act in European territories but that was no reason it wouldn't play in halls across America.

Billy made the effort to climb at the doctor's pace, then almost crumpled on the top landing. He leaned against a guardrail, giving a remarkable performance in the role of a man whose lungs weren't bursting.

My brains swam. I'd not ascended this high this fast on my first training flight. The staircase was a miracle of design. An earthquake wouldn't shake it. California architects worry more about seismic incidents than whether passers-by will claw out their eyes at the sight of their buildings.

Going round and round while going up and up is against nature. At least, it's against my nature.

I would have liked a jolt.

A couple of ounces of Scotch. A measure of vodka.

A gimlet. A Manhattan. A quart of Gracia's punch.

There comes a point when you don't drink to make the scenery spin, but to make it stop still.

It wasn't yet ten o'clock in the morning. I licked my teeth but the bitterness wouldn't go away. The taste of Papa Heim's coffee.

The lower levels of the Lamia Munro Clinic smelled like an insurance office – ink, boredom and air-conditioning. The top floor landing had a saccharin sick-room whiff. Gallons of violet water couldn't obliterate antiseptic soap and ripening rot.

A Bim guarded a frosted-glass door. Maybe he was a Rolf or a Werner. I'd stopped taking names. You can't individuate every hood and barfly. Sometimes, a Bim is just a Bim. He did the shoulder-twitch salute as Dr Vaudois monkey-scuttled up to the door.

The physician turned to us and said, 'The patient is in a delicate condition.'

'You mean he's pregnant,' I said.

'Not at all.'

That dart missed the mark.

'Hah,' he said a few beats too late, acknowledging the gag as a gag but not allowing that it might have been funny.

Fair enough. He's not my only critic.

Was Dr Voodoo thinking in another language and mentally translating?

'We understand Mr Home was severely burned,' said Billy. 'An incident with an electrical device?'

Dr Vaudois didn't want to go into that.

The Bim opened the door. We followed the doctor into a light, airy suite. Only a patient whose family owned the joint rated such accommodation. The Princesses Royal would scorn the place as too ostentatiously luxurious. A hundred-and-fifty-thousand dollars' worth of smudge hung on the walls, mostly right side up. Paris in the rain. Sunsets at sea. A clown with no eyes. You'd want to recover just to get away from the art.

More waxy floral tributes were on display than at a gangster funeral. Helen Twelvetrees and Gustav von Seyffertitz had sent signed photos to cheer up the patient. Cards from Junior's enemies wished him speedy recovery. Refreshingly, Groucho had scribbled 'please die soon' on a caricature of the Marx Brothers dressed as dancing undertakers. W.C. Fields, for reasons only he could explain, had sent a brand-new spade with a floppy green bow tied around the handle. The shovel blade that had never turned sod shone like a chrome bedpan.

A radiogram powerful enough to draw in signals from Mars emitted noises from *Say It With Tubas*. If Marlowe were on the case, he'd figure the racket was a fiendish scheme to drive a victim to suicide. Ten minutes of burbling brass and I'd poke pencils in my ears.

The suite still stank of hospital.

Opaque white curtains hung on a steel frame around a bed wide enough for Siamese twins who'd been run over by an ice truck. A china vase shaped like a conch shell was propped in a stand made from twisted metal tubes. The flowers in it wanted changing. The peach roses had rust spots and the white Asiatic lilies were curling and dry.

A blonde sat by the curtained bed, in a chair with zebra-print upholstery. She reminded me of the girl in uniform stationed in the lobby whenever *Dracula* was staged. 'For the benefit of those of a nervous disposition' or for patrons who'd rather make time with a fake nurse than listen to a ham in a cape and a tuxedo whine about 'chee-e-eeldrain of the nai-i-ght!'.

Obviously a less discriminating reader than Nurse Anne, the blonde had her nose in a publication to which I'd never contributed – *Rangeland Romances*, a pulp for Western fans who liked sheriffs smooching gals in calico rather than gunning bad hats at the OK Corral. It takes all sorts to fill a newsstand.

Noting our entrance, the nurse tore off the corner of the page she was reading and dumped the magazine. She stood and clicked her heels. She wore shiny make-up and had lady wrestler thighs. I reckoned she could knock Joh Devlin on his beam as smartly as any lawyer.

'Let's see the patient, Gretchen,' said Dr Vaudois.

She tugged a cord. The bed-screen crinkled out of the way like the curtains of a puppet show.

Ward Home Junior was propped on a stack of pillows.

He wore a turban of starched bandage. His face was blotched. Black-red scabs glistened with ointment. The rest of his fizzog was pinkly healthy as if he'd checked into the Lamia Munro for a beauty treatment. He usually sported a William Powell moustache. Even in publicity shots, the lip-brow looked more ratty than natty. Now, it was burned or shaved off.

White-mittened hands lay on his bedspread.

He wore black silk pyjamas with 'Jr' monogrammed in silver on the breast pocket. His feet stuck out of the cream coverlet as if he'd mistakenly been given child's blankets. He must buy his Persian slippers at the store where Dr Frankenstein got the Monster's asphalt-spreader boots.

Junior's chest rose and fell steadily. His breath was easier than mine after ascending the indoor Matterhorn.

'Mr Karloff has come to visit,' said Dr Vaudois, enunciating clearly. 'And brought a writer with him.'

The patient's eyes flicked open. The left was bloodshot.

I jumped a little. It was what Billy called a 'boo!' moment.

I squelched an urge to gasp, '*It's al-i-eve!*'

My instinct for what Joh called *wrongness* kicked. I wanted to swing W.C. Fields' get-well-soon present and wedge its shining blade so firmly in Junior Home's skull young King Arthur couldn't pull it out.

I squelched that urge too.

'Boris, Boris,' said the patient, focusing on his famous visitor, 'so you want to make a picture at Pyramid? That's a switcheroonie. We offered you a good, good script last year and you passed. *The Fiend of Fog Lane*. Very fine picture. Seven weeks at the Rialto. We gave away ten thousand cardboard masks. Last Hallowe'en, every trick or treater wanted a Fiend Face. Way more brats than wore Frankenstein masks. Way, way more.'

Billy's gast was flabbered. Dr Voodoo was smug.

The quack had, of course, *known*.

Having his head catch fire had done something to Junior's vocal cords. His voice was like a sixth-former's, broken but bell-clear. And he was *loud*, the dial on his horn turned up all the way.

As he spoke, a jug of ice-water rattled on a bedside table.

'We can *talk*. We're always happy to talk. We're ever on the prowl for new, new ideas. Know what I say – every picture starts with a new idea.

Schubert, I said. No one's done Schubert! Everyone knows he didn't finish, but no one knows *why*. Let's tell *that* story. Good, good example. *Unfinished Symphony*. Made its money back in Europe. Shut out of theatres here, because of the Jews. Well, we expect that. The Mayers and Cohns and Warners look after their own – while they can.'

A penny-sized scab peeled off his cheek. Nurse Gretchen picked it up with tweezers and put it in a steel container that was either custom medical equipment or a novelty cocktail shaker.

'So, you have a picture idea, Boris,' he went on. 'Good to hear. I'll weigh ideas from anyone. Even an actor. But, what with this limey spooker prohibition, I'm not sure Pyramid can use a film with your name on it. BOP, they say. Box Office Poison.'

Dr Vaudois was inexpressive.

Billy and I had banked on Junior being a mummified basket case who couldn't contradict everything we'd said in order to get into the Lamia Munro.

'I heard you were… in a coma,' said Billy. 'Burned to a crisp.'

Junior motioned to touch his face, then remembered the mittens and flopped his hands down. Were the bandages just to stop him scratching?

'I recover fast. The experimental procedure was a success. A great, great success.'

'The experimental procedure?'

'Yes. You'll want to know about that… for the script, right? An idea is a gift, but it needs wrapping. The script. That's what the clerk's here for, right?'

Junior looked straight at me. I couldn't look away from his clotted iris.

'This is…' began Billy.

'Raymond Chandler,' said Junior. 'An unimportant writer.'

Unimportant but known to Ward Home Junior. I wasn't sure that was an improvement on being Artie Chandelier – Nobody of This Parish.

'*Are* there important writers?' I said.

'Maybe Ben Hecht,' said Junior, pretending to take my smart aleck remark seriously. 'But we can't get him. Too rich, too busy, too picky. We tried to sign Bernard Shaw for *Maisie and Minnie in Piccadilly*. Get the

English touch, you know. He cabled back regrets and said the trouble was Hollywood was only interested in art and he was only interested in money. So we couldn't get him. But Pyramid *can* get you, Chandler. We can get you and have you any way we want.'

That wasn't threatening at all. Except it was.

'You're a pony with one trick, right?' he continued, patches reddening on his face. I felt warmth coming off him, as if extra coal were shovelled into his boiler. 'Go on, do it now. You know what I mean…'

'I'm really rather afraid I don't.'

'Listen to him, Dr Vee! "Ai'm weally wawther afwaid I doeoen't!"'

At school, chaps made fun of my 'colonial' accent. I could never hear it. I was mostly trying not to sound bloody Irish. Junior wasn't a good mimic. He just brayed viciously. I don't have a recessive R.

'The whatchumacallit figure of speech you're big on,' he continued. 'The one thing is like another thing whatchamacallit… What do you call that?'

'A simile?'

'Yeah, the *sillymillies*. Like "fit as a fiddle", only cleverer… *too* clever, our reader said about your *Big Snooze* book… like a, whatelsechumacallit, a *mannerism*… yeah, "mannered", that was the word. Or it could have been "laboured". Smart cookies, our readers. They get to skewer *everything*. Still, hop to it, Chandler, dish us a sillymilly. What other thing am I like?'

I was flustered. I knew galleys of *The Big Sleep* were out in the wild, but not that they'd circulated around the studios. I'd written in dope fiends, smut rackets and every sex perversion on record just so the movies would never, ever touch the book. Cut the stuff the Hays Office wouldn't pass and there's nothing left to point a camera at but Philip Marlowe failing to solve chess problems. The virgin prudes of the Hays Office made the British Board of Film Censors look like drunk French sailors on shore leave in Tijuana, to coin a sillymilly.

But I still resented the unknown skewerer. Perhaps the prick pierced the skin? Even *Dime Detective* told me to use fewer similes. 'Cut the fancy-schmancy and just come out and say it' was the usual note.

Similes are like spices – best used sparingly.

'You're like… ah…'

'Yeah, come on, hit me with a zinger. "The movie mogul was as… crispy as a pancake." No, that's rotten. Routine. 'Sides – pancakes are soft, mostly. Just burned in spots. Though that's me, isn't it? Burned in spots. Come on, Cha-ahndler… "like…" give with it… "as… as a…"?'

'I'll work on it,' I said, feebly.

Junior's mask of disappointment was a gloating snarl.

Victory was his!

The perfect snap-back would occur to me three days later, when it'd be no more use than a girdle on Pitcairn Island.

That's what you get when I'm pushed. Something put down in the hope something better occurs by the next draft, which gets left in by mistake. Whole paragraphs of my magazine output make me want to puke green onions.

'The movie mogul was like ten gallons of shit poured into silk pyjamas tailored to hold five,' I said.

Get *that* past the Hays Office!

Junior's bloody eye bulged. He barked something like a laugh.

'That's the spirit, Wittle Waymond. There's hope yet. You might be movie material after all. We could toss you a rewrite on *Tubas on Parade*. Nathanael West is having third act issues. You could fix it by having two guys with guns barge into the bandstand. Or we could grab the *Big Snore* rights for five hundred bucks, ditch your no-name dick and use what plot there is for one of our series stars. Imagine that – a "based on" credit on *Trooper's Mystery Ranch*. Hell, kick it up a notch! *Maisie and Minnie's Bed-Time Burlesque*. Throw Boris a bone. He can play the Stranglewood butler. Who'll turn out to have dun it. We can't use *your* miserable excuse for an ending. The slut sister goes to the nuthouse! Who wants to see that?'

His crimson eye was a cherry about to pop out of a pie.

Which is a meteophor, not a sillymilly.

'Oh, one other thing from our reader. She wants to know… *Who killed the chauffeur?*'

That again.

'It's obvious, isn't it?' I said. 'It was…'

I tailed off. Billy arched an eyebrow.

He'd asked the same thing. So had Cissy. And Joh, while giving tips on the professional conduct of the well-dressed dick. And a sub-editor at Knopf, to whom I penned a curt note I later regretted. Sometimes, when Taki looked at me funny, I thought she was miaowing, 'Who killed the chauffeur?'

I'd talked them all round... but, now...

I had the answer. I had *an* answer, which I'd formulated and was happy with. Nice and polished. Easily jotted on a crib sheet. Life, you see, isn't like a green-jacket mystery where a boring Belgian explains every detail so you know exactly what happened but don't care a damn about it. Crimes are swept under the rug with the dust. In life, you never find out who killed the chauffeur – and it hurts. That was what I meant all along. Owen Taylor died to prove that point.

I wasn't just careless.

But now, staring into Junior's eye – grown to the size of a grapefruit injected with mercury – I was voiceless.

With a drink in my hand – not even in me, but close by, cool against my grip – I'd trot out my set answer and that would be that.

I'd turn down Junior's dial. Damp his boiler.

I'd tell him where he could put his money. I wouldn't have Marlowe ditched or my ending changed. And it's *Sternwood*, you moron! Read a book – not the coverage!

'Come on, Chaaa-aahndler, give with the solution! I've a good, good deal for you – Pyramid will pay for a rewrite! To fix your busted book. Need an automobile? Next year's model. How about a new liver? I own a clinic, you know. Want a date with Minnie or Maisie? Or the both at once! Hell, Dry Bone *and* Trooper could be delivered hogtied to the hotel suite of your choice. Just go back and write a proper solution. One that makes sense – no cheating.'

Only now did it strike me that *The Big Sleep* – not overlong by anyone's measure – might not have needed the waterlogged corpse in Chapter Nine to hold the reader's interest. Owen Taylor turned out to be more trouble than he was worth.

Junior was shaking – not with sickness, or rage, but vitality.

Dr Vaudois expressed concern without saying anything.

I assumed his patient was on five kinds of legal dope. Even Hollywood studio heads didn't usually fly this high.

'This experimental procedure?' said Billy, interrupting my humiliation. 'What exactly was its purpose?'

'The conquest of death,' said Junior, clearer eye gleaming.

He reached out as if he wanted to clutch a lapel and make someone listen. He shook his swaddled fist like a caveman's club.

I breathed again, relieved at the change of subject.

I was still parched. The bedside jug looked like a desert oasis.

Water, ice… just add Scotch… or a pinch of whatever hop Junior was juiced with.

'To beat the Reaper,' Junior went on. 'That was the idea. Science starts with an idea too. A bright idea. The brightest. One day, it was just there. In my brain. Hear me out. It's a big, big question. Who wants to die? No one – except suicides, of course. They're stupid idiots. When people told me not to make the Schubert picture, it roiled in my insides. So I made *Unfinished Symphony*. When people – the same people – said I had to die, eventually… it didn't sit right. Not at all. Why? I said. You know, like kids say when they're told things they don't like. No more candy. Apologise to the gardener. Kiss Oma Lamia on the mouth. Why why why? Kids are smart, smart people. Gets knocked out of 'em. I guess I never took that knocking. Good thing, as it turns out. I decided I didn't want to die. Not now, not ever, *never*.'

Junior was enthused. Joh Devlin was on the money about what the Clinic was for. He must have inside sources. Those who slip dossiers under doors and try to stay in the shadows when the sacking – and, in extreme cases, the shooting – starts.

Junior leaned forward. His whole face was reddish now.

'Who wants to not be around?' he said, stabbing with a forefinger. 'Who wants to leave their symphony unfinished? Their mystery unsolved. I'm no science genius. But I have money and science geniuses are for hire. They're not too rich, too busy *or* too choosy. That's a fact. I can hire Einstein for less than I'd pay Goldwyn to get Anna Sten. I had the money to make a Schubert picture. I figured I had the money to opt out of dying. To book a ticket on the stay-alive train. So, I went to the market for science geniuses… like Lionel here. The original Dr Voodoo.'

Dr Vaudois clicked his teeth at hearing the nickname.

'A big, big brain is Lionel R. Vaudois. Colossal in the cerebellum. I have him under exclusive contract. Norman Quin, too. *Engineer* Quin. That's a thing the dictator nations are smart about. In Europe, the title "engineer" commands as much respect as the title "doctor". Build a dam in Europe and you get laid as often as Gary Cooper at Christmas. Quin is *Engineer Quin* at Pyramid. Not a bum like he was at Universal. I don't know what it is, but the guy is aces in places where most don't have spaces. Publicity came up with that and I pay them so I own it. I like it. It's got internal rhythm and a triple rhyme.'

Did Junior talk like this *before* electricity shot through his skull?

'Lionel,' he said, temporarily spent, 'explain further… in words they can understand… tell them what we did and how we did it. You and me and Quin and the others. The true, true Talents. You'll want chairs. Karloff, Chandler, I tell you… you are about to go weak at the knees. Your noodles are about to be smacked six ways from sideways.'

Gretchen stuck Finnish folding chairs under us. Three sheets of plywood and a hinge. A day's back pain guaranteed for every hour sat on one.

We were turned into an audience.

Colin Clive did the same thing to unwelcome visitors in *Frankenstein*.

A thing about Junior's new, new ideas – they had mostly been used, used already. Two years before Pyramid's *Unfinished Symphony*, an Austrian outfit made the same story as *Liese Flehen Meine Lieder*. *The Fiend of Fog Lane* was *Murders in the Rue Morgue* with a Bow Bells accent. *Say It With Tubas*, so far as I know, was an 'original'.

'Gentlemen, what do you know of death?' began Dr Voodoo.

Billy and I looked at each other.

'Come, come,' said the doctor, 'you must know someone who's died… a parent?'

'My parents are dead,' said Billy.

'My mother is dead,' I said.

I didn't know – or care – whether my father was. If he had died, I wouldn't want anyone bringing him back.

'… and three or four hundred boys I served with in the War,' I added, hastily. 'They died.'

'What is death, my friends? What is dying?'

The doctor looked at us, as if expecting answers.

'You, Mr Karloff, must have an insight. You have returned from the dead many times on the talking screen. In *Frankenstein* and *The Mummy*. Recently, you made *The Walking Dead*, which involved resuscitation of a dead man by scientific means. That made Quin and I wonder if our work was known at Warner Brothers.'

In *The Walking Dead*, Billy plays a sap who's railroaded into the electric chair. His corpse is claimed by a kindly old inventor whose revivification process needs testing. Risen Billy is a changed man – a human spectre with a white streak in his hair. Billy stalks the bad hats who framed him and brings about their irreversible deaths. At the end, wouldn't you know it, Billy dies again. As the lights go out for a second time, he passes on the news that God doesn't appreciate infringement on his copyright. He would prefer Kindly Old Inventor give up on revivification devices and work on a non-stick waffle iron instead. The upshot is that science shouldn't mess around in the domain of the deity.

I imagined Dr Vaudois and Engineer Quin booing that humbug.

The doctor wasn't wrong about Billy's special insight. His eyes had seen much and the camera caught that. He hadn't needed to go to war to learn that the world was dark. He didn't need a medium to know about the sundered veil, the glow that lingers after the candle's blown out. I think the dead don't care. They sleep their sleep and dream of nothing. Billy disagrees, but doesn't argue. He saves it for the cinema – the pain, the wonder and the magic.

The Walking Dead is a punk movie, no better or worse than a hundred others – but it shows off the shine in Billy's eyes, the light of knowledge it's best not to share for fear of driving others mad.

'Warner Brothers brought you back from the dead in under sixty-five minutes,' said Junior. 'Dr Vee works slower. And costs more.'

'Trial and error,' said the doctor, with a tiny lips-pursed scowl Junior didn't notice. 'False pathways. That's research.'

Junior grunted. The payer of bills was entitled to poke the hired help.

'He's right,' he admitted. 'It's like the picture business. Papa is a great, great oilman – but doesn't understand the picture business. He knows you sink ten wells before you get a gusher, but not that you make ten pictures before you get a hit. "Just make the hits," he says. "Don't make the nine no-goods." If only… Science is like that too. Nine nutty notions – bicycles with flapping wings, giant exploding corkscrews – before the Wright Brothers take off. Wind-up hearts. Clockwork brains. Preserving gases. Pituitary glands? Hell, we tried all sorts of glands. Human glands, even. You can get 'em fresh if you really want 'em. Serums and elixirs. The works. Some of the flop ideas we used in horror pictures. You should have made *The Fiend of Fog Lane*, Billy. It was *educational*. We found the little Chinaman through open casting.'

Which hadn't been a blessing for the late Mr Chick Chang.

Nurse Gretchen plumped pillows. Then, while her bosses talked of the mysteries of life and death, she got back to *Rangeland Romances*.

'Mr Home sponsored the Clinic with this end in mind,' said Dr Vaudois, 'to circumvent death. Not to reverse it, or delay it… but to abolish it entirely.'

'I don't want to die,' underlined Junior, grinning.

Another of his scabs flaked off, showing healthy skin beneath. Gretchen let this one lie on the counterpane. Action must have been hotting up down at the Sweetheart Spread.

Ward Home Junior might not have been raised from the dead – though Dr Vaudois was maybe leading up to claiming so – but a miracle had been worked for him. He fairly glowed. He was so *alive* people who cared about him should worry – if there were any.

'We began, of course, with cures for death.'

'Of course,' I said.

Dr Voodoo still missed the dig.

'We looked to precedents in history, folklore and fable. Jesus raised Lazarus from the dead, we're told. Not a repeatable experiment, sadly. The Messiah was not available to us at the Clinic.'

'… under exclusive contract to DeMille,' said Junior.

'So we looked at other pathways to our desired end.'

'Voodoo,' said Junior.

'Yes, we considered the Haitian concept of the zombie.'

'Bela made that movie,' said Billy. 'Not me.'

'And I've drunk that cocktail,' I put in. 'Often.'

That was a lie – for effect. Zombies are vile. I'm a gimlet loyalist.

'Contrary to lurid popular imagining, zombies are not the undead. They are living men dosed with a drug that erodes the will, enslaved to work in cane fields. They are not the walking dead, but they walk like the walking dead. In fact, they walk like you do, Mr Karloff… in your films, and, as I notice, off the sound stage too. The monster walk.'

Billy shrugged. Dr Vaudois should see him run up to the crease.

'Interesting as the properties of puffer fish toxin might be, we abandoned our friend the zombie…'

'Voo-doo a no-no, as *Variety* might say,' said Junior. 'Zombs Bomb in Fish-Dust Bust.'

'Which brought us to *Frankenstein*. His project was not ours – at least, not entirely. Dr Frankenstein set about to create artificial life. In your film, parts of dead people are used as components. There's a confusion about the brain. Is the Monster a monster because he has been given an "abnormal brain", or – as in the book – is the Monster monstrous because the world rejects and torments him?'

'Can we hurry this along?' I said. 'My grandmother has eggs that need sucking. You're explaining *Frankenstein* to *Boris Karloff*!'

Dr Vaudois allowed the point, but resumed the lecture.

'What caught Quin's imagination in *Frankenstein* was the use of lightning to spark life. As you know, he created the electrical equipment for Universal. Those gadgets were made to add visual excitement to a motion picture. Not to *do* anything. We chuckle at such things. But we, too, are susceptible. Ideas, as Mr Home says, grow anywhere. Even in a Hollywood studio…'

He paused for laughter that didn't come.

'Electricity was the idea, of course,' he said. 'The human body generates electricity – in the brain, particularly. Thoughts are like lightning. Life is, in a sense, an electrical process. We use an electric current to kill… a modern replacement for the guillotine. But a stopped heart can also be started again by calibrated shock. Full revivification through electricity has been done with dogs for years. A humane asphyxiation and then, moments later, a charge to restart the heart… but not just the heart, the brain… the lungs… all the processes of life.'

'We're not interested in dogs,' said Junior. 'Though there's a fortune in it for anyone who wants to open a parlour on Wilshire Boulevard where they zap run-over poodles and fed-to-death cats back to life.'

The studio head fiddled with the high collar of his pyjama top, scratching his throat. A metal plate was inset into his sternum – not at the side of his neck like Jack Pierce's rusty old bolts. Rather than protruding terminals, the plate had a plug socket. He could wear dressier shirts than the Monster.

'See, I'm an Electrical Man,' said Junior.

'Does that hurt?' asked Billy.

'According to Quin, it hurts less than having bolts glued to your neck. You'd know about that.'

Billy had another set of tiny scars under his ears – from having the Monster's terminals attached day after day. Jimmy Whale and Jack Pierce gave him a career, but did him much lasting damage. Another *Frankenstein* picture might cripple him.

'We pursued electrical reanimation three years ago,' said Dr Vaudois. 'Using unclaimed bodies from the morgue. That was not fruitful. An issue with dead people is that immediately before they died they were damaged. By murder or accident. Even in so-called natural death, bodies are riddled with sickness. We developed simple methods for restoring life, but our subjects were dying all over again. There are applications for temporary resurrection. If you can get past the shock and confusion, victims could identify murderers… though a lawyer might argue those momentarily brought back from death are in no fit mental state to furnish testimony that'll hold up in courts. That's not my field.'

'That's the plot of *The Face at the Window*,' said Billy. 'I've played that on stage. They keep filming it in England.'

So, another stolen idea.

'No good news for the I-don't-want-to-die movement then?'

'Not at all, Mr Chandler. There's quite a bit of good news. You could – ahem – call your next book *The Short Nap*. Yes, we can bring back the dead – but only those killed in a very specific and limited way. Drowning is good. Asphyxiation too. Anything that stops the processes but inflicts minimal damage to the system. We have to murder you carefully to be certain of reviving you in working order. That we've learned. I've undergone the process myself. My heart stopped for a minute and fifteen seconds. I don't know if I can say I have died and risen, any more than if I held my breath for the same length of time.'

'Did you see…?'

'The light, Mr Karloff? An effect of the optic nerve shutting down. No more. Sorry to disappoint.'

'Not at all, not at all.'

Billy spoke in the offhand tone a Boris Karloff character might use to lull someone into turning their back just as he slipped a knife out of his sleeve.

'You wouldn't catch me volunteering for *that*,' said Junior.

'It was a necessary step. Now, a routine. Gretchen has died, in that sense. She doesn't lurch like a zombie. Quite the contrary.'

The nurse looked up, smiled. Her eyes were ice marbles.

They were changed, these reanimates. But they didn't *know* they were changed. Not even Dr Lionel R. Vaudois, who ought to be objective enough to see what everyone else would. I remembered his brisk walk. He was quickened in every sense.

I had an idea many at the Lamia Munro had nipped through the Dark Curtain and been yanked back by electrification. The Running Dead.

'What manner of resurrection *did* you volunteer for?' I asked Junior. 'And how did it go so wrong?'

'Who said it went wrong?'

'Three – no, four – people who aren't sitting up in the morgue.'

'They're not saying anything, Chandler,' said Junior. 'That's what dead people say. Nothing.'

'Saying nothing can be a forceful statement.'

Junior was impatient. He didn't like having holes poked in his story. I bet he fired writers who pointed out inconsistencies in his picture ideas. He brayed about my unexplained chauffeur, but had signed off on *The Fiend of Fog Lane*. The explanation of the piano duet heard from the locked murder room after the crime – not because there are two killers, but because the ape accompanied himself by playing the second part with his feet – is absurd. Gorilla fingers are too thick to do anything more refined than mash the keys.

'We moved on from reanimation,' said the doctor. 'Another sidetrack, I'm afraid – though an intriguing one, which will bear development. No, I had misheard the question put to me...'

Junior chuckled.

'The problem I was given was not how to return the dead to life...'

'The dead are losers. Who needs 'em around, eh?' said Junior.

'... but to ensure that the living do not die in the first place. To *vaccinate* against death, to make man immune to dying.'

'By "man", he means me,' said Junior. 'I paid for it.'

'Quin's device accomplished this,' said the doctor. 'There were regrettable side effects... as a result of some participants failing to heed instructions given for their own safety...'

'... but the procedure was a success,' said Junior, sitting up straight and clapping his mittens like a seal. 'I can't die! Go on, try to kill me. You can't! No one can. Nothing can.'

He threw off his covers and leaped out of bed.

Billy stood up, hands out to support Junior if he fell.

Ward Home Junior stood a full six inches taller than Billy Pratt.

Billy looked at Junior's broad chest, then up to his beatific face.

'Weren't you... ah, shorter?'

Junior roared a laugh and clapped Billy on the shoulder – a friendly blow that fell like a hammer. A plaster cast inside his mitten cracked.

Dr Vaudois showed concern.

'You mustn't...'

He remembered his position as minion and shut up. Men like Junior

Home – though, it seems, few were like him – hated to be addressed with sentences that began 'You mustn't…'.

Around town, people called Junior names like 'shrimp' and 'Mighty Midget'. I remembered Joh's story that he only signed tiny actresses so he wouldn't look a pipsqueak when photographed with a starlet on his arm. Billy Pratt, *sans* monster boots, was an inch shy of six feet. The new Junior Home crested that by a hand-span or more.

Electricity had done him a world of good.

(but killed four other people)

Junior smashed his other hand-cast and shook off the mess of bandage and plaster.

His big pink hands flopped, as if boneless – like the bloated, impossibly bendable hands of a cartoon character. He reached for Billy's aghast face, fingers lengthening like white worms, then knotting into a bricky fist. He knuckle-tapped Billy's forehead and made him stagger.

'Who's the big, big man now?'

13

Ward Home Junior stepped away from the bed. He scrunched his neck like a turtle but still had to hang his swollen head to get under the curtain rail. Then, he stood up straight. His custom-made pyjamas were too short, exposing hairy, muscular ankles. The jacket didn't button across his broad chest. He experimentally pressed fingertips against the ceiling, wondering at this new sensation – a simple thing he couldn't have done last week.

A new-made monster was raring to rampage across the countryside, smiting woodcutters and ravaging blondes. He was stiff-armed and -legged, as if his joints didn't work properly yet.

Dr Vaudois wasn't happy with his patient.

Nurse Gretchen took away our folding chairs so we didn't fall over them as we retreated from her boss.

Junior needed *space*.

He wasn't just taller and wider.

He was healthier. He wiped off the last of his scabs. His skin was ripe apple-rosy. His eyes were neons.

And he was *flexible*.

I couldn't look away from his fingers, which flattened against the ceiling like unbaked dough.

He noticed my fascination and held out his hands.

Their plasticity delighted, then irritated him. His hands were happy squid, tentacles writhing and entwining. I shuddered. He grimaced.

Flexibility was all very well but twisting too far out of true *hurt*. His transformation was fresh enough that he hadn't got his limits yet.

Junior concentrated. The squid became hands, like puffed-into gloves turned right side out.

He wiggled his fingers like a practising pianist.

'Hah,' he said, pleased.

'You should be careful,' began Dr Vaudois.

Junior's right forefinger extended by an extra phalange. He wagged at his doctor's nose.

It was clear that 'You should…' was on the list with 'You mustn't'.

'You're still healing… we don't fully understand the processes.'

'I'm not healing. I'm healed.'

Dr Voodoo pursed his lips at that. A thrall with special knowledge, insight or ability must purse his lips a lot. And end up with mouth wrinkles like my unpleasable grandmother.

'I was sick all my life,' Junior continued, unsteady on tree-trunk legs, 'the way you're sick. You're all dying. Only I'm not.'

Gretchen supported her boss, putting one hand against his lower back, fussing over buttons with the other. She looked like a ventriloquist with an oversized dummy.

He glanced at the nurse and grinned like a five-year-old.

'I can see the top of your head,' he told her.

That was it. More than immortality, Junior Home wanted to see the top of an ordinary-sized woman's head.

He looked down at us, hoping to be congratulated.

Honestly, I was impressed. And terrified.

The world's first self-made *Übermensch* was the mind behind *Say It With Tubas*.

Billy took it differently. He was *deducing*.

'Quin's machine didn't just *give* you something,' he said. 'It took away from Herbert Holloway.'

'Who?' said Junior.

That irritated Dr Vaudois.

'The giant,' he said. 'Groto the Gargantuan.'

'Ah, yes... the big freak.'

'It's what the others were *for*,' Billy went on.

I saw sparks in Billy's haunted eyes. *He had figured it out.*

Staggering monster... dried-up mummy... horn-handed truck driver and ditch-digger... but also educated in schools, libraries and life, with a keen mind and sharper intuitions. People saw that drawn, worn face and forgot how very, very clever he was. Steeped in Latin and Greek and Conrad.

He was the sleuth in the last act of an English mystery, explaining a culprit's wicked plot to him. In *Boris Karloff, Master Detective*, I'd be the less perspicacious friend and biographer. Not R.T. Chandler of Dulwich College or P. Marlowe, Esq., but Poor Old Watson. Egad, you astound me, Pratt.

'At first, I reckoned the dead men were guinea pigs,' said Billy. 'To test the process and see if it was safe for you – which it obviously wasn't for them. But why submit to a device that killed people? You wouldn't. No one would. They weren't there to try out Quin's machine. They didn't go first. They were components of the process. Vital components. You all had to be wired *together* for it to work.'

Junior smiled, as if praised by a better man.

Dr Vaudois backed into a corner. Did he expect his boss's heart to go off like a grenade if he got over-excited, filling the room with bone shrapnel and ribbons of human meat?

'You were there to take and they were there to give,' Billy went on. 'You needed their talents. You got that trick with your fingers from Chick Chang. India rubber bones? Elastic muscles? How far can you stretch? Amthor the Mystic Yogi could cut himself and heal quickly. Swallow pins and needles. Wounds instantly knit and smoothed over. Look at your face – it's brand-new. That's Amthor, isn't it? His healing knack. You're taller because of Holloway but not crippled because of Chang and Amthor. Holloway's gigantism was a burden, enfeebling him. You'd not want to be tall if you couldn't stand up by yourself, so you needed to be able to stretch flesh and bone and then set it – to break and remake and heal. Those capacities you got from the contortionist and the fakir. Still, it must have been agony.'

'I wouldn't know,' said Junior. 'I was distracted.'

'Of course, your head was on fire.'

'Some dishes you have to pour brandy on and set light to. I wouldn't usually recommend doing that to yourself... but – what can I say? – it worked for me.'

He posed with his hands on his hips. Gretchen stepped away from him.

'You missed a trick,' said Billy. 'If you'd wired in Paderewski, you could play the piano to concert standard without practising.'

Junior wiggled his fingers again.

'A bright idea, Boris.' He smiled. 'Why didn't you think of that, Dr Vee? What do I pay you for?'

Dr Vaudois cringed.

'A friend said you were more like Dracula than Frankenstein,' said Billy.

'Smart friends you have.'

Under the boyish bigness was unmissable threat.

Junior the Shrimp had been Dr Jekyll. We were meeting Mr Hyde.

He was having big ideas. Things he could do. Untrammelled by physical constraints. As for moral constraints – he was third-generation Hollywood money... qualm was bred out of him.

'Can you speak Chinese?' Billy asked.

Junior thought about it but the words didn't come.

'So it's only physical attributes you swallow. In your mind, you're still you... not you, diluted by three other persons.'

Junior nodded. 'I'm particular about that, Boris. I'm me, but *more*.'

The big man *liked* having it explained to him. Even though he knew what he'd done – rather, what others had done for him. He loved hearing it aloud, like a child who wants *Goldilocks* or *Puss in Boots* every bedtime. He needed to be told he was clever. If a Pyramid picture was a smash, it was all down to his vision. If it died, it was the director's fault, or the star's, or the writer's. They failed, not him. It was Chang and Amthor and Holloway's fault that they'd died.

He wasn't even the mad scientist here – he thrived on the madness of others. He was the experiment – the Monster, not Frankenstein.

Dr Vaudois wouldn't come out and claim credit. Besides, it was too early to determine how successful the process was. Three dead people bothered him on some level – flaws in the procedure, if not pricks to his conscience. But he hadn't paid for the experiment. If there was a Nobel Prize in this, it would end up on Junior's mantel, in the spot where he'd planned to put the Best Picture statuette *Unfinished Symphony* hadn't won (because of the Jews). The results were Junior's to bruit from the top of the Hollywoodland sign. He could climb up there with Gretchen in one paw, posing in the criss-cross of gala premiere searchlights, and bawl his success at the whole town. It would take more than airplanes to down this beast.

'So you're immortal, now?' Billy asked.

Junior winked his clear eye.

'The only way to prove it is by not dying,' he said. 'I've done well so far.'

'After, what, two days?'

'Nearly.'

'Capital, excellent, well done… do you know how long Herbert Holloway – Groto the Gargantuan, Bertram Halleweigh, the Windmill-Man – lived?'

Junior didn't and didn't care.

'Doctor…?'

Dr Vaudois didn't want to be caught knowing something his boss didn't.

'Now he's dead,' I put in, 'couldn't you saw through his leg and count the rings or something?'

'He wouldn't – or couldn't – give us dates,' said the doctor. 'He claimed to be older than America.'

'Historically or geologically?' asked Billy.

'He wasn't a caveman. He was physically and mentally weak by the time he came to us. Enfeebled, as you said. He had deteriorated greatly in recent years. He was born in the Middle Ages. He was English. Your old country stock.'

'Yes. Of course. My old country stock.'

'I *can* speak English,' said Junior.

I knew schoolmasters who would have debated that point with him.

'I don't feel any limey in me. No thirst for milky tea... no lust for crumpets.'

His red eye was contained in its orbit – more sinister when not threatening to burst. It suggested an intellect its owner otherwise lacked. I was frightened by this blustering, blundering giant child, who'd be forever smashing furniture and banging his head on the lintels of his built-to-shrimp-scale castle. It'd be much worse for the world if he were *cunning*.

'I won't go senile like Groto,' he said. 'Thanks to Chang and Amthor. You were dead right about what I drew from them. Being immortal isn't enough... you got to stay in shape and in your right mind. That I'll do.'

No *struldbrugg* he – though I'd bet the studio head only skimmed the first two books of *Gulliver's Travels*, with the little people and the giants. The rest of Swift is not movie material. The eternally senile, wretched immortals of the Land of Luggnagg bore red dots above their eyebrows. Junior had their curse-mark *in* his eye.

'Are there others like Holloway?' Billy asked Dr Vaudois. 'Very old people.'

'He couldn't point us to any. I imagine the unnaturally long-lived get very good at hiding...'

... in plain sight. According to Joh, Junior had a portrait of one on display in his house. Though Ariadne was Another Thing Again. A fifth book might have brought Gulliver to shores where such as she were spawned.

The desirable package was 'immortal, and...' Swift understood the universal wish was for 'immortal, and hale'. Holloway was 'immortal, and tall'. Ariadne was 'immortal, and...' many, many other things.

'We only found Holloway because of his *other* distinguishing feature.'

'That he was a giant?'

'Yes, easier to find than men who don't die. Giants are remembered.'

That file delivered (mysteriously!) to Joh must have come from Dr Vaudois' archives. He'd had research done. Studios had departments for that, staffed by people with library cards and crossword puzzle minds.

'So Holloway *was* immortal?'

'Until he died, Mr Karloff. Until he died.'

'Yes, there's that. Does his death give you any concerns, Mr Home?'

Junior didn't look troubled, except a flicker under his good eye. Gamblers call that a 'tell'. The boy had spilled an inkwell and prayed no master's gaze would alight on his blue-black guilty hands. He put up a front of innocence.

Billy noticed the tell too. He was practised.

'You didn't know they'd die,' he continued, reasoning. 'You haven't the stomach to be a cold murderer. If you'd fully appreciated the danger, you'd have taken more precautions. There wouldn't have been so much panic. That flap when you blundered onto Sunset Boulevard with your head on fire was more than unfortunate. It was foolish, a bad mistake.'

Dr Vaudois' pursed lips were more a shout than a tell.

He hadn't been at Home House on the night of the experiment. He'd called in via television-telephone, and then only after the damage was done. His main concern was mopping up.

Someone had gone ahead against advice. Small rich boys are not known for their patience. They get bored and want to unwrap their presents in early December – then ask for new ones on Christmas Eve, preferably gifts taken away from some other boy or girl.

This wasn't just Junior, though it was his ultimate say-so. Quin was in it too. Even those contract-signing, fee-pocketing test subjects. Joh saw no signs of struggle. They'd willingly wired themselves to the Great Electric Vampire Device.

Dr Vaudois must have been the nay-saying spoilsport.

The test-it-on-monkeys wallah. The wait-till-the-observers-from-Sweden-are-here delayer of miracles.

The grown-up.

'You thought you could take their talents and leave them alive,' said Billy. 'Diminished, perhaps – but living.'

'And paid,' Junior said. 'Don't forget that. They got their money up front.'

'They were supposed to die only for a moment, as you leached from them… then wake up, *electrified*, like the doctor and nurse here… and, I think, very many others. *All* of the staff at the Lamia Munro?'

'We don't bother with the janitors.'

'It's done wonders for my complexion,' said Gretchen, like a radio commercial for Lady Esther Four-Purpose Face Cream.

The nurse slipped a dressing gown over Junior's broad shoulders. His arms no longer fit the sleeves, so he wore the gown like a mid-length cape. A Dracula cloak, of course – the colour of dark wine. The mogul needed an entire new wardrobe. The Pyramid costume department would be stretched.

'I'm torn up about those guys – Groto, the Chinaman, the other one. I'll have their families traced and take care of 'em.'

'Herbert Holloway's descendants may be legion,' said Dr Vaudois. 'In the thousands.'

'Well, not *his* family, then. But the other two. They won't want for anything.'

Junior arranged his face to seem sad. His story required the briefest pause to acknowledge the sacrifice of minor characters. Two nameless Merry Men were cut down by Sir Guy's blade. Robin would frown for a trice then vault out of the ambush with a grin, bursting to rob the rich, feed the poor and climb Maid Marian's ivy. The peasants could rot.

'But they didn't *all* die?' said Billy.

Junior's new face froze. He was too expressive for a poker player. Probably too expressive for a Hollywood deal-maker.

'We're anxious to locate Miss Ives,' said Dr Vaudois.

'The odd-looking one,' said Gretchen. 'I wish my hair would do what hers does.'

Witch-Eye, Joh called her.

'We're concerned for Miss Ives, of course,' said the doctor. 'There's no way of knowing how the process has affected her. Like Mr Home, she should be at the Clinic, where we can observe and treat her for any… symptoms.'

'Laurel Ives,' I said, rolling the name around.

A monster was hidden in the name, or at least a seductress. Lorelei. I'd thought of her often since Joh talked about her.

'That's not her real name,' said Junior. 'Any more than yours is "Boris Karloff". "Laurel Ives" is a stage name, a moniker…'

'A *nom de plume*,' I suggested.

'Yeah, what you said. Nominal plumage. You'll like this… her real name is "Stephen", like a guy who'd be called Steve. "Stephen Swift".'

Any relative of Jonathan, I wondered?

'Don't trust women with the names of birds,' I said.

Junior didn't understand.

'A swift is a type of bird, like a swallow,' said Billy. 'You've heard of birds' nest soup? That's made out of swift spit.'

'Huh,' said Junior.

'Women with the names of birds – Lark, Swan, Dove – tend to be… *flighty*.'

I'd just made that up. I am a writer. It's what we do.

'Good to know,' said Junior. 'Good to know. Like a bird, Stephen Swift – Laurel Ives – has flown.'

'She won't stay free long,' said Dr Vaudois. 'The police…'

Junior spat at that. A substantial glob landed on his bed-curtain and ran down a fold.

'Your full resources are deployed,' the doctor said, a Minister telling the Old King his men-at-arms were searching the countryside for that defiant milkmaid who scratched his cheek. 'I expect results imminently. Confidently expect.'

'"Confidently" is a superfluous qualifier,' I said. 'Double underlining. A sign of trying too hard. A confident man wouldn't need to say so.'

Junior loomed over his minion.

'Waymond has you there, Dr Vee. And finding the birdie isn't the same as catching her, as bringing her in. Not at all it isn't. Not if she's…'

Then he shut up.

I wasn't as confident – that word again! – as Billy that Junior Home hadn't the stomach to be a cold murderer. I worried he'd grown just such an organ and was as eager to test it as he was to look down on a woman's hair-parting.

'That's the thing I *can't* figure…' said Billy. 'What you needed – what you got – from Holloway, Chang and Amthor is obvious. What did this poor woman have that was part of the process? Since she's alive, is it still hers?'

'Not exclusively,' he said.

His red eye – his own witch-eye – didn't expand, but glinted.

In that blur of a crimson iris, something whirled.

The bedside water-jug exploded, soaking Dr Vaudois' coat, sticking glass splinters into his wet sleeve.

The bed-curtains tore off their rails and knotted in mid-air, then hung, with no visible support.

I felt a *push* at my chest and was driven to my knees.

Junior Home turned his eye to Billy.

I saw Billy grip invisible hands that were clutching his throat. His shoes lifted on tiptoes, then rose off the carpet entirely. He floated, struggling.

'I can't tell you how *good* this feels,' Junior shouted.

'Mind over matter,' I said.

Dr Vaudois wanted to calm Junior down, to have him rein in whatever hoodoo that was now an innate talent.

So, Stephen Swift was one of *those*.

Was she a *lorelei* after all?

But suddenly having Paderewski's fingers wasn't the same as learning all the concertos. Junior couldn't keep holding Billy up and me down at the same time. I felt the *push* go away.

Billy was tossed across the room.

He landed on a model of Notre Dame made of flowers. A get-well-soon tribute from RKO.

Billy tried to get back on his feet but was knocked down.

'I just imagine a big boxing glove,' boasted Junior. 'And *POW*!'

I was about to cough up a lecture on onomatopoeia and why it should only be used in prose as a last resort... but then he turned his *struldbrugg* eye on me.

The red light grew to the intensity of a small sun.

A firepit yawned open beneath my feet and I dropped into it.

Everything went away. Including me.

14

My hands throbbed with phantom pain. I opened my eyes a crack, expecting to see stumps at the ends of my arms. No, there were my hands. White and cold as boned chicken. Severed by guillotine then sewn back on by the undertaker.

I was not to upset the mourners, if any.

I heard ghost music.

Tannhäuser. Half the musicians hadn't clocked in. The horn section was thin. The percussion made do with ash-can lids. Beats of silence interrupted the Wagnerian swell. What was up with the no-shows? This was a German orchestra. Had the FBI seized them as spies? The trouble could have been with my ears. I worried that half my hearing was burned out.

I wasn't vertical.

I'd not drunk for days. Not through exercise of will-power. I'd been absent from myself. Coming to in my aching body, I was afraid the driver I'd lent it to had run down a cop and crashed into a beer truck.

Or gone off a pier.

Damn it – that was what had happened!

I'd enacted that damn Owen Taylor's last minutes, scalp streaming from a cosh wound, pedal wedged under my foot, wheel wrenching in my grip.

The sea came up fast. The driving wheel evaporated. Twisting in my hands was the greasy stick of my old training plane. I'd lost control. The instructor couldn't cut in. RFC cadets got called Huns because we pranged more Allied kites than enemy groundfire.

I heard the scream of air over wings. Canvas tearing.

Then I slammed into cold wet darkness.

Not saltwater, not Flanders mud, but oil – black, black gold. The stuff gets everywhere and stains everything. Too rich for anyone's blood. The windshield blotted black instantly, like a skyscape a-swarm with passenger pigeons. Foul sludge oozed into the car interior, viscid on my face, a hundred tons on my chest. My throat was forced open, my lungs filled.

This was how I would die.

I wouldn't sleep in an oil sump.

Or burn in a firepit.

I'd just be crushed.

The medium-sized room smelled like hospital, only without *eau de violets* or flowers from well-wishers. So I knew where I was with wishers in general. Well-wishers kept away. Ill-wishers supervised my treatment. Ticks were chewing into my arms and back. I tasted soap and medicine. My mouth wouldn't water enough to wash the tang off my teeth.

I had what the Irish call a powerful thirst.

Not for water.

I felt my face – I could move my hands now – and found I'd been shaved. Cuts on my chin were clotted. Someone was looking after me. My spectacles were within reach on a night-stand. I put them on.

The room came into focus.

A bulb big as those used on shooting stages burned behind protective wire mesh. A sun in a cage, throwing heat and light. The room was anonymous but clean, painted within the last few months. A line ran round the wall at mid-point between floor and ceiling. Below the line, the paint was aquamarine; above, the colour of fresh cream. My bed was shoved in a corner, head and long left side neat against the wall. Not a proper hospital arrangement. Nurses need to get at you from any angle. This was more like a drunk tank. Another bed fitted into the opposite corner, neatly made up and without even a ghost lying on it. There was no window. I thought for a panic-clutch moment there might not be a door...

… for the love of God, Fortunato!

But there it was, in the wall opposite – a blue panel and a cream panel. The reason I hadn't spotted it was that the handle on this side had been removed. A hole, plugged with putty, showed where it had been. At eye-height was a sliding peephole. Again, like jail.

On the bedside table was a bottle. I rolled over to focus on it.

Not Amontillado.

A pint of Wilson Blended whiskey. On the label, it said 'that's all', to assure the high-liver that any crushed beetles mixed in were barely perceptible. 'Regardless of price, no better whiskey in any bottle'.

Not my brand… indeed, not my drink.

Whoever furnished refreshments in this hostelry was thinking of Philip Marlowe. But, any port in a storm… it would suffice, as they say. Sufficiently suffice. 'Sufficient unto the day' – *thwack across the palm for mumbling, Chandler!* – 'is the evil thereof.' Matthew, Chapter Six… verse – *another thwack for hesitation, Chandler!* – thirty-four. Six blends in the blended, or thirty-four… how many breeds of beetle are there in Relay, Maryland, where Mr Wilson works his mixing magic?

By the bottle was a clean glass beaker. Something from a laboratory.

I sat up in bed, which involved flaring general pain, and discovered I was wearing a green paper gown. What I had taken for ticks were flecks of wood-pulp in the rough, cheap stuff. My clothes were on the floor, at the foot of the bed, folded on top of my shoes. Neat enough to pass barracks inspection.

I reached for the bottle. It was cold and heavy as stone.

Yes, I am a drinker. On occasions, I am a drunk. But as even the reverend master who beat scripture into me was forced to concede, I am no dunce. Hospitals, even the shadiest, do not provide liquor to the recovering. County jails can be more accommodating, but slipping a Sheriff's Deputy a ten-spot gets you 99 cents' worth of paint-stripper. Only a valued repeat customer would rate Wilson.

So, this was a more nefarious institution.

Give Chandler booze and he'll swallow any medicine you like in it.

I'd have to be dry for a good while longer to fall for that.

The seal was unbroken. I ran my thumb over the crimped tin cap, feeling for a hypodermic puncture. That hymen was intact too. I was safe from the Fiend of Fog Lane.

But I was still invited to poison myself.

Just more subtly. I was trusted to turn to drink.

It was time for my medicine.

After the week – the *life* – I was having, I had earned a jolt.

I broke the seal and unscrewed the cap. A thundercloud of alcohol fumes rose like a genie from the bottle. My eyes stung. Inhaling would get me squiffed.

I saw the appeal. I'd regret abstemiousness later.

But I screwed the cap back and put the bottle down. My palms were wet from the cold glass. I still couldn't get spit in my mouth.

The smell didn't disappear. It was in my nostrils, burning my sinuses.

I went over the story so far, the voice in my head more Marlowe's than mine. I'd visited a movie monster and heard out an ex-detective. A case fell in my lap. Billy and R.T. – sleuths about town. Murders in a mansion. A girl runaway. German breakfast. The Lamia Munro Clinic. The exhausting Dr Voodoo. The risen Ward Home Junior. Son of the Windmill-Man. Stolen talents. Mind over matter. A fall into the fire.

It wasn't a story *Dime Detective* would buy.

Maybe *Unknown*. Or *Weird Tales*.

The door opened outwards and a Bim came into the room. He wore a shoulder-holster over his white tee shirt and under a doctor's coat that was too big for him. He was built to scale for Junior's former height. A muscular, blond shrimp. He toted a chart on a clipboard.

'Bugs, you're awake,' he said.

'Evidently,' I replied.

He grinned. One shiny tooth caught light like a signal mirror.

'We weren't sure, for a while… Mr, ah…' He glanced at the chart and said, 'Marlowe.'

So that was how they were going to play it.

He paused for a tiny moment, expecting a protest. I didn't give it to him. So he knew that I knew that he knew… let's call the whole thing off.

We could cut this whole scene, but – no – he ploughed on.

He held the bottle up and saw liquid still level with the neck. He stroked the broken seal with his thumb.

'Most of 'em don't pass the temptation test. Glug this down and you're not serious about treatment. Dr Vaudois tosses you out on your rear.'

'Treatment?' I gave him the prompt.

'Sobriety in three weeks or your money back. The Lamia Munro Clinic has a great success rate. With those who want to succeed, at least. Famous names have been through the treatment. You wouldn't believe who's a slave to the bottle. Movie folk, oilmen, writers…'

'Ever heard of a writer by the name of Raymond Chandler?'

'No. I'm a couple of hundred pages into *Gone With the Wind*. Have been for a few weeks, to be honest. If you ask me, that wind is taking its own sweet time about going. Still, there's the War to come. I'm sure that'll goose the wind no end. Get it into a going frame of mind.'

'Is the actor Boris Karloff here?'

The Bim grinned again, slyly this time. He looked at the empty bed.

'In the room? Is that what you see when you're coming off the sauce? You've been getting vitamin shots, and they can mess with your mind too. Frankenstein sitting up in the other bed. It's bats, usually. Sometimes spiders. I guess DTs dress up for Hallowe'en any how they like.'

I had an idea this Bim had no real experience with drinkers.

The Lamia Munro didn't really administer the Cure. Many places offered differing quackery for the well-heeled and well-oiled. Sobriety farms. Temperance Temples. Dry gulches. The only institutions that could boast real success in the field were morgues.

Dr Voodoo would like me to write off what I'd seen as a booze hallucination. Not a bad approach, given that he'd been forced to come up with it on the hoof.

How were they trying to convince Billy he hadn't seen what we both had? The only thing he drank too much of was tea.

'Would you like to be up and about, Bugs?'

'Stretching my limbs might do me good. I feel like a beaten carpet.'

'I'll just bet you do. Well, in a day or so, if all goes to plan…'

'Oh, I could manage sooner than that. Why, I could—'

'Hold your horses, Mr Marlowe. The state you were in when Dr Vaudois admitted you, the things you were saying. It's not likely we'd let you up till we're sure you've got your head screwed on right way round. You could toss away hard-won progress by starting up on that again. Monsters. Zombies. Giants. Now Boris Karloff! I'll be much further into *Gone With the Wind* by the time we're ready to get you in circulation. Probably clear through the War and into the Reconstruction. A lot of Johnny Rebs are going to bite Southern dust. And Miss Scarlett has a closet full of gowns to wear. I'll keep looking in, see how you're doing. Before you know, you'll be in your right mind and ready to get back to work. You're a...?'

'I ride a unicycle. In a carnival.'

'I reckon you need a fine sense of balance for that.'

'No one wants a lopsided trick cyclist,' I admitted.

The Bim looked at his chart again. I'd swear hieroglyphics were printed on it, like the scroll that brought the Mummy to life.

'Strange circumstance,' he said. 'We don't have "circus artiste" listed as your profession.'

'Carnival, not circus.'

'Shouldn't make a difference. It says here you're a gumshoe.'

'What? An overshoe?'

'An eye. A dick. A hawkshaw. A man with a magnifying glass.'

'... and a pipe?'

'Yes, that's it exactly. It's with your clothes. And other effects. The ones you can't hurt yourself with.'

'The tobacco pouch is there?'

'Yes. Not the lighter, though. We're wary of fire in the Lamia Munro. Too many secure doors. For patients' safety. Are you a firebug, Bugs? We've had them here too. Some folk never grow out of playing with matches. Wouldn't want a conflagration.'

'I can see how you wouldn't.'

'We've taken your shoelaces, belt and necktie too. After a few dry days, the itching starts. And a gnawing thing, like rats in your guts. You get to thinking about ending it all. That passes. Most cases.'

'I could fashion a rope out of twisted sheets.'

'You could try. The sheets are treated paper, like the gown. Tear if you put any weight on it.'

'So, the would-be suicide is handily thwarted?'

'Part of the treatment. No use being stone-cold sober if you're hanged.'

'I can't argue with that.'

'Few can. Many try.'

'I'd like to ask again about Mr Karloff…'

'We could get you powders if you have night terrors real bad. Most regular drying-out souses only get spooked enough to see Bela Lugosi. That's no fright at all, really. Barely a pinch of powder sees off Lugosi. If you see Karloff, that's serious. A three- or four-pinch problem. It'll be the Fiend of Fog Lane next. Did you catch that, Bugs?'

'I prefer musicals.'

'That'll be the carny in you. Me too. *Say It With Tubas?*'

'Saw it five times the weekend it opened. With the live act.'

Bim oompahed alarmingly – something like a tune. A lively, up-tempo copyright infringement of *Tannhäuser*.

'Is Mr Karloff still in the Clinic?'

Bim stopped mooing through his nose. He took a pencil from his top pocket and squiggled on the chart.

'What you have, Mr Marlowe, sounds like an iday fixay.'

'Amscray to your iday fixay, Mr…?'

'You can call me Bim.'

'Mr Bim… hmm, familiar name. No, you mistake me, deliberately I deduce…'

'A deduction. See, you're a dick after all. Not a unicycle jockey.'

'I'm not asking about phantasms of alcoholic withdrawal. I mean a flesh and blood British actor. Known for playing demons and dastards on the silver screen.'

'We have many clients from show business, as I told you. It's right stressful, bein' in the movies. Their names are confidential, of course. You never know when Louella Parsons is listening. She employs shabby private detectives to ferret out and pass on her Tinseltown scoops. Eyes like you, Mr Marlowe. Snoopy snoopers who snitch.'

He was pleased with that.

I wasn't enjoying the talkaround.

'What's the gun for?' I asked.

'Rambunctious patients.'

'So it's "kill or cure"?'

'Not in that sense.'

He pocketed his pencil and pulled his rod.

It was red plastic. A Flash Gordon blaster. Collect enough box-tops, mail them in to the station – and you, too, can defy Ming the Merciless.

'A squirt gun loaded with lemon juice,' he said. 'I aim for the eyes. That'll unrambunctuate a patient any day of the week. Twice on Wednesdays and Saturdays. See how I've notched the barrel? Those are times I didn't get a bloody nose or a busted arm because I was mighty fast on the draw.'

The Bim fired a stream of liquid like an old-timer hawking chaw at a spittoon. A stain lay across my paper top-sheet.

He still hadn't told me about Billy.

Someone rambunctious – and a good deal more – had exerted their mind over Billy's matter.

There was a new undying monster in town.

Junior Home.

Billy's Florsheims had kicked in the air. He was hauled up to the ceiling, by his neck. A lynch mob victim strung up on an invisible rope.

The Bim holstered his toy.

He knuckle-tapped the door in a Morse sequence and it opened.

I assumed he was leaving. Instead, another Bim – the original, I thought – and Nurse Anne carted in a stretcher. They put in little apparent effort, as if the bulky patient were a couple of bolsters arranged to fool the night-monitor. I wondered if it were a papier-mâché dummy, then remembered the staff were as freakishly strong as they were abnormally quick.

Thanks to revivification by electricity.

Which hadn't been done to me. I was weaker than a kitten. If the young Taki was any representation, kittens can look after themselves in most fights. They are sharp of claw.

The new patient was hefted onto the other bed, then tucked in by Nurse Anne.

'You're getting a room-mate, Bugs,' said the pistol-packing Bim. 'Meet Mr Frankenstein. Frankie won't be any trouble. He's having a long rest.'

'Frankenstein' turned his head to me, as if rolling over in his sleep.

The patient's head was so completely bandaged he looked like an uncarved Irish Hallowe'en turnip. He'd had museum-quality mummification.

'What's his problem?' I asked.

The Bim flashed that steel tooth.

'Life has got him down.'

'I sympathise.'

'I'm sure you do, Bugs.'

The Bims and the Nurse withdrew – I fancied Nurse Anne gave me an encouraging little wave – and the door shut.

My new cell-mate didn't move.

'Billy,' I asked. 'Is that you?'

He tried to raise himself on one elbow but could only lift an inch or two off the mattress. His long, swaddled body was taut and arched.

He gave a Monster grunt.

'Rrrrr.'

Then he slumped on the bed. Sweat seeped through the bandage, creating the damp shadow of a face.

Was it Billy?

We were back in the opening credits of the first *Frankenstein*.

'The Monster…?'

Question Mark had returned.

I looked at the night-stand. Bim had taken the bottle of Wilson Blended with him, the louse. I lay back and studied the ceiling.

Miss Scarlett and I would have a long wait till the wind got gone.

15

Hours passed. Maybe days. Without a window, it was impossible to tell time. I don't wear a wrist watch. I'd been asleep and I was awake... but it could be any hour of the clock.

The caged light stayed on. Even if I shut my eyes, they hurt. You shouldn't stare at the sun and by instinct you don't... until the man in your head *tells* you not to. Then you can't help squinting and turning your face to the light for a moment, burning crescent-shaped neon blobs into your vision for minutes.

I lay immobile, not looking at that mesh-covered bulb... but unable to look away either. My eyes were drawn again and again towards the white-hot spot. I tried taking my glasses off, but the blur still seared. Every six dozen breaths, I'd glance again, burn again. If I screwed my eyes shut, a neon squiggle blazed in blackness.

Then I went through the whole cycle again.

Much more of this and I would be blind. Which still wouldn't turn off the light.

I wanted darkness more than I wanted drink.

Darkness was cool, safe, comforting. The light in this place was stark, abrasive, minatory. The useless paper sheets shredded as I shifted and itched. Sharp wire springs prodded through the mattress, inscribing stitch-and-blood patterns on my back.

I couldn't sleep but I couldn't get out of bed. My hands were mine again, if sluggish and heavy. It would take an age to reacquire my legs.

And I was in better shape than the other fellow.

Question Mark breathed like a mustard gas casualty. He made no attempt to rise.

I was semi-sure, now, that it was Billy.

The Bim called him Frankenstein, but the patient wasn't Colin Clive. For one thing, Mr *it's al-i-eve* Cl-i-eve died soon after *Bride of Frankenstein* came out. The Bim had made the not uncommon mistake of confusing the doctor with the monster.

Of course, the deeper meaning of *Frankenstein* is that Frankenstein is the Monster and the Monster is Something Else. Even schoolboys, perhaps *especially* schoolboys, know this. It's a young person's book – a three-volume novel penned by Mrs Shelley before she was twenty. Some writers don't scrape together enough for a single-volume novel before they're fifty.

The sweat pattern on his bandage mask formed the face of the movie Monster. Hollow cheek (where Billy took out a partial plate), deep forehead scar, flat-top skull. Changing Billy Pratt to look like *Boris Karloff* would be a cruel plastic surgery joke. Question Mark was Frankenstein's Monster in a Mummy wrapper.

Had they torn out his tongue too? Or filled his mouth with cotton?

The Bim tried to tell me I was a detective. They had made Billy into a Monster. We were at sea in our own made-up stories.

'Write what you know', correspondence course teachers say. Those dusty fakers mean the mundane trivia puked up in wedge after wedge of critically lauded prose no one reads by choice. Leave the idyllic farm for the corrupt big city. Hate your dull wife and fool around with a racier, sleeker model. Get drunk in Paris and whine about the War. Always the bloody, bloody War. Such is what they mean by 'what you know'.

But what if 'what you know' is… terror by night… daggers in the back… duplicitous dames… haunted mansions built on graveyards… resurrection of the dead by electrical device… wholesale murder, ignored by cops and politicians… hooded master fiends… and Monsters?

What should the conscientious author write then, to stay honest?

Mr Posterity, do you want to know what the twentieth century was *really* like? Leave Booth Tarkington on the shelf and watch *King Kong*. Start a fire with Edna Ferber and read *Red Harvest*. Prop up that wonky table leg with John Galsworthy and riffle through the horror magazines where the truth is really told. Toss Edna St Vincent Millay in the trash and tune in to The Shadow. The man with the cackle in his crackle *knows* what evil lurks in the hearts of man… the evil that swirls all around, formless and deadly as poison mist.

America isn't social realism. At its rare best, it's an adventure story. As Joh Devlin knows it, with skirts lifted and garter showing, it's a crime drama. As Boris Karloff stalks its woods, it's a horror story.

I shut my eyes.

The curling filament burned crimson in the night inside my head.

It pulsed and crackled like the machinery in *Frankenstein*. The gadgets made by Norman Quin that did nothing but produce sparks and arcs. Glowing scorpion tails inside glass tubes.

I heard a choral swell. Wagner, of course. Voices and trumpets.

Not in my head. Piped, throughout the Clinic. And it wasn't trumpets. This was the Pyramid Pictures arrangement, with tubas substituted. No Home could have enough tubas.

That woke a determination in me. I couldn't just lie here and take it.

I have never shirked difficult work.

I didn't need to be shouted at or whipped. I only needed to be asked, politely. I say, old man, would you mind awfully getting out of bed?

Of course, my friend. Anything for a fellow English public school chap.

Is today good for you?

Absolutely ideal, chum.

… then?

I concur. It's a perfect day for getting out of bed (and finding and smashing the speaker grille!).

Then why haven't you?

Haven't I? I thought I had.

No, I'm afraid not. Not a sign of it. Nary a twitch.

I opened my eyes and had to concede the voice in my mind – my voice, or P.G. Wodehouse's, I forget which – was correct in every detail.

I had not got out of bed…

… though I conceded that, at bottom, it was a mighty swell idea.
I should give it every consideration at the earliest possible opportunity.

Like now?

You again, eh? Yes, now. That would make sense, only…

…

Only nothing. And there's nothing for it. Stuff those tubas!

I shifted my stiff legs, ripping sheets that should have been changed for
fresh. A nurse was neglecting her duties. My feet dangled over the cliff-edge
of the bed. The hundred-pound fishing weights tied to my ankles dragged
me to the ocean floor. I slid out of bed and fell onto cool linoleum.

My escape plan had not involved bumping my seat on the floor and
banging my head against the bedframe.

But I was the conquering hero who had got out of bed.

Now – *excelsior!* – I must be the intrepid mountaineer who stood up
straight.

Then I would be the engineering genius who put on his pants and
buttoned his shirt.

There were punishments for misaligned buttons.

Five circuits of the parade ground with full pack on the back and lit
cigarette in the gob. An extra circuit every time the fag blew out. That'll
learn you, Chandler. That'll learn you!

A little rest, first.

No, rest later.

If you insist, old man.

Rather afraid I have to, R.T.

The room's clocklessness was now a mercy. I couldn't be embarrassed
by how long it took to dress myself. I made a futile search for my belt,
even under the bed where dust gathered and shadows tempted, before
remembering it was kept elsewhere as a precaution against self-slaughter.
My pants rode low on my bony hips. My unlaced shoes flapped when I
walked the five paces to the door and the five back to the bed.

I buttoned my shirt but that small victory didn't satisfy. I didn't usually
care for the fuss of a tie – old-school or bow – but now the choice was

withheld, I'd have liked to show off dexterity by tying a perfect knot. Mama used to tie my tie before school but I learned to manage by myself before I became a man. I had relapses, though – becoming the small boy again. When I was at Dabney, my hands shook in the morning and Cissy had to render me the kindness of a proper bow, and made the three points of my display handkerchief match too.

Men marry their mothers and chase their daughters. I'm sure Freud said that, or a wise man I met in a speakeasy during Prohibition… or a sinister shrink in a yarn too bitter for *Dime Detective* to run.

That brisk stroll to the door and back did me a power of good.

I'd earned a nice nap. Possibly a steam and a massage.

No, miles to go yet. The brave boys in blue and grey had to march off to war, leaving the womenfolk and slaves behind. It was a long hard slog to the last page of *Gone With the Wind*. Selznick would get the picture out before Bim could get there – to 'tomorrow is another day'. The book, and my recuperation, would not be over by Christmas.

Not at all at all, as the Irish say.

I considered the monster in the room. Question Mark.

'Billy,' I said. 'Boris. *Frankenstein.*'

The head-lump moved slightly.

Underneath several thicknesses of linen, the patient's eyes fought to open. Would he panic and think he was blind?

No doctor would advise me to take off his bandages.

He was swathed for a reason. He should be given time to heal.

But no one got better in the Lamia Munro Clinic – except Junior. He got better and better and the rest of us got worse and worse.

Wagner kept sounding out. Some chunk of *Rheingold*.

I had a panic spasm that my essence might have been drained.

My waistband was loose because I had shrunk – the way Junior Home had grown. The Windmill-Man hadn't been enough. Now he needed to feed again, taking sustenance from captive patients. On the menu for tonight: Chandler, R.T. – substantial, satisfying entrée. With a slice of starlet for dessert. Not with wine. He never drank wine.

Not Frankenstein, Joh said. *Dracula.*

Junior was the King Vampire of the Lamia Munro Clinic.

I learned Keats by heart at Dulwich College. His 'Lamia' was a species of vampire, a snake turned into a wicked woman. Now the connection came to me, something irritating was explained. The statue above the door of the Clinic was that Lamia of antiquity. The snakes in her hands were her former skins. Keats fingers Hermes as the rat who transformed snake into seductress. He peeled off her scales to show silky skin, but didn't warm her blood. Tearing apart a caduceus – the staff of Hermes – was her revenge play.

The Munros, the hill folk who birthed Old Man Heim's wife, might not be as up on romantic poets as we were at Dulwich College, but they saw something in the child and named her accordingly. The baby must have had a caul or a talking wart.

Lamia was the third of three in this tale of terror. Always the trinity – the Furies, the Fates, the Gorgons, Macbeth's witches, Dracula's wives. Ariadne sat on the highest throne, as Queen or Papesse. Stephen Swift-Laurel Ives, of the witch-eye, was the maiden. Lamia Munro was the crone.

I looked down at my cell-mate, who was still in distress.

Question Mark groaned in short bursts – the guttural, halting, pained attempts of a speechless creature to communicate.

I must help the mumbling mummy.

My fingers sought the tied or taped ends of the bandages – as hard to find in a hurry as the end of a roll of sticky tape. An elegant purist might wind a single mile-long bandage round and round, with a single bow behind the ear to keep it in place. Another purist would gently tug that bow and let the bandages spring undone as if of their own accord, freeing the captive with a conjurer's flourish.

No one as pure as that was in this room.

I thumbed through the seams and wrenched apart the bandages over the eyes.

The Monster's grunts rose in agitation. Strong hands – also bandaged – gripped my arms.

'I'm not trying to blind you,' I said. 'I want to help you see.'

'Rrrr… *arrrr!*'

'I'm a friend,' I said. 'Friend... *goood*!'

It had worked in *Bride of Frankenstein*.

'Frrr... *grrr*!'

'That's the idea.'

Like that screeching ninny who snatched off the Phantom's mask, I tore away the bandages. I backed away from the horror as the Monster sat up in bed.

He was *al-i-eve*!

Question Mark was wearing a grubby white bandage balaclava. He unwound the rest of his dressing. His brows jutted like callused heels. His eyelids were swollen as if injected with venom. His lips were stained black.

I *still* didn't know if my room-mate was Billy or a stand-in.

... but it certainly was the *Frankenstein* Monster.

'What have they done to you?' I asked, unthinking.

Question Mark felt his face and growled.

He touched his hollow cheek, his forehead-cleft, the metal clips at his scalp-line. He discovered new, permanent contours.

The bandages around his hands came loose.

His tapering, black-nailed fingers looked like someone else's. I thought of the murdering mitts Peter Lorre grafted onto Colin Clive's wrists in *Mad Love*. Had Dr Voodoo kept the late actor's hands packed in salt until Billy came under his knife? It would be a nasty joke to stitch parts of Dr Frankenstein onto the body of his Monster.

Those liquid, pitiful eyes – what had been done to the eyes! – implored me.

'Rrrr...'

In my inside jacket pocket, I kept a comb and a sliver of vanity mirror. Anticipating this moment, the ruthless bastards in charge took the comb but left me the mirror. I daren't show the Monster his face... yet I couldn't hold back. Better pain now, rather than later.

I'd seen worse in the War. Honestly.

I held up the mirror, expecting an angry shriek.

He took it from me with surprising daintiness and considered himself as if peering into the still surface of a pool.

Would he dash my brains against the wall?

He angled the mirror this way and that. He pulled a scarf of bandage away from his throat. This year's model didn't have neck terminals. He smiled, slyly. He saw his face and was not entirely displeased. He fingered his horse-shoe jaw.

Had his mind gone?

Or did he breathe a sigh of relief? If they made another *Frankenstein*, he was spared untold hours in Jack Pierce's torture chair. He could clump on set in his big boots at ten o'clock and – after a light dusting with grey ash – be ready for shooting by five-past.

He handed me back my mirror. I stood away from his bed.

He threw aside the paper covers. It was much less effort for him than it had been for me.

He put bandaged feet on the floor and stood.

He was bigger now – or, that panic again, was I smaller? He was tall and wide as the Monster seemed on screen.

Question Mark's breath strained the bandages around his chest. The Billy of 1931 was a soup kitchen refugee. This Monster was built like a weight-lifter, not a slat-ribbed hobo. He could tear off your arm and slap you with your own hand. In *Frankenstein*, Jimmy Whale shot Billy from low angles. Other actors – even those not playing hunchbacked dwarfs – slouched and bent to emphasise the Monster's height. Now, no movie magic was necessary.

Junior Home expanded after electrically vampiring the Windmill-Man. It could have happened to Billy too. Or – the thought struck me like an ice bullet – was someone else wearing Billy's stolen face? There could be another Quin device in the Clinic. To become Question Mark, someone – a Bim, an understudy, a desperate Bela Lugosi? – might have absorbed the magic that made William Henry Pratt into the Demon King Karloff.

He growled like Billy.

Folded at the foot of his bed was a khaki greatcoat. I picked it up by the collar and it flopped open, heavy and malodorous. War surplus with rank and regiment insignia unpicked. It certainly wasn't what Billy – a nattier dresser than most of his screen characters – wore on the street.

A huge hand lowered onto my shoulder… and gripped.

It was agony. Exploding agony.

I dropped the coat.

After accidentally drowning the little girl, the Monster's dismay and confusion were heartrending. The expression I now saw – through tears of pain – came later in the film. This Monster was wiser. Having learned cunning and cruelty by example, he was bent on revenge against the man who made him misshapen. He feared fire, but tingled at the thought of burning down the world that rejected him. His abnormal brain lit up with a torturer's delight.

Dr Voodoo's little joke had gone too far.

Dr Frankenstein and Jimmy Whale could retire. The Lamia Munro Clinic had made a real Monster.

16

The grip on my shoulder was a bone-crushing vice.

Question Mark wasn't even angry. He was testing his strength on something within reach. A hatstand would have done.

No, it wouldn't. A hatstand wouldn't squirm, squeal, grit teeth, buckle at the knees.

The Monster wanted to hurt something alive.

I couldn't see Billy in those eyes. The kindness was gone.

I tapped his hand, like a wrestler submitting. No response.

'You're going to have to stop that,' I said, with difficulty.

No reaction.

I talked to him how I talked to Taki and got the same response. The cat didn't care if her claws sank in.

'That *really* hurts,' I said.

Maybe a flicker of understanding.

The grip eased but didn't go away. I stood straighter and put my hand against his chest to brace myself. His bandages were hot and damp.

He looked around the room and – inevitably – his gaze was drawn to the light fixture. Deep shadows etched into the Monster's face. He didn't blink.

He let go of me – blessed relief! – and reached up. A gesture from *Frankenstein*. Bandage strings hung from his fingers. He could almost touch the light. He made a fist, as if to punch the sun... then turned to look at me.

Tiny fires burned in his black pupils.

Because he wasn't wearing pore-clogging make-up, this Monster could sweat. A droplet crept from his raggedly cut hair and slalomed down the scars and clefts of his face.

Despite what censorial prisses say, horror films are polite about monsters. No one ever mentions that a living dead man *stinks*. Village mobs cornering the Monster don't hold their noses. Dr Frankenstein lectures with his creation laid out on a table and no one's eyes water from the *stench*.

Zoo-animal smell boiled off this Monster. I choked back sick. An undertaste of rot had me licking the roof of my mouth. The miasma of cesspool, slaughterhouse and oil sump could fell a man.

Question Mark looked around. His swift, darting movements were disturbing in someone so big. He took in the lack of windows. The beast got the measure of his cage.

'There is a door,' I told him.

I touched the jammed-up hole where there wasn't a handle.

He understood me. He had a brain.

An abnormal one? Anyone's brain would curdle if they woke up in that cage of a body.

What's a normal brain anyway? How is it any use?

He sized up the door.

You've seen it in pictures... the raging Monster crashes through balsawood, shatters sugar-glass and lurches into the blonde's boudoir.

Off movie sets, doors are sturdier.

He punched the handle-spot and bloodied his knuckles.

Dark red blood, not green. He licked it off like a cat and considered the smear on the door. The wadding was loose in the hole. The painted-over metal plate was dented.

He punched again. Something splintered.

I still didn't think he could get out. But he made a noise.

He threw himself against the door.

Again, you've seen it in the movies. Hero splinters puny door off its hinges with nary a sprain and skips on to adventures new. As opposed to: Hero breaks own fool shoulder on solid, unimpressed oak and collapses screaming on the mat.

In this case, it was a draw.

The door didn't break but neither did the Monster.

There were new cracks. Some of that ugly paint flaked away.

The Monster looked at me, expecting me to pitch in.

'Brute-work is your department,' I said, holding my still-sore shoulder. 'I'll advise on strategy. I was an officer and know strategy. I think you've jarred the lock mechanism. One more sound blow, and – who knows? – we might be in business.'

The Monster pummelled with both fists – as if systematically working on the other fighter's cut eyebrow.

The door was pulled open.

Question Mark hadn't broken out, but had got attention.

He drew in breath to roar defiance. A squirt of lemon juice got him in the eye. He screeched like a bird with a wrenched wing.

Bims rushed into the room.

The Bim with the squirt gun was backed by two more with riot sticks. One was wider than he was tall. He would have had to look up to the old Junior, but had the muscle mass of two Shrimp Homes mashed together.

Another Bim held up an oversized (custom-made?) straitjacket like a Turkish bath attendant approaching a steaming fatty with a towel the size of the parking lot. They should have got the restraint garment on Question Mark when he was out cold.

The Lamia Munro Clinic was not run terribly well. Quality leg-breakers made good dough under contract to loan sharks and protection mobs. Top-drawer thugs rated a clothing allowance. They stood outside nightclubs in ritzy duds, tipping silk hats to drunks they'd toss in garbage cans hours later. Bims weren't in that league. Dr Voodoo didn't have his pick of the town's bully brawn.

What was left was gunsels.

Double-Shrimp Bim pointed his club at me. I stood by my bed, at attention.

Chandler, R.T., reporting…

Yeah, even a gunsel could make me back down. I gave out no smart remarks. Philip Marlowe would have had a cutting line. But Marlowe repeatedly gets knocked unconscious after his wit irks lesser intellects… so I was ahead of the game.

The Monster rubbed his eyes, whimpering.

'Back, Frankie, back…' said the Bim with the Flash Gordon gun.

The Bims closed on their prey.

They handled one thing at a time – not necessarily in the right order, with no real expertise. I saw an open door and a corridor beyond. While Bims surrounded the Monster, I just left the room. I didn't even expect to get far…

… my escape distracted Flash Gordon Bim. He half-turned to see me walking free, giving the Monster a clear shot. Question Mark jabbed a knuckly punch at the back of the Bim's head. He'd nearly shattered an iron lock. This time, he dented bone into brain.

Flash Gordon Bim went down. Double-Shrimp Bim was under him. The other Stick Bim's club was wrenched out of his grip. The Monster swiped him with it, dislocating his jaw. A splatter of blood hit the wall. The Bim stayed on his feet – that unnatural strength again, apparently with high tolerance for pain to go with it – and spat teeth like bullets. He got a jiu-jitsu hold on the Monster and threw him back on his bed.

As Question Mark bounced on springs, his Frankenstein face was quizzical. He was surprised any hunchback or peasant put up a fight when he roared and stamped and scythed.

No-Stick Bim got a grip on the Monster's throat and Flash Gordon Bim – his squirt gun trampled to bits – got back on his feet. His caved-in head popped back in shape. He got a hold on the night-stand, which was bolted to the floor, and tore it free. He raised it over his head and brought it down heavily on the patient's face.

'Fuck you, Frankenstein,' he shouted.

He had liked that Flash Gordon squirt gun. The offer was closed and they didn't make the boxes with the tops any more.

In the corridor, I hesitated.

I felt a chill breeze. A door nearby was open. I smelled petrichor – that tang of recent rain on stone. The literal breath of freedom. A few steps, that was all – and I would be out of the Lamia Munro Clinic.

Leaving Question Mark – perhaps my friend Billy – to the mercies of people who had no mercy.

I did not run – forward or back.

My mouth went parched again.

I thought of the taste of Wilson. Not just the taste – the softening of the world that came after a few measures, the warmth inside and out, the sudden gushing ease of conversation... the way secretaries perked up and responded to lines they'd scorn if spoken sober... the sparkling lights in a velvet night-sky, without the prickling of frost... the indefinite deferment of that cold, hungover dawn and the rinds of wormwood between my teeth.

That fellow – Chandler with a few in him – I liked him a lot.

More than I cared for this one – Chandler stone-cold sober and no help at all.

Drunk Chandler might have swung for a Bim.

Okay, he'd have been knocked down. He'd be in that inky pool of oblivion Marlowe knew so well. But he'd have ached and bled with masculine pride.

Sober Chandler I wasn't sure about, damn him.

I couldn't see Question Mark for Bims. Three were whaling on him. The valet Bim still held the long-armed canvas waistcoat, ready to wrap the bleeding remains when his pals were through. Double-Shrimp Bim hunched like a sumo wrestler, ready to bounce on the patient. If he came down hard, he'd stave in the Monster's ribs.

While pummelling Question Mark with a broken-off night-stand leg, Flash Gordon Bim turned to me and said, 'Hold it right there, Bugs – we'll get to you in a moment...'

I still didn't run. From school, from the War, from marriage, from the oil business, from cat-parenting... I was used to obeying, going along with, not standing up to.

I am not P. Marlowe, Esq.

I stood, dying inside.

The sustained assault was exhausting, the Bims were flagging. Their whiny chesty grunts sounded as if they were taking rather than dishing out a beating.

The Bims stopped and stood away.

Question Mark lay bloodied. Streaming face wounds would heal into new additions to his scar collection. Bright, sly eyes opened in his mask of blood. His black lips drew back to show white, sharp teeth.

He got out of bed, dripping.

Dislocated Jaw Bim came at the Monster with a bloodied length of nightstand leg. Jagged nails protruded from wounded wood. Question Mark grabbed the Bim's shoulders and spun him round like a top, then snapped his spine over his knee. He died with a look of astonished irritation. Death is always a surprise – though in this case he'd died before.

The Monster picked up the rag-doll corpse by the waist and flailed its booted feet at the other Bims. They were strong and quick but not strong and quick enough. After their electric resurrection, they thought they were gifted. They hadn't learned to fight for their new lives.

Cops and crooks who think the gun in their armpit makes them the equal of a street-fighter were like that too. One good punch to the solar plexus… the throat… the kidneys. Or – that old schoolyard favourite, even on the playing fields of Dulwich – the boot to the balls. The tough guy goes down, holstered iron gouging into his side, most likely whimpering that it wasn't fair. Where was the fear, the *respect*?

The Monster battered two Bims senseless and dropped the third Bim's broken body on top of them.

That left the other Bim holding up and hiding behind the canvas wraparound.

It wasn't enough.

Question Mark tore the straitjacket away and grabbed the last Bim by the throat. That grip could squash an Adam's apple. The Monster laid into his prey with a retrieved riot stick, which broke after a few swipes – then jammed the splintered stub into the attendant's mouth with the heel of his hand.

The Bim choked and dropped.

All but one were still breathing and moaning. None were getting up again and fighting.

The dead Bim jerked to life again, galvanised.

My skin crawled. His backbone snapped back in place, and he rolled off his battered pals. His dislocated limbs worked like crab-legs. The scuttling thing had eyes like a boiled fish.

I couldn't look away.

The Monster kicked Crab Bim into the corner, where he got tangled up with himself.

'Come on,' I said, from the corridor. 'What are you waiting for?'

The Monster looked down on his beaten foes.

Even without his big boots, he could stamp their heads to paste.

'We don't have the time,' I told him.

This was my contribution – sensible advice. If he didn't heed it, we'd both be caught. If we lingered for revenge, more Bims would come. They'd bring long guns rather than short sticks. If they fire from twenty feet away, it doesn't matter how dirty you fight.

Question Mark decided he agreed with me.

He picked up the khaki greatcoat and towelled blood and sweat off his face. Wounds from the fight were healing already – the Vaudois-Quin Process in action! It didn't make him prettier. He put on the coat and lifted his bed to fetch a pair of army boots in his ridiculous size. Laceless, of course. Slipping bandage-stockinged feet into the boots, he gave a 'loose shoes... *goooood*' happy grimace.

'Bugs,' gasped the lead Bim from the goon-pile on the floor, 'don't be fooled by Frankie... he ain't...'

The Monster backhanded him to silence.

We walked down the corridor. My friend weaved from side to side to avoid bumping his flat head into coolie hat lampshades. A bright orange line was painted down the middle of linoleum that was otherwise the colour of diarrhoea.

I held Question Mark's arm and pretended to steer him along the line, as if I were a consulting physician and he a star patient. The imposture wouldn't hold up for more than a few seconds, but was a gesture.

At the end of the corridor was an open door.

Roofless blackness beyond.

17

The ground was freshly wet and so was the air. I looked up and saw no stars. I knew what time it was.

Fatheads who sleep easily say 'it's darkest before dawn' – as if that were a comfort. I've stayed awake with a book or a bottle through enough nights to feel the weight of the long silent hours. It's darkest when it's dark, that's all there is to it.

I'd hoped we'd stumble back onto Los Feliz, with passing cars, cabs and cops. We didn't. The Clinic's back door should lead to the Home Estate, a gated enclave but big enough to get lost in. We weren't there either.

The sky flashed bone-white. Clouds were boiling up there. Seconds later, the percussion section came in. A drum-roll up in the hills.

A storm was about to hit.

On occasion something called 'the North American Monsoon' gives the lie to cracks about California papers running 'sunny all day/balmy all night' copy until the type wears out. Thunder and lightning rip the sky. Dr Frankenstein flies box kites. Taki hides under the bed. We get the sort of deluge that drowned a dozen extras the last time Hollywood made a Noah's Ark picture.

Such spells come on quick and go away fast.

By the time the rest of the country hears about our wet weather, the flood has disappeared into drains, raising the level of the reservoirs by not one fraction of an inch. Mudslides wash tar-paper mansions off hillside estates and new ones are up before the week is out. Houseboys scoop saltwater fish out of swimming pools and drown them in running gutters. Sidewalks bake dry by lunchtime. Traffic cops draw pensions, invalided off the force by sunburn.

We were out of our cell, but still in the jail.

Another sheet of lightning let me see we had escaped into a closed quadrangle. High walls on all sides. Raked gravel underfoot. In the open air, but in no sense free.

Why had Question Mark been put in my cell? The Clinic must have enough locked rooms to keep patients apart from each other. I suspected a cruel experiment. That would be just like Dr Voodoo. Our escape was an illusion. We hadn't paddled away from Alcatraz or Devil's Island. We were rats who had worked a lever to get out of one box only to find ourselves in a bigger box. A maze of boxes.

Either that, or the Monster was supposed to kill me.

More lightning. Thunder closer.

My eyes got somewhat used to the dark. Hills were outlined beyond one roof, so I knew which way was north.

Question Mark turned his face up to the sky and licked his lips. I breathed in, wetting the roof of my mouth.

Rain started up again. Soon, it would pelt down.

The dark slab walls had no windows – not even frosted glass.

This hidden courtyard was like a prison's place of execution. Instead of a scaffold, its centrepiece was a twenty-foot-tall structure that could have been a futurist memorial to martyred factory workers. Rain pattered on steel blades. The whole thing creaked. With lightning striking closer, it would be advisable to get well away from this mass of twisted metal.

'Oh, it's you,' said a woman.

Turning, I saw a red pin-light.

Nurse Anne was by the door, holding up a cigarette.

So, prosaically, this was what the courtyard was for. Staff could smoke here, out of the sight of patients. That explained the lack of windows. Rich sick people don't want views of healthy poor folk enjoying themselves.

Nurse Anne stepped away from the wall.

Her waterproof cape glistened like serpent skin. A cellophane hood went over her wimple. Rain spotted her transparent turban.

The cigarette below-lit her face, giving her feathery insect eyebrows and a mouth like a black-red bruise.

Question Mark snarled at her.

She didn't raise the alarm.

Friend?

Or afraid?

'The doctor told me who you were,' she said. 'Your name isn't Artie. It's Raymond… Raymond Chandler.'

She stepped closer to me and exhaled smoke plumes.

'You're the best writer in America,' she said. 'Better than Carroll John Daly.'

I couldn't have been more astonished if she'd sucker-punched me.

Which, of course, is what she did next.

I glimpsed her tight face as my wind was knocked out. She jammed me good in the gut. Her clenched fist sunk in like a little cannon ball.

I doubled over, wanting to be sick – though there was little in me to come up. I'd been on vitamin shots, Bim had said. I might not have tasted solid food since Papa Heim's bee sting cake. I retched clear fluid.

Question Mark snarled and stepped towards Nurse Anne.

Her lighter flicked and a long, hissing flame spouted.

The Monster hesitated.

Fire bad!

Not only was Nurse Anne a connoisseur of fine literature, she also went to the movies.

'You really are a terrific writer, Raymond,' said Nurse Anne. '"Killer in the Rain", "Guns at Cyrano's", "Noon Street Nemesis". Other *Black Mask* writers run together. They give you thrills enough while you're reading… but a half-hour after you've finished the magazine, you've forgotten which story was which. Yours stand out. Stick in the mind. "Mandarin's Jade" is your best yet. You should write a book.'

My thorax – where several organs were burst and leaking – wouldn't let me tell her the good news.

The Big Sleep would be out from Knopf, soon.

Though I might not be around to read the notices.

Her lighter flame shrank. Question Mark lurched in her direction. The flame grew again. The Monster cringed away.

'You stay there, Mr Tall Man.'

The Monster stood to attention.

It was official. A single Nurse Anne was worth more than four Bims.

The rain was serious now. My clothes were soaked.

The lightning strikes and thunder peals were almost simultaneous. The storm was coming down from the hills like enemy artillery getting their range. Shells would soon drop right in our laps.

The fused metal mass began to turn on its axis like a merry-go-round. It wasn't another ugly sculpture, but a machine.

I straightened, still clutching my middle.

Whatever damage Nurse Anne had done didn't immediately kill me.

Lightning flashes gave me a better look at the revolving contraption.

Rods and cables were welded together seemingly at random, with radiogram boxes wedged in. The heart of the beast was a dynamo. Motion generated power, bringing the machine to life. Dials glowed and needles twitched. Big, shielded bulbs lit up.

Dancing shadows were cast around the courtyard.

Doors opened. I worried that we'd be recaptured – or worse.

Question Mark was distracted from the lighter flame. He looked at the machine with something like awe. Did he remember being born – or reborn? – on an operating table as something like this crackled and sparked?

I recognised the hallmark style of Engineer Norman Quin, the mad genius who cobbled Dr Frankenstein's laboratory equipment. He'd crafted apprentice work for Universal. This towering machine was his masterpiece. A Frankenstein set-up that wasn't just for show. It was at once a generator, a meat-grinder and a magic lantern.

Bims in hooded raincloaks filed out of the Clinic like monks called to prayer. They all had places to stand and proceeded accordingly to their positions. Parade drill all over again. I was bumped off my chess-square and shoved – gut pain burning again – closer to the machine.

The staff didn't show any interest in capturing or killing me.

Some other horrible thing was in the air.

'No, Raymond,' said Nurse Anne. 'You should be here.'

She took my arm – I flinched, of course – and guided me to a spot next to Question Mark. He was rapt by the increasingly lit-up, fast-spinning machine. It generated sound – a symphony inscribed on a giant wax cylinder, played backwards at the wrong speed.

If there were places for us, that meant we'd not escaped.

We'd been *allowed*. Where was the rats' reward?

The lights burned brightly now. Sparks cascaded. Electricity discharged into the ground.

'Is that thing safe in the wet?' I asked.

Someone was crucified upside down on the machine like the Hanged Man in a tarot deck. Maybe this was a place of execution after all. A steel butcher's hook spiked through one of his ankles. The wound didn't bleed, so he was most likely dead. His head was encased in a bulbous metal shell like a diving helmet – another Quin touch. Otherwise, he wore only soaked pants. Rain coursed over his sunken belly and scrawny chest. Copper wires tangled around his arms and legs, the ends plugged into wound-scabs.

Was this corpse test subject or sacrifice?

Jimmy Whale was right. This wasn't science. This was a ritual.

Lightning struck on the other side of the courtyard, fusing gravel into black glass. Bims, who were at least human, shifted out of the way in alarm, though they uneasily settled back into formation.

The nightmare carousel was a giant knot of lightning-rods. Arcs crackled between ball-tipped steel bars. Fire thieved from the heavens was trapped in faraday cages.

Electric jags burned into my vision. My ears rang from thunder.

With a mass shuffling, everyone but me and Question Mark put on green goggles. Nurse Anne had emerald-lens sunglasses with horn-rims. I made do with my poor old specs.

I was better off than the fellow they'd hung out to get this started.

The obeisance to the machine felt Egyptian or Aztec – though, according to B horror pictures, those snake-handlers and heart-rippers shed blood for the sun rather than night and the storm.

Big shutters, which I'd not noticed before, rolled open half-way up a wall. A balcony emerged, ratcheting out of the building. A waterproof canopy unconcertinaed above it. Anyone whose place was up there would get less wet than the slicker-clad peons below. I could guess who was about to make an entrance.

The machine's avant-garde cacophony gave way to a proper orchestra.

Huge His Master's Voice gramophone horns hung at the corners of the quad. The harsh Pyramid Pictures fanfare boomed out.

Then… music.

I expected more Wagner.

Instead we got Grieg. 'In the Hall of the Mountain King'.

The piece – jokey-ominous, unlike Wagner's knit-brow solemnity – was forever changed for me when Peter Lorre whistled it as the child-killing creep in *M*. Grieg intended teasing merriment but I always heard bone-scraping terror underneath the light touch.

That German film showed how feeble Hollywood pictures were.

Billy's Monster and Lorre's M both killed little girls and were tormented afterwards… but *Frankenstein* is about the horror of being ugly, strong and clumsy in a fragile world. The Monster means well, at first. *M* says a man might *need* to ravage the way he needs to eat, drink and breathe. A man might *enjoy* ripping apart small bodies. It didn't take lightning and grave robbery and crackpot inventions to create Peter Lorre. This monster was just an ordinary man.

The machine spun to the beat of the conductor's baton – the Grieg went faster and faster, louder and louder.

The music projected pictures in my mind. A single rat crawled along a gutter. Joined by more and quicker vermin. A living carpet swarmed over rooftops, dividing around chimneys, flowing together again. Rats bit each other, chewing and spitting flesh gobbets that sprouted and grew into more and bigger rats. A morass of tails and feet and fur and teeth. Burying a house, a street, a town, a city… the *whole world* went under a sea of wriggling, ravening rat-kings.

Faster and *faster*, louder and *louder*, faster and… STOP!

A child's balloon floated up against electric wires.

No, that wasn't real. That was from *M*.

Roving spotlights converged on the balcony.

Junior was there, an emperor in burnished armour. His bandages were off. He was bare-headed and shaved bald. His swollen dome gleamed like a dinosaur egg. Room in there for extra brains. Abnormal ones, of course.

After the Grieg stopped, we heard grinding metal and the rattle of the rain. The machine was a giant, breathing painfully. Goggled eyes looked up at Junior. I half-expected heiling.

He was no longer alone.

Beside him, but three steps back, was Dr Vaudois, in white coat and wide-brimmed hat, a green visor over half his face.

And then – in one of her own shimmering gowns, impervious to wind and weather, hair like white phosphorus flame – there was *her*.

Ariadne.

I couldn't help it. I sank down on my knees.

18

The Monster looked up, transfixed.

I understood.

The first sight of that face is a silver fishhook in the heart. It stays stuck, years later. Even a stray memory is a cruel tug on the line.

It was a physical sensation above all. But also a brand on the soul.

All who saw her, she possessed. For life.

Like me. And Billy.

I shall always remember Ariadne touching a finger to her Cupid's bow lips while wearing an elbow-length scarlet glove. Then the liquid velvet thinned to show white, white skin and I realised the red wasn't a glove. I was so beguiled I scarcely noticed the dead boys at her feet. One had a cricket stump through his chest. Another's face was wiped off his skull. They were blurry, background details. Her shushing smile, perfectly lit, was in focus.

After that night, Billy and I were hers – no matter how far away we ran… to Canada, to the War, to America, to oil and money and drink and dreams. Wherever we fled, there she was. Patient as Penelope, demure as Demeter. Old, beautiful, constant. Our moon and stars. Licking her red fingers. Like a child or a cat. Not caring about the corpses – which someone else would always tidy up for her. If not us, somebody… there was no shortage of willing minions. Hunchbacks, fly-eaters, gunsels, fall guys, patsies.

I always recognise her special friends.

The time I met Hammett, at a *Black Mask* writers' dinner, I knew Ariadne had marked him too. We didn't even need to trade stories. Joh Devlin took a photograph of assembled happy hacks. Dash and I eyed each other from either side of the line-up, uncomfortable and haunted. Knowing what we knew set us apart from the scribblers whose stories Nurse Anne wouldn't remember. Ariadne gave us something to write *about* – someone to write for – but of course it didn't make us happy. Or easy to get along with.

I don't blame her.

She didn't make us the way we were. But she found us.

She lit a fire in us. Taught us lessons.

In *She* – another book passed around at Dulwich, frowned upon but relished by masters who'd read it themselves as boys and were still under the spell – the immortal Ayesha goes veiled in public because all who set eyes on her face fall in love with her. This curse ruins her victims, because to love Ayesha means hating oneself for being unworthy. A love impure, a love that ruins, a love that scars like razor-sharp kisses.

Rider Haggard must have known Ariadne too.

And Keats, dead at twenty-five, who wrote 'Lamia' and 'La Belle Dame Sans Merci'. The quiet girl in the corner, spinning *Frankenstein* for a ghost story contest. Beethoven and Wagner, of course. Peter Lorre, for sure. Bill Faulkner. The weirdest of the *Weird Tales* writers. Poets, painters, musicians. And murderers.

She has, of course, been here all along.

Sat beside the story tree, dripping beautiful poison.

You can see that face over and over, if you look for it. Even when the artist gives her raven tresses or spun gold rather than her coronet of frost. Once you start looking, you can never stop.

A beautiful face, but also a hole burned in the world.

Whenever there's terror, she's present. Whenever art goes too far, it's at her urging. She loves the riot as much as the premiere. When machine guns rake a field, she cultivates the poppies that spring from the bloody soil. When a poet chokes his last or an actress takes a header off the Hollywoodland sign, Ariadne dips the hem of her garment in the mess and walks away, unquestioned but culpable. Hers is the face pilots see as they crash in flames.

I have glimpsed under the veil and am still in love with Ayesha.

In the first chapter of *The Big Sleep*, Philip Marlowe idly considers a stained-glass window showing a knight rescuing a lady tied to a tree. Here's the secret – the lady isn't a maiden who needs to be rescued, but the dragon who'll breathe fire on the knight, the court, the kingdom. There on page one, the mystery is blown. Marlowe is hired to rescue Carmen from blackmail, but the girl is the monster of the story. The narrator-hero finds that out thirty-two chapters later, but the oh-so-clever author told you so already.

Carmen Sternwood... Ayesha... Ariadne...

I bare my throat to you and invite your seashell-sharp teeth.

Please end it for me. End my story.

Ariadne looked across the courtyard. Did her glance linger on my rain-wet moonface for even a shard of a second? No. She paid me no special attention. She gives no favour. She doesn't need to. Those who love and dread only her will always be on their knees wherever she looks.

This most terrible thing of all leaves me haunted and alone and awake at four in the morning... her indifference, once she has passed on to newer, riper throats. It is not cold or unkind, it is her way.

I have Cissy, Taki, other comforts.

They will never be enough – that's why Taki scratches, Cissy turns out lights after the radio concert. They understand without knowing.

Lightning struck again, straight into the machine. Even the corpse juddered.

The flash bleached Ariadne's pale face so that – for a moment – she was a skull carved in snow. Her hair rose like porcupine spines, haloed by a bluish corona. Static started to give her a *Bride of Frankenstein* permanent.

She touched her lips.

I could have screamed, but my mouth was dry again.

And she was gone.

19

Question Mark growled.

I got up off my knees.

Ariadne had put in her appearance and left the stage. That didn't mean the show was over. She was the match that lit the fuse. There would still be fireworks.

The machine whirled faster.

The hanging man kept coming round, arms swinging loose.

The all-new Junior Home commanded the balcony. He was the Green Knight returned for the second round of the beheading contest, but with the wrong noggin – a meagre poke-snatcher or pig-thief, executed and forgotten before the feast – set where his properly titanic crown should be. His corded neck and expanded cranium made his face look too small.

Dr Vaudois cringed in his shadow.

Junior came forward. His tin tuxedo was a lightweight studio mock-up. Painted fabric or silver foil. Ben-Hur muscles sculpted into the breastplate. Fascist fancy dress, patterned after Roman legionaries and Teutonic knights. Add a goldfish bowl helmet and he could be a pilot of the future, steering rocket ships to the stars or vaporising cities with wonder bombs dropped from outside the atmosphere.

I itched for Junior to get too close to the edge of the balcony and tip over, crashing on his stupid little face. I'd forgotten the Vaudois-Quin Process hadn't just made him taller and wider. He possessed stolen talents too.

He stepped off the balcony and stood stock still in mid-air, gauntleted hands on metal hips.

Junior Home had conquered gravity. Here was Nietzsche's Overman come to California in a fanfare of tubas.

Bims thumped their chests – right fist raised, thumb-side to the breastbone. They gave themselves three quick blows.

It figured Junior would have his own salute. I bet he'd had one of the studio's indentured writers come up with it.

Junior saluted the crowd in return. His triple-thump put a dent in his Pyramid logo-marked chest-plate. He puffed and the dent sprang back with a wobble. Despite his ascent to demi-divinity, Junior was ridiculous. Most tyrants are. People only stop laughing when the pile of corpses reaches the roof. Even then, the temptation of black humour remains.

The jokes we told about the mangled dead in the trenches don't bear repeating. Never let the civvies back home find out how callous we became wading through mass murder.

Junior floated gently to the ground. His bootheels crunched into slushy gravel.

He had mastered the old conjurers' trick of wireless levitation. The Home House experiment gave him the power of mind over his own matter.

Dr Vaudois stayed up on the balcony, alone.

We had been blessed momentarily with the presence. Now we had to endure the pain of fresh memory. Ariadne wasn't inside the building, out of sight. She was gone. Junior Home was left to get on with his rigmarole. The rest of us were extras. After her, even miracles were an anticlimax.

I felt Ariadne's absence the way philosophers feel the absence of God. An ache in the heart, a bleeding into a void. Her image was a hot coal that hurt to retain in the mind. If held too long, it would do real damage. Nevertheless, it was hard – if not impossible – to let go.

No matter how bad things were when she visited, they got worse – much worse – when she left.

Even the weather turned fouler. The wind dashed gritty rain in my face. I cleaned my glasses on my lapel. They blobbed over again by the time I put them back on. My waterlogged clothes shrivelled. I wasn't dressed for a night like this. Question Mark had scavenged a coat in his outrageous size. I'd been too keen on making an exit from the Lamia Munro Clinic to pick up wet weather apparel. Cissy would be scornful if I shuffled home with pneumonia. It would be my own fault for not wrapping up warm.

My wife likes to play a game where I'm the absent-minded one. She delights in those instances – involving drink, though she takes care not to mention it – when I slip and give her ammunition. Alas, poor Raymio. What would he do without me?

A couple of Bims wrestled a giant umbrella in a valiant attempt to keep the rain off Junior's head. A vicious gust caught the fabric and dragged them across the quad like hunchbacks holding down the tethers of a box kite. They let go and the umbrella turned inside out, then scythed through assembled ranks like a broken-winged condor until it got trampled and kicked into a corner. Bims shuffled back into formation. The two who'd lost their battle with the brolly slunk to their places in shame.

Uncomfortable as I was, the rain fell on everyone.

Junior had to put up with it too. Water must be pouring into his armour. It was hard to bestride the earth like a colossus when you squelched.

His small wet face showed he was in a sulk.

Lightning struck repeatedly, charging the heart of the madman's merry-go-round. Bulbs exploded. Magnesium rods melted. The dead man glowed as if coated with luminescent fungus. Wind whirled around the courtyard.

I covered my ears and looked at the ground. The quad didn't drain well.

A chunk of flaming something spun off the machine and hit the wall.

The Monster wrung out my shoulder again and grunted, nodding urgently at the contraption. I peered through my wet spectacles. I realised what he wanted me to look at.

The hanging man was having convulsions. Electricity whipsnapped around him. The wires stuck in his skin were live. His copper helmet radiated heat like a stove.

Who was he? Some hapless patient or a willing volunteer?

Was Junior stealing something else? Fluency in foreign languages… a head for sums… x-ray eyes. Maybe not. The leaching trick was worked by the machine in the basement of Home House. This carousel was not the same device. Junior wasn't plugged in. Even with all he had gained, he didn't want to catch on fire again.

Was this how Bims were made? Killed, then sparked to life.

The body jitterbugged upside down. The kick reflex. Even a corpse dances when electrified. It's not life, it's galvanism.

Then the hanging man jackknifed like Houdini wriggling free of a straitjacket while suspended over the Hudson River. His hands scrabbled at the hook piercing his ankle. He didn't manage to duplicate the escapologist's feat, but...

He was *al-i-eve*!

No one else was surprised.

Question Mark looked quizzical, curious. He couldn't understand what he saw but it prompted memories of things that had happened to him. He knew this machine. It had made him. No, that wasn't right. But it was close. I nearly saw something, but it slipped away.

Now a new monster was stirring. A son of Frankenstein.

This couldn't just be another Bim. The Clinic turned them out the way Pyramid made Dry Bone and Trooper Westerns. This was a bigger deal. An A-feature. A mass gathering in a storm at dead of night. It was a high ceremony, one of the major sabbats in the witches' calendar. Ariadne wouldn't show up for the opening of an envelope. This was a gala premiere. *A Star is Born*.

The crowd watched the hanging man struggle.

His helmet had no faceplate, so he was blind. The hook speared through meat, between bones. He had no leverage to pull himself free.

The machine turned too fast for anyone to get to him. I had an idea a human man who tried to touch the device would be a burning, smoking ruin within seconds – and not in a way there was any coming back from. The Vaudois-Quin Process made four or five corpses for every Junior Colossus.

The Monster let me go and staggered, stiff-backed, towards the machine.

The hanging man kept coming round, still fixed on his hook.

Question Mark weighed up the prospects of snatching the ring.

He hunched his shoulders and moved his head from side to side like a cobra. Here again was the sly, calculating brain that sometimes overruled his blundering innocence. When the Monster let slip that he was *clever*, he seemed more dangerous, more terrifying. If he drowned you, it wouldn't be an accident.

A Bim – one of the larger ones, with ape-long arms – tried to get a wrestling hold. Question Mark shrugged him off with a snarl and turned to plant a boot on his face.

Junior Home held up his hand.

Question Mark felt a touch. Junior was using his mind over the Monster's matter. Question Mark went up on tiptoes, pulled towards the sky. His forehead scar throbbed and bled. I remembered the exploding vase.

As evolution fits us for survival, all mankind will move, create or destroy things with mind power. Some fortunate freak – Eustis Amthor, Chick Chang or Stephen Swift – had been born with the talent a few centuries before its time. Now it was wielded by the New Windmill-Man of Beverly Hills.

With a roar, the Monster tore free of the invisible grip.

Junior was affronted. He could do magic, but still got slapped down. That wasn't what he'd paid for!

The revolving machine slowed. The carousel ride was ending, the calliope's tune almost done.

When the hanging man came round next, the Monster grasped protruding rods and wrenched the whole apparatus to a halt. He took an electric charge that would have felled him were he a killable man. He shook and his coat smoked, but he held on. Bulbs burned out and popped. White smoke poured from the works.

Bims shrank at this sacrilege.

The congregation relied too much on their high priest's miracle powers. If anyone had thought to tuck an automatic under their oilskin, they could have just shot Question Mark in his flat head. Dr Frankenstein didn't bullet-proof his Monster. The story was written when muskets were useless without powder-horns and ramrods. If the peasants had Lee-Enfield rifles and a Maxim gun, the Monster wouldn't pose much of a problem. Handmade pitch-and-cotton torches, unreliable in wind and rain, were obsolete. We had the flamethrower now.

In stopping the machine, Question Mark ripped his hands open on sharp metal. Rain-thinned blood dribbled from his stigmata.

The hanging man still writhed.

The Monster took hold of the poor creature's leg and *lifted*...

Wires were pulled out but electricity still played across his wet torso. The gashes sparked like broken wall-sockets.

Now his heart pumped, his ankle wound bled. He yelled inside the copper helmet. He banged his fists like a silent movie comedian with his head trapped in a moonshine jar.

The Monster turned, holding the hanging man upside down by his leg.

The guy stopped squirming and making noise.

Question Mark right-sided his catch and set him down.

The resurrected man stuck his arms out for balance. He propped himself against the Monster's chest. He tried not to put his weight on his injury. The hole in his ankle had already scabbed over. A benefit of the process? He'd be strong too.

Junior thumped his chest again, three times.

The massed Bims responded. Thump thump thump.

Overdone, that routine became comic. Had it been dreamed up by a gag-writer for Pyramid's hoke farces? Unlikely. No Sparx Brothers routine was as solemnly funny as this charade.

Question Mark made an impatient waving away gesture. He wasn't joining this game. Junior stuck out his bottom lip.

The man with the helmet raised his fist, thumb-side in... but stopped short of saluting.

Another recalcitrant, ungrateful Lazarus. Good. The world needed more like that.

Did I solicit thee from darkness to promote me? Nertz I did!

His hands went to the helmet's ruff. He felt for a catch but had no luck. The Monster understood. He took considered hold on the metal bowl, then strained. The helmet popped open like an Easter egg. Question Mark threw it away in pieces.

I again remembered the unmasking of the Phantom. That skull face, horrible when blurred, worse in sharp focus. The madness in Chaney's eyes.

And the looming shape in the doorway, turning round. The camera cutting progressively closer on the Monster's face.

This time, there was another turn of the screw.

I had the same shock of recognition as when I saw *Frankenstein*.

The hanging man – face paler than ever I'd seen it, water on his chest glistening – was Billy Pratt.

So who was Question Mark?

Billy stamped a little, steadier on his feet. He looked at his rescuer, who stood by patiently, protectively.

Could this be the *original* Frankenstein Monster, returned from the ice floes Mrs Shelley packed him off to in 1818? Bent on persecuting his upstart screen impersonator the way he once hunted his creator's family and friends – playing the long game, waiting for Billy to recover enough from the Quin-Vaudois Process to pay attention and understand why he was having his brains beaten out. In the book, the Monster keeps insisting his murders are supposed to be educational.

The machine still shot out sparks.

Did the device reach into the realm of imagination and conjure its denizens to life? If so, and I'd been consulted about it, I'd have suggested testing it out with Mr Pickwick or Becky Sharp. Maybe even one of the smaller, less dangerous dinosaurs from *The Lost World*. Making a Frankenstein Monster was, as every version of the story reiterated, a bad idea. It always starts with a crackle of electric inspiration and ends in fiery or icy doom, with a catalogue of incidental fatalities that would shame a Jacobean Revenge drama or a *Black Mask* novella.

I worried my imagination was overheating. With so much madness in front of me, was anything impossible any more?

Wrestling Bim got to his feet and contemplated rushing the Monster again. He saw Boris Karloff giving him the Mummy stare and backed down. He wasn't tougher than two Frankensteins.

Question Mark was probably another stand-in. Pyramid preparing to undercut Universal's Monster the way they had the Marx Brothers – getting an arrant imitation into theatres the week before a big release, riding the winds of another studio's ad-pub build-up.

Billy had enough to be surprised about, what with his round trip to that bourn from which no traveller returns. Now he stood in the rain, bare feet on wet gravel, face to face with a distorting, enlarging mirror.

This Monster was taller than him so Billy had to look *up* at his living reflection.

Whom he *recognised*.

'Norman,' he said, astonished, 'what have they done to you? You look like… *Boris Karloff*!'

20

Question Mark was Norman Francis Quin.

One mystery solved. More mysteries raised.

Quin reached out to touch Billy's face but stopped short.

His hands. Yes, of course! The dainty, spindly, all-wrong-for-his-build hands. Billy had talked about them. Fit for needlepoint, not throttling grave robbers. I'd thought of that Colin Clive picture. *Mad Love*. A pianist's hands, not a murderer's. I should have put it together. P. Marlowe would have seen straight off that Question Mark was Quin. Poor Old Watson had missed a clue.

In writing mysteries, Dash Hammett and Joh Devlin had the advantage of real-life investigative experience. I had to stress other qualities, like my well-tuned ear for American speech. Which wasn't much use to anyone now.

'Norman,' said Billy, trying to get through to the towering lump, '*Norman…*'

So Quin was finally playing the Monster. Made over rather than made up.

How? Why?

Don't ask me. I'm not a detective. As I had proved.

If my body worked like Chick Chang's, I'd kick myself.

At the Clinic, they had killed Billy Pratt. The machine brought him back to life. Like in the movies.

He saw me, standing next to Quin.

'R.T.,' he said.

I was relieved he recognised me.

'What was it like?' I asked.

'Dark... for a while. Then the lights came up. *She* was here, wasn't she?'

I nodded. 'She's gone now.'

'Yes,' he said, with regret. 'She would leave. Still, we must play on, eh? Play on and play the game.'

Billy's ankle unkinked and he stood straight. I couldn't even see a scar.

He was barefoot and shirtless. Rain mussed his hair into spikes. His chest was scorched where wires had been attached. Blackened patches remained even as the wounds closed.

His eyes glittered with life.

Electricity ran through him. He didn't feel the cold.

He considered his wet hands. They shone.

He looked at Junior Home, smiling. I knew that expression from *The Invisible Ray*. There was something about *his* hands now. Not a pianist's hands.

'Boris,' said Junior. 'Welcome to the Pyramid Family. You understand, now, what we have to offer... and what you can do in return to show your loyalty.'

Billy kept looking at Junior. Kept smiling.

His glance took in the studio head's big boots, metal two-piece and shaved head.

'What *are* you wearing?'

Junior's face went dark for a moment. He was a giant but still couldn't command respect from a star. Raising Billy from the dead didn't put him under contract.

'I *made* you, Karloff.'

'Are you sure? Didn't you only *pay* to make me? With your father's money too. Oil money. Pyramid lost seven million dollars last year.'

'And I'll lose seven million more this year... and the year after... then things will change. People will pay for what I can do for them. You're the example, Boris. You're the proof. You're *advertising material*.'

That was Hollywood all over. Some fools were made immortal on celluloid – though nitrate stock is unstable, flammable stuff – but bigger fools sought immortality in the flesh. They would stump up any price, even if it meant robbing the poor box or the pension fund.

'No, you won't do that,' said Billy. 'You might think you want to, but it's not about money for you. It's not really about money for anyone born rich. It's about the love, isn't it? Being admired, envied, feared. You can't have all that if you share too widely, even with those who can afford it. *Especially* with them. They've always looked down on you… you're not really one of the club, you know. It's why you've never won an Oscar…'

I remembered Junior whining about 'the Jews'.

'You'd never give *them* a leg up. Mayer or Jack Warner… or – who else? – Hearst and Rockefeller. Oh, and your father, of course. You can't sell your miracle to them. If any of them got what you have, they'd look down on you all over again. The things your father would do with your new gifts! No, you can only make *one* you. Like there's only one Garbo. You'll never sell what you've made of yourself. If you're not unique, you're nothing.'

Billy was buzzing with insights. They spilled out of him.

It wasn't about dogs not barking in the night or stopped watches in a corpse's pocket set to a time when all the suspects had alibis. It was about understanding people. Seeing inside their heads and working out the particular ways in which they were rotten. Junior's swollen cranium might as well be glass. We saw his abnormal brain, throbbing like a clumsy carpenter's just-hammered thumb.

It still might not be wise to give voice to all this character analysis. The Overman wanted worship not diagnosis.

Junior shot a look over his shoulder at Dr Vaudois, who was still up on the balcony.

This drama was not unfolding according to his script notes. In front of the massed ranks of his employees and acolytes and creations, he looked small again. A shrimp.

His big idea was to be big. Everything else was goofy gravy.

He had been *persuaded* to make monsters.

He made Quin into Frankenstein. He made Billy into… 'Boris Karloff'?

Junior's moment of doubt passed. He gave an imperial thumbs down, jabbing three times. Water trickled out of his cuff.

'Remember this, Chandler,' he said, directly to me. 'I'm going to leave you alive to tell the tale. Jesse James did that when he killed a bunch of people on a train he was robbing. He made sure a single survivor knew his name, so it would get about that he was not a man to be messed with. That was in a picture, anyway. You won't be able to prove anything. You'll be taken for a drunk and a cuckoo… but you'll tell the tale. You won't be able to help yourself. Whispers will go round. People will know it was me, know what I've done. But they won't believe your crazy story. The police, the DA – they'll pin everything on Quin. Look at him. He's the perfect patsy.'

Does Hitler explain himself to people he's having shot? Or Stalin? Even Jesse James. Real villains don't deliver monologues. Junior only knew how to be a movieland arch-fiend. He mostly saw Pyramid Pictures, where cliché was king. If Louis B. Mayer or William Randolph Hearst became an Overman, they'd have flair. They'd be an A-feature villain, like Laughton as Captain Bligh – with smarts and nuance. That Junior was a joke terrified me. He'd burn down everything if he felt he wasn't getting his due. And he could never get enough because there wasn't enough in the universe for him. So long as anyone else had a speck, he wasn't happy.

He pointed at Billy.

'I have to make an example of you, Karloff. A name player has to die. Those basement freaks were nobodies. Not that you're so special. Not really. Remember, I replaced you with *Mischa Auer* and no one cared. Your funeral will be strictly a programmer. Not a class attraction, like Valentino's. Or Lon Chaney's. They were *real* stars. Irreplaceable. When you're gone, we'll still have Bela Lugosi.'

See – one minute, he raises Billy from the dead to serve as testimonial to his mad science process… the next, he's ordering minions to kill the unkillable man all over again to prove another point. His people just went along with it. If you pointed out the contradiction to a Bim, you wouldn't be speaking in a language they could understand. This was Junior's audience, people who accepted Jannings' Bismarck romancing Mae West's Lillie Langtry and hummed along with the big numbers of *Say It With Tubas*.

Two Bims approached Billy with nightsticks.

Billy took hold of their throats with shining hands.

He lifted them off the ground. They kicked, choked and died – eyes cooked white. He laid the corpses gently on the ground.

'A Death Touch!' exclaimed Junior, delighted.

Then he frowned and turned to his court magician.

'Vaudois, why don't *I* have a Death Touch?'

Dr Voodoo tried to back off the balcony.

Bims gave Billy a wider berth. He held up his hands and showed his teeth.

He shook his longish, rain-wet hair. Since I last saw him – how many days ago? – he had gone unshaven long enough to sprout grey fur on his cheeks and grow a darker, definite moustache.

His dental plate was missing. The gap in one side of his grin gave his face a leaner, more Monster-ish look.

He wasn't just resurrected. He was transformed.

He had taken on attributes of his screen characters. An unexpected bonus of the Vaudois-Quin Process? It wasn't just mechanics, it was magic.

How would Billy explain his Death Touch to Mrs Karloff?

He'd have to stop petting Violet the Pig.

'I hope you can turn that off,' I said.

In *The Invisible Ray*, he couldn't.

Billy wasn't unduly concerned at the moment. He was excited – the way he was onscreen when the urge to kill took over… or on a pitch after his loping run-up as terror sparked in the eyes of a batsman about to bungle a ninety-mile-an-hour bouncer.

It was possible to get drunk on electricity.

I was the one who had to remember we were in a courtyard in the middle of the Clinic, deep inside enemy territory, surrounded by fanatics bent on doing us harm. We were an irritant to a tyrant who had ordered Billy's execution and would quickly forget that he wanted me alive to spread his story. Everyone else was just too damn impressed with their own performances.

'We should be leaving,' I said.

Bims cautiously closed on us. No one wanted to be on the receiving end of the Death Touch even if Junior would like to see it demonstrated again so he could work out how to steal it. Quin snarled – not quite Billy's Monster snarl, but close enough. Bims held their line.

There were three of us now. In the midst of our enemies.

Inside the Monster's skull wasn't a grunting moron brain but some species of genius. The resurrection machine was his invention. I pegged Vaudois as a partial fraud, yoking his name to the creator of the Quin-Vaudois Process and stealing top billing to boot. Was Quin becoming a monster part of some great plan?

No, it was haphazard.

I'd seen Junior's pictures. I knew how he put plans together. The Lamia Munro Clinic produced wonders, but they weren't thought through. Billy had seen at once that Junior's supposed scheme – immortality for a price! – wasn't something he'd actually do. The picture was in production and he didn't have an ending he was in love with. Costs would pile up and the banks would tut over his line of credit. Even with undying monsters and Death Touches and levitation, this was more mess than mystery.

Who killed the chauffeur? Least of our worries.

Billy held up his right hand, fingers slightly clawed.

The crowd parted. Bims cowered like a colony of vampires before a gleaming crucifix.

Billy walked through the cleared path. I followed.

Quin brought up the rear, growling and batting away Bims.

I kept my head down and wished for a big overcoat.

Billy faced the Overman, deadly hand raised.

'You'll never work in this town again,' Junior shouted.

His roar was turning into a squeak. When he got angry, he sounded more like Mickey Mouse than the Voice of Doom.

He reached out with his extensible arm – stretching rubbery bare flesh beyond his non-extensible metal sleeve – but hesitated before slapping

Billy. He had Amthor's healing knack. Apparently, that was general issue. But the ability to recover from harm might be nullified by the Death Touch. If two unnatural phenomena collided, instant putrefaction and instant health might race around his body in competition, extending the agony of death forever as he screamed his mind out.

I'd not want to test that either.

He drew back his hand and knit his brows. Blood swirled in his red eye. He was thinking hard. Using mind over matter was a great strain. If he exerted himself too much, he'd rupture something. Wet gravel shook under our feet. Was he trying to whip up an earthquake? His mind surely couldn't shift that much matter.

Overman and Risen Billy locked invisible horns.

Junior should have had sharpshooters on the roof with rifles.

A director, who has to be a general and bent on victory, would have seen to it. A producer is only an accountant with a bigger cigar and a better-looking girlfriend. He'd fuss about the cost of extras, flash powder and guns.

Lightning struck the big machine.

Without a human component to pour into, current ran through the carousel, exploding lamps and bursting dials. The turning mechanism lurched into motion and a few Bims' robes got caught up. They fell and were dragged as the machine half-revolved before halting again. A large iron mill-wheel rolled out of the heart of the thing and barrelled across the quad.

It was a helpful distraction.

Billy led us to the nearest open door.

Nurse Anne stood there, barring the way.

She dared Billy to try his Death Touch on her. She pushed back her hood the better to show her face.

It struck me then that Billy couldn't have known what his touch would do to the Bims. Unlike me and Quin, he'd not been in the War. He'd killed countless people, but only in films. Karloff took delight in indiscriminate homicide. Men, women, children. Billy wasn't Boris. I knew he wasn't squeamish – we'd left Prospero Prince behind his wall – but what he'd done to those Bims shocked him to his quick. He'd been defending himself. The lethality of his hands was unexpected. He'd had a few moments to think now, to become frightened. He wasn't ready for cold-hearted murder.

Nurse Anne was clever. Not just because she liked my stories.

She looked at Boris Karloff – eyes of the Mummy, sneer of the Monster, deadly hands of Invisible Ray – and saw gentle, regretful Billy Pratt. Kind to cats, small children and his roses.

Billy held up his hand. It wasn't glowing any more.

He didn't want a Death Touch.

Again, Nurse Anne proved her worth to the Clinic. In a just world, she'd end up running the place. And Pyramid Pictures too – which would be good news for me and my agent, since her first priority would be to cut a Selznick-sized cheque for Philip Marlowe's film rights. She'd have to cast Cary Grant, of course.

She raised her finger like a schoolmarm. Billy looked at his toes, shifty.

Bims grew more confident. I glanced back and saw Quin tussling with two or three. He snapped arms, but they just set their bones and came back at him.

Several rolled up their robe-sleeves and wrenched bludgeon-like components off the machine. Once they got going, they wouldn't remember Junior said they should leave one alive. Enthusiasm would get the better of them. I bet the James Boys were the same.

'Nurse Anne,' I said. 'I should have told you something. I *have* written a book. It's being published in a few months. It's called *The Big Sleep*. It's the best thing I've ever done... with a new detective, Philip Marlowe... and a mystery to end all mysteries...'

Her eyes sparkled with interest.

'*The Big Sleep*,' she said, rolling it around. It was still strange, hearing one of my titles on a beautiful woman's lips. It sounded good.

'I can send you an advance reading copy.'

I thought Anne was going to laugh in my face. But her smile was gentle, unreadable.

She stood aside. If all the proofs were gone and the mail was disrupted, I'd type the blessed thing out again and have it delivered to her care of the

Lamia Munro Clinic by St Bernard rescue dog. If I lived to write again and Marlowe ever met a doll who wasn't a killer, she'd be called Anne.

Billy led us past the nurse.

She closed the door behind us, against the crowd.

We were back in the Clinic. Ochre linoleum, sickly light, clocks with no hands.

'You need some clothes,' I told Billy.

'We need to find another door,' he said. 'One that leads outside.'

21

Twenty minutes later we were outdoors again, somewhere on the Home Estate. The downpour was over but the ground was sodden. Loose earth was on the move. My laceless shoes filled with mud. A reminder of the last time well-resourced people were prepared to devote apparently infinite effort to murdering me. In the War, I'd had a rifle to shoot back and a tin helmet that made me harder to kill. Now I only had my wits. I wasn't sure my hold on them was firm. Not after this night's work.

We three huddled in something like a slip-trench. A fast stream ran under us.

I had worried the white doctor's coats Billy and I filched from the Clinic would stand out in the dark. They were already so grubby they might as well have been dyed grey-brown.

Billy was alert, hopped up on electricity. The Vaudois-Quin Process made him hardier – and sharper. For someone who'd been hung like a side of beef earlier in the night – let alone been dead – he was in excellent condition. Given a moment's respite, I'd worry about his jumpiness.

Like Junior, he was changed.

I shivered uncontrollably and bit down to keep my teeth from chattering. I didn't know if I was shuddering from fear or just soaked to the bone. I wondered a little why I hadn't collapsed completely. What had been in those vitamin shots they gave me at the Clinic? I couldn't help but look anxiously from Billy's face to the caricature of it worn by the next man.

Quin showed dog-like devotion to Billy, but sometimes glanced at me with a snarl that showed a glint of tooth.

Original and stand-in should not be in the picture at the same time. Quin was Billy's echo or shadow. I had no sense of him as a person in his own right. He was still a Question Mark.

The mutilated inventor was a savant. Billy was alive again because of him, though I took it he also had a hand in him being killed. Now he could – or would – only grunt and moan. He was the Monster from *Frankenstein*, not the more articulate creature of the sequel. I didn't anticipate Milton quotations from him any time soon.

We'd scavenged what we could from the Clinic – coats from a rack, slip-on ward shoes for Billy. Then Quin smashed an unbarred window and we climbed out. Just our luck – we were further from Los Feliz and freedom than ever. The grounds of the Lamia Munro Clinic were part of the Home Estate. Like Junior with his head on fire stumbling onto Sunset Boulevard, we'd made our exit on the wrong side of the building.

I remembered Joh's descriptions of the fiefdom. The lawns of Home House must be nearby, watered to death by the storm. The Pyramid backlot, with its faux-Egyptian glass centrepiece, was an enclave within an enclave. People would turn up there before dawn. Make-up, wardrobe and lighting calls were set for hours before the day's shooting started. I had half an idea we could get lost in the crowd. Odder-looking people than us wandered around studio backlots.

Mountains rose above us, locations for numberless cowboy films and alpine adventures. Up there sat La Casa, the Old Man's house.

We rose from our crouches and soldiered on, wading through flowing mud to a thicket of trees.

Billy told us to tread only where water ran, so as not to leave easy-to-follow footprints. He'd learned the trick from Northwoods melodramas he made in the twenties. For a spell, he'd been typecast as a wicked French-Canadian trapper with a check shirt and a slick moustache.

'There's a door in the woods,' he said, pointing.

I only saw trees, then realised one conical shape was more regular than the others. A spire among the firs.

'It's Heim's German church,' I said. 'Joh told us about it.'

'Sanct-u-ary,' said Billy.

We struggled to the doorstep, bedraggled pilgrims or giftless Magi.

The door was locked but Quin yanked it open. We stumbled into the church, wet coats heavy as handicap weights, and sat on cold, hard, dry pews.

Quin shut the door behind us.

The church was small – low ceilinged with heavy, arched beams. The pews took up too much room.

I remembered Joh said the Old Man brought the church over from Germany stone by stone. It was a plutocrat craze of the twenties – re-erecting Scottish castles and Italian villas in California desert. Barely a decade on, structures that weathered centuries in their original climes were cracking under the sun and sinking slowly into soft sand.

The process of dismantling was far easier than the process of putting the pieces together again. From the result, I guessed Home's artisans had a few diagrams upside down or were stumped for what to do with extra bits and pieces left over after the job was finished. This interior might have shrunk in transportation. The walls closed in like the crushing trap in Prospero Prince's basement. One window depicted a falling angel, nose-diving in flames like a shot-down air ace. I realised it was put in upside down. Some flagstones had unreadable inscriptions – they were gravestones, laid flat. The font looked like a well. In German forest style, antlers and horns and glass-eyed animal heads were stuck up wherever there was space for them and in several spots where there really wasn't. Was this a pagan survival or had a shipment of décor got mixed up with the church fittings? Was a lodge on the mountainside festooned with images of the saints?

'There must be candles,' I said.

It was a Catholic church, after all.

'A moment,' said Billy.

I agreed with him. We needed to draw breath before we lit a candle, which might give us away. Any light behind the tall, thin stained-glass windows would draw attention. Was there anything we could use as a blackout curtain?

'Why haven't they come after us?'

'I'm sure they will, R.T.'

We'd fled as if pursuers were at our heels. Now we were holed up, it was obvious no mob was closing on us. I wasn't reassured. It just meant someone was confident we couldn't get away. A plan to recapture or eliminate us was in motion, more sophisticated than turning loose the Bims and hoping they caught our scent.

'Are they waiting for morning light?' I asked.

'I doubt it. This is night work.'

'What happened to you?' I asked. 'How long were we at the Clinic?'

'I don't know. Days, at least. A week? For a time, I was… not conscious.'

'Dead?'

'That would be absurd. I'm talking to you. The dead don't talk.'

'I didn't say you were dead. I implied you had been dead. But aren't any more.'

'A fine distinction.'

A little light shone in the church. Silvery, shimmering. Billy's hands, glowing again. Deadly.

His face was underlit.

Boris Karloff's face. The way it was on movie posters.

His eyes – the Mummy's eyes – glistened.

'I doubt I was shot or stabbed. I'd remember that. I have a sense of a great weight pressed on my chest. Air forced out of my lungs. Something over my face. I was pushed into the darkness. Cold and quiet. I couldn't hear myself breathe. I had no sense of a heartbeat, a pulse. Everything was turned off.'

'You might have just been unconscious. In a coma. Slowed, but not stopped.'

'Oh no, I was dead, all right. You were right when you wrote that the dead don't care. They sleep your big sleep. The only thing is – the thing you got wrong – they aren't alone. There are so many. While they sleep, others are among them. Not the dead. Quick, sparking things. Imps, perhaps. I almost understood death's mystery. But it's gone now. A dream that comes apart like cobweb when you wake. Coming to *hurts*, R.T. When the heart and lungs and mind start up again, they're *loud* – like giant engines and furnaces and boilers.'

'Aren't you stronger? Like the Bims, like Quin?'

The hands were reddish – black charcoal bones clad in flesh like solid flame.

'Oh yes, I'm limber and supple. But it still hurts.'

'Your hands?'

He concentrated for a moment. Their light went out.

'Safe now,' he said.

'Let's not test that.'

Quin mewled like a hurt animal. He had a panicked, whining tone. I heard thumping. He was hitting the flagstone floor, smacking with his great open hands.

'He's afraid of the dark,' said Billy.

'Are monsters really terrified in the night?'

'Monsters most of all are afraid. It's why they're monsters.'

Billy got up. I thought he might try to calm Quin like a baby or a dog. Billy was good at that. Or he might summon his Death Touch and shut him up before he got us captured. That would be a temptation for me.

Instead he found candles and matches.

Light flared – hurting my eyes, even after only a short time in the dark – and Billy touched a taper to a tall, red candle, which he propped in a crack in the floor. He lit several more. Keeping the burning candles close to the ground meant less chance of them being seen from outside.

The candlelight showed us we weren't alone.

I felt like I'd taken a punch to the heart. I reacted audibly.

The altar was fit for a cathedral, with a lectern fashioned like a spread-winged golden eagle. Behind it stood a sombre-faced priest.

At the foot of the altar knelt a scarved woman.

In the front row, bundled up in furs, was another parishioner.

Had we interrupted some secret nocturnal service? Home had brought over the villagers with the church.

'They're not alive,' said Billy.

I saw this was true. The figures were posed, unmoving.

I breathed again.

'They're not people,' I said.

'No, they are,' said Billy.

He held up a candle to show the priest's face. It shone, waxy and pale.

Norman had his hands over his eyes. He knew enough about this place to be more frightened than curious.

But Billy and I were cursed.

This was a strange thing. We needed to know *how* strange.

I joined Billy and examined the priest and the other two figures.

Their clothes were stiff, crudely stitched. Their eyes were glass and their hair was crinkly wig material. But their skin was tanned and varnished, not painted wax.

These were preserved corpses.

'Does this look like anyone we know?' said Billy.

He meant the priest. He held the candle close so I could look.

I saw it.

'Home. He looks like Junior Home.'

'Doesn't he, though?'

Junior Home could have been the priest's brother…

… though, since we'd no way of knowing how long this figure had been posed here, the family relationship could have been father to son or, more likely, ancestor (great-grandfather?) to descendant. This tableau was the root of the family tree.

'The woman is Sigurd Heim's mama, I think,' said Billy. 'The fellow in the skins is her husband. Look at his coronet.'

From his fur hat sprouted horns. Cuckold's horns.

'I do believe this display is telling the story of Home's ancestry. A family album in three dimensions.'

I looked at the priest's face. A smug mask of pious lechery.

'The church is the same in Ireland,' I said. 'If you've a red-headed priest, half the altar boys will be ginger.'

Billy walked round the altar.

'You have to wonder about a family who go to such lengths to put their past in aspic,' he said. 'I wouldn't keep a display like this. Would you?'

I'd happily have Maurice Chandler pickled, but wouldn't give his corpse house-room. I gathered Billy felt similarly about certain Pratts.

'We knew the Homes were insane in their marrow. Is this such a stretch? They happily threw a mad science pageant. *Frankenstein*, staged by Busby Berkeley. This is just a minor horror. What was it called? *Mystery of the Wax Museum*.'

'I wasn't in that. Warners cast Lionel Atwill.'

I was getting used to the gloom. A face loomed as if in a mirror.

'Look who's above the altar,' I said.

Billy shifted the candle. A painting hung, wreathed in ivy.

I presumed the artist intended Ariadne to represent the Virgin Mary. In this depiction – more an Orthodox icon than a Catholic image of veneration – she looked like Salome in a blue dress. Hell, she could be Medusa with her snakes tucked into a wimple.

'Of course she'd be here,' said Billy. 'She's always been here.'

'Do you suppose she's visited herself on the Homes or Heims, and whoever this sky-pilot is, the way she's blighted our lives?'

'Indubitably.'

I felt sick. Also jealous.

'We're as stuffed and puppeteered as these poor boobies,' I said.

She had been in their lives longer than in ours. They were special to her.

Billy took the candle away.

He brushed the priest's vestments, which were inset with chunks of coloured glass. The dead man creaked and moved like a figure in a mediaeval town clock. His head turned and his right arm lifted, forefinger stuck out like a baton.

The horned congregant stood and shook. Dust fell out of his furs.

The woman – shamed and abused mother of the Home line – tore at her scarf with fingers that had flaked away, showing armature bones and claw-tip nails.

Billy and I were between the three of them.

Surely, they couldn't be rigged up to give us a fight.

I took up a pigeon-chested boxer's stance – not a sport I excelled at in school – and gave the priest a pre-emptive jab to the nose.

After the evening's ordeal, I was curious.

Would I feel better if I punched someone?

I certainly got a surprise – along with scraped knuckles.

The priest's face came apart. The flesh had been peeled off before varnishing, in segments like a peach, then pieced back together on the skull. When my jab landed, the face came apart and fell on the floor. A death's head looked at me. Huge glass eyes shone in bony orbits. Veins threaded over bone plates and the jawbone was fixed in place by copper wire. Half the teeth were gold. Was that a sign that a nineteenth-century German country priest could prosper off his living, or a post-mortem gift? The Homes could afford to do what they wanted with the Father who was their father. They could have encrusted the skull with precious stones and lapis lazuli if they'd had a mind to.

'What a *frightful* horror,' shuddered Billy.

'Look who's talking, Boris.'

The mechanisms wound down. The peasant who'd contributed nothing but his name to the bloodline shrank into a seated position, but missed the pew and fell on his side, bending at the waist. The mother's finger remnants got stuck in her scarf. The skull-faced priest slumped forward on his lectern.

Shoddy workmanship, I supposed. Or long years of disuse.

The floor was swept free of dust – some of the gravestone names would have been legible if they'd not been cut in elaborate Gothic script – but no one had prayed in this church in a long while.

It might be a good time to start.

Quin was still whining. Not just in hurt self-pity. His keening had a new urgency. He was trying to attract our attention.

We saw he was motioning his limp hand at the shut door.

Billy heard the noises outside before I did.

Low whistles. Not bird-calls, but close. Hunters' signals.

Someone had followed our trail.

22

'**C**oo-*eeee*! Y'in there, Frankenstein?'

For an extended moment, none of us breathed.

Two of us might not have had to. I gasped first.

The voice came from outside the church, but close to the door. We hadn't obscured our tracks well enough.

'We've come a-callin', Frank-en-stein!'

The voice was thin, flat, high. A Western drawl, but snotty as if a passage were clogged. I didn't get an impression of a straight-shooting, clean-shaven, tall-in-the-saddle Gary Cooper Westerner. The man outside sounded more like a sly, claim-jumping, plug-you-in-the-back-with-a-rifle-from-cover varmint. Walter Brennan in a mean mood. A hoodlum with a different hat.

'Frank-en-stein…'

Had he seen any other Karloff pictures?

I chewed my lips.

I wanted to shout back at him. We didn't have Colin Clive holed up with us. Frankenstein was the name of the man, not the Monster. A mistaken literary allusion would have merited a ruler over the knuckles at the schools Billy and I went to. One master at Dulwich gave 'the Old Testament' as punishment for such slips. A boy had to recite the books of the Old Testament, receiving a lash of the knout – a length of knotted rope that hung from a hook by the blackboard – across the posterior for each name. If an error was made, the miscreant had to start over again. It could take all afternoon. Genesis, Exodus, Leviticus, Numbers…

No wonder I stayed away from chapels and churches in later life.

Quin cowered. For a monster, he was easily spooked.

Billy had said monsters were always afraid. I understood. It was a distinction between villains and monsters. Villains were fearless, or took precautions. Villains knew life wasn't like the movies. They often left the white hats hanging from a tree and rode into the sunset with the leading lady tethered to their saddle, dragged ragged across sagebrush.

Out there, cooing at us, was a villain. It didn't take the detective know-how of Philip Marlowe to work out he wouldn't be alone.

Now there came a knocking.

Not skinny knuckles, but something heavy and wooden.

The stock of a shotgun? A weighted blackjack?

Why didn't the knocker just barge in? Did he need to be invited?

'Frankie, c'mon now, this ain't *sociable*,' said a voice. 'We sees your lights…'

I'd known they would.

I picked up the plural first person. *We* sees. Confirmation that our caller wasn't alone. Heroes walk alone into devil's dens. Villains have gangs. If the villain wears a badge, they have a posse. Every gangster in my *Black Mask* stories has an obligatory goon entourage. It's not enough just to have them there like menacing furniture. You have to individuate the bastards. A man comes through a door with a gun – my get-out for when the plot stalls. But a man has to be a man, not a hatstand for a Luger.

Now, I didn't care how many gunmen were out there. I'd happily never know their names.

'Our Hubert can *smell* you,' said the caller. 'He's got a fine sniffer on him. Led us straight to your hideaway hole.'

I did not think 'Our Hubert' was a hound.

'You wouldn't be able to tell us apart,' he went on. 'Our Hubert and me. We's twins. Triplets, would be – only Our Horatio got snakebit in the womb, and throttled hisself on the belly-cord. I itch sometimes and reckon Our Horatio's still with us. In spirit. Understand that, Frank? Flesh ain't all we got. 'Sides meat and bone, there's the spirit. Shining and glorious is the spirit.'

'Hallelujah,' said another voice, deeper.

Hubert? Or another sibling?

'I cain't sniff a skunk on Sunday morning,' said the more garrulous caller. 'I didn't get the smellin'. I got the sight. Can make things out from a long way off. Critter rolls over in its sleep half a mile away and I can shoot out its eye – not spoil the skin if you want a trophy or taint the meat if you want fry-up breakfast. 'Course someone has to walk the half-mile to fetch the dead beast. Often ain't worth the effort. Ever do that, Frankie? Kill a thing just to keep in practice?'

Again, I was affronted.

Billy spent the War marrying actresses and performing *East Lynne* in Canadian barns. I was the trained killer this side of the church door. Though I was out of practice and Billy had his just-acquired Death Touch if he had the heart to use it. It wouldn't work from a mile away… or through a door. Neither, I reckoned, would Junior's mind over matter trick.

Junior wouldn't be out there now.

This was a job for his people. Specialists.

Not Bims.

'Say, d'you reckon Our Horatio would have had the ears in the family? If he'd lived. There'd be a *symmetry* to that. Eyes, nose and ears. Hal, though – cousin to me and Hubert – he's got the tongue…'

'Hallelujah,' shouted the cousin.

The cretin of the family?

What family? The Homes? Heims?

No. But close.

The stress on *symmetry* told me something. He wanted us to acknowledge that he knew such words, though he was using them imprecisely. That'd have got him the Old Testament in Knouty Knox's classroom. Or told to grasp a cinder at Uppingham. He meant logic, or at least poetic logic. Senses are abstracts. Symmetry is for concrete things – objects that are exactly alike or mirror images either side of a divide. He meant something intangible but fitting, a rule of three.

'I ain't introduced myself, Frank. I'm Hector.'

H-names all.

How had Joh described them? 'Snake-handling Pentecostalists who clung to the shady side of the hill.' Lamia's folk. The Munros.

'Hector Munro,' I called out. 'Like the author.'

A pause.

'Yes, like the writer.'

A longer pause.

He now wanted acknowledgement that he knew who H.H. Munro was. The Englishman who signed his work 'Saki' was a great influence on my generation of *littérateurs*. A genius, the missing link between Poe and Wodehouse. What a *Black Mask* man he'd have made. You can hear him in Hammett. They both use words like little scalpels. So sharp you don't notice you're bleeding out. I can't match that, so I work on the similes and play down the chilliness. H.H. Munro was dead in the War. Saki's last words were, 'Put that bloody cigarette out!' Another soldier's fag, a glow-worm in the dark, alerted German snipers. Shot for practice by someone of a mind to, like our new friend.

There were no prizes for having heard of a namesake in another field. If there were a champion yachtsman called Raymond Chandler, it'd come to my attention. I wasn't convinced this Hector had read a word of Saki.

'You ain't Frankenstein,' he said. 'You're the other one. Got your name writ down somewhere.'

'I'll wait,' I said.

Hector chuckled. 'You do that.'

While I chatted with the man outside the door, Billy searched for another way out of our trap. He moved quiet as a cat and didn't take a candle. The church was built on a steep slope, back wall set into the hillside. It was too much to hope for a hidden panel leading to an abandoned mine or natural cave. Billy lifted a rug behind the altar. The floor was solid rock, with nary a trapdoor.

I picked up a candle and waved at the corpse-automaton priest.

'If we burn this place,' I whispered, 'they'd find three skeletons…'

… which would throw the Munros off the scent. The stink of the smoke and burned corpses would confuse Hubert's nostrils.

'No,' responded Billy, 'they'd find *six* – because we haven't found a way out.'

'Have you tried the ceiling?'

Billy looked up. That was promising. Any rear exit would have to be twenty feet above the level of the front door. Above us was a forest of antlers and glass eyes.

'Raymond Chandler,' said Hector, at last. 'Printed neat as you please. Easy name to forget. Be even easier tomorrow. Hate to break it to you sudden, but you're the one they don't want brung back alive. Guess you ain't worth the long walk and the haulin'.'

So much for leaving one man to tell the tale.

'Still, I'm a fair man and all,' Hector went on. 'I like that straight off you thunk of Hector Munro the writer… I'll give you a long count before I unsling Old Jerusalem – that's my shooting rifle – and take aim.'

'Your shooting rifle? Do you have any *other* kind?'

A long pause.

'Huh? Guess I don't. Ain't no use for any kind of rifle that don't shoot. Is a redundancy is what it is. Like saying "fetch me a pail of that wet water". You don't need no adjective.'

'Saki never wasted a word,' I said.

'Reckon he didn't. You'll get the full count, Mr Chandler. Talking with you is improving and I owe you a kindness for that. The full count. *Both* books of the Bible… Genesis, Exodus…'

'… Leviticus, Numbers…'

Hector laughed now.

Knouty Knox and Hector Munro. Two sadists continents apart, with the same use for scripture. That was symmetry for you.

'Joshua, Judges… but we'll get to that when you come out.'

'Why don't you come in?'

Quin covered his head with his forearms. He was terrified. Hector's voice scraped his last nerve.

'Me, step in a Roman church? I'd as soon dare venture into Hell Itself.'

That's not how I'd have expressed it but I understood the sentiment.

Billy gave a stage *hisst*. I turned and saw he had shinned – with new agility – up a wooden support and was in the eaves. He had his hand splay-fingered against a wooden panel unadorned by dead game. He pushed and it gave.

A back exit.

Billy flapped his hand in front of his mouth.

Keep him talking.

'How many should we set the table for?' I asked.

Hector snickered. 'Enough.'

'We're three in here,' I said.

'I know.'

'We're armed, of course.'

'I doubt that.'

'You're welcome to.'

'Not that I'm calling anyone a liar, you understand. I was raised better than that.'

There were Munros out there we hadn't heard from – or heard of – yet. More cousins. Henry, Hogmanay or Hob. Older and younger brothers to the Sight and Smell twins. Maybe a sister with a skinning knife between her teeth. Heloise or Hepzibah.

Why the H-names? Did that start when Lamia hooked into a Home?

Billy dropped quietly to the floor and assembled pews into a pile we could climb easily and quickly. It was impossible to manage without scraping the stone – a sound like scratching a blackboard. With every scrape, my teeth hurt.

'How about we send Quin out?' I said. 'Would you be satisfied?'

'We'd appreciate the gesture greatly. But we'd still require Frankie.'

'How about if we send Quin and Mr Karloff out... could I get, ah, lenient treatment if I were to *persuade* them to meet with you?'

They wanted Quin and Billy alive. So I could in good conscience hand them over...

... though, of course, I knew alive didn't mean unharmed.

And it was wrong to peach on a comrade, whether an old friend or an acquaintance of this evening. Knouty Knox offered to spare a minor infractor who named two greater offenders. In the history of Dulwich

College, no boy ever took him up on it. That was the lesson he was trying to impart – which didn't mean he didn't take an unholy joy in his Old Testament.

Hector Munro didn't see the world like that. He killed just to keep his eye in. He didn't understand that an English public school man would rather take a knouting of both Testaments than betray a fellow.

'Let me think on that,' said Hector.

An advantage in dealing with villains is that their ideas are limited.

They believe everyone is like them.

Cowardly, cautious, eager to take advantage.

Billy had erected a climbing frame. We could get out quietly. He beckoned.

Quin stood up.

'I reckon we could be amenable,' said Hector. 'I always get them Letters to the Ephesians and the Corinthians mixed up and have to be set straight. Who knows, by the time I reach Revelations you could be clear over the hill and out of sight…'

I knew precisely when he'd shoot me in the back.

It'd take 'Genesis, Exodus, Leviticus, Numbers' to raise the rifle to firing position.

Deuteronomy. Finger on the trigger.

Joshua. Sight on me, thirty paces away.

Judges. Intake of breath, calm moment to enjoy it – probably with a hot little thrill in his water.

Ruth!

If I went through with the dirty deal, I'd have eight books to live.

So, it was a climb out through the roof and a scramble up the hillside… with Sniffing Munro and Seeing Munro after us.

'What do you say, Ray? Time's a-passin'.'

Quin began climbing, with Billy pulling him up.

I stepped away from the door.

More knocking. Impatient?

'Don't be playing no monkey tricks. I can't abide a monkey trick. Say, did you see that picture? The Sparx Brozz in *Monkey Tricks*? The Sparxes is funnier'n them other brozz, if you ask me. I'd see them Jews in court if I were Cousin Junie. Or take 'em huntin'. See how hi-larious they is when they's runnin' with targetses on their backsideses. 'Specially that dummy. I'd get him a harp to play, all right.'

Not impatient. Excited.

Like he knew things we didn't. Or knew we knew things we thought he didn't.

I went to the altar and talked quietly – thankful that Horatio of the Sharp Ears hadn't lived…

'They know about the door in the roof,' I said. 'They'll have hooks and ropes. Men with guns in sniper-nests.'

Billy was disappointed.

He was proud of his improvised staircase.

'They're practically begging us to scuttle out the back,' I said. 'So that's where they're strong. This Hector isn't the Eyes he says he is. He's the Mouth. We're being sweet-talked into their trap.'

Billy didn't argue. He cottoned on quick.

Quin was confused. He pulled down one of the pews. That made a racket anyone could hear.

'You folks okay in there? Sounds like a rumpus or a ruckus. If there's a difference.'

'Quin tripped over his feet,' I shouted. 'He's big and clumsy.'

'That's Mr Norman for you,' said Hector. 'A galoot. You have the measure of him right and proper.'

'Indeed.'

Billy came down again. We were in a huddle.

He looked at his glowing hands. He was getting over the horror of the Death Touch. Immediately, that was a good idea. In the long term, I'd worry. The talent could prove addictive – a terrible temptation. It was easy to become a monster by increments, taking small, awful steps.

'You can do now what you can do in pictures,' I said, quietly.

Billy thought about it. 'Some things, yes – I believe I can. The hands from *The Invisible Ray*. Bits and pieces from other films. *The Walking Dead*.'

It was a side effect of the Vaudois-Quin Process. An innate talent, dosed with salts. Unexpected – and new. What might all those Bims and Nursies be able to do if they thought about it.

'The more times you've played it, the stronger it is… you've come back from the dead over and over, so you heal fast.'

He nodded.

Bullets would only slow him down. Me – they'd kill.

'It's chilly out here, after the rain,' said Hector. 'Could be we light a fire on your front step. Big old wooden church door ought to catch light fast. Ain't no sin burnin' down a Popish Temple of Idolatry. More like a duty.'

'Billy, in *The Mummy* you could exert your will over lesser minds. Glowing eyes and mesmeric influence.'

Billy nodded. His eyes glistened.

'As Fu Manchu and in *The Black Cat*, you had similar business.'

'I also played the hypnotist in *The Bells*, with Lionel Barrymore.'

'That's the *Boris Karloff* we need now, Billy. The one who can cloud men's minds.'

An invisible Jack Pierce went to work on him.

His cheeks dried and withered like parchment. And his eyes lit up. Not reflected light, but light from within. In an early poster for *Frankenstein*, the Monster shot death rays from his eyes. It was too much to hope that Billy could do that. But he didn't need to. He just needed to exert his will, like a three-thousand-year-old sorcerer… a diabolical oriental mastermind… a high priest of Satan.

'Mr Karloff is coming out now, Hector,' I said. 'I'd appreciate it if you didn't make use of your shooting rifle…'

'Old Jerusalem is slung away safe,' he lied.

'Long may it stay so.'

Billy walked down the nave as if he were risen from the tomb. Quin and I crept after him, hiding in his shadow.

He was calm now, relaxed as a cat…

The door opened before him.

He stepped out of the church.

'Good evening, friends,' he said.

23

That mendacious cur, Hector, had Old Jerusalem's stock against his shoulder. He peered down the sight, aiming at Billy's breastbone.

He was a short fellow in cowboy duds and muddy boots. A silver rim around his black hat. He hadn't lied when he said his brother got the family's nose. Where his ought to be was a patch of rough skin and a single nostril – which might have been made with an implement for puncturing leather. The deformity gave his voice that high, flat, snotty tone.

Cousin Hal was two sizes bigger, with a wider, but not flatter face.

'Hallelujah,' he said.

'Yes,' said Hector, 'that does get irritating. That you, Ray?'

I did my best to stay behind Billy and Quin, to make me harder to shoot.

'I'm not the one you should pay attention to, Hector.'

I couldn't see Billy's face, but I felt something coming off him. A calming influence. The full force of it was turned on Hector and Hal, like headlamps.

Watch the watch... are you feeling sleepy? ... you are in my power.

'Hallelujah,' said Hal, in a different tone.

'Ha...' said Hector, lowering Old Jerusalem.

'You want to throw that dirty thing away,' said Billy.

'Yes, sir,' said Hector, chucking the rifle against a tree. He rubbed his hands against his pants.

'You can all come out now,' said Billy.

And they did. Five or six Munros.

Brother Hubert was easy to identify. Hector lied when he said we wouldn't be able to tell them apart. Hubert had a Durante-sized nose but regular eyes. The imbalance of senses and sensory organs wasn't a general trait spread across his clan. I'd imagined Munros with tiny or no arms, compensated for by mighty legs and feet. If Tod Browning ever made a Western, this would be his outlaw gang.

'Throw away your irons, gentlemen,' suggested Billy. 'They're unhealthy, heavy, unpleasant things.'

They laid down their guns before Billy as if he were a great chief accepting their surrender.

From the pile of donated weapons, I picked up a pistol. A Webley, like the ones issued in the Canadian army. I checked that it was loaded and was satisfied. Now I had a Death Touch too.

Hal was the first to go down on his knees before Billy.

The others followed suit. None took their hats off, though.

Was this draining Billy? I worried he'd snap out of it and we'd have a ruckus – or a rumpus – on our hands.

For the moment, the spell held.

Quin experimentally knocked the hats off a couple of Munros, as if tipping coconuts at a shy. He enjoyed that, so he tweaked the noses of them that had them and cuffed the ears of them that didn't. His childish malice disturbed me out of proportion. Whatever had been done to his face, worse had been done to his mind. This man who could work miracles seemed hardly brighter than Hallelujah Munro. Hal at least had a vocabulary of one word.

Surely, Junior Home and Dr Vaudois *needed* his genius. They had dreams of building empires on his work.

Why would they make a moron of him?

Jealousy. Arrogance. A belief that they had all the miracles they needed out of him and he was now an embarrassment, like a writer trying to take credit for a hit picture.

If I were Junior Home – Overman – I'd be wary of Norman F. Quin – Man-Made Monster. They'd shot I don't know how many *Frankenstein* pictures and still nobody learned the lesson of the story.

Don't make Monsters. Just don't.

Quin picked up the smallest Munro – some nephew or son or foundling, with a hat and gun-belt too big for him – and twisted him at the middle. He quacked with delight at the kid's yelps.

And that was what distracted Billy and broke the mesmeric spell.

I shot Hector in the leg before he could get Old Jerusalem back.

It was as if I'd had my hand on an anvil when the hammer came down. I'd not fired a pistol since 1918 and had forgotten how they kicked. I didn't put a bullet in Hector's thigh because I was a white hat who shot to wound and knew the rustler would reform by the end of the picture. I'd aimed at his no-nose but the percussive blast was like a blow to my wrist and the shot went wild.

Killing Hector Munro wouldn't have troubled my nights more than they were. He'd been only too happy to share his plans about murdering me, and even then he'd lied to lure me out. A bloody crevice in the middle of his face would have served him right.

Billy trampled and kicked the guns at his feet, then took off at speed.

Munros bumped heads as they scrabbled for their shooting irons.

I tore off after Billy, getting a stitch in my side before I'd gone fifty yards. At least I hadn't been shot yet.

Quin flailed after us.

The sky was getting lighter. Dawn was nearing.

I hoped the Munros were still confused. They had known about the church's escape hatch, but not that Billy could issue hypnotic commands. Even Billy hadn't realised that. I'd only guessed.

Billy ran through the forest like the *Last of the Mohicans*...

I ignored the pain in my side and my mangle-wrung hand and tried to keep up. Billy dodged trees and I smacked into them. The Webley weighed as much as a car battery.

But the Munros chasing us were a motivation.

We outran them. Billy led us downhill and out of the trees.

I stopped and turned – unwise as Orpheus – to look back. Unlike the ancient crooner, I had a gun. Shooting another Munro might turn them into a scattering rabble. I had an itch to kill again. A secret kinship with

Knouty Knox and Hector and all the other sadists. I raised my gun but the person in my sights was Quin. He huffed down the trail, picking up his knees and pumping his arms like a hurdler.

He ran past me. I didn't want to be left behind, so I followed him.

The trees had been cleared from a muddy mess of a field, which was criss-crossed by barbed wire and studded with water-filled depressions I recognised as shell-holes.

Billy stood looking at a shining cylinder that stuck out of an anthill.

Lucky, clever fellow – kissing the girls and taking the bows in the North Woods. He had no idea what he was looking at.

I did.

'For Christ's sake, don't touch that.'

He turned at me, smiling. His eyes weren't glowing now.

'It's an unexploded shell,' I said. 'They're never complete duds. They always go off. That one could take us all with it.'

He looked back at its shiny point. He couldn't resist. He put his finger close to the needle-tip and strained as if it were exerting a magnetic pull.

Then he laughed and gave the thing a heavy kick.

24

The shell didn't explode. It wasn't a dud. It was a dummy. A prop.

We weren't back in the War.

We were on the Pyramid lot. On an exterior set.

When the Munros caught up to us, their guns would fire real bullets that could kill real people.

Well, they could kill *me*.

Pressed into the mud were small dummies. Not children, but half-sized adults in crude miniature uniforms. Even a flattened hobby-horse. The battlefield was half-scale. Several acres of No Man's Toyland stretched in front of us. Not for staging play-fights, but for flying planes over. Too many air ace pictures offered spectacular, authentic 1918 aerial jousts flawed by glimpses of 1930s California traffic trundling on roads below.

Quin seemed even more gigantic in this setting. A sickening funk came off him. He smelled like six dead men sewn together. The British Board of Film Censors would have broken their scissors to get rid of scenes where Frankenstein scrapes rot off ripe body-snatched odds and ends. Quin also looked *worried* – not an expression his carved, frightening features assumed easily.

I understood. Billy didn't.

All of us have this dream where we're back in the War.

Even the early morning quiet was authentic. Heavy guns couldn't fire round the clock. They had to cool off and be maintained. The still quiet spells were torture by hope. A lull you couldn't help but take as a sign it was finally all over. A lie that would end with the first whistle and bang of the day's bombardment. The Kaiser's Cock-Crow. I bet they called it John Bull's Wake-Up Bell in the trenches opposite.

Going mad in the still quiet hour was an invitation to be put up against a wall and shot by your own men. A case of nerves was punishable by summary execution. Only the English poets got shipped off to Dottyville and the head doctors. Canadian Highlanders got a dose of something vile and told to pull themselves together.

I don't write much about the War. General Sternwood, Marlowe's broken old man client in *The Big Sleep*, must have been in it. An officer who loved and indulged his lads but slept easily when they were dead and he wasn't. The character isn't autobiographical. I've not slept through a whole night since 1917. I tried writing blasted war poetry once. It was like scratching scabs. I'd rather drink.

Quin had a look I'd seen on a thousand faces.

Not on monsters. On men roughly my age. When a car backfired or an old song came on the radio or the garden got churned into mud. The fear. That it didn't end with the Armistice, that it would happen again, that we'd be rushed through call-up and muster and be back in the mud and the din. Thanks to goose-stepping fools in Europe, it's not even an *irrational* fear. Some would volunteer, to get the agony over with. Some felt a duty to finish it properly this time. I'd told Cissy I'd enlist if England went to war again. She said they'd be lucky to have me in a tone that implied she didn't believe the King would put a superannuated sot like me in uniform even if the SS were marching up the Mall.

Billy wondered why Quin and I were so spooked.

For him, this was a breather. We were out of the woods. No Munros in sight. He was in a place where he was comfortable. A film set. Movie make-believe. Not a real battlefield.

'We can't go to ground again,' he said. 'When the sun's up, they'll track us by sight.'

I didn't disagree.

The sky to the east was reddish.

We could make out a large structure bordering the battlefield, like a Nebraska barn covered with a camouflage net the size of a circus tent. Disguised from the air.

I had an idea what it was for. Which gave me another idea.

Not a good one. But we were out of sensible options.

Sensible options ran out while Rutherford B. Hayes was President, around the time Sigurd Heim struck oil. The twentieth century offered precious few sensible options.

'This way,' I said, and struck out towards the barn.

The trick of hopping from one solid patch of ground to the next came back to me.

Quin and Billy waded through quagmire, making slower progress. I tried not to get too far ahead.

The faceless half-pint dummies made solid little islands, so I trod on as many of those as possible.

As we neared the barn, a vehicle approached from the other direction. A fire truck, painted green and brown like a tank.

I stopped in my tracks, gesturing to the Monsters to crouch low. I could just about pass for a lost extra who'd fallen asleep drunk on the battlefield. Quin and Billy were out of a different movie. Billy was too recognisable. Anyone on this set would know Erich von Stroheim was playing the 'Boris Karloff' part in this picture.

The truck parked by the barn. A man scrambled out of the cab onto the back.

Leaving Quin and Billy in a huddle, I ambled over – affecting a casual air of belonging.

The fireman wore olive drab overalls and a railwayman's hat. He unspooled a serpentine length of grey hose and fixed the nozzle to an extensible ladder-arm. By the time I reached the truck, water was spraying over the sodden ground. It splashed and seeped and pooled.

I could have sneaked past the fireman. He was in his own, happy world pouring gallons and gallons of water onto earth that had been thoroughly deluged by nature. He swung the ladder-arm around in an arc. The artificial rain made pleasing squiggles in the air.

But I had to know. I was fatally curious.

I reasoned that talking to the fireman made me *less* conspicuous. Someone who had any business being here at this hour of the morning wouldn't skulk past the fire truck.

'Is that really necessary?' I shouted.

He looked at me. I couldn't see his face.

'Mr Home's orders,' he said, with a German-Dutch sibilance on *Home'ss* and *orderss*. 'Field look not like mud in rushes. Too damn dry. California dirt. For Mr Home, everything must be *just so*. This is Class A picture.'

'It's not dry now.'

'Mr Home has not countermanded his order. Every morning, before shooting, the battlefield is to be watered to make mud. Nothing is said about when field is mud already.'

'You could have taken the day off today. Your job's been done for you.'

'With Mr Home, there is no "take the day off". There is getting fired. I have orders. I am following them.'

I couldn't decide whether that was admirable or insane.

I left the fireman adding water to mud – in a desert where potable water had to be stolen at great expense. Saltwater was cheap and easily to hand in the Pacific, but that wasn't Class A enough for Junior's mud. No flapping fishes in the No Man's Land of *Flight of the Red Eagle*.

As I said, sensible options are off the menu.

The barn was a huge curve of metal with no walls. Inside I saw what I'd hoped for. Planes.

I looked back.

The battlefield nearest the barn was swamp now. Any half-pint Hun stepping onto this corner of France-Faux would sink up to his *Pickelhaube*. The fireman got back in his cab and drove off to inundate some other patch of the set.

I waved, trusting Billy's eyes.

The Monsters loped out of the thinning darkness.

I proudly pointed out my discovery.

Front and centre of the squadron was a Fokker triplane. When the sun was up, it would be vivid scarlet. In shadow, it was brown. In the RFC, we trainees studied a shot-down tripe, dissected and pinned back together. A 'know your enemy' lecture went with it.

How much better was this plane than our Camels?

On his final flight, Baron von Richthofen, the deadliest ace of the War, was shot through the chest. He died instantly in the air. His Fokker landed in a field on its own, unharmed. His plane was torn apart for souvenirs before the RFC could get hold of it.

'I can fly one of these,' I said.

Billy looked appalled. After everything that had happened in the Clinic, *this* was what struck him as insane.

'But… but…' he said.

Quin didn't look too happy either.

The Fokker wasn't built for three. It was designed to get one man and his guns in the air and give him speed and manoeuvrability. Anthony Fokker specified how heavy the pilot could be. Hermann Göring flew a tripe in his slimmer days. He might command the Luftwaffe now, but he'd never be cleared to fly. No room in the cockpit for beer-and-sausages bellies.

I led them past the Fokker – the hero plane, centre-screen in the battles – and similarly restored Spads and Camels. What I was looking for wasn't a fighter.

At the back of the barn was the most important bird in this squadron. A two-man spotter, much like the modified Bristol F.2b I flew in training. That had dual controls, so the instructor could take over whenever it seemed likely I'd kill us both. This German plane was also modified – as a flying camera mount. I hoped the equipment needed to film air battles – which wasn't left here overnight – weighed approximately as much as two Frankenstein Monsters. The rear cockpit would be a squeeze for them.

'They'll have all the gates guarded,' I said. 'But not the sky.'

'Didn't you transfer to the RFC at the *very end* of the War?' asked Billy.

'Yes,' I said, not seeing the point.

'You never flew in action?'

'The Armistice was declared while I was in training.'

'Which, as a consequence, you didn't complete.'

We were part-way through the course. But it was only a ceasefire – an Armistice, not a victory. We kept taking lessons, working towards flying certification. A cadet on my course died in January 1919, firing at a practice target pinned on the ground. The synchronising mechanism went out of whack and his gunfire shredded his own propeller.

'I can fly this,' I said.

I'd not had the knout since 1905, but I could still recite the books of the Old Testament (flinching at each name). I'd not sat in a cockpit since I was mustered out and packed home to Mother, but I could still fly.

Put me in a modern plane and the instrument panel would be as baffling as one of Quin's mad science machines. This old bus was different. Anthony Fokker made aircraft for Prussian aristocrats who knew everything about shooting but had little people polish, clean and load their guns. Murderous fatheads who couldn't put their boots on by themselves. Fokker had to design planes that could be flown by idiots and children.

And we didn't have to fly far. This was little more than a hedge-hop.

I checked there was fuel in the tank.

Then I had my brawny Monsters push the spotter out of the barn. On the other side, away from the battlefield, was a paved runway. Shorter than I'd have liked. I trusted Billy and Quin wouldn't pay too much notice to the strip's puddles and cracks.

Once the plane was in the air, I could fly it.

I had some concerns about take-off. And more about landing.

In the RFC, landings had never been my strong point.

25

Half the sky was light now.

Beyond the runway I saw the studio's glass pyramid – which must glint in the distance and spoil many shots. An eye-shaped balloon gleamed in the early morning sun. Other buildings appeared in the dawn light. Humped sound stages. Warehouses for scenery and costume storage. A row of dainty bungalows for favoured serfs. A commissary where the five thousand could be fed rolls baked by the ton and coffee brewed in vats a child actor could – and probably should – be boiled alive in.

My body remembered to be hungry.

And thirsty. After this, I might allow myself a breakfast belt. I had earned it.

Or would have…

Once I'd played the lead in *Last Flight of the Greyish Eagle*.

I had my strange mechanics point the plane at the runway.

Quin wanted to open up the nose – a tinkerer's brain still sparked in that squared-off skull. Billy stopped him getting his tiny fingers in the engine.

It would have been a blessing if jackets and helmets had been stowed in the cockpit. No such luck. This trip might freeze our ears off. I didn't mention that. Billy and Quin could discover the disadvantages of flying in an open cockpit for themselves.

I fetched chocks – big wooden triangles linked by a single pull-chain – from the barn and wedged them under the front wheels.

'Yank these away when the engine turns over,' I told Billy, giving him the chain. 'Then, pretty sharpish, climb into the rear cockpit. You should both fit...'

'If you say so, R.T.'

'Relax,' I said, which made him tense up.

We'd learned what scared Boris Karloff.

I reached for grips in the fuselage and hauled myself up, putting weight on the step reinforced specially for my right foot.

It had been seventeen years since I last did that. I remembered it as an easy, simple pull-up. Once, it had been. Now, I was older. Since Cissy stopped playing tennis, I'd given up my Athletic Club membership. I could no longer take physical ease in minor exertions for granted.

I wrenched my shoulder and tried not to show it.

As I swung from the wing-step to the cockpit, I put my foot through the canvas flank. In the RFC – 'when Pontius was a pilot', as moustached bores in the Hollywood cricket club put it – we'd had planes made of exactly this stuff. Sailcloth stiffened with paint and plaster. A cadet duty was going out every morning with thick nine-inch needles and sewing the tears up with string.

'Nothing to worry about,' I said, making Billy feel worse.

He hadn't the experience to know this was normal.

I settled comfortably into the pilot's seat. I've eaten fewer sausages than Göring. In front of me was the stick, which notched into my lap – and a panel with four switches and a button. My Bristol had sported a slightly different configuration. That was a bit of a facer.

'Someone's coming,' said Billy.

This was a *German* plane. I flicked what I presumed was the fuel switch and pressed the starter button. An engine rumbled and gave out petrol stink. I hoped the no expenses spared approach that dictated adding water to mud extended to making sure the flying stock – virtual antiques – were maintained in Class A working order. Fuel lines were always leaking on these things. RFC mechanics were more valued and cossetted than cadet pilots. They were harder to come by.

A plink and a ping cut through the drone of the motor.

A shot had ricocheted.

'The Munros are coming,' said Billy.

Another shot. In the asphalt by the wheels.

The propeller turned a couple of times, startling Quin into standing back – then whirred properly. You could slice ham with it.

That was a good whine, a familiar whine.

I knew what a prop in working order sounded like. This was it.

They came from somewhere – down from the hills, or across the battlefield set – and fired wild. If they'd wanted to shoot the Monsters, they could have. Billy and Quin were standing out in the open with no cover. But they had orders to bring them in alive. My survival was a matter of indifference to anyone. Huddled over the stick, I hunched to make myself harder to draw a bead on. The camera plane was a great big target. I hoped the Munros had standing orders not to destroy Pyramid Pictures equipment.

The plane strained at the chocks.

'Okay,' I said, '*now…*'

Billy yanked the chain and pulled the chocks away.

I held back the throttle and felt the plane's weight shift as Billy climbed into the rear cockpit. He didn't tear through the floor of the bus.

'Norman,' he shouted.

I looked over my shoulder.

Billy was snug but Norman failed to get a grip on the handles. His silly, small hands were greasy from mud. The beast he was trying to board was too powerful.

Munros were here.

First came Hal, fast for a big man – a charging bear, yelling 'hallelujah' as he got a rassling hold on Quin. Others were close after him, hollering. Munros I'd not seen before and didn't care to make the acquaintance of. More Munros than the world really needed.

A neat bullet-hole appeared in the wing above me.

A rip in the flank was a joke. We used to tear funny shapes out of the planes so they'd make obscene silhouettes when sewed up. Holes in the wings were serious. Enough of them and we'd be footnotes to the list of

Great War Dead. It's never too late to die. A saleable pulp novelette title – though it sounded more Cornell Woolrich than me.

Munros swarmed over Quin like villagers assailing the Monster. He twisted at the waist, snarling and battering them off.

Billy stood up in his seat, ready to climb down and fight.

Hector took aim with his shooting rifle. A tourniquet was bound around his leg. He was just mad enough to ignore orders. Junior Home wasn't boss of him, but *kin*. Too big for his boots even before he turned himself gargantuan. Who was Cousin Junie to tell him who to shoot and who to leave be? He had a bone to pick with Chandler, R.T., RFC. A little matter of a bullet he'd like to return.

Quin swiped at Hector's weapon, putting a kink in the barrel.

I heard more shots but had to look at the controls.

Holding the plane back made my elbows ache. Smoke came from somewhere and pooled in the cockpit. I realised half the controls were disconnected. They were for the guns the peace-time plane didn't have.

Billy called out to Quin.

The Monster growled and fought. *The Munros Meet Frankenstein.* He would hold out longer, but eventually they'd pin him. From the corner of my eye, I saw Quin waving – flapping his left arm in a signal…

… go without me… I'll hold them off… fly and live…

Or maybe he was just pleading for us to stay and help him.

Billy wouldn't understand – but Joh would. If he still had his mind, Quin would too.

You have to save who you can and leave who you can't. As an officer, I'd done it a dozen times.

Oh, you got beastly drunk afterwards.

But you told yourself you'd saved who you could.

I wasn't one of the poor devils who wrote the letters. I kept quiet about being a published writer, though I'd had scraps in the *Westminster Gazette* and the *Academy* before the War and scribbled miserably through several months on the *Daily Express*. I'd rather fly against von Richthofen with a squirt gun loaded with lemon juice than have to write the letters. To parents, wives, children…

'*Norman*,' shouted Billy.

The plane bounced along – almost playfully, like a big toy train or sledge picking up speed – and put yards between our tail and the Munros… and Norman Quin.

'R.T.—' shouted Billy.

He said something else but the engine was too loud.

There's a moment when the bouncing stops – when air rushes fast under the wheels and over the wings. When your stomach unknots and there's an exhilarating *whoosh* in your vitals.

That's when you're in the air.

We took groundfire but not much.

The plane didn't handle well. I'd hoped for the simplest possible flight plan. Up, up and away – a straight shot above the glass pyramid, over the walls of the Home Estate, then landing on the nearest open stretch. This early in the morning, long straight roads not too far away ought to be relatively traffic-free. Still-lit street-lamps that would serve as landing lights.

I'd reckoned without the wind. Fifty feet off the ground, there's a maelstrom.

We were tossed like a kite. I gripped the stick hard and we didn't turn over.

I could only imagine Billy's face.

The sky disappeared and I had a view of the ground. That was one of the first lessons – be sure you're looking at clouds, not at dirt. Crash into a cloud and it won't hurt. Crash into dirt and a bill comes due. The aircraft is property of His Majesty's Royal Flying Corps and thus worth more than your hide, cadet.

Norman Quin was still fighting. Broken and crawling Munros were at his feet. When they were down, he kicked them.

Someone with a pistol shot him in the small of the back. I saw a vivid splash of scarlet – more like the paint on a Fokker tripe than blood. Being shot only made him angry. Some broken Munros weren't crawling any more.

Other people emerged. Film crew folk. We had made a noise.

A couple of fellows in leather flying jackets and fleece-lined helmets looked up at their bird flying away. Their enviable gear reminded me I could no longer feel my ears and couldn't hear the engine. A small man with a beret screamed silently at us through a megaphone. He must be the director. This day would be a write-off.

We swooped low over the runway. Everyone except the director threw themselves flat on the ground. The martinet kept shouting. I couldn't tell whether he was venting his fury or giving instructions. Cameras couldn't be rolling.

I used the horizon as a guide and got the wings level.

The bullet-hole wasn't neat any more. It was a ragged tear, and spreading like a crack in a plate.

At last, there was more sky in view than ground. Eighty per cent sky was reckoned the best view from a cockpit. As we rose, even La Casa – Old Man Home's clifftop fortress – looked like a model that could be stuck in Junior's pretend battlefield. The rush and the roar went quiet. It was peaceful – but I could have just been bleeding from burst eardrums.

I pushed the stick.

We flew out of the fiefdom of Home.

26

IT'S NEVER TOO LATE TO DIE: A MADCAP MYSTERY
STARRING J.D. DEVLIN – PRIVATE INVESTIGATOR

T WO DAYS AFTER FITTS TOOK AWAY HIS BADGE, Devlin called in a
favour at City Hall. The District Attorney often raided unaffiliated
vice dens at the request of the million-dollar industry's controlling
interests. The last time he shut down the Hot Lunch Box, Devlin let
a little fish slip through the net. Now, courtesy of a grateful unfired
clerk, a document was folded neatly in his wallet. The provisional
licence authorised him to practise as a private detective in the State
of California.

Just like Ray Chandler's man, Marlowe.

At night, he checked under bedcovers for nymphomaniac little
sisters. None had turned up so far.

His only client so far was himself.

His only case was Home House.

But he put in the hours and wore out shoe leather. He showed his
licence to citizens who had no idea what they were looking at. Some were
intimidated enough to answer questions.

Tasso, Norman Quin's landlord, was sick of the sight of him. No, the
bum had not come back to his lodgings since the last time Devlin asked.
No other callers, no mail, no nothing. When Devlin first dropped by
the three-storey rooming house on Descanso, a Rampart dick was sitting

in a Plymouth outside doing a terrible Someone Who Is Not a Cop impersonation.

Devlin slipped Tasso a ten-spot and tossed Quin's room. He found clothes, science books and magazines and stills from *Frankenstein* movies. He pulled down the murphy bed. No nympho there either. He was beginning to doubt they were as thick on the ground as they were in Ray's head.

A medal was on display in a frame above the sink. The kind awarded to those who got mangled in the line of duty rather than fought with especial valour. A 'sorry about your face, soldier' nod from Uncle Sam. No tools or half-built wonder gadgets lay around. The genius must have a workshop somewhere else. Probably on the Pyramid lot.

On the second visit, Tasso's price dropped to five. The hawkshaw had gone and not been replaced. Rampart Homicide didn't think Quin would be coming home for a shave and a shower. Devlin took another look-around. The place was stripped. Most of Quin's things – including the medal – were in a trash can round the back of the rooming house. Two of his reasonably new coats were in the window of the pawnshop across the street.

On the third visit, Devlin refused to hand over even a single. With the scrying eye common among landlords, Tasso saw he was tapped. Someone else was living in Quin's room. A high school quarterback from Hot Coffee, Mississippi who thought he had a shot at being the next Tarzan. He demonstrated his yodel-yell, which went about an octave too high for the king of the jungle. Devlin wished him luck.

Quin was his less interesting quarry anyway.

He had even fewer leads on Witch-Eye.

Laurel Ives was not leasing a house or apartment in Los Angeles. She owned no property. She wasn't registered under that name at any residential or transient hotel.

At the Screen Extras Guild, he asked after women who wore their hair over one eye. The French-Canadian *maman* in charge of the register wasn't fazed by the question. Devlin was impressed. She came back in twenty minutes with seven files. The fourth contained a photograph of

Laurel Ives. When she signed up for the long slow road to stardom, she was blonde and calling herself Philippa Zhan.

Devlin then went back to contacts he'd hit up already. All were a mite less pleased to see their old pal, the ex-city investigator. Word around town was that he had pride of place on Fitts' Shit List. Wearily and warily, they opened the same ledgers and sorted through the same files. He could have guessed the results.

Philippa Zhan was not leasing a house or apartment in Los Angeles. She owned no property. She wasn't registered under that name at any residential or transient hotel.

Until he could arrange premises where prospective clients were less likely to get food poisoning, his office was a booth in the Tramline Diner on Sunset Strip. He sat there and went over what he had so far: a photostat of the file his new mother at the SEG let him have when he asked nicely in French and five copies of the Philippa Zhan headshot. He flattened one out on the tabletop and blacked the hair with a pencil. Having a gap in his sleuthing schedule, he made a good job of retouching. It took all of half an hour.

There, that was his Witch-Eye, all right. Little Miss Wrongness.

On the SEG file, her age was listed as 'early twenties' and her height as '5'6"'. He believed her height. If she was early twenties, then he was late thirties – and he was born in 1888. The only significant notation was 'owns own evening wear'. A short list of films she had worked on included Jimmy Whale's *Show Boat* (Universal) and the Sparx Brothers' *Hockey Puckers* (Pyramid). He didn't remember her in *Show Boat*.

He'd take the photo around booking agencies. Witch-Eye was too distinctive for extra-work. Her face looked like a profile even seen straight-on. She'd draw too much attention from featured players. You weren't supposed to notice a background girl. Joh hadn't thought she talked like an actress – four or five brain cells were working, even after electrocution – but she knew her way around the business. In carny lingo, she was 'with it'.

She must be some kind of freak, or she wouldn't have been in the Home House basement. Did she work tent shows or middling variety halls? See the Amazing Electrical Girl! Or… Madame Philippa – Her Mystic Eye

Sees All! Laurel Ives was no Chinese contortionist or Windmill-Man, but she wasn't wired up to Quin's machine because she owned her own evening wear.

One sign that he was on to something was that he'd picked up an extra shadow. Three, in fact – working as a team. He knew when their shifts ended. They always bumbled handovers. He didn't flatter himself that Fitts would call in favours from the FBI to keep up with a just-canned employee. If they were Pyramid Security, they weren't Ysidro's jackboot cowboys. They could be oil company dicks, sanctioned by the Old Man.

Being off the city payroll, he had lost his spot on the unofficial register of Los Angelenos it wasn't safe to knife in the kidneys. He could cash in favours – though it didn't do to rely too much on the gratitude of folks who had the ridiculous idea that a badge-less Joh Devlin wasn't someone they should be afraid of. Many and varied were the folk he'd annoyed in the course of his former duties. The city had enough Devlin Haters to form a club with a monthly bulletin and membership cards.

He still carried his Colt Super .38. He'd already filed new papers on it. Not being cop-affiliated meant more hoops to jump through before he could do his job. Ray never spent a chapter on Marlowe filling in forms and scaring up six property holders to give him a reference.

A Remington .41 single-shot rimfire derringer was holstered to his ankle by an elastic sock. An antique in working order, only for use in desperation. Firing the doodad guaranteed a couple of broken fingers.

He also kept a folding-knife in his pants pocket. If anyone asked, it was for fruit – though Devlin ate his apples with the peel on. Someone had honed its edge fine enough to shave a lady's legs.

He propped Witch-Eye's photo against the sugar shaker.

This case had Gothic trimmings – secret passages, voodoo, mad science, circus freaks. Devlin left those angles to Ray and Boris. They were at ease with the spook stuff. He was the meat and potatoes private eye.

Strip it down and he was left with a simple game.

Find the Lady.

A shadow fell over the table. He looked up.

A lady had found him.

'BIG MAN,' SHE SAID. 'The cop's dead.'

Fritzie Minikus slid into the U-shaped booth, skirt squeaking on upholstery that hadn't started life as a cow. She sat opposite him, shoulders hunched, blonde frazzle pinned under a blue beret. She wore sunglasses indoors, like someone who didn't want to be recognised.

'Cops die,' he said. 'They get Irish wakes, even if they're Italian.'

Fritzie called for coffee and a plate of pickles with a side of sour cream.

The coffee came quickly. It took a little longer for Chef Holbein to arrange a pickle swastika and scowl at a jug until the cream turned.

'He's paying,' Fritzie said to Lotte, their waitress.

That was news to Devlin.

Fritzie emptied the sugar shaker into her mug. Coffee sloshed over the sides and stained Witch-Eye's photo.

'Was that important?' she asked.

'I have more.'

She glugged as if the coffee were her first beer after three days in the Mojave Desert. She wriggled a balled-up handkerchief past her cuff button and dabbed her chin. Then she glugged again.

Lotte presented the pickles and cream with pride.

Fritzie did a magic trick and made them vanish in thirty seconds. She used the last pickle to scoop the last of the cream.

'Are you pregnant?' he asked.

'What?' she said, in disgust. 'No. Just hungry.'

Like a good publicist, she'd led with an attention-grabber. The dead cop. Devlin was still waiting for the body copy.

'You were talking about a policeman,' he prompted.

'Cardigan Trapnell. Card. Officer Trapnell. Need his badge number?' Devlin didn't. He remembered Trapnell.

'Five of us went down to the basement,' she said. 'Too many of us are dead. Any more and there'll be a "No Vacancies" sign outside the morgue.'

Devlin took her seriously – which, women being women, upset her.

She'd come to him hoping he'd dismiss her worries as hysterical. He should convince her Trapnell's death was a coincidence. Other members of their exclusive party – Devlin, Ysidro, Witch-Eye, herself – were perfectly safe. She resented that it broke another way.

'How was Trapnell knocked off?' he asked.

'He was walking his beat. There was a disturbance in the Dutch bakery on Franklin. The shop with the big windmill over the door. Some characters were throwing food at each other like in a Mack Sennett two-reeler. Trapnell stepped in to break up the hullaballoo and took a pie to the face. The fixings were dosed with something – cyanide or arsenic. He was dead in thirty seconds. The comedians folded up their act and vanished. No, Trapnell wasn't allergic to cream. A one-in-a-million shot didn't clog his mouth and nose and suffocate him. A kid sneaked a lick of pie filling off the counter before the ambulance came. He got instant bellyache and had to be carted off to have his stomach pumped. It was an assassination. Professional job. Neat as you please.'

Moritz Stewart – the butler. Now, Card Trapnell – the cop.

In addition to the freaks. And maybe Ward Home Junior.

Enough corpses for a *Dime Detective* novella. Enough even for *Morticians' Monthly*.

Fritzie distracted herself from her jitters by reading the tabloid-sized menu. The poison pie incident hadn't put her off her feed.

Every diner on the Strip had a gimmick. The Tramline's was meals from around the world that sound like something you wouldn't want to eat. Chef Holbein's fare mostly turned out delicious – but some patrons regretted it later.

Fritzie ordered toad in the hole.

Devlin indicated to Lotte that this would be on the lady's cheque.

'Fine,' she snapped. 'If you want to play it that way. Are you aware that the uproarious farce *Minnie and Maisie's Argentine Adventure* is shortly to open in motion picture theatres across the country?'

'I am now, though I don't see the relevance.'

Fritzie took a notebook out of her purse and jotted down a figure.

'I am a publicist for Pyramid Pictures. I have just publicised Pyramid's latest – and some have said finest – production. This is now a business lunch…'

'… which you can claim on expenses.'

She smiled. 'Bright boy. You should be a detective.'

Her food came. Fritzie was disappointed no actual amphibian was involved. The French eat frogs, after all. Devlin, well-travelled, knew what toad in the hole was. Fritzie ate up anyway.

Lotte brought the coffee jug back. They had refills.

'Laurel Ives is in the wind,' said Devlin. 'Dan Ysidro has a private army. And I've not yet rented office space, unless you count this booth…'

'… where I found you. After only three phone calls. It takes four to get a hair appointment for a Chihuahua.'

'A fair point. I'll rotate booths from now on. What I'm getting at is that they clipped Trapnell because he was easiest to locate. A cop walks a beat. You know where he'll be at any time. A few minutes after the first cop walked the first beat crooks memorised his schedule and knew to thieve at the other end of the street from where he was. Trapnell got ambushed easily.'

'We, however, are *forewarned*!

Encouraged by that, she swallowed the last of her sausage pudding.

'You can get me onto the Pyramid lot,' he told her.

'Sure. I can throw on a screening of *Trooper for the Prosecution*. We're seeking testimonials from law enforcement professionals.'

'"The most accurate screen depiction of the workings of the Los Angeles District Attorney's Office to date!" – J.D. Devlin – Private Investigator".'

'You want on the lot so you can talk with Chief Ysidro?'

'A wearisome task – but we can't really duck it. I would sleep poorly if he were splatted with a deadly dessert before we could warn him.'

They settled up with Lotte. Devlin took a cue from Fritzie and put the cheque in his wallet. Now he was working for himself, he must be fastidious (and inventive) with receipts and expenses.

He took his hat and trenchcoat off the hooks by the door.

'I can recommend a spotless dry cleaner,' said Fritzie.

Devlin knew the coat was moderately grubby.

'It's going to rain,' he said. 'This is my raincoat. It only comes out of the wardrobe twice a year. You know, when it rains. Coat gets wet, coat dries. Goes back in the dark for another six months. Whenever I fetch it out, I think "I should get this cleaned" but it's about to rain and I need it to wear, so… it's a cycle.'

'So you *don't* wear a dirty trenchcoat just to look like a hardboiled shamus on a detective magazine cover? To go with the gun I see a-peeping out of your jacket.'

'I rarely wear it at all. This is California. It's notoriously sunny. Eskimos wear Bermuda shorts here.'

'Okey-dokey, Big Man. The coat is let off, on the condition it's cleaned and pressed after its next soaking. What's the hat's excuse?'

'I'm ending this interrogation,' he said, holding the door open for her.

As they stepped out onto the sidewalk, Devlin heard a whistling.

On instinct, he shoved Fritzie forwards and himself backwards. She opened her mouth to protest…

… and a safe dropped out of the sky. It took its own sweet time about falling – or else the last split seconds of Devlin's life were slowed down enough for him to reflect on the many errors and missteps that had brought him to the point when he was crushed under a heavy object.

Only he got out of the way in time – and his perception sped up.

The safe thunked into the asphalt. Black tar oozed up through cracks.

It was a huge, old-fashioned, icebox-sized affair. Brassbound and stamped with a curlicued Wells Fargo logo. A three-man job to heft it to a window and tip it out.

But the Tramline Diner was a single-storey building.

Devlin looked up and saw a dinosaur-neck crane, with a still-swinging hook. The crane had been mothballed on a shut-down construction site next to the diner. It was some New Deal development where graft ran out before the job got finished. The safe had been dangling in a sturdy net until an unkind soul let it fall.

Somewhere, someone was laughing.

It wasn't Devlin. When he threw himself on the ground, his pocket-knife broke. He was lucky not to open an artery.

His coat would have to go to the cleaner's now.

Fritzie was more terrified than angry.

A flung pie. A falling safe. Slapstick gags. Groaners.

This was a theme crime spree. Like the Mystery and Imagination Murders, inspired by the immortal works of Edgar A. Poe. Fritzie called the characters who rubbed out Trapnell 'the comedians'. She was a fine, instinctive detective.

Prospero Prince was a madman. This was a different can of Looney Tunes. It'd have been a cinch for any sensible torpedo to stake out the Old Dutch Mill or the Tramline and spray lead at folks other folks wanted got gone. With a tommy gun, no one hears a whistle and dodges out of the way.

In that scenario, he and Fritzie would be dead. But it wouldn't be *funny*.

Not that these gags were funny. They were tired. Corny.

Laurel and Hardy could get laughs with a pie fight. Comedians who weren't geniuses couldn't. But they still flung flans.

'I know who's after us,' he told Fritzie.

They were in his Studebaker, rolling up to the Home Estate.

'Pray tell,' she said.

'You won't like it.'

'I can't imagine I'd like it whoever was trying to kill me.'

'Pinky and Gecko,' he said. 'The Sparx Brothers.'

'Not Screwball?'

'He's in the pokey.'

'Not any more. Orders came down to pull strings. I had him bailed on the recognisance of his family yesterday.'

'But they're not his real brothers.'

'He *might* have a family.'

'You won't see the funny, but as the Sparx Brothers go, this is a half-decent gag.'

'What – the falling safe routine? Felix the Cat would turn up his nose at such material.'

'No. The joke is getting you to spring the button man so he can aim a safe at your head.'

'Oh, I get it. I ain't laughing, but I get it. I know you – like everyone else in this burg – think my job is ridiculous. Making nice with mean drunks and vicious fairies and Hedda Hopper to get stories in gossip rags about Dry Bone Mullins or the Tuba Tearaways. But it's a job and I'm good at it. The other part, the worser part, is keeping stories *out* of gossip columns. Not just who's running round with who else's wife – frankly, we circulate those ourselves. No matter what the bluestockings say, audiences like a screen star who cheats. The worser part is the messes you have to mop up. Messes that make you sick to your stomach. A hot-foot cripples a chorus girl. Some joker sets fire to her slipper for a quick laugh and ends her career so she has to limp back to Fresno. A prop man wakes up hogtied in a trunk, with a piano wire noose round his neck attached to his ankles. The sucker was savvy and didn't struggle – not wanting to cut off his own head for a punchline. That's the Sparx Brothers for you. Whatever you want to call them, the lowest and dirtiest names… they're worse.'

'French intellectuals prize *les Frères Sparx* above all other cinema. Even Soviet operas about tractor production come a distant second.'

'Jean Cocteau doesn't have to dole out hush-money to the victims.'

Fritzie was recognised at the Home Estate gate. Devlin drove onto the Pyramid lot.

'Three inconspicuous fellows are tailing me,' he told her. 'The Sparxes without make-up?'

'Their stand-ins,' she said. 'Slaves, more like. When a court ordered Gecko to take the cure, his stand-in spent a month drinking celery juice on a dry-out farm. The poor sap came home clean and sober to find Gecko flicking his long tongue into Mrs Stand-In. Know Gecko's catchphrase?'

'"You have to laugh, chum!"'

'Yup. Gecko never stops saying it. "You have to laugh, chum." The gag-writer who came up with that cut his own throat. Couldn't live with the guilt.'

Devlin parked the Studebaker outside the low, anonymous building that was the movie studio's own police station. Above the lintel was an old-timey sign that read 'Sheriff Dan's Jail'. It had bullet-holes in it.

Fritzie opened her door.

'Watch out for banana peel,' he told her.

She didn't laugh.

Ysidro wasn't seeing the funny side either.

'This you, Devlin?' he snapped.

'What me?' Devlin responded.

They were in an outer office. A woman in a tailored black shirt sat at a reception desk. A couple of Pyramid goons milled about, polished belts and boots creaking.

Their boss was angry. Red-faced.

Devlin was supposed to break down and confess, but had no idea of what he was suspected.

Ysidro had to be reminded of Fritzie's name.

A distinct smell of the stables circulated.

A whinny and a snort came from behind a door with 'Daniel Ysidro, Chief of Security' lettered on it.

Devlin remembered seeing photographs – which Fritzie had probably taken – of Ysidro posing in a mock-up of a Wild West Sheriff's lair, decorated with props from the Dan Starr Westerns. Roll-top desk, iron stove, rack of long guns, wanted posters. In his shiny black blouse and peaked cap, Ysidro didn't match the design scheme. The set dressing wasn't his idea.

Ysidro couldn't get into his office and wasn't happy about it.

A cowboy arrived – in jeans, boots and hat, not the uniform of one of the dictator nations. On second glance, Devlin saw the cowboy was also an Indian – olive face, black braids, scalping knife in bead-decorated buckskin sheath. He walked oddly, as if he'd taken a gutshot forward dive off a livery stable roof but missed the mattresses. Another casualty of the quickie Western production line.

'Standing Pat, it's about time…' said Ysidro.

'Stunt pays twenty dollar,' said the Indian.

Ysidro was so mad, a shakedown couldn't make him angrier.

'Pay the man.'

The receptionist took a lock-box out of a desk drawer, opened it with a key she wore on a chain round her neck and counted out twenty singles.

They stayed in a pile on the desk. Standing Pat looked at the money and at Ysidro. Sheriff Dan lost the staring contest. He stuffed the bills into the Indian's front shirt pocket.

Ysidro and his men stood aside.

Standing Pat opened the office door a crack.

A whinny came from inside.

The Indian shut the door and turned to Ysidro.

'Stunt pays forty dollar,' he said.

Devlin had been wrong. Ysidro could get angrier.

He drew fast. He'd been a trick-shot in the rodeo. It wasn't his gun-slinger skills kiddies laughed at.

He didn't shoot Standing Pat, but aimed at his own office door.

Suddenly, all his minions were pleading with him. The receptionist was particularly upset.

'Don't do it,' she said. 'Don't kill Trooper!'

'Think of the children, Chief,' said one of the goons. 'That nag gets more fan mail than Clark Gable.'

'Trooper is beloved of young and old,' said Fritzie. 'I speak for Publicity in saying the front office would take a dim view of any Pyramid employee – most likely any *former* Pyramid employee – who caused him harm. What's he doing in your office anyway?'

Ysidro holstered his iron but had no answers.

'It's a gag,' said the other goon. 'Has to be, right? A nutty gag.'

'"You have to laugh, chum,"' quoted Devlin.

That brought a chill to the room.

Standing Pat's hand went to the handle of his knife.

'Those rat-bastards,' spat Ysidro.

Devlin opened the office door and peeked. Ysidro's cosy inner sanctum was almost entirely filled by a large horse. On his hindquarters was a cavalry insignia – a shield with what looked like the silhouette of a chess knight burned above a diagonal bar. Even Fritzie couldn't sell the story that the brand was a birthmark. Trooper's studio bio claimed he was descended from a mount that survived Custer's Last Stand. Lately, he had been fed with something spicier than oats and hay. Quantities of near-liquid faecal matter had exploded out of his rear end and redecorated the entirety of the room, including the ceiling. You couldn't read wanted posters for crap.

Trooper made a nasal, throttling sound and convulsed. A large bolus of solid dung shot out from under his tail.

Devlin shut the door promptly.

'We'll leave you to it,' he told Ysidro. 'And come back later.'

'Stunt pays *sixty* dollar,' said Standing Pat.

'Pay off this extortionist,' Ysidro told the receptionist. 'And fire whoever was on duty last night.'

'Hump Conroy,' she said. 'Have to find him to fire him. He wasn't where he should have been when I came to work.'

Devlin took Fritzie's arm and guided her to the outer door.

'Hold your... hold right there,' said Ysidro. 'I want answers from you, Devlin.'

They agreed to stick around.

The receptionist went through the rigmarole with the cash box again. Thirty-eight dollars in singles and two in piles of coins. The Indian was cleaning them out.

Ysidro took the money and handed it nicely to Standing Pat.

The Indian could have asked for Ysidro's father's pocket watch and got away with it.

He opened the door and squeezed into the office, clucking as he approached Trooper. It was supposed to be calming.

'You've heard about Officer Trapnell?' said Devlin.

Ysidro nodded. Most of his attention was on the horse being coaxed out of his domain – which would now need a thorough clean-out. A snag was hit. Trooper couldn't take two steps because he was hobbled by a wire looped around his ankles like the 'running W' rigs used to make horses in battle scenes take spectacular tumbles. It was also similar to that nasty trick played on the prop man who kept his head. Standing Pat had to kneel – carefully avoiding the stinking pools – to deal with the wire.

'A safe fell on the sidewalk this morning,' Devlin told Ysidro. 'Missed us by inches. And a cop was killed by a pie.'

'Get the picture?' said Fritzie. 'This isn't only a joke.'

Ysidro was short-fused, not stupid. He knew this was serious.

Standing Pat took out his knife.

Ysidro stood in the doorway of his office, impotently supervising.

Trooper was skittish and unhappy, but everything that could come out of him had.

Standing Pat cut the wire... the length now not attached to the horse's legs was snatched away on a fisherman's reel. Gears turned and weights fell. The rack of guns behind the chief's desk flapped down and went off. The wire was wound round the stocks and through the trigger guards.

The horse panicked and bolted – tightening the rig, falling painfully, neck banging against the rim of the desk.

Ysidro turned around. His chest was a red ruin.

He made it two steps further before he dropped.

Written at the back of the case where the rigged-up guns had been stored was 'You have to laugh, chum'.

—

'How did they know Ysidro would be standing in the right place to get shot?' Fritzie asked.

'I doubt they cared,' said Devlin. 'If a gag flops, they spring the next one. They're cruel, not cunning. We dodged the safe. That must have been as much effort to set up as Ysidro's office.'

'We should still be worried?'

'Very much so. The next joke could be a thousand-volt joy-buzzer or an exploding cigar packed with nitro. Don't shake hands with a clown. Or accept a smoke. Or sniff a boutonnière.'

'A boutonnière?'

'It'll squirt vitriol.'

They were back in the car, getting out of Dodge before sundown.

With Sheriff Dan dead, Pyramid Security was in a state of collapse. Luise Driss, the receptionist, pinned on the badge until a man willing to fill Chief Ysidro's boots stepped up. She discovered her second corpse of the day. Propped in the supplies closet, feet in a bucket, throttled with a rubber snake. Hump Conroy, the night-guard. Someone had painted a red nose on him.

Fritzie wouldn't leave until she was sure Trooper was okay. The shotgun volley hadn't done anything to calm the nag. Standing Pat had to work carefully to remove the rest of the tripwire without cutting his hooves off.

Fritzie was half soft-boiled. A horse being mistreated upset her more than several murders.

She kept adjusting her sunglasses. They pinched her temples. In the basement of Home House, she'd seen corpses. In Sheriff Dan's Jail, she'd seen someone die. Feeling bad about harm done to an animal might be her way of getting through today and the next day and the rest of her life without screaming herself into a cell with quilted walls.

They needed somewhere safe to hole up.

Fritzie ran through options, but Publicity's usual stash house for persons the studio wanted out of the headlines for a spell was well-known to the Sparx Brothers. That the comedians had permission – orders, frankly – to kill the Chief of Security suggested Ysidro's posse were just for keeping autograph hounds away from Erich von Stroheim. Rougher stuff was authorised by other departments. Devlin looked up at La Casa and shuddered.

He had to slow the Studebaker. There was a hold-up ahead. It was usually easier getting off a studio lot than getting on. Now, this side of the gate, a line of vehicles created a tailback.

A guard was checking trunks and back seats for stowaways. A Pyramid Security cap was slapped on his mop of red corkscrew curls. Pinky Sparx. One of his props was an ice-pick. The running gag was that he couldn't pass a balloon without popping it. He also jabbed pompous diplomats and dignified dowagers in their rears. Pinky opened trunks with his left hand, ice-pick gripped in his right fist – ready to stab throats or shoulder joints.

Devlin didn't join the exit queue, but swerved into the entry lane and aimed the Studebaker at an oncoming flock of dress extras. They were just off the bus, spiffy in evening wear (their own, presumably). The crowd parted either side of the car's prow, feathers and finery in disarray.

Devlin stepped on the gas and sped away from the Home Estate.

⌒

HE DROVE SOUTH BY SOUTH-EAST, from Hollywood to Bunker Hill.

Fritzie twisted to peer out the back window, then faced front.

'No one's following us,' she said.

'No one *new* is following us,' said Devlin. 'Our old friends are still on the job. The stand-ins.'

She turned again and gave the traffic behind them another good staring-at.

'I can't see anyone.'

'That's because they're in front of us. It's the smart way to hang a tail. The mark is so busy doing what you just did – looking over their shoulder – they don't notice they're seeing the same rear bumper all day.'

'Which car is it?'

'The midget,' he said.

'The American Austin,' she said, spotting it at once.

'The shrimp on wheels. A comedy car, of course.'

Their tail guessed they'd take Figueroa, but didn't foresee Devlin turning off into Court. It took fancy driving to catch up. Devlin had to dawdle at a traffic light to let the tail reattach.

'Don't hunch in your seat or stare as they overtake, or they'll know we know they're there.'

She saw the sense and suppressed her instincts.

The Austin trundled past. The modified British car design wasn't popular. Americans liked their cars like they liked their football players, movie cowboys and gang bosses… big, loud and violent. But if Devlin were in the Austin and the stand-ins had the Studebaker, he'd have an advantage. A longer car couldn't have got back on them after missing Court Street. The silly little thing could hide in traffic. But, once spotted, it was a wasp bothering a picnic. Hard to shoo off by hand-flapping, easy to swat with a rolled-up newspaper.

From Court, Devlin turned onto Olive. At this hour of the afternoon, the thoroughfare was busy.

He idled at the kerb near Angels Flight. People huddled in heavy coats at the boarding station of the funicular railway. Its two cars, Olivet and Sinai, crawled up and down the three-hundred-foot track between Olive Street and Hill Street all day.

'Get out and grab attention,' he told Fritzie. 'Adjust your stockings or something.'

'You see too many movies.'

'Everybody sees too many movies. Whose fault is that?'

'Publicists,' she said, pushing the door open.

Fritzie sashayed up to a gent who looked like an Anglican priest but was probably a runaway bigamist and stock swindler. She wagged a cigarette at him, asking for a light.

All eyes on the half-pint blonde. Excellent.

Devlin cruised on, scouting for a parking spot.

The nippy Austin had squeezed into a gap between two block-long roadsters. Devlin seriously considered the ridiculous toy as a work vehicle. The potential for sneakiness was possibly a worthwhile trade-off for the jibes from colleagues with more manly automobiles. A body wouldn't fit in the trunk, though – unless you specialised in murdered dwarfs.

As he passed the Austin, he saw two stand-ins in the front seats. Both wore natty straw hats. The car must be cramped as a diving bell. That ruled it out for him. With his frame, he needed something roomy. In the driver's seat of an Austin, he'd be a big bear in a small cage.

One stand-in was his tail. The other must be Fritzie's. So they'd been following her too.

When he and she got together, their tails had teamed up.

A mistake. Devlin still couldn't tell how smart they were.

Had they expected to clock off after the falling safe? They might be on overtime. When he ran tail-jobs, Devlin made sure his ops worked relatively short shifts. It was a boring job, for the most part. The most placid, dogged sleuths got edgy after a couple of hours at it. Also, a turnover of faces meant the mark was less likely to spot a shadow.

He found a parking place by a flower stall. Getting out of the car, he saw one of the stand-ins strolling towards Angels Flight, where a bit of a fuss was in progress. Fritzie was making her scene.

Devlin bought flowers – the posy of the day, black-red roses.

He took out his broken pocket-knife. He slid the long, thin snapped-off blade into the posy, careful not to slice his fingertips.

He walked down Olive, silently whistling a jaunty air.

As he came up behind the Austin, he did a hop, a skip and a trip… and jammed the roses against the rear tyre. He swore in French and German to cover the hiss of escaping air. Satisfied the rip was good and irreparable, he left the blade stuck where it was. He dumped the ruined flowers in the gutter.

The stand-in behind the wheel was red-faced.

The little twerp was so intent on not looking at Devlin that he fixed his eyes down and pretended his mark didn't exist – though no sighted, hearing person could fail to notice the idiot blundering against their car. Devlin had put a dent in the rear fender by kneeling on it. Austin must use tin-foil for their bodywork.

He walked rapidly back to the Studebaker.

The stand-in got out of the car and discovered the damage. A regular citizen would call out to have Devlin stopped. A cop was standing right on the block. The stand-in got redder and kept schtumm.

Devlin drove the short stretch to Angels Flight. The bit of fuss had escalated to something of a kerfuffle. Fritzie was making accusations. Gallants just off the up car formed an impromptu mob to prevent the reverend gent from escaping on the down car. Fritzie played a wronged woman scene that would have been too unsubtle for an out-of-town *Lucia di Lammermoor*.

The stand-in tailing her stopped in his tracks.

That convenient cop was about to notice the kerfuffle blossoming into a full-blown howdydo.

Devlin swung the passenger door open and whistled.

Fritzie withdrew from the howdydo and slid into the Studebaker.

'The nerve of some people,' she said, still in character.

Behind them, chaos escalated. Two small, undistinguished men took out their frustration on their straw hats.

The car picked up speed along Olive. This neighbourhood had sprung up in high-button shoes days. The wooden houses were decorated like cakes, with Gothic spires or minaret-like cupolas. After the War, the fashionable and wealthy moved up the coast, leaving behind sub-divided mansions rickety enough to slide three streets down when the next quake hit.

They had shaken their tails. Just to be sure, Devlin took random turns up and down the hill. Finally satisfied, he headed back north by north-west. There must be a third stand-in. He didn't appear to be on this job. Was he looking for Laurel Ives? And having any luck?

'Where are we going now we're alone and fancy-free?' Fritzie asked.

'A place I know,' he said.

———

THE SCUFFED-UP MESS around the bungalow used to be a Japanese garden of raked sand and artfully arranged rocks. It had been ravaged during the crimes and trampled in the investigation. Only one track gave access to the property, a steep driveway off a side road in Laurel Canyon. The place had a garage that would do for the Studebaker. The Duesenberg Torpedo Phaeton that used to live there had been impounded. The blood soaked into the upholstery would knock a slice off the value when it came up for public auction.

'Where are we?' Fritzie asked.

'Somewhere something happened.'

'Do I want to know about it?'

'Possibly not.'

'Worse than what we've seen lately?'

'God yes.'

She sank in the passenger seat and adjusted her glasses.

'Take them off if they pinch,' he said.

She was affronted by the notion. Which was odd.

He got out of the Studebaker and walked around it like a chauffeur, opening the door for her ladyship. She was rubbery on her legs and he stopped her falling. He had a notion she'd not be unhappy leaning on him longer than was strictly necessary for her health. He had another notion he might not object too strongly. It was only in Ray Chandler's stories the private eye couldn't trust the dame in the case – and in *The Maltese Falcon*. He might not write English as well as Hammett and Ray, but he saw their tics. When J.D. Devlin, Private Investigator, typed the yarn, the scenario was more like the real world, where the dame shouldn't trust the detective.

A sliding door led to the bungalow. It was padlocked but he had a fold-out wallet of burglar tools. Every investigator on the DA's staff had a set. Whenever a cracksman got convicted, his lockpicks went missing from the evidence room. It didn't do to skimp on the tools of the trade.

'Are we breaking and entering?'

'Hard to say. No one owns this place. That makes this a grey issue.'

'This is America. Everywhere is owned.'

The padlock clicked and the chain fell away. They stepped into a small, stale kitchen. Fingerprint powder was congealed on Formica surfaces.

'We made a thorough search of records,' he told her. 'This isn't an address. On city plans, it's a vacant lot. The family found here had no names we could pin to them. It's an interesting point of law. If we couldn't verify they were ever alive, was killing them really a crime?'

'How did you know they were a family?'

'General resemblance.'

Fritzie wandered out of the kitchen.

The bungalow was mostly one big room for sleeping and eating in. A picture window afforded a view of the garden. A front door, easy to unfasten from this side, led to a canopied porch. Swords had been hung on the wall. You could see the spaces where they were missing, white and unspeckled. The only furniture was a table so low every cop who went through the place bruised their shins. The people who died here must have sat on mats or leaned against each other.

'Have you got any theories?' she asked.

'A million of 'em. None the DA wanted to hear. This was my second strike with Fitts. It nearly got me fired. He waited till Home House to award me the Order of the Boot. It takes juice to make a place or person invisible. Pay-offs have to be made. Thing is, no bribes had been handed over. The city employees who could expedite such a miracle were furious it had been accomplished without them getting their taste. Complaints were made. Nothing came of them. We kicked around for a week or so, because what was done here was an *affront*. We couldn't determine the names of the dead but were motivated to avenge them. Even cops have kids and parents and best friends. Fitts got a telephone call while he was in a restaurant. I have no idea who from. He doubled over and was sick in the booth. We all got reassigned. This isn't a case. The bungalow isn't here. The people who died were already ghosts. By moving in, we become ghosts too. When that storm they're predicting hits, it won't rain on this plot.'

'Really?'

'No. That's poetic licence. But we are gone from mortal ken.'

Fritzie looked around. 'I could really go for a chair,' she said.

Devlin chuckled. 'There's lawn furniture stacked in the garage. We can haul it out when we bring in the groceries.'

They'd stopped at a market for supplies. Fritzie had been puzzled when he told her to pick up a sheaf of magazines – pulps, slicks, general interest – from the newsstand. The bungalow didn't have a radio. They'd need entertainment. Sitting on a folding chair or lying on a mat thinking about who wanted them dead would get enervating after an hour or two.

'You guarantee we're safe? No one can find us.'

'Ay-up. The cops who worked this scene were told to forget directions to the place and if asked, deny it ever existed. I was too.'

'But you came back.'

'Because of circumstances. Unique circumstances. I half-expected it not to be here. Like the hostel in the ghost story where the traveller goes back the morning after being scared off in the night and finds a ruin where once long long ago there was a coaching inn…'

'The ten shilling note he used to pay for his supper on a rock, paper-weighted by a pebble.'

'You know that one? Yes, like that. But it's still here.'

She was already pacing the room. And she hadn't seen it when the original occupants were strewn around like torn-up cushions.

'You know, I feel strangely *privileged*,' she said.

'I understand. All the tension goes away. You can breathe here. You could take off your glasses.'

'I could,' she allowed. 'But won't just yet.'

It was getting on for evening. One of the electric lamps still worked. He suggested she fix food.

'Yes, Master,' she groaned.

'Hey, I opened doors for you,' he said. 'Cuts both ways. After we eat, we have to hike up to the Boulevard. Best to get it done before full dark. We'll most likely have one night's real sleep before the hilarity resumes.'

She selected a can of tomato soup and was about to pour it into a pan.

'Just for my peace of mind,' he said, 'rinse that out before putting in anything that'll end up in our stomachs.'

'Looks clean enough,' she said, examining the pan.

'Humour me,' he said.

Without further argument, she ran water and rubbed imaginary spots with a dishcloth, pretending to be Lady Macbeth. Fritzie thought that was funny. Devlin knew it wasn't.

She got the soup on the burner.

The kitchen was too small for them both, so he fit into the doorframe and watched her fuss – putting cans and packets in cupboards, scouting out bowls and cutlery, which she made a show of cleaning. She wiped the fingerprint powder away without asking what it was.

'No knives,' she said, looking in a drawer.

'There wouldn't be,' he said.

'No need to cut soup anyway.'

She still wore those sunglasses. Devlin knew wives and girlfriends who did that, to hide the bruises. He presumed Fritzie wasn't married. She hadn't mentioned any steadies. Her job was like his, murder on romance. Twenty-four hours a day of unsocial activity.

'What's this about a hike?' she said. 'I'm not dressed for mountaineering.'

'I have to make a phone call. So do you. Just one each should be enough. If it isn't, we wait two days and try again.'

She was puzzled.

'This place isn't just invisible,' he said. 'It's defensible.'

'You couldn't tell that from the former residents, if I understand what you've implied.'

'No. That was an unusual feature of the case. One of many. Mart Maxwell said I was nuts, but I got the feeling they *invited* what happened... sat here, in limbo, awaiting the fall of the axe... calm, even, when it came. There was, as they say, a ritual element.'

'I'm not reassured.'

'Don't be. I want you on your guard.'

He got his foot up on a stool, hiked his pants-cuff and pulled the Remington .41 out of his sock.

'Cute,' she said. 'For me?'

He handed it over.

'Most girls prefer mink.'

'It's a last resort,' he told her. 'For close-work. Best you press it against someone's ribs when you fire it. Someone else's ribs.'

She twirled the gun.

'You know, if I use this, I'd worry about breaking my fingers.'

She knew something about firearms. Good.

'This is a forest idyll,' he said. 'Peaceful and away from the cares of the world. But we can't stay here forever.'

'To me, this is not news.'

'We have a problem – *three* problems – and we need them to be over...'

'Pinky, Gecko and Screwball.'

'"You have to laugh, chum!"' he shrilled.

Her mouth went tight.

'Don't *ever* do the voice again,' she said. 'I mean it.'

The soup simmered. She put the single-shot pistol down and poured from the pan into bowls.

To prove a point, he reached for the gun.

With her free hand, she picked it up and pointed it at his nose.

'That was a rehearsal,' she said. 'On opening night, I'd toss hot soup in your eyes before shooting you.'

'You work in *publicity*?'

'Rough game, Big Man. Hell of a rough game.'

Now she was intimating horrors. It was becoming a competition.

'You've solved murders,' she said.

'A few,' he admitted.

'Fritzie Minikus has *covered them up*.'

She spoke as if she was proud and cynical about it – but using the third person was a tell. She was distancing herself from dark deeds done. Nobody in this business was content with just the one face.

'Soup's on,' she said.

———

FROM AN ALL-NIGHT DRUG STORE on Laurel Canyon Boulevard, Devlin called Mart Maxwell at home. He said he expected an important parcel to arrive at the DA's office addressed to him and asked Maxwell to forward it. In strictest confidence, he admitted he was hiding out in Blood Bath Bungalow. He told his former colleague he'd pay him back with passes to a preview of the new Robin Hood picture. Mrs Mart could meet Basil Rathbone. Maxwell was reluctant until Devlin dangled that offer. He might go through with the deal, rather than just say he would and forget it. Of course, he'd have a long wait for the parcel.

'That should do it,' he said, after he hung up.

Fritzie understood the play. She made a call, giggling all the way through it. Devlin wondered what had been wrong with her screen test. She was a pretty good actress. He could see her as Heroine's Best Friend.

'Who did I ring?' she asked him.

'No idea.'

'Fraulein Driss. Ysidro's receptionist. Loosest lips on the lot. I asked her to cover for me when I'm not at work tomorrow. I've confided that I'm cosied up to a no-good guy in a love nest in the Canyon. She swore not to tell.'

He knew that song.

'Funny thing is,' she went on. 'I believe she believes it when she promises. A blot on her brain means she believes she really truly can keep a secret. Whenever she tells anyone, it doesn't count... they wouldn't pass it on, would they? Then they do...'

That was the plan.

'Know what Fritzie always says? "If you really want to publicise something, tell people *not* to talk about it." Trade secret.'

She was doing that third person thing again.

And still giggling, carrying on the phoney act she'd sold the receptionist.

Did terror make her light-headed?

He would have to watch that.

'Why did we go to all the trouble of ditching the stand-ins, not to mention ruining the day of an amiable old cuss who wasn't hurting anyone, if we want to be tracked down?'

'Because throwing off tails is what people like us would do in a situation like this.'

'Clever,' she said.

'If – to a certain extent – you do what people expect, they get comfortable. They presume they know what you'll do next. Which is when you do something else and they regret their lazy assumptions.'

———

HE WOKE IN THE MIDDLE OF THE NIGHT, padded quietly past Fritzie to use the tiny john and silently checked doors and windows. Not wanting to wake her, he went outside to smoke. He couldn't resist walking to the steep drive. When they returned from their hike, he'd raked over the tyre tracks and their footprints. He held his lighter aloft like a torch and looked up the slope. The road was cut off from sight by the gradient. Thick chaparral grew from the roadside edge of the property to the shore of the sand lagoon. Weeds hadn't invaded the Japanese garden.

Word couldn't have reached the Sparx Brothers yet. Devlin guessed it would take most of tomorrow to get around the watering holes, squad rooms and pool halls. The day after, there'd be items in the trades. The day after that, there'd be headlines in the *Los Angeles Times*. One way or another, there'd be obituaries.

The night was so cold he couldn't smell the sage, usually so strong here many denizens of Laurel Canyon got permanently woozy. This hillside had inhabitants you couldn't avoid labelling 'denizens'. Musicians, artists, gurus, indoor bums. Renegades had holed up in mountain shacks with shotguns around the turn of the century, expecting law at their door any minute, only for the haphazard city to grow around their hideouts until their beards were so long and grey they no longer looked like their wanted posters.

The bungalow wasn't the only abandoned house in the neighbourhood. Los Angeles only seemed too new to be haunted. Here was where its ghosts moved.

Wet specks on his face and hands weren't quite rain. That storm was coming. Good cover for a slaying, but the killers would get wet.

He saw grim justice in God dumping buckets on the murder clowns.

Back inside, he watched Fritzie sleep in a nest on the floor, head on a pillow. Her folded sunglasses were placed carefully on her blue beret. In the half-light, he saw her eyes weren't blackened. They moved under closed lids. She was dreaming.

Something was up with her.

Asleep, she didn't look like herself. He felt his lighter in his pocket but let it go. The flint strike would wake her. The derringer was stashed under her beret, in easy reach. She might plug him on instinct and then where would they be?

He returned to his own nest and got a few more hours' shut-eye.

THE NEXT DAY, it started raining in earnest. If he had been here, it would have rained *on* Ernest. And all around him. He would be a glum, wet Ernest.

'Morning, Big Man,' said Fritzie, from the kitchen. 'Wouldn't it be funny if a mudslide got us before the Sparxes did?'

She was cooking again – breakfast. And had her dark glasses on.

Fritzie hadn't worn cheaters in the basement of Home House. They were a new thing.

'What if they find *her* first,' said Fritzie, angling a hand over half her face to show who she meant.

'Witch-Eye?'

She nodded. 'Laurel Ives, wasn't it?'

'Or Philippa Zhan.'

'Stephen Someone, I've heard,' she said. 'Like a guy's name.'

'You know more than me.'

They sat cross-legged at the low table and ate.

'We had files on them. In Publicity. The giant, the contortionist, the mind-reader. And your wall-eyed wench.'

'I've seen a file on Herbert Holloway, the giant. Not from your department – from the Lamia Munro Clinic.'

'Same diff. We publicise the Clinic too. You think screen stars are vain, you should try quack doctors.'

'Someone delivered said file to me. Anonymously.'

'Mystery deepens.'

'I had wondered whether the unknown giver of gifts was you.'

She splayed her fingers on her chest like a silent movie flirt and said, 'Little old Fritziekins?'

'I know. Stupid idea. You have to suspect everyone. It was probably Dr Voodoo scattering bait…'

… which might have netted different fish.

He'd not heard from Ray or Boris in nearly a week. He'd phoned Ray's apartment two days ago, to share what little information he'd turned up. Cissy told him her husband hadn't been home for a spell – which, he gathered, wasn't unusual. Devlin liked Cissy, who was older than she looked and not as daffy as she pretended to be. One way to get along with a drinker was to take no notice. Then he'd called Casa Karloff and Beata answered. She was minding the telephone while *Tía* Gracia scooped fronds out of the pool. The child urgently wanted Devlin's professional opinion on who would win in a fight between the Lone Ranger and Flash Gordon. The matter was undecided when she accidentally cut off the call – and he hadn't phoned back.

'Where have you gone?' Fritzie asked.

Her 'little old Fritziekins' bit had fallen flat.

'I was weighing up strategy, weapons and skills.'

She was impressed. Which gave him a guilt pang, so he fessed up.

'This girl I know…'

'Romance in the air? Should I be jealous?'

'She's all of nine years old.'

'Some Oscar-nominated featured players no one wants to work with any more wouldn't care.'

'She asked me who would win in a fight between the Lone Ranger and Flash Gordon.'

'This is a subject you dwell on?'

'It seemed important to her.'

'Go on, then… who *would* win?'

'The Lone Ranger.'

'A man on a horse in a fight with a man in a rocket ship, Big Man? I can't see it. Doesn't Flash Gordon have a disintegrator ray? No amount of Hi-Yo Silver stands up against that.'

'Flash Gordon has space weapons but isn't trained to use them. He's from Earth. His ray-gun is from the Planet Mongo. He's been lucky so far but if he tries a fast draw he could vaporise his own thigh.'

'A fair point.'

'The Lone Ranger uses silver bullets because – he says – killing a man should have a high price.'

'He might also be loaded for lycanthrope.'

'That would be a different radio show.'

'Conceded.'

'Fancy ammunition or not, the Lone Ranger has the advantage. He grew up on the planet where his guns were made. He has familiarity with his tools. He was trained to use them. He's a Texas Ranger, driven to work outside the law. Flash Gordon is a polo player who got press-ganged on a rocket ship. Ever see a polo player try to shoot skeet? Or tie their own shoes? In a straight-up fair fight, Flash Gordon bites the dust with silver in his heart.'

'Wouldn't happen,' she said, definitively.

'What would you tell Beata then?'

'The Lone Ranger and Flash Gordon would *never* get in a fight. They're good people. They'd be on the same side. They'd be friends. They'd team up and fight, oh, I don't know, Professor Moriarty… or Dracula.'

'I doubt Beata would be satisfied with that.'

'Now who would win in a fight between Dracula and, say, Bluto from the Popeye cartoons?' Fritzie warmed to the subject. 'That's a question. They're bad people, right? A vampire and a bully. Bad people make alliances of convenience, like Hitler and Mussolini. But they're not friends with each other. Bad people hate other bad people because they hate themselves. They always fall out. Good people team up. It's why they win.'

'You'd be surprised how highly some bad people think of themselves.'

'Go on, spoil it, why don't you? Tell a little girl everything is rotten and there's no point in growing up.'

He didn't know which little girl she meant – Beata Sol or Frederica Minikus.

Dracula would win in a fight with Bluto, he didn't say. It would be wasted. Fritzie would play contrarian and say what if the fight happened in daytime in a field of garlic bulbs. She was in a mood. They'd had these sorts of conversations in the trenches. He remembered the waiting-for-the-attack mix of tedium, terror and whimsy.

Fritzie skittered back to an earlier thread – important, practical matters from before his thoughts got in the way of his thinking.

'Why are they coming for us now and not the woman with all the names?'

'I'm a detective and I couldn't get any good leads on Witch-Eye,' he said. 'The Sparx Brothers are trigger men. They need someone else to do the legwork. It'll take ops smarter than the stand-ins to track her down. I get the impression she's been on the dodge a long time. So she's left till last. We're next on the to-do list because we're findable. We made sure of that, remember?'

'Think they know where we are yet?'

Devlin wavered his hand.

'Maxwell will have snitched. He feeds tips to the press for favours – cash, column inches, party invitations. His tongue just can't hold still. If he told Mrs Mart before bed last night, she'll have spread it to her sewing circle. Better than jungle drums. If my leak doesn't run up against your gossip by sundown, this town is not what it used to be.'

'So, tonight?'

He weighed it up.

'Depends what their gag is and how long it takes to set up. And the weather, of course.'

'I like the rain,' she said. 'Reminds me of…'

'Home?'

He thought Fritzie was from Chicago. Windier than rainy.

'Nowhere,' she said. 'It reminds me of nowhere.'

'That's what this place is. We're the King and Queen of Nowhere. How would you like to spend the day, your majesty?'

'Not dying, sire.'

'That goes without saying. Anything else?'

She picked up a magazine. *Dime Detective*.

'"Lullaby in Lead", a novelette by J.D. Devlin – City Investigator." I'm catching up on my reading.'

'I could tell you how it ends.'

'I don't mind. It's not the ending, it's who gets killed along the way that's the thrill.'

'Now you're frightening *me*.'

'See, you're not so tough.'

He left her to it and checked the driveway again, just in case the jungle drums had got an early start.

He hoped she'd like the story, though.

If she skimmed it then read every word of the Ray Chandler story that came next, then he'd consider letting the Sparxes get her…

… except he wouldn't.

⸺

EVERY TIME HE WENT OUTSIDE, he put on his hat and trenchcoat. Both were wet now. The coat was in such a state Fritzie stopped making jokes about it. The rain soaked the sand and formed rock pools.

It was his turn to make lunch. He served his speciality. Franks and beans out of a can along with coffee Chef Holbein wouldn't use to clean a griddle. After that royal repast, he planned on trudging up the driveway and scoping out the road again. He didn't get off the porch.

Hung on the exterior knob of the front door was a white straw hat.

'Fritzie,' he called.

'What's up?' she said. 'I'm just getting to a good part. The dick's slapping the doll around. It's only the third beating this story.'

She lay on a sun lounger in the big room, devouring pulps. With her glasses on, she looked summery.

He shut the door behind him and held up the hat.

'We've had a visitor,' he said. 'He left his card.'

She paid attention and tossed her magazine on the table.

He felt the reassuring weight of his holstered Colt .38. He wasn't the antsy type to pull it at the first sign of trouble.

Which was a good thing – because this was the first sign of trouble.

He spun the hat across the room. It skittered off the table.

Whenever a Sparx Brother saw a stooge wearing a straw hat, they'd snatch it and punch through the crown, then slap it back on the victim's head. For variety, Screwball sometimes took off the brim with a can-opener. Pyramid must buy the hats by the gross.

A knock came at the door.

Shave-and-a-haircut… two bits!

Devlin pulled it open about half-way.

A boyo he'd never seen before stood outside, sodden newspaper folded into a sailboat on his head. He was a compact little guy.

'Have you seen my hat, pally?'

'We're all out of 'em. You could try walking on your hands? Shoes are wonderful for keeping out water.'

'There, now, you see – that's smart thinking.'

The boyo did a deft backflip, landing on the heels of his hands. He waddled away from the front door, body and legs curved to keep balance. His soggy makeshift headwear fell off. He made it a few yards, then got into trouble on the wet ground and right-sided himself with less ease – smiling as if he'd intended that all along. He danced up the driveway and out of sight.

'Cute,' said Devlin.

Fritzie joined him at the door. She was less taken with the boyo's act.

'That's the third stand-in?' Devlin said.

'Uh-huh, the new one. Fresh from vaudeville.'

'What happened to the old stand-in? Pinky get too enthusiastic with the ice-pick?'

'The old stand-in is the new Pinky. The old Pinky died of itching powder.'

'That how it works in Sparxland? Succession through assassination?'

'No one saw it coming. No one will catch the new Pinky like he caught the old Pinky. He's the mean one. The old Pinky used to use rubber ice-picks. The new Pinky likes sharpened steel. Don't let him get close to your eyes.'

———

THE BOYO CAME BACK with a different hat. An alpine number with a quill pen tucked in the band.

'Is this the residence of Mr Carlton Cinfuegos,' he began. 'C. I. N. F. U. E. G. O. S.... C. A. R. L. T. O. N.... r. e. s. i....'

'... d. e. n. c. e.'

'So you know your ABC?'

'Uh-huh.'

'Tell me what you think of me.'

'Not much.'

The boyo pointed at his heart.

'To the quick, pally,' he said. 'The quick.'

'It's a hard, cruel world.'

The boyo wiped his brow with his sleeve as if he were sweating out a heatwave rather than dripping in the rain.

'Nice place you have here. Very… isolated. Calm and cosy.'

'We like it.'

'You and your lady wife?'

'Me and my Colt Super .38.'

'I trust you're happy together.'

'Delirious. The honeymoon never ends.'

The new stand-in showed sudden interest in the doorjamb, reaching out to a brownish mark on the white wood. When Devlin first visited the bungalow, a human ear was nailed to that spot.

'I seem to have been sold a pup,' said the boyo. 'I may have the wrong address. Tell me, do you *know* Mr Carlton Cinfuegos. C. I. N. F. U.…'

Devlin cut him off. He knew the routine from W.C. Fields.

'No, sir, I do *not* know a Mr Carlton Cinfuegos. C. I. N. F. U. E. G. O. S.… And if I did, *I wouldn't admit it!*'

He slammed the door.

⁓

THE STAND-IN CAME BACK as a singing telegram man.

Devlin didn't open up this time.

The boyo slunk off in a sulk, muttering that he'd written special threatening lyrics to the tune of 'Smoke Gets in Your Eyes'.

'We're not going to die laughing,' Devlin told Fritzie.

She was more rattled by the routine than he was.

But she knew the Sparx Brothers better than he did. If she was rattled, then being rattled was the appropriate thing.

He took out his .38. Still loaded. Like the last five times he'd checked.

—

For his next trick, the boyo wore a big white Tom Mix hat and flapping chaps. He did a bow-legged cowboy walk, thumbs in his belt.

'Hey, sheepie,' he shouted.

A cowboy in the rain was a sorry spectacle.

'Sheepie, you got sheep in there?'

'A whole flock of fluffy little lambs.'

'Move on, sheepie. This is cattle country!'

He turned and waddled back up the drive.

—

Devlin was impressed enough by the next quick change that he stepped out of the bungalow to admire the full effect. He stood on the porch, out of the rain.

The boyo sported a complete Astaire rig. Top hat, white tie and tails. Even a white dress scarf.

He twirled his black cane like a quarterstaff.

Devlin warily stood back. He had an idea this was about more than counting coup.

Fritzie said the new stand-in came from vaudeville. He displayed a broad range of talents. It would be juggling soon. Or, more likely, knife-throwing.

The boyo danced to music only he heard. He splashed through puddles.

The cuffs of his dress pants got muddy.

He tossed his cane away with a flourish and swarmed Devlin, grabbing him by his right wrist and left hip. He pulled Devlin off the porch and forced him to stumble backwards around the garden – overgrown, clumsy Ginger hustled by trim, confident Fred.

Who would win in a fight between Johnny Weissmuller and Fred Astaire? Not Tarzan.

Dancers were strong and skilful. They could kick you in the head while you were standing up. They had the stamina to keep punching hours after your second, third and fourth wind ran out.

The pinch-grip on Devlin's wrist was firm. He was held so close he couldn't reach for his gun with his free hand.

Still, size told in the end. Devlin headbutted his dance partner, who let him go and had to steady his top hat.

Devlin almost felt bad about breaking up the act.

The boyo whirled away, scooped his cane, tipped his hat (brim dented) and exited as if pulled by a giant hook.

Devlin stood in the rain, squirming in wet clothes. His forehead was bleeding.

He went inside.

'Happy now?' said Fritzie.

'We should have put down bear-traps.'

'Let me see to that cut. You shouldn't be using your head… you should be using your head.'

He agreed with her.

⁓

AN AUTOMOBILE ROLLED DOWN the drive and into the rock garden. Devlin watched its approach through the rain-washed picture window.

The Austin, with a fresh rear tyre. Dancing Boy was in the front seat. Hatless. The windshield wipers struggled.

The boyo waved, as if suddenly seeing an old friend. Devlin didn't feel inclined to wave back. He must have scowled. The stand-in made a sad face and knuckled his dry tear-ducts.

'What is it this time?' Fritzie asked, from her lounger.

'Dancing Boy's come in a car.'

'Alone?'

'It's that little clown car from yesterday. I only see him in it.'

She got up and clutched his arm.

'A *clown car*,' she said.

Devlin realised what he'd just said.

Doors, hatches, the trunk and the hood flew off the Austin. People exploded out of the car. More than three… no, more than six. He couldn't see how they'd all been folded to fit in. Dancing Boy stayed at the wheel – though the car was stripped to a frame skeleton, wheels and the engine. Including the boyo, nine people were outside, gurning at Devlin and Fritzie.

The Sparx Brothers, their stand-ins and… their stand-ins' stand-ins?

It was like seeing triple. A mirror maze in a nightmare carnival.

Pinkys – wild crimson ringlets attached to the rims of derby hats, tartan jockey tunics, hairy jodhpurs, ice-picks in each hand.

Geckos – snakeskin zoot-suits, lizard-flicking tongues, monocles, sombreros hung with chicken bones, razor-edged watch-chains.

And Screwballs – untied straitjackets flapping, doctor's reflectors stuck to their foreheads, cheeks puffed with a dozen marbles that could be spat like machine-gun pellets.

Devlin reached for his .38 – which squished as he pulled it from his holster.

This is what that 'Cheek to Cheek' routine had been about! Dancing Boy must have an extra hand. He had spirited away Devlin's gun and substituted a past-its-best banana.

Fritzie at least had the derringer.

He coughed for her attention.

'Item: who would win in a fight between a troupe of homicidal maniacs and us? News flash: we only have one bullet. Remember, though – we're good people.'

'Are we? I never said that.'

She stared at his banana and didn't laugh.

The Sparxes surrounded the bungalow and raised a racket – hammering and banging and scratching on walls. They used whatever they'd brought with them and whatever was lying about. Rakes and spades, ornamental rocks. Ice-picks, straight razors. Surgical instruments, musical instruments.

Devlin couldn't see guns. He supposed they weren't funny enough.

A Gecko took a tuba from the trunk of the disassembled Austin. He settled it around himself and played 'Humoresque', aiming the bell at the picture window. A missile flew out and cracked the glass. The brass section was a musical mortar.

The Sparxes yawped like apes. They knocked into each other, took pratfalls, pretended to be hurt, then sprung up again, gloating. Dancing Boy honked his horn. A Screwball – not *the* Screwball, because this was a Black man with a whited-up skull face – played a set of chimes that were scalpels hanging from a frame.

Fritzie backed into the centre of the room. A Sparx was up on the roof. Clomping in Karloff boots.

'Hey, Dieffenbach,' shouted someone.

So they knew his original name.

'What?' he replied.

Fritzie pressed the derringer into his hand. If they had one shot, he might as well take it. He was the professional hired gun.

'Oh *Dieff*-en-bach…'

He tried to aim at the right patch of ceiling.

'You have to laugh, chum,' came the screech.

Gecko! He inhaled helium to get that voice.

'You have to laugh, chum!'

Devlin didn't. He really didn't.

———

ANOTHER TUBA–LAUNCHED MISSILE struck the window, which shattered.

Cold rain blasted into the room.

A full set of stand-ins – a Pinky, Gecko and Screwball – leaped through the breach. The Screwball jammed his shins against the low table and pitched forward. Devlin grabbed the front of his straitjacket and stuck the derringer's barrel-mouth into the soft underpart of his chin. He held him close enough to smell the greasepaint.

'Back off,' he told the Pinky and the Gecko. 'Or the whack-job loses his marbles.'

They laughed at him. He figured they'd snorted more than helium.

'We don't like him,' the Pinky sang. 'No one likes him. We don't like each other. And we certainly don't like you.'

The Screwball was heavy and limp. Devlin saw ice-pick handles sticking out of his back. The Pinky was empty-handed. He made an 'oops, silly me – where did I leave those things' face.

'You h-h-h-have to laugh, ch-ch-chum,' said the Gecko.

Devlin hefted the dead Screwball like a shield and took aim at the Gecko.

Then, as if he'd changed his mind or gone nutso himself, he set the dead Screwball down on the table, mumbled an apology and handed over the Remington.

Even the Gecko was surprised.

He looked at the toy he had been given.

He had the drop on Devlin. He posed like a duellist with a sword, left hand held up over his head like a shadow-puppet snake, gun-arm outstretched. Devlin looked down the barrel of his own hold-out piece. What *had* he been thinking? It took him moments to catch up with himself.

The Gecko swung around and aimed at Fritzie, who held her hands up and cringed. The Gecko stuck out his fat tongue and sucked it in again. He only did the tongue-flick when he remembered. He was as bad at it as he was at the voice. He looked like the main Gecko – enough to be his actual brother – but his impersonation was lousy.

Fritzie must think Devlin was out of his mind.

This Gecko had come through the window smugly, sure he'd be the craziest cluck in the room. He was reassessing the situation.

Was it a trick?

Of course – but what sort of trick?

The besieging Sparxes quieted a little, intrigued. The real Gecko crawled down from the roof. The percussionist Screwball kept tinkling his blades. Devlin knew the reigning Pinky straight off. The mean eyes gave him away.

The Pinky in the room began to sing 'Stardust'.

A glint of ambition showed in the Gecko with the gun.

But who to shoot? Devlin or Fritzie.

How would Devlin have played it?

Kill the girl in front of him, and the guy would feel less a man – a failure as a protector, a coward in his guts. Plus it'd be gruesome fun – blondes die best. Kill the guy in front of her, and the girl would be shocked and terrified – realise no one would stop them doing to her anything they had a mind to.

But did the Gecko dare kill either of them?

He was a stand-in. He might have ambitions, but no Sparx Brother got where he was by leaving an upstager unpunished. This uppity minion should last no longer than the bleeding, backstuck substitute Screwball. Stuttering Gecko was a warm-up act. Tire 'em out a bit before letting the main attraction swing in on a Peter Pan harness. He didn't get to sell the punchline.

'Are you the stand-in with the wife who likes being flick-licked,' Devlin asked.

He had no out for this. He was just stalling.

The Gecko aimed at Devlin, squinting down the sight, thumb-cocking the piece…

only one w-w-way to get back that c-c-c-craziest cluck in the r-r-r-room paper hat

… he swung round and shot the singing Pinky in the head.

Red matter exploded out of the Pinky's wig, which came off along with his hat and a segment of his skull. Sympathetic pain sang in Devlin's silver cranial plate.

I did th-th-that to my pal – imagine what I'll d-d-do to you…

The Gecko hadn't expected the recoil.

He sh-sh-shrieked and dropped the hot gun.

Firing the derringer had broken more than one or two fingers. His whole hand was shattered. There were a lot of bones in the hand. Breaking just one of them was more painful than many serious injuries.

The sh-shriek became a wh-whimper.

Devlin slashed the Gecko's throat with a sharpened spoon. The best he'd been able to do with the cutlery left at the bungalow.

Now he was out of bullets. And ideas.

And six more killers were on his case.

———

'ALL RIGHT,' SAID FRITZIE. 'Come in, boys. We're spent. That was all we had.'

She didn't even put her hands up. What would be the point?

The puff went out of Devlin. He shifted dead stand-ins out of the way and sat on the table. The razor spoon had buckled as he used it. Like the Remington, it only had one death in it.

The Sparxes stopped capering. Even the percussionist.

While the cameras aren't rolling, comedians become sad, lost people. Irked that their small gags are ignored by grips too busy arranging the next set-up to fake a laugh. Deep down, they're terrified one day they'll wash off their face-paint and find themselves staring into an empty mirror.

Fritzie opened the door so their assassins wouldn't even have to climb through the window and risk the remaining shards of glass. Devlin contemplated snatching one and using it as a dagger. That seemed an awful lot of work, and likely to cut up his hands.

Killing someone always made him feel spongy.

Like he ought to ache more, somehow. He usually tried to learn their names afterwards.

This time, that might not be on the cards.

The Gecko stand-in was probably the last person he'd kill.

They came into the room, through the door and the window.

White-face Screwball, the percussionist. Tuba-cannon Gecko. And Dancing Boy, who wasn't content just to reprise Pinky's act – knowing not to compete with someone who'd killed for his featured spot. These were the stand-ins.

The other three were the real thing.

The real Pinky cast a cold, sceptical eye over the punctured Screwball. He didn't approve of the ice-pick placing.

'That's a poor job of it,' he said.

'Killed him straight off,' said Devlin.

'Exactly. You can stick a man dozens of times without killing him straight off. This was banal.'

'You're the expert.'

'Any famous last words?' asked Screwball. 'I like to jot them down before the screaming.'

Devlin could only think of obscenities.

But there was a lady present.

'Fritzie,' he said, 'do you speak any foreign languages? German or French?'

'Only Latin and Classical Greek, from school.'

He nodded. He'd swear in German and French, then.

Wait a minute? What kind of school had Fritzie Minikus gone to? Latin and Classical Greek! That sounded more like the curriculum of the snob academies Billy and Ray always droned on about. Not Chicago's PS 101.

'You're next, chippie,' said Pinky, aiming his ice-pick at her. 'And why the shades? It's raining, in case you hadn't noticed.'

'And what is it *you* haven't noticed, Gerald?'

Pinky – whose real name must be Gerald – looked around the room.

White-face Screwball and tuba Gecko were leaning against walls, knees bent, sliding downwards.

'Don't worry about them,' said Fritzie. 'They're dead.'

Dancing Boy hurdled the windowsill and made a run for the driveway.

Half-way across the garden, he stopped in his tracks. His spine broke like a breadstick. The upper half of his body bent at a right angle to his hips and legs. For a moment, he was taken with the way he could put his palm against wet sand while his other arm stuck up straight in the air. Then he fell in a heap.

'He's dead, too,' said the killer.

Her voice had changed. A red tear sparkled on her cheek.

They were down to the main trio.

Screwball whipped a trailing sleeve of his straitjacket at Fritzie's face and tore away those sunglasses.

Her right eye was bright red and leaking blood.

'Witch-Eye,' said Devlin.

———

SHE KILLED the Sparx Brothers quickly.

She reached inside their bodies with invisible hands and twisted hearts, scrambled brains, popped eyes.

Screwball first. Then Gecko.

'You have to laugh, chum,' she whispered.

Last, drawing it out just a little, Pinky.

She took hold of him like a puppeteer. She could have made him dance or levitated him up to the low ceiling. Instead, she worked his arms and made him stick ice-picks into his chest. Not stabbing in a frenzy, but easing thin blades between his ribs. After a few minutes, her mind was the only motive force holding him upright. She let him go. He fell forward, slamming onto the table. Pick-points stuck out of his back.

The executions over, she made gestures like Stokowski wringing 'Night on Bare Mountain' out of the Hollywood Bowl Orchestra and conducted the corpses into the air. They hung limp and she swam them out of the window. She dumped them among the rocks. A new kind of ornamental garden.

She didn't look at all like Fritzie Minikus.

She arranged her black hair over her bloody eye.

'Did you prefer me blonde?'

———

FRITZIE MINIKUS WAS POCKET-SIZED. Stephen Swift was five foot six. Fritzie's clothes were too small for her.

'They got Fritzie first,' she told him – that third person thing made sense now. 'Even before the cop. A heart-shaped box of exploding chocolates, delivered with a "from an admirer" note. It took her face off.'

'So you put it on.'

Swift kept dabbing blood tears.

Whatever she'd done had taken a lot out of her.

'They thought they'd killed the wrong woman. Didn't even care who.'

'They're not who's terrifying me now.'

She looked at him. He flinched, expecting a stranglehold.

'You want to know how. I ate her ghost.'

Devlin wondered whether he might not have been better off with Pinky Sparx.

'Ghosts don't last long,' she said. 'I wouldn't have been able to keep the act up for another night.'

'Just looking like her wasn't enough. You talked like her. Knew things she would know. You weren't acting.'

'That's the ghost. With a ghost inside, you're not entirely you. It works best if you're not even mostly you. But you can get into trouble. Eat the wrong ghost – a *dybbuk* – and you're not in disguise, you're possessed. Fritzie wasn't a *dybbuk*. I let her have a loose rein, or else you'd have seen through it. You're a detective. You kept banging on about those bloody dark glasses. I couldn't have kept them on much longer.'

'You can't change your eye?'

She looked at a bloodspot on her handkerchief.

'No. Not the witch-eye. That's an old wound. A reminder not to rely too much on the mentacles. What I just did, I can't do often. I shouldn't do it at all. The Lone Ranger is right. Killing *costs*. I don't know how many more silver bullets I have. In the end, I'll rupture my brain. Have a full-blown aneurysm. That's what happens with people like me when we overstrain our talents.'

'There are other people like you?'

'There'll be more of us if Dr Vaudois gets Engineer Quin's machine working again. And there are others like me who aren't strictly people.'

Devlin had an idea who she meant. Billy and Ray's beloved nemesis.

'Home put a bounty on us,' she said. 'I turned myself in just to see what it was all about. I also needed the money. All the things I can do that you can't and I still have to make a living. When Dr Vaudois explained the process, I assumed it wouldn't work. It's a ridiculous idea. Quin conceived something like blood transfusion but for unusual attributes, with electricity as a conduit. That's why Home was hooked up, to drain us of our specialities, to snaffle them for himself. Then, when it seemed it *would* work, I was curious to see whether it would work for me. Obviously, I had to lay my shekels on the table… but could I scoop them back, along with a few extra talents? Eustis Amthor's constitution for instance. With his knack for self-mending, maybe I could fix my eye? Rupture-proof my poor, buzzing brain. You see why that was worth the risk.'

She tugged Fritzie's skirtwaist down to her hips, but still didn't cover her knees.

'No such luck, by the way,' she went on. 'All I gained was a smidgen of Chick Chang's elasticity. That's how I managed to be Fritzie's height. The woman was practically a pygmy. It hurts, though. Everything worth doing hurts. Haven't you noticed?'

'So it was all about stealing… What, magic powers?'

'No one calls them that – except witches. Yes, that's what Home wanted… to take from us. We were paid, of course. Or would have been, if we lived. Which I did, though – wouldn't you guess it? – Mr Moneybags didn't honour the contract. The pay-off was to be delivered by his hired killers.'

'You *were* trying to cheat him.'

'The prize was worth it. Not Amthor's get-better-in-a-trice trick. Holloway's not-dying trait. That was the gold ring here. We'll have to get used to Ward Home Junior, because he's likely to be around indefinitely.'

'Holloway isn't. He died.'

'He gave up what he had.'

'You're sure you weren't the lucky winner?'

'There's only one way to find out… and I'm not going to be talked into it. If in fifty years I walk under a Number 19 rocket ship on Shaftesbury Avenue – or if next week my brain bursts like a boil – and I jump back up like a jack-in-the-box, it'll be a nice surprise. I'll have a laugh at Home's expense. But I'm not counting on it. And I'm not letting you subject me to a test under laboratory conditions. I've had enough of laboratory conditions.'

'Did you slip Holloway's file under my door?'

'A brilliant deduction, Holmes. Yes, I took it from Home House, when none of you were looking. Tucked in the back of my knickers. I come from a long line of smugglers.'

'Really?'

'No. My family aren't like me at all. I'm a perennial disappointment. No one calls a child "Stephen" if they are happy to see her pop out female. Know what they called my little brother? "John Stephen". When he was born, they started pretending my name was "the Girl" and called him "Stephen". Is it any wonder I've become a woman of many names?'

Devlin sat in a corner and looked up at her. He was tired and had a million more questions.

The one he asked was, 'Why me?'

'You're a big, strong man. And a detective. Given Holloway's file, you had enough to make a start on the case. I thought you'd keep up pressure on Home and Vaudois while I laid low. It didn't work out that way. You got fired, you idiot. And you started looking for me, which was annoying. I reckoned it made sense to tag along as Fritzie and keep you from harm. I knew you trusted her more than you'd ever trust me. But you can thank me for deflecting the falling safe, by the way. I've had a splitting head ever since.'

He remembered her as Fritzie, practically jitterbugging into the Tramline Diner with bad news.

'Teaming up with you was Fritzie's idea,' she said. 'She saw herself as Fool to your Lone Ranger.'

'Fool?'

'Like King Lear's Fool. Isn't that what "Tonto" means in Spanish? I only know rude words in Foreign.'

'But you're fluent in Latin and Classical Greek.'

'Not ruddy likely. I was a near-complete dunce in languages. I stagger through *amo amas amat* then can't tell my *amatis* from my *ulna*.'

'So you did know what toad in the hole was?'

'*Everybody* knows what toad in the hole is.'

'You eat it all the time for high tea in Potters Bar?'

'With crumpets and kippers? I'm not that sort of Englishwoman, Mr Devlin. That was the first toad and the first hole that e'er passed my lips. It's what miners' mothers serve them in tins.'

She'd stopped crying blood.

She padded around the bungalow. Fritzie had done something similar – or was this a Witch-Eye tell? She was high-strung as a thoroughbred who's won by seven lengths. A handful of sugar lumps weren't reward enough. She craved more of the dope that'd whizzed her over the finishing line.

Was she hungry for more ghosts? Nine of them must be fluttering around – counting only the latest crop. He didn't want to look at Stephen Swift and see her wearing a Sparx Brother face.

Small, broken objects – cups, hats, scalpels – lifted up from where they'd fallen.

In the War, her brand of intoxication was dangerous. Surviving a battle doesn't make you invincible. It's all too horribly likely you'll be shot by some Tommy who can't make out the colour of your uniform. After you've won is not a good time to be careless.

She realised she was doing conjuring tricks, concentrated a little and gently set everything back where it had been.

She claimed to be people. Not people like Devlin but people all the same. Somewhere at the farthest edge of the definition of people. Like the Windmill-Man. A border must exist, and beyond that were what she called the not strictly people. Like the roles Boris played. The Monsters.

'Who would win in a fight between you and Popeye?' he asked.

She made a fist and flexed her bicep. 'Who do you reckon?'

'Who would win in a fight between you and me?'

'It wouldn't come to that.'

'Because we're good people?'

'Because we're not. I wouldn't let you fight me.'

'You let *them* fight me.'

'Only till you couldn't fight any more. Then I stepped in. At school, girls called me "Miss Steps". I didn't have the bloody eye then. I burst something in it when I first overstrained. A long time ago. "Take that as a warning," I was told. No more wicky tricks for Miss Steps. Those incredible, wonderful, terrifying things you can do – don't do them. Or else your brain will pop like a blister. I have stopped, for the most part. Eating ghosts is something else. It uses other muscles. I don't do that often either. Not just because of *dybbuks*. When the last rags disappear, it's as if they're dying for a second time, dying inside me. Not something I care to put myself through every week.'

Rain came through the broken window, soaking the floor matting. It was past sunset. Thunder and lightning announced that the promised storm was here. A witch walked in Laurel Canyon, but didn't stop the rain. It kept pouring down. The rain it raineth every day.

'Do you want to say goodbye to Fritzie?' she asked.

'She's still here?'

'Very little of her. She's nearly gone.'

Most of the time he'd known Frederica Minikus she'd been someone else.

'She liked you, you know,' she said. 'Big Man.'

'You don't?'

'Not really. Don't take offence. We're alike. Smile too much, think too much, talk too much. Here we are, alive, surrounded by corpses, merrily chatting away. Have many evenings like that?'

'A few.'

'I'll bet. Me too. I can live with this. I can live through this. I can live after this. You, I imagine, will say the same. Who wants to be friends with someone like that?'

Devlin felt no remorse. Pyramid would grow more Sparx Brothers.

He did wonder, as he hadn't much over the last week, how Billy and Ray were faring. They'd set out to visit the Lamia Munro Clinic and quiz Dr Voodoo. Devlin hadn't spoken with them since they got back. Now it came to mind, he didn't know for sure that they had got back. He should have checked regularly. He'd figured that if they'd had anything to report, they'd have reached him at the Tramline. He didn't want to think about the risks they'd taken on his say-so.

He had to look after himself first.

He stood up. He considered the bungalow as a crime scene.

People who did the job he used to would eventually arrive.

'Dancing Boy still has my Colt,' he told her. 'On him or in what's left of his car. I need it back. If the cops ever sort through the mess of dead comedians, I'd like for them not to stumble over a gun registered to me. I wouldn't even know what lies to tell about all this.'

'You wipe your prints off the banana,' she said. 'I'll get the pistol. I know where it is.'

Exhausted, he went along with it.

If she was willing to go out in the storm for him, she was more like good people than she claimed.

She took his coat and hat. She angled the hat to set off the hair falling over her tell-tale eye.

'Is this hardboiled enough for you?' she asked.

His coat was too big for her. His hat settled comically around her ears. She wasn't having wardrobe fortune today.

He forced a smile.

'See you around, Big Man,' she said.

That came out wrong. She couldn't do Fritzie's voice any more.

When she left, he went through the room. He wasn't worried about prints unless they were in recently spilled stuff. If the bungalow were dusted again, they'd find his prints, Mart Maxwell's, half a dozen cops' and the coroner's. But he didn't want to leave anything that could be traced to him. He left the Remington where it had fallen. It wasn't licensed to anyone and a paraffin test on the Gecko stand-in would tie him to the slug that had passed through the brain-pan of the Pinky stand-in. This could wind up looking like a comedy orgy gone wrong. A massacre of all the Sparxes.

Had stuttering Gecko really been that crazy – or had he been *pushed*? Was that another of Stephen Swift's 'wicky tricks'?

Lightning kept flashing, bleaching the room bone-white.

Thunder cracked like the Devil's coach-whip.

The noise rumbled on. Not just thunder. An engine was starting up. He had a spurt of anger.

He felt for his keys – chained to his belt – and found them still there.

Before his indrawn breath could be let out in relief, he realised what she'd lifted. His burglar tools. When she broke Dancing Boy in half, had she gulped down his fleeing spirit to gain his pickpocketing skills? Or was that something she learned at school while flunking Latin and Classical Greek?

The Studebaker departed up the driveway. Its lights were on.

If Witch-Eye turned to wave, he couldn't see her through rain and rage.

His impulse was to hurl himself through the window frame and spread-eagle on the trunk of his car… but his Colt .38 floated out of the storm, as if on wires. The gun wobbled, not really aimed at him, and dropped onto the table.

At least she'd left him something to remember her by.

———

27

E vading Junior Home's army of the electric undead was no easy task. Escaping from the murdering Munros in an obsolete plane presented many challenges. Bringing the kite down in La Brea Tar Pits was deucedly dicey. Then we had to do something really difficult – get across Los Angeles without any money.

Our billfolds were back in the Lamia Munro Clinic, as were our street clothes and our keys. I was out a hat I liked and a spiffy topcoat recently bought with Knopf money. We'd parked near the Clinic too. Had Dr Vaudois shifted the cars to delay the filing of missing persons cases?

To get away from the downed plane, we waded waist-deep through bitumen. A casual observer would figure the angry mob had done a half-way decent job of tarring us but been let down by the local feather supplier. Probing trouser pockets for forgotten coins was impossible.

We couldn't ride the Red Cars.

We couldn't call a cab.

We couldn't turn ourselves in. Any cop would take one look and tell we'd been in several fights. No story I could invent would satisfy the police.

Billy and I walked along Wilshire like lost souls, leaving sticky footprints. In any other city, we'd be netted by dog catchers.

This was a coming district. The May Company was building a streamlined department store at Wilshire and South Fairfax. The plans featured a dirigible mast. No one seriously expected airships to dock here. It was a cheap way of adding extra height and claiming the title of Los

Angeles' tallest commercial building. When I arrived in California, this was an unpaved track where cowmen and bean-planters shot each other on Saturday nights. Now they call it Miracle Mile. It's a miracle if you get off it without being robbed.

There was local excitement.

A patrol car drove by, siren yammering. Several people – mostly in states worse than ours, after a night outdoors in a storm – spread the news.

Some damn fool had crashed a plane in the Tar Pits.

'It's that Howard Hughes,' a scarecrow-dressed hobo told us. 'He's always crashing something.'

If I hadn't known better, I'd have believed him.

The hobo's wayward eye was drawn to Billy.

'Do I know you?' he asked. 'Your face is…'

Billy shrank. He was always gracious when recognised, though public praise embarrassed him.

'You look like *Boris Karloff*.'

Billy shammed hurt. 'Is that a nice thing to say to a fellow?'

The hobo was apologetic. 'I guess it ain't, mister. Can't be a picnic with a map like yours. I should hate to bear such a burden in life. I resolve to think on things more before I blurt 'em out.'

A middle-aged Black man came out of a shed and set up a food stall. He wore a white apron and a chef's hat.

'Hey, Nick,' said the hobo. 'Hear about the plane crash? It was that Howard Hughes.'

Nick set up a coffee urn and laid out trays of pastries and pretzels. A sign offered '10¢ Breakfast Special – 5¢ Just Java'. The smell was a reminder – much needed – that there was beauty in this world, even if it was out of the reach of the penniless.

The hobo buttonholed other people and told them about that Howard Hughes.

I didn't know what I'd tell Cissy. When a husband leaves in a car and comes back on foot days or weeks later wearing someone else's clothes, even my wife's powers of non-observation falter.

'You *are* Mr Karloff, aren't you?' said Nick.

Billy relented and admitted it.

'I thought you were you,' said Nick. 'We were in a serial together. *The King of the Kongo*. You won't remember me. I do extra-work. Whenever there's an African tribe, I'm in it.'

'I've done extra-work too, friend,' said Billy. 'I'd still be doing it if it weren't for this face. It's my fortune to look... well, like Boris Karloff.'

Nick had a striking face too – rangy, with prominent cheekbones. A bronze Gary Cooper. He might be a star in race pictures. At the studios, the best he could hope for was being out of focus behind the singers in *Show Boat*.

'Would you and your friend like breakfast?' Nick asked.

I could have eaten mammoth-meat from the Tar Pits.

'I'm afraid we are... ah, temporarily embarrassed.'

Billy indicated his sticky pockets.

'On the house, Mr Karloff. I know this town. Not making horror pictures any more, are they?'

Nick filled paper cups with his java and handed them to us. It was the best I'd ever tasted.

Billy wouldn't take a pastry.

He'd been as broke as Nick thought we were, more than once. When troupes went bust in the North Woods, he'd hitched or worked his way back to civilisation. Since *Frankenstein*, he'd looked after his finances to ensure he would never be on his uppers again. No lavish birthday parties for Violet the Pig. No retinue of hangers-on talking him into get-poor-quick schemes. No bathroom remodelled in Carrara marble with silver faucets. If studios didn't want Karloff the Monster, he'd play other parts. Inventors, warlords, detectives. He had a healthier bank balance than many a higher-paid, faster-spending star...

... and he hated going along with the lie that he was broke.

'I'll pay you back,' he assured Nick.

I knew he would. And I'd send Nurse Anne an advance copy of *The Big Sleep*. It was the thing that was done. Keeping one's word. Even when no one expected you to.

'Know who this is?' Nick told his next customer. '*Boris Karloff*.'

Billy was ashen with shame. I admit I slightly relished seeing him squirm. A small cruelty warmed me after a spell of cold terror.

'Mr Karloff will sign autographs for, ah, ten cents,' I said.

'No, no, no,' said Billy, affronted.

I overruled him. A crowd formed. Nick's customers were construction workers from the May Company site and shopgirls and secretaries working in buildings that were already completed.

Billy was news on this block, even in a town where gods and goddesses of the silver screen were as commonplace as double-decker buses in London and broken windows in Berlin. A movie star drinking Nick's five-cent java! They'd remember this. It was the same morning Howard Hughes made like Icarus. Folks produced scraps of paper, wrappers, used tickets. They proffered pens and pencils.

Billy was uncomfortable. Charging for the small courtesy of an autograph went against his nature.

Still, if I could steal an airplane, Billy could turn signature tricks.

We netted a little shy of five dollars in twenty minutes. People walked away with a glow, not so much for the scrawl but for the memory of a moment shared with a star. Not that half of them believed Billy *was* Boris Karloff. Why would Karloff be in Santa Monica this early in the morning, covered in muck and out of funds? He was just an ugly tramp who could do the voice. Still, it'd been a magical, unexpected encounter.

No one wanted my autograph.

No one even asked who I was.

Billy insisted on paying Nick for the coffee out of his take. There was back and forth. Billy had to snarl a little Karloff menace to make the stallholder take the coin. I worried he'd accidentally summon his Death Touch. He refilled our paper cups and Billy left it at that.

'See you at the movies, Mr Karloff. Next time you make a picture with an African tribe.'

He shook Nick's hand and we left.

We found a working phone booth.

A reporter was in it, calling in the plane crash story. He told the copy-taker Howard Hughes was still missing. Probably at the bottom of the Tar

Pits. Preserved alongside the mammoths. The world of aviation was in shock. Many starlets would wear black. A new, experimental model aircraft was lost. An autogiro. A hush-hush government project. Spies and sabotage were suspected.

Item filed, he yielded the booth. He was so caught up in invention he didn't pay us attention. A muck-raker with passing interest in the facts might have noticed the state of us and asked why we'd taken an early morning dip in semi-liquid asphalt. We reeked of the stuff. A smart aleck, on-the-ball newshound would have made connections. This Front Page fiend was happier making things up than chasing down a story.

We wondered who to ring.

Neither of us thought it a good idea to spring anything on our wives. We'd have to give long, carefully crafted and edited explanations that would take time to finesse between us.

Billy suggested calling his agent. Always an actor's first instinct.

I was tired enough to go along with that, but suggested we try the Tramline Diner first. Joh said we could leave messages with Lotte.

I made the call and got through.

The waitress told me she didn't need to take a message and summoned Joh to the telephone. He was having breakfast.

'Ray, where have you been?'

'I'll get to that. I'm more concerned with where we are now. Billy and I are at Wilshire and South Fairfax and need to be anywhere else.'

'Did you see Hughes crash?'

'About that… I'll explain later. Could you pick us up? We've no money.'

'Have you been robbed? I've warned you about Bay City… Santa Monica. Always keep a fifty in your shoe.'

'That's the least of it.'

'I understand. I've had a strange, terrible night. Big developments in the case. You won't believe what's been happening.'

'I think we will. It's you who won't believe what's been happening with us.'

'This isn't a contest, Ray… but I've been with Laurel Ives – Stephen Swift – and she's… well, she's a witch, or a kind of a witch. She do hoodoo.'

'Billy was killed and brought back to life.'

A long pause. I heard breakfast clatter at the other end of the line.

'Okay, Ray, it *is* a contest,' said Joh. 'And you've won.'

PART FOUR

CASA KARLOFF

28

...   nd what I liked best was Marlowe never finding out who killed the chauffeur. Never even thinking about it for the rest of the book. That's not like a mystery story – that's like life! You never find out who killed the chauffeur.'

Nurse Anne – out of uniform – had a great deal of praise for *The Big Sleep*, but that comment stuck with me even after her face blurred. I knew there was such a person, but had been given the hype over and over at the Lamia Munro Clinic. Who knows how much of what I remembered was real?

The day after the storm was Hangover City.

Joh Devlin provided a taxi service from Santa Monica.

I needed a bath and a change of clothes. And hours of undrugged sleep. I was not in good odour at home. Taki took hours to forgive me and settle in my lap. Cissy indulged in more refined torture. She acted as if I'd not been missing and continued conversations she'd been having with me all the time I wasn't there. She had one of her heads. They always made her vague and distant. Her project was rearranging the *animaux* – the little china figures of giraffes, elephants and bears we collected. She had renamed several and would sometimes quiz me about their characters and traits. I was expected to add to the mosaic of story pieced together around them.

After a few days with the *animaux*, the call from Nurse Anne was a sweet little lure. She suggested we meet in the bar of the Hotel Cecil.

Lures are just to distract you from hooks.

I should have remembered that.

Or, maybe, in the world revealed to us – the world with Junior Home and Stephen Swift and Norman Quin – hooks were the least of our problems. We tried to get on with our lives.

Warners had given Billy a start date for his Chinese warlord picture. He had a script to learn. For a six-page stretch, characters named Wu Yen Fang and Chow Fu-Shan were called Pancho Lopez and Pedro Gonzales. The writer had accidentally left in a scene from the Mexican bandit script he was retyping. Ever wonder why you feel you've already seen a movie that's only just come out? Hollywood files off the serial numbers and sells it to you again.

On that morning in Santa Monica, Joh turned up in a ridiculous rattletrap – an American Austin with much of the bodywork hanging loose, bolted on upside down or missing altogether. At least he didn't care that we got tar on the upholstery. Even with his own car missing, he got shot of the lemon double-quick. It was left across the street from a Lincoln Heights repair shop known to the DA's office as a front for a hot car ring. No self-respecting auto thief would waste time boosting the comical car, but they'd cannibalise the wreck for parts. It came partially disassembled to make stripping it down easier.

A few days later, Joh found his Studebaker parked outside his apartment house, with a full gas tank and his hat and coat – cleaned, pressed and blocked – piled on the driver's seat. Billy and I never saw our cars again. I surreptitiously spent the last of my Knopf money on a blue Packard roadster to match the one I'd mislaid. Cissy wasn't fooled. It smelled different. Billy bought a new Chrysler. His wife asked no questions.

Cissy often raised the subject of why I'd changed the Packard, especially in company. Our casual friends thought she was dotty. That I had vanished without excuse for over a week was never mentioned. But she harped on about the car for months, years. Why did you change the Packard, Raymio? Why why why? She didn't like the new car's smell. Something about the sound of its motor was untrustworthy.

After an exchange of tall tales about the night of the storm, we entered a state of anticipation and dread. At least I did. Joh was too hardboiled and Billy too British to be quite so nakedly terrified. Though it told on them too. Joh was short-tempered and less able to hide it. Billy had changed more than either of us. Cissy would have said he smelled different. He sat quietly sometimes, retreating into himself, eyes shining like they did in *The Mummy*.

Powerful, dangerous, unnatural forces were aligned – and knew our names and addresses. They even had our house keys. People had been murdered to keep a lid on the story. Joh stressed how ill-disposed the authorities were to our cause. The Home pull extended throughout the city – the police, the judiciary, the press, the studios. If we told what we'd seen, the only people who'd believe us would be the ones who already knew. They wouldn't think twice about doing us harm.

Or, more insidiously, favours.

Interest in film rights to *The Big Sleep* was definite. Anticipation for *Farewell, My Lovely*, the next Philip Marlowe, was keen. Mysteriously large bids were made for paper-bound editions. Another fortune was offered by radio networks. Marlowe could roust blackmailers between commercials for ironised yeast and blue coal. It wouldn't do to get too used to the income. A man with something is a man with something to lose.

Universal Pictures contemplated a run around the British horror blockade. A reissue of *Frankenstein* had made money. That explosion at the end of *The Bride of Frankenstein* might not have finished the story after all. The studio registered the title *Son of Frankenstein*. If it got made, there'd be bumps in pay, billing and benefits for the only actor in town who could pull on the Monster boots.

Overtures were made to Joh, dangling the possible return of his badge and job. To make the offer more tempting, breaks came in cases that long frustrated him. Lost evidence turned up. Witnesses finally talked. With Joh back on those investigations, innocents might see justice. People called Home were beyond the reach of the law, of course, but other grade-A rotters were liable to see the inside of a gas chamber.

Every day we weren't murdered prolonged the agony.

I haunted a block-long newsstand run by one of the dwarfs from *Freaks* and bought every paper. Storm damage was a running story. Blistering editorials railed against Roosevelt's foolish notion of governing in the interest of people who didn't have funds enough to buy their own politicians.

Howard Hughes' autogiro crash generated headlines. Pictures of the incident were few and hard to make out, so papers ran artists' impressions. The moustached inventor-tycoon piloted a Flash Gordon rocket ship into the jaws of a dinosaur that was roaring out of the primeval stickiness. Hughes strangely didn't speak up to deny he'd flown an experimental aircraft into La Brea Tar Pits. Had they got to him?

After that first time at the Hotel Cecil, I had several further meet-ups with Nurse Anne. She had more insights and adored the title *Farewell, My Lovely*. Drinks were involved. Sobriety seemed less important these days. Carnal episodes ensued, which spurred guilt and shame. That led to more drinking, which led to more mussed sheets. And bruises – Anne had that Lamia Munro Clinic staff trait of not knowing her own strength. I deserved the punishment, though. I was a rutting hound who deserved no sympathy. When Taki licked my hand and tasted perfume she hissed. The cat knew of my treacherous liaisons. Cissy took no notice, unless the pain in my digestive tract came from small quantities of ground glass introduced into every meal.

Of us all, Joh was most likely to do something foolish or brave or dangerous. He still took the crimes of Ward Home Junior and Associates as a personal affront. And he had an obsession with wrongnesses of several stripes. I tried to act as a cautioning influence.

We took a drive out to Laurel Canyon but couldn't find the turn-off that led to Blood Bath Bungalow. Annoyed at this failure, Joh hammered his head with the heel of his hand, as if trying to dent his silver skull-plate. He said Witch-Eye had got into his mind and fogged vital pieces of information. He no longer knew the sign posts.

Joh took me to a drug store they had used. He recognised the coot behind the counter. The druggist had no memory of him or of a lady who might be a short blonde or taller and darker with hair like an eyepatch. Joh sputtered with an annoyance that warned me against asking more questions. Could anyone else alive confirm that Stephen Swift was a real person? Frederica Minikus had been of this earth – dead in what the stop press box on page fifteen called a gas burner accident. Laurel Ives was a name cited twice in coverage of the Home House case. The late Fritzie's crime scene photos, developed too late to be much use to anyone, all managed not to have Laurel Ives in them. Far be it from me to say witches weren't real, but this one had departed on her broomstick. All Joh had to testify to her existence was her 'Philippa Zhan' head shot, and she was blonde in that.

Joh and I met often, in the Tramline and sundry bars.

He pored through even more papers than I did. And pressured 'sources' to supply him with official reports not released to the press. Any that didn't support his theories he dismissed as forgeries to throw us off the track. We talked around the whole thing till I worried we sounded like that booby who spun Howard Hughes' autogiro out of thin air and sold it to his editor.

Joh became, unbelievably, a bore on the subject. He insisted items obviously unrelated to the case were secretly parts of the picture. Political movements in Europe… an earthquake in Japan… strange flying creatures over the Tower of London… new discoveries in the temple of Angkor Wat… a craze for irritating nonsense songs that might be secret codes – 'Hut Sut Rawlson on a Rillarah Wi' a Braw a Braw a Suet', 'Flat Foot Floogee with a Floy Flogged'. All rang bells strung to a cat's cradle of conspiracy.

Joh insisted something should be done and we were the boys to do it.

The worst thing was that he was right.

Walking away would be shameful. What had been done – what had been done to *us* – was a crime. I stung at the reproachful looks Billy still gave me for leaving Norman Quin to the mercy of the Munros. Engineer Quin was still in the papers, as 'Frank N. Quine', the Monster of Home House. If the press had photos of what he looked like now, they'd put out extra editions. I presumed he was dead, buried on the fake battlefield where Pyramid were still filming their wretched air ace picture. The patsy took the heat for all of it – the dead freaks in the basement, near-fatal injuries to Ward Home Junior, the murder of Dan Ysidro.

One rag tried to make out he was the secret mastermind behind the Lindbergh Kidnapping.

The other subject Joh got heated about was Billy.

Because he was learning his lines, having costume fittings and shooting make-up tests, Billy wasn't with us often. His famous face would have attracted too much attention. Joh and I would rather keep a low profile.

Joh was fascinated by how Billy had *changed*.

He asked me more about Billy than about Junior – who had grown to giant-size, levitated and demonstrated the power of mind over matter. Billy had come back from the dead. And he was less Billy Pratt, and more the imaginary creature he had named Boris Karloff.

Sometimes, you could tell Billy was still electric. Metal door-handles sparked when he touched them. He had to be careful, learning his own strength. He'd played the blundering Monster on screen and knew to be cautious in real life. I knew he was testing his limits in private. Lifting more and more weight. Holding his breath for longer and longer spells. Bending and re-straightening fireplace pokers. His old injuries no longer bothered him. The relatively fresh ones – sustained when Jimmy Whale tossed him into a water-filled basement on *The Bride of Frankenstein* – went away entirely. Free from pains he'd lived with most of his life, he was careful to walk his old bow-legged walk, not bound across a lawn with a spring in his step and a flex of his muscles. He could have skipped *Son of Frankenstein* and gone up for *Tarzan Joins the Circus*.

Billy couldn't resist using his prowess on the cricket pitch, brutally bowling out Errol Flynn, David Niven and Robert Coote in quick succession. A gossip column hinted that Billy had received monkey gland transplants on the sly.

Yes, he paid Chef Nick back – disproportionately. Wu Yen Fang was a rare Chinese warlord with an African hatchet man. A featured role, not extra-work. Nick had a fresh sideline serving java to film crews on location.

Billy's generosity, exerted without making the beneficiary self-conscious, beggared my own in slinging Nurse Muscles a bound proof. He didn't sleep with Chef Nick either.

Billy took to wearing gloves, in case the Death Touch came back.

'Witch-Eye can kill without a Death Touch,' said Joh.

He talked often about the woman with a dozen names. She wasn't on our side or their side, he said. Nobody's side but her own.

'That's all of us, in the end,' he said.

I had grown too weary to argue with him.

What did it matter? Joh didn't want to hear that. I'd seen Junior Home play *Übermensch* and *Führer* and Mandrake the Magician. For all his stolen talents, he was a shrimp inside. He could no more take over the world than run a successful film studio. He wasted the profits of *Say It With Tubas* on overstuffed historical duds that earned him not respect but ridicule. Radio comedians said, 'In case of an air raid, take shelter at Pyramid – they haven't had a hit in years!'

When the Old Man was gone, Junior would squander the oil money. He'd use the Vaudois-Quin Process to make more of himself without ever really becoming anything. He'd be as grotesque as those beach chunks who lift weights until they look like colossal sculptures made by tying boiled hamhocks together.

Joh still wanted something done about Home House.

His big idea was that Billy should do something.

Use his *Boris Karloff* powers. His Invisible Ray Death Touch. The hypnotic eyes of Fu Manchu. He should unchain the Monster. Storm the castle. Bring down Junior.

Joh couldn't understand how Billy could just go back to acting. Not with all the things he could now do.

'Are you sorry it wasn't you?' I asked.

'Damn right. If I had what Boris has, I'd use it the way Witch-Eye uses it. I'd sit outside the offices of the bastards and strangle them by mental radio waves. I'd set fire to the oil deposits under the Home Estate and watch the place burn.'

'She won't notice,' I said, trying to be kind.

Joh was startled to shame, as if caught being beastly in private.

'Your witch won't notice,' I went on. 'Our witch is the same. You can't do enough for her. She might still, on a whim, stop your heart in your chest. They are not like us.'

'Women.'

'Witches. Sirens. Lamiae.'

'Lamiae?'

'Plural of lamia – an ancient Greek variety of vampire.'

'You studied Classical Greek?'

'Classics. Of course.'

'Modern German?'

'Yes, we had modern languages. Dull, after Classics. I lived in Germany for a few months after school, to learn by usage.'

'Enjoy the old country?'

'Germany? At times. At times, not. I wonder how many of those bank clerks and café waiters later took shots at me. There's this little flash of hate when they hear you speak German.'

'Who can recognise your accent, Ray? American-Irish-English-Canadian?'

'Germans can. It's an Allied Accent.'

'What happened to you and Boris at school? When you met her for the first time? Your her. Ariadne.'

'Now there's a story. We've told it to you.'

'Yes, but what *happened*? What *changed*?'

'Some boys – and a master – died for her. They weren't murdered. They died of their own accord and were happy to. She was embarrassed, as if she'd invited friends to afternoon tea expecting them in cricket togs and sun hats only to open the door and find them in evening dress with a Rolls Royce full of roses and champagne on ice. But she accepted. She *exulted*. Billy and I didn't die that time. But we were captivated. She brought us together. We weren't at the same school, you know. It was a cricket fixture. The Pratts sent him to Uppingham so he wouldn't be a day boy at Dulwich, like I was. He was there because of a match. That's how I met him. We were together when she put her mark on us. She could have picked two other fellows. Or maybe she had her eye on us before. Did she know who we would be or are we who we are because of her? Mr Mystery and Mr Horror. I've turned that over and over. It's unsolved. It was a bloody, messy business. I can't say it changed us, because we were already changing – both of us. At that age, everyone is. We've changed ourselves over and over ever since – our names, our countries, our jobs, even the colour of Billy's skin. It's possible she chose us because we were wet clay – suitable for moulding. Or it could just have been random. We aren't unique. We aren't even uncommon.'

'You saw Ariadne on the night of the storm?'

'She was there. To see Billy die. Or see him rise from death. I don't know which would please her most, if she can be pleased. She's not like a woman. Cissy, who God alone knows has her strangenesses, or Nurse Anne, or any other skirt you could chase. She is most like Taki. She can adore you for hours when you're smelly from pipe smoke and busy with something else. Or you can give her a whole tin of tuna and expect a nuzzle then get scratched through your socks. My advice is to forget your Witch-Eye. You're not stuck on her. You're stuck with her.'

Joh didn't say anything to that.

Lotte came to our booth with a telephone message – not for Joh, but me. It was from Nurse Anne. She said, 'Go see your friend.' The waitress confirmed it had been a woman on the line. She wanted to leave a message, not actually talk with me.

'Your nurse works for Home,' said Joh.

I couldn't deny it. We knew which friend she meant.

We took Joh's Studebaker up to Coldwater Canyon.

I wouldn't see Nurse Anne again. I'd known all along that she was reporting on me to Dr Vaudois, even as she gave me tidbits about the Clinic. Junior, exhausted after the storm, was back in his private room. Dr Voodoo was worried about his eye, which was the size of a tangerine. I remembered what Joh said about how his Miss Steps got her witch-eye but kept it to myself. That Junior's brain might boil over like a pan of milk left too long on the stove would solve problems. I wouldn't say anything to urge caution. If the shrimp wanted to play Russian roulette with the universe, it was his look-out.

Nurse Anne had saved us – or at least, stood aside to let us escape – but she worked for them. Now she was delivering their messages.

I didn't want to think about other things she might have done because she'd been told to. I could bear it if Nurse Anne had acted under orders when she went to bed with me. It'd be profoundly disappointing if her praise of *The Big Sleep* was a put-on.

Night fell as we neared the Karloff residence.

Lights were on in Billy's house.

Violet was outside, truffling through scrub. That wasn't usual.

When we got out of the car, we heard howling. Something nearby was in pain. At first I thought it was a siren. The howl echoed back from the hills. It set off dogs, coyotes and – for all I knew – mountain lions. Neighbours must be trembling in their bathtubs. The keening was a banshee wail or the cry of *la llorona*.

A pure note of sustained grief. Scarcely identifiable as human.

Joh unholstered his Colt .38.

That gave me the job of pushing doors open and stepping aside so he could aim through them.

No one in the hallway.

The howling filled the house.

In the den, a large mirror stood on the mantel over the fireplace. Billy and his wife would catch sight of themselves when ritzed up for their rare nights on the town. Joh and I saw ourselves reflected, unhealthy and afraid. A message was scrawled on the glass.

MUNROS WAS HERE.

The daub was so red it could only be paint. Outside of green-jacket mysteries, blood goes brown or black and runs. Words scrawled in gore by dying men are unreadable – a torment to loved ones or cops hoping for answers.

The Munros had smashed urns and chinaware. They'd shot chunks out of the beamed ceiling. They'd knocked over lamps and trampled shades. They'd let loose a sack of rattlers – though they'd also stomped the snakes' heads flat, so they were more a disgusting mess than a danger.

We followed a trail of debris through the house out into the garden.

Billy was on his knees by the pool, back bent, bony shoulders heaving. He was the howling thing. He gave raw, inarticulate voice to the Monster…

the wretch torn from the grave, rejected by his maker, tortured with fire, despised and hated and feared. Misshapen, ill-used and determined to be a villain. Racked by horrors wrought with his own hands.

A child floated face-down under the hanging willows.

Billy heard our steps, reined in grief and turned to look at us, which set him off again. He'd torn his cheeks open with his blunt fingernails. On the flagstones in front of him were black soot handprints. He had discharged current from his fingers.

The girl in the pool was Beata.

29

A scene from *Frankenstein*. A dead child in the water. Part of the ritual. Another message.

The Munros were fiendish. In their daily lives, Home's kin were morons who could barely button their shirts. When it came to torture, they were inventive geniuses – prodigies of the imagination to rival Poe.

This was the worst they could do.

Billy could – and had – endured great pain. He had even been killed. That hadn't broken him. To torture him, they had to hurt someone else. Someone he couldn't protect. To the Munros, killing Beata was vandalism. Done to upset Billy, not because of who she was or anything she did.

Wary of touching him for fear of electric shock, I tried to comfort Billy. His howl ran down, possibly after tearing something in his throat. Wordless, agonised sounds still came out of him.

Joh searched the house. Billy's wife and Gracia were upstairs in their rooms, asleep. They'd been put out with chloroform. Joh left the women as they were but brought down a rattlesnake he found nestling on Gracia's pillow, carefully gripping its neck so it couldn't turn and fang his hand. He tossed the snake into the garden. It slithered off about its reptile business.

I stood by the pool, looking into dark water.

'Should we leave her there?' I asked Joh.

'It'll be suspicious if we do. We should haul her out and try to get her breathing.'

'Too late for that,' I said.

'I know. I'm thinking of the story we'll need to tell.'

Billy covered his face with his arms as Joh used the long-armed pool-scoop to pull Beata to the edge of the pool. I dragged her onto the flagstones. She was heavier than expected.

No heartbeat, pulse, flutter of breath.

Her eyes were open. They saw nothing.

She was heavy because her lungs were full.

I tried to arrange her with some dignity.

A wet black scrap of cloth was around her neck, fixed by elastic. A domino mask. A white hat floated against the fronds. She wore a cloth gun-belt, with empty holsters.

Billy crawled over and hugged the small corpse. One cold grey arm flopped out of his desperate embrace. I worried he would snap her bones. That would be hard to explain. Joh was right. We needed a story we could sell.

There are things a movie star can get away with in Hollywood.

Drowning a child isn't one of them. Especially if the star is famous as a murderer of little girls. Fan magazines love to profile a screen villain who is at heart a gentle soul, cultivating rose bushes and reading fairy tales to orphans. Other rags seek seamier stories. They show film stars as the worst of us. Drunks, hit-and-run drivers, wife-beaters, degenerates, drug addicts... Monsters. Billy had posed for enough scowly stills, face twisted by collodion and Jack Pierce, to illustrate articles that would run under House of Horror headlines.

His career being over was the least of it.

He pressed his hand against Beata's chest and tried to will her to life.

Nothing happened. He'd never played a character with a healing touch. The Vaudois-Quin Process hadn't made him that kind of miracle worker.

He was lost in anguish. Next would come wrath.

When he got angry, he'd be impossible to stop. If Junior ordered this, he'd sent the wrong message. Killing Beata wouldn't scare Billy off. The Frankenstein Monster would batter down the doors of the Lamia Munro Clinic and tear off arms and heads. Even if Junior survived, little left would be worth keeping. His stolen talents wouldn't count.

But we'd lose Billy Pratt too.

My thoughts turned to Billy's liquor cabinet, where he kept enough varieties of gin to keep the whole British Raj pickled through monsoon season. When it came to cocktails, Billy was a martini man. The house had a wine cellar too. Katharine Hepburn left stock behind when she fled the ghost who turned lights on and off while she wasn't in the room. That spook knew better than to bother Boris Karloff.

'Someone's coming,' said Joh, gun in hand.

We went quiet and listened. Noise drew us to the reception hall. Slow, heavy footsteps came up the drive. We looked at the door.

Joh raised his gun. Billy wiped froth from his thin lips.

The door opened.

A familiar silhouette showed us its back. Flat head, broad shoulders, long arms. Norman Quin had shoved the door open with his back because his hands weren't free. He carried two large silver cases, like the kind used to transport camera equipment. He turned, like Billy in *Frankenstein*, bringing his awful, greyish face into the light.

Joh had his first sight of the Monster. It was one thing to be told what had been done to Engineer Quin… it was another to see the stitched-together ruin for himself, not in black and white on a screen but in the flesh and getting closer. The smell hit me again. Joh had to resist an impulse to shoot on sight. Quin wore new blue overalls and custom-made boots. The cleft in his forehead was infected by rust-coloured fungus.

He wasn't alone. Dr Vaudois came into the house too, along with a woman I didn't know. She wasn't dressed as a nurse. An ambulance was parked in the drive. Hector Munro grinned at the wheel and waved at me.

If Joh had known who Hector was, he'd have clipped him then and there.

The way the private investigator told it, he hadn't gunned any Sparx Brothers – just shivved one of their stand-ins with a spoon. The rest of the clan got notched by Stephen Swift. Since the banana switcheroo, Joh had taken more care of his .38. It must rankle that he hadn't shot anyone in this case. He was supposed to be the professional. The hardboiled, two-fisted dick. Not the fainting, shrinking maiden in need of rescue.

Dr Vaudois fussed over Quin's cases. The engineer was being used as a beast of burden – not the Monster, but the hunchback. A mad scientist's minion. Qualified to rob graves and fly kites.

'Gentlemen,' said Dr Vaudois, 'we meet again.'

'You should cackle when you say that,' I advised. '*B'wa-ha-ha-hah!*'

He responded with something terrifyingly like a laugh.

Another human sound of absolute insanity.

Joh levelled his gun at the doctor. Quin put down the suitcases and loomed into the line of fire, inviting Joh to riddle his chest with slugs. If that scene played out the way it does in the movies, bullets would barely slow the monster as he crossed the room, reaching out with tiny, flexible, strangling hands.

It finally reached Billy's brain that Beata's murderer was here.

Not Dr Vaudois. He was complicit but delegated to others. Had Quin re-enacted the scene from *Frankenstein* with the girl floating flowers in the lake? Where the Monster tosses Little Maria into the water, expecting her to float prettily. I couldn't see it. It was probably a Munro – most likely Hector. Yes, definitely Hector. When he'd waved, I saw his cuffs were wrinkled and water-stained. From holding the girl underwater. The Littlest Lone Ranger would have fought. If I'd had a brick in my hand and Hector was within reach, I'd have battered his brains to paste. So angry I could barely see, I still filed the clue that gave him away as a killer. It's the curse of mystery writers. We always jot down clues. Lipstick traces. Second stains. A black mask. Anything we can use. It's no surprise that people get uncomfortable around us. They're carrion. We're ghouls.

Billy's Mummy eyes glistened with sorrow and rage. Veins in his neck and temples pulsed as if his blood had turned luminous. His hands had an *Invisible Ray* glow.

He was no longer squeamish about his Death Touch. He would end the life of Dr Voodoo. He would reclaim his title as the Only Frankenstein Monster. Then he would rampage. The quality of Billy's everyone remarked on was his kindness. It was burned out of him. By the time he was spent, there'd be fewer living Munros than Sparx Brothers.

'Stay where you are, if you please, Mr Karloff,' said Dr Vaudois.

'*Or else what?*' said Billy.

That hung there. Snarled with venom.

Not the words of a grunting brute – a cold, defiant threat.

'*Or else…* the little girl stays dead.'

That's when we remembered the Vaudois-Quin Process could bring Beata back…

… and all three of us caved in.

We competed in begging and pleading, offering silence, mercy, money, fealty, pathetic gratitude. Even as we gabbled, I had contempt for us. We grovelled at the tennis shoes of a parasite. Dr Vaudois wasn't even a tyrant. Just a better-dressed minion. A grifting vizier, translating his master's whims into execution orders.

'Shush,' he said, like a schoolmaster. 'Norman…'

Quin opened the cases. One contained harnesses of wire and leather – related to those galvanic belts and corsets quacks used to hawk as salve-alls. The other held an array of batteries and glass receptacles packed in straw. Quin assembled a device, slotting parts together and fixing connections. His seamstress fingers worked deftly. This model was considerably more compact than the machine at the Clinic. He had made refinements since his recapture. Had he been forced? Or was he back in the fold? Once, he'd tried to escape.

What was in it for Norman Quin?

Was it a compulsion to make these things, to achieve these wonders? Without qualm. So long as the laboratory bills were settled, his backers could do what they will with the products of his genius. Not to care took a remarkable, curious vacancy. His conscience was dead in him, while other qualities thrived – imagination, desire, invention. I saw why he had put on the face of the Monster. I had no doubt that the alterations had been made at his request. What frightened me was that I understood Quin. A dead little girl upset me, but not so much I forgot to take notes for future mysteries.

'This is a transaction,' said Dr Vaudois. 'Mr Karloff, it is felt that we have been overgenerous. Our intent in demonstrating the process was not to bestow quite so much on you.'

'Junior wants his Death Touch?' I said.

'It's not as simple as that, Mr Chandler.'

'It's exactly as simple as that. The shrimp is not complicated.'

'Perhaps, as you say, it is just that. It's not my part to opine. More interesting than the specifics, as I'm sure you'll agree, is the precedent. This is another stage of the great experiment: to siphon an intangible attribute and store it so it can within the hour be conferred upon our benefactor. Don't you see how exciting this is? For science?'

'Junior doesn't even have to be in the room when he rapes you?'

I was only snotting the doctor to snatch back some crumbs of self-respect. I'd begged and pleaded with the others.

'Fetch the girl,' said Dr Vaudois. 'We will show good faith by treating her before you submit.'

'Big of you, Doc,' said Joh.

They could trust us. We couldn't trust them.

Is that why we always lose?

Billy loped out to the pool to fetch Beata.

The woman who hadn't spoken went to the mirror above the fireplace and rubbed at the Munro message with her sleeve.

'Hagar,' said Dr Vaudois. 'There's a simpler way to get rid of evidence. No one is that good at jigsaws.'

The woman – Hagar Munro? – pulled the mirror down and stepped away as it smashed on the hearth. She smiled an imbecile smile, delighted by breakage. I could imagine her giggling as she emptied the sack of rattlers.

Billy came back with Beata, like the peasant carrying his drowned daughter. He laid her on a table, stroking her hair away from her face. A funny thing – in Mrs Shelley's *Frankenstein*, the Monster *saves* a girl from drowning. He still gets grief for it. Quin attached his apparatus to the corpse. If he touched her roughly, Billy growled.

'Are we sure about this?' asked Joh. 'We could be signing up for something worse.'

'There *is* nothing worse,' I said, nodding at the dead child.

'You say that now, Ray…'

'Now is when we have to deal with it. This is simple. A little girl. Should she be alive or dead?'

Joh thought it over.

That he agreed with me in the end was a stone picked off the path and thrown away. That he had to think it over was a problem to be dealt with later.

Quin fitted a bell-shaped helmet over Beata's head and attached wires to terminals in its ruff. The helmet had bulbous glass eyeholes.

'Did you tailor one of these in a child's size especially?' I asked.

Quin looked at me. I remembered the time we'd spent together, the odd little hints of intelligence. He was a moral imbecile. I was right to leave him behind when we flew off – though I wondered if that betrayal had been used to persuade him back into the service of Home House.

He fixed the wires, checked all the connections.

He unrolled an ordinary flex, like one you'd use for an electric fan. Hagar plugged it into a power outlet. Lights came on. Dial needles twitched. The carousel of resurrection at the Lamia Munro Clinic was a futuristic pagan idol. This was a household appliance. A vacuum cleaner or a radiogram. Quin waited for it to warm up.

Then he flicked a toggle switch. A whining hum sounded.

The lights burned so brightly I had to look away.

Beata didn't kick and sit up.

Of course it wouldn't work. Why would it? This was all crackpot nonsense. Any real science was incidental.

Billy made guttural noises, alarming Hagar.

Quin nodded a silent count of ten, then flicked the switch again.

The whining hum resumed. Still nothing.

Joh was about to shoot someone.

The glass eyes misted. Beata was breathing.

'Get that off her,' I said. 'The helmet.'

'… is perfectly safe,' said Dr Vaudois. 'It ensures…'

'Her lungs are full of water, you dolt.'

Billy tore the helmet off, yanking out wires, breaking lights.

He hugged Beata from behind and exerted a crushing grip on her ribcage. He let her go limp, then squeezed again. She spewed water, choking. She thumped against his arms, hesitated and threw up again. Then her hands went to her neck and she put her mask on properly.

'Hi-Yo, Silver, away…' she said – and slumped.

'See, she's fine,' said Dr Vaudois, prematurely. 'Now, if we could move swiftly to the next phase. Mr Karloff, if you would consent…'

Billy handed Beata to me – she was still wet, but warm. She fell asleep. Being dead all evening had tuckered her out. A white streak threaded through her long, dark hair. Would she dye it or flaunt it? Was the Beata who came back the Beata who went away? She'd be able to crack walnuts between her knuckles. Billy had come back with other talents – which was why we were going through this transaction. Would Beata now be as sharp a shot as the Lone Ranger?

Quin held up another harness, tailored for a full-grown man.

That's when Joh gunned Dr Vaudois.

Hector Munro limped towards the house, pistol in hand. He was still slow from the bullet I'd put in his leg.

Dr Vaudois' wound was in the upper chest, between heart and shoulder. An artery was clipped. Bright blood gushed like a crimson oil strike.

Joh shot Hector too – in the throat and then the right eye.

Hector dropped at once, dead on the doorstep. Dr Voodoo took about thirty seconds to empty out.

Hagar's mouth opened. She was certain Joh would kill her next.

'What's the matter, doll,' he said. 'Quin can cure death, right? So bring them back.'

That plainly wasn't going to happen.

I'd been wrong. They couldn't trust us. One of us.

Somehow I was shocked. Joh had broken his word. Of course, he'd been to a different school. He'd learned to get things done.

Billy was even more determined to go through with his part of the deal. He'd give up his gifts to be free of the Death Touch. He'd accept crippling back pain as his lot. He felt he deserved it. He tried to strap himself into the harness. Quin had to undo misaligned catches and show him how do to it properly.

'You might want to hurry,' said Joh. 'It's been a rowdy soirée. Even up here, neighbours will complain.'

Quin kept on. He knew what he was doing.

Hagar backed towards the open door, then dodged round the ambulance and took off into the night. She ran like someone used to uneven ground.

Quin fit more components into his apparatus. Sturdy flasks containing curls of glass tubing, like inert neon signs. He threw switches. The tubes glowed violet – a colour not found in nature. It was hard to look away. Something had been drawn out of Billy – something at once fluid and gaseous. Ectoplasm? An essence of the Vaudois-Quin Process?

Quin removed the flasks and carefully packed them back in their straw. Billy tried to tear off his harness without undoing the straps. He was no longer strong enough. I helped him. His face was ashen and he kept wincing. He had changed back – if that was even possible. Going forward in agony knowing it was by choice must change a man in another way.

Quin was gone in the ambulance with his damned flasks by the time we heard sirens.

Joh was gone by the time the cops showed. One of them kicked a rattlesnake off the doorstep before coming into the house.

The corpses had to be explained. Billy could talk only at the level of 'friend good… fire bad'. It was my responsibility to lie my socks off. To tell a story.

I sold an attack by crazed horror film fans and showed the damage they caused before I shot them. At least, I thought I shot them. I'd been drinking all day and couldn't be sure. Whoever shot them, it was self-defence. Or accidental discharge. The unwelcome guests had let snakes loose and there had been a mess of shooting. I pointed out the bullets lodged in the ceiling beams.

Then the cops should have asked for the gun – but didn't. They didn't even sniff my liquor-free breath, though I planned to shore up that part of my fairy tale as soon as possible.

Yarn-spinning was a waste. The fix was in.

The police went through their lines like B players at the end of a shooting day. The collection crew came from the Lamia Munro Clinic, not the morgue. They acted as if they knew this scene wouldn't be in the final cut.

The only detail that excited much interest was the broken mirror. Seven years' bad luck, but not for Billy and me. We hadn't smashed it. I explained there'd been a woman with the dead men. A wild-haired harridan with an autograph book. She'd toppled the looking glass. A cop picked up the empty gilt frame.

'When someone else breaks your mirror,' he said, 'you get seven years' *good* luck.'

I'd not heard that before and didn't believe it now.

PART FIVE

THE MAN IN CHAPTER 30

30

I never knew his name, but he was rather tall and handsome for a detective, which is what he must have been, partly because he was there, and partly because when he leaned across the table to fit in a puzzle piece, I could see the leather underarm holster and the butt end of an automatic pistol.

He didn't speak much, but, when he did, he had a nice voice, a soft-water voice. And he had a smile that warmed the whole room.

'Wonderful casting,' I said, looking at him across the puzzle.

It was at least a thousand pieces – if they were all there, which I doubted. The jigsaw had come from a thrift shop, loose pieces collected in a cigar carton. The box was long-lost, so there was no picture to guide in the puzzle's completion.

We were doing the jigsaw. Or he was. I was just there, watching his small and very neat and very clean hands go out across the table and select a piece and fit it in. When he did this, he pursed his lips a little and whistled without tune, a low soft whistle, like a mature engine that is very sure of itself.

He smiled and fit in the last edge piece.

He had an oblong, with a few busy patches of vivid red spreading into the jumble of the interior. It wasn't even apparent which of us was looking at the picture the right way up. It wasn't quite a fifty-fifty chance. The oblong could have been on its end, if the picture were a portrait rather than a panorama. The pile of pieces didn't have enough flesh tones to suggest we were going for that. It couldn't be as simple as Ariadne, posing to show off her long neck and looking slightly beyond the artist – and the theoretical viewer – to stop him noticing her hunger, masking her serpent self with a sham of melancholy.

The picture was never just Ariadne…

… though she'd be in it. She was in every picture ever painted.

'What do you do in your spare time?' I asked him.

'I write a little,' he said. 'I use a noiseless Underwood, though I have my eye on an Olivetti.'

'Perfect casting,' I said, and fit in a piece. Cold dark blue, with a half-fleck of yellow that matched an edge piece. Sea or sky.

A thing I've said before and will say again came to mind.

When in doubt, have a man come through a door with a gun in his hand.

People remember that, but not the context. I was talking about the kind of writing I started with, not the sort I aspired to. *Black Mask-Dime Detective* yarns, where the need for action was constant and if you stopped to breathe you were lost. I acknowledge this could get silly. The real advice in the paragraph, which isn't funny and is harder to take, comes at the end. 'A writer who is afraid to over-reach himself is as useless as a general who is afraid to be wrong.'

Here was a man with a gun. Not at the door – now I looked, I couldn't see a door – but sat there across from me. I have trouble getting people into and out of rooms. Best just to end the chapter and start the next one somewhere else.

He clicked together an archipelago of pieces. A figure, falling or flying. Perhaps an animal – a pig or fat dog – in a human's jerkin with boots over its hind legs? The assembled figure didn't connect with any of the edges. He pressed it flat against the desktop and turned it around as if winding a mechanism. With no other guideline, he tried to make out the prevailing direction of the picture to guess which way up this section was supposed to be. The result, as ever, was inconclusive.

Outside the frame were islands of pieces, sorted into colours.

His nails were bright but short. You could see he was a man who loved to move his hands, to make little neat inconspicuous motions with them, motions without any special meaning, but smooth and flowing and light as swansdown. They gave him a feel of making headway. The picture emerged. The puzzle was getting solved, methodically. Even if pieces were missing, you would see what it was supposed to be. The sky or sea would be dotted with wobbly squares of absence that gave away that the world had once been taken apart and jumbled into a box.

It was about five-thirty. The sky behind the screened window was getting light. The roll-top desk in the corner was shut. The room was anonymous but familiar. The furniture could have come from a scenery dock. The dust on the desk might have been puffed from a can. The room was somewhere I knew. Were we in one of the many, many apartments Cissy and Taki and I had taken in our long evasive manoeuvre across the map of Los Angeles?

Or was this a building just across the street?

Set up by the window was a tripod. A telescope would fit on it. So would a camera.

This was a detective's room. One of the rooms I went to when I sat down to write.

He was a handsome man. More than a dick would be.

If he were a movie star, he wouldn't be Billy. Cary Grant.

He had a boyish aspect – a singer in a musical – and a shark-smile of menace – a tough guy in a gangster picture. A little of him was Dash Hammett, prematurely grey in a way that suited him and drew admiring glances. A lot was Joh, without the wrestler's bulk. It was a face I never bothered to imagine. The way I write – first person singular – he never needed describing, unless he caught sight of his fizzog in a mirror and was compelled by self-regard and wry amusement to examine his latest cuts and bruises. He took plenty of beatings, but it didn't do him lasting harm – not on the outside.

'I should be angry with you, Chandler,' he said.

'I know. I apologise.'

'You shouldn't get involved in these elaborate messes. No point in it that I can see.'

'They pass the time on long journeys.'

'Is that a metaphor? The Long Journey of Life… the implication being that no one wants to get to where we're all going, that we'll take any chance to dawdle.'

'No, it's a literalism. Train journeys, bus journeys, afternoons in rooms like this… waiting to be seen by doctors or lawyers or editors. Empty afternoons.'

'That's a title for one of the books you imagine you'll write.'

'Empty Afternoons. English Summer. Good point.'

His smile was sharp, bright and engaging.

'I get why you'd rather leave this room,' he said. 'But I know you won't.'

He wasn't being cruel.

If I were him – which, as I'd learned painfully, I was and wasn't – I'd want to get my own back on Chandler, R.T. I'd slapped him about with no mercy. I'd bopped him on the skull so many times that only story requirements lifted him back out of those black, black pools. Everyone he met lied to him, shot at him, wanted him jailed or dead, shook him down, roughed him up. Women all went for his pan – not a one didn't swoon. He pushed them away, knowing they'd chew off his head like lady praying mantises on their wedding nights. He had few friends. No family. I didn't even give him a cat.

He rented space in my head.

Was that where this room was?

'You're introspecting, Chandler.'

'You're not human, Marlowe,' I said.

'No. I'm not. I'm something else.'

His smile darkened.

Suddenly, he saw it. Like an endgame that prompts a spurt of energy from a challenger who sees how he can best the tired old master. Pieces fell in place. His hands moved so fast I couldn't see them. If he went for his gun, he was quicker on the draw than any cowboy. Western gunslingers would be terrified of him, because he was their successor. Who'd come after? Flash Gordon and Buck Rogers, with ray blasters. Miracle monsters like Stephen Swift and Junior Home – stretching limbs, x-ray eyes, mind over matter, deaths that never take. Gaudy angels and parfait knights, striving against the fall of endless night.

He was satisfied with the patch he'd made.

From my side of the table, I couldn't make out what it was.

I'd been waiting an age to meet the Man in Chapter Thirty. From him, I was supposed to get the answers.

'Who killed the chauffeur?' I asked.

'You know,' he said. 'But no one wants to hear it. When they ask, tell them you can't remember. They'll think it funny. That you're cavalier. If you own up to taking it seriously, there'll be no mercy. Blood in the water. Say you killed him, but it was long ago and so complicated you can't remember. It's not what's important anyway. You'd still while away the long journey with pleasure if the last chapter was torn out.'

I felt cold, tired and hungry.

Also uncomfortable. How long had I been in this room with a window but no door, with the shut desk and tripod with no camera? The place had the whiff of the classroom. Chalk and chemicals. The knout hung in the corner. If I turned, I'd see it there.

Genesis, Exodus, Leviticus, Numbers...

Tearing out the last chapter was a temptation. It meant ducking the hard work of finishing the jigsaw, avoiding the disappointment of readers who wanted the killer to be someone else... not the vampire woman, but the professional gambler... or the little poisoned man who might not be dead... or the narrator, the detective, the author... yes, blame that many-headed bastard for all the ills of the world. Anyone but *her* – the girl on the cover with hair over one eye and long, silk legs. Save the dame and chuck the rest to wolves.

The detective took a pipe out of his vest pocket. He tipped in tobacco from a pouch, lit up with a match from a book – the cover said 'Florian's', which struck me as a clue – and sucked.

I didn't have my pipe with me and now missed it terribly.

Was he smoking my pipe? I'd not be surprised, though it was a low trick. Beneath him, really. I should know.

'You know how difficult an Olivetti is?' he said.

'All typewriters are treacherous. When you're up at five in the morning and the rest of the apartment is dead, the "noiseless" Underwood chatters like a tommy gun. If words come easy, your fingers bleed. If they're still-born, you want to jam your hands between the keys. Who writes well?'

'Hammett.'

That stung. Writers should never ask civilians who they like.

'Cornell Woolrich?' I countered.

He shook his head. 'Too convoluted. Too crazy. Too many witch doctors and head-shrinkers. Mystery is just life. No editorial needed.'

'Is that a dig?'

'Not at all.'

He puffed happily, putting together pieces without looking at the puzzle. A bit of a show-off. He had inside information he wasn't sharing, which is classed as a cheat in how-to-write-a-mystery articles. Sometimes the puzzle got done just because it had to, not because anyone helped.

'How do you feel about Mary Shelley?' I asked.

He stretched and sat back in his chair. His holstered gun flapped in his armpit like the dead hand of an undeveloped twin attached to his skeleton.

'Writers love *Frankenstein* so much they tell the story over and over again,' he said. 'You make a monster and kick it out of the apartment because it's not the beauty you wanted… and your hideous progeny gets smart and vicious, then wrecks your life, kills your family and friends and finally leads you on a dance that can only end when you die. But *it* goes on without you. Years after you're dead, the monster is earning money. It's more famous than you are. You get off the train and freeze to death on the platform, but its journey goes on… books, plays, motion pictures, radio… comic books, television and whatever they come up with next… say you swallow a lozenge and the story runs through your head, and you can be whoever you want in it… or that machine you half-imagined which sets fictional characters free from Flatland… the guy with the gun… the cop on the beat… the woman in the window. Whatever, there'll still be *Frankenstein*. And me. In some form, in an old hat and coat or armour and a cloak. The question, Chandler, is whether there'll still be you.'

He looked at me with that goddamn movie star come-hither smile, pipe clamped between teeth as perfect as Clark Gable's china falsies. He had a tracery of pieces in his hands, a crucial section that would spark recognition of what the picture was. He fit it into the puzzle. The pieces seemed to pour through his fingers, in a blur.

'Are you the man at the door or the eye in the room?' I asked. 'With a gun.'

The stream of pieces stopped. Without apparent motion a gun took their place. He held it lightly in his right hand pointed at a distant corner of the room. It went away and the pieces started flowing again.

'You're wasted here,' I said. 'You ought to be in Las Vegas.'

'That should be my line, Chandler.'

'It will be, Oscar. It will be.'

'I know.'

He tapped out his pipe – my pipe? If it was a pipe. 'Pipe' was a word we agreed upon to signify a smoking implement… but a pipe was also a length of lead tubing handy as a bludgeon. Very easily classified as a blunt instrument. Wielded by Colonel Cummerbund in Lady Araminta Trent-Fussey's library with an antimacassar wrapped around it to preserve someone else's fingerprints… or by a brainless hood in an alleyway who didn't even bother with gloves because prints never broke a case and cops could be bought to look the other way.

The smuts spilled into a bowl made from a sawn-off, upturned human cranium. Three plates meshed together with squiggle sutures infinitely more intricate than jigsaw pieces. One plate was not bone but silver, engraved with a name and a date.

The picture, downside away from me so it was right side up to the man with a gun, was maybe one-third done. If it were a map, the continents would be there, in unfamiliar configurations, but the oceans were irregular holes of scuffed brown tabletop.

I could make out the picture, though.

A car – not a Buick – was being pulled out of water.

Men stood on a pier.

In the clouds above, the pre-dawn/tinged-with-crimson masses, was the shape of a huge face.

Mine, of course. When you put the picture together, you see yourself. Not clearly.

Something clicked and the window shutter rolled up. Light assailed the room, making me flinch and blink and shudder.

I looked from the window to the square-shouldered man across the table. But he wasn't there any more. The puzzle pieces weren't there any more either. Nothing was there but a chair pushed in neatly to the table and the skull-top ashtray he'd emptied his pipe into, now cleaned to a shine.

For a long moment I had that creepy feeling.

Then I wasn't in the room any more. I was back in coptown.

PART SIX

MYSTERY AND IMAGINATION

31

We spent most of the day at the Malibu Sheriff Station. Lieutenant Corder grilled us in his office, not a featureless room. With the windows open, you could smell the sea and hear gulls. He asked questions about Joh, most of which we answered honestly.

Corder's bookshelves were like a writer's: not a neat display according to size or author, suitable as background for a posed photograph, but a jumble of books of all shapes and sizes in a private system of use. Law, philosophy and history; almanacs, manuals and directories; a Bible, *Brewer's Dictionary of Phrase and Fable*, Roget's *Thesaurus*. No fiction, as he'd said – except a mint *Gone With the Wind*. A gift from someone who'd want to see it spine-out when they visited. A wife or a Mayor or a wife of a Mayor. On the slim ledge between books and shelf-edge were placed odd-shaped seashells.

If it weren't for the photographs of Corder in uniform, it could have been the office of a popular college professor. Our conversation was more like a seminar than an interrogation. He saw us individually, then all together. Billy, me and the English woman, Stephen Swift. We talked around the subject. Each student gave an edited account of their association with Joh Devlin, sticking close to what was on the public record. Obviously, we left a lot out – which, equally obviously, Corder knew we had. At the end of the session, the prof was benignly disappointed in the class but kicked us loose anyway.

While walking us out of the station, just to show off, he solved a mystery.

'Devlin didn't have to be conscious – or alive – at the wheel of the car, with his foot pressed on the accelerator,' he said. 'A murderer could have wedged the pedal down with a cake of ice. In the sea, the evidence would melt. You're scowling, Chandler. Don't like it? Too "Agatha Christie"?'

'It makes me squirm,' I admitted. 'People don't kill each other like that. Not really.'

'People also don't kill themselves like this. So where does that leave us?'

'Not in a green-jacket mystery.'

That was what Joh called them. Refined English entertainments, written by and for dons, old maids and horrid bright schoolboys. Now, putting him in his place, Joh was a green-jacket corpse. He even had his head blown off, all the better to delay formal identification and allow the unlikely-to-ridiculous turn-up that another tall, wide party with a silver plate in his head had been murdered in his place. The real Joh Devlin would return from a brass-rubbing tour of the Hebrides in Chapter Eight to take over the investigation and justify the title *The Man Who Solved His Own Murder*.

'I don't suppose that, when we ask around, any of you will turn out to have ordered an extra block from the iceman this week.'

'In a truly insufferable whodunit, we all would have,' I said.

'This was *arranged*,' said Corder. 'It's personal. The car roaring off the pier, the unresolved murder-or-suicide conundrum, the mutilation of the body. That's from your book, Chandler. But open up the trunk and out pops a mermaid. Who does that come from – Thorne Smith? The shotgun contraption is a taunt. The sort of trick you think is beneath you, that you'd never put in your mysteries. Come back when you figure it out. Or don't. If I don't catch the gunnie who got Devlin, I'll catch the gunnie who gets you. It's easier to see a pattern after the second or third corpse.'

'And that's beneath you, Lieutenant,' said Billy.

Corder shrugged, admitting it. He was tired.

We all were.

He left us at the door of the Sheriff's Station. We stepped out into hard daylight.

I knew in my bones where this was going.

First Joh Devlin and Stephen Swift.

Then… Raymond Chandler and Boris Karloff.

I knew whose list we were on. Corder was at least half-way decent. Telling him the whole story would put him on the list too.

He'd have trouble enough with this case.

The woman who hadn't drowned would bother him. No theoretical cake of ice explained her. She wasn't one of the delightful magic minxes Thorne Smith put in his books. She was a *wrongness*. Another Joh Devlin expression. Any circumstance that provoked what I called 'that creepy feeling'.

I looked at Stephen Swift – Laurel Ives – Philippa Zhan – Leila Bostwick – Witch-Eye. She'd suggested we call her Steps. She'd said her eye injury went back to her school days. Not from a cricket ball or a hockey stick. From 'overstraining' the talents Joh told us about – what had she called them? – her 'wicky tricks'.

I judged she was not often seen in sunshine. Her uncovered eye blinked as she adjusted to the outdoors. She was dressed for a night out, in a gown that had dried on her. A gown by Ariadne.

Billy, gallant as ever, lent her his coat.

How much did Miss Steps know about us? As much as we'd heard about her?

Her story, which we didn't necessarily choose to believe all of, was that she'd received a telegram, purportedly from Joh, asking her to meet him in the Polo Lounge. The telegram was addressed to Leila Bostwick, a name she'd only been using for a week, and presented to her at the front desk of a hotel she hadn't checked into yet. It would take a detective to pull that off. A dogged sleuth who'd been on her case for two years or more. She arrived early – to scout her escape routes, I'd guess – and ordered a Manhattan. There must have been something in it besides the cherry. She tried to leave under her own steam but didn't make it. Her legs stopped working. A helpful soul escorted her through the lobby of the Beverly Hills Hotel and into the trunk of a Studebaker. She couldn't make out whether the helpful soul was Joh or not. She said she'd no way of knowing how much he'd changed. But she knew his car well enough to recognise it.

Though her vision was getting artistic, she made out someone Joh-sized slumped in the front passenger seat. It'd have been fairer to a theoretical reader if she'd also noticed a set of ice-tongs on the floor of the car... a detail that'd need to be mentioned sixty or seventy pages before the smart cop came up with the accelerator wedge theory. But no tongs were there.

In the dark, the venom really took hold and she relaxed into deep, dreamless sleep. She'd have to be knocked cold, if what Joh had told us was true, or else she'd have used one of her remaining mental silver bullets to break the trunk catch and visit death on her assailant. Next thing she knew, she was in icy water, scratching at her metal coffin-lid. Light burst in on her and she fully came to flopping on the deck of the recovery barge, with saltwater rising in her gorge.

Now the three of us stood in front of the Sheriff's Station.

Out of official earshot.

'Joh told us there was a side effect of what happened at Home House you didn't want to test,' said Billy. 'He said you said you'd "had enough of laboratory conditions".'

She looked at him. He wasn't what you expected before dusk either.

'Has it been tested now?'

She let that lie for a while.

It sank in that what Joh had told us about her was all true – about Blood Bath Bungalow and the Sparx Brothers and the Vaudois-Quin Process. After hours of tiptoeing around parts of the tale Lieutenant Corder wouldn't be able to use, it was a relief to her to talk with people who were under no obligation to disbelieve the fantastic.

'If that was the idea, it was unnecessary,' she said. 'I've been "accident-prone" lately. This wasn't my first fatal car crash. And there was a suspicious gas leak in my digs last year. It really did kill the canary first. Yet here I am, the undying woman. Afraid of me yet?'

She touched a forefinger to her temple. Her hidden eye was on us.

I had a chill, remembering exploding vases and Death Touches.

'Don't worry,' she said. 'I keep a low profile. There are things I still don't want to test. In some circumstances, not dying could be a handicap. They used to say being born with talent was a curse. They might have been right all along. How do you think Junior Home is enjoying his gifts?'

Not at all, I thought.

Which might explain the house-clearing. Got to check off names on that list while you can still get a sick kick out of sending gaudy floral tributes moistened with crocodile tears.

The thing Ward Home Junior hadn't seen coming was the War.

The war America wasn't in. Yet. The war they wouldn't let me in. A few loud voices were selling America First and isolationism and let-the-Europeans-settle-their-own-mess… but that wasn't the mood of the country. Especially with Japan – a fully paid-up Axis Power – making aggressive moves in the South Pacific.

Hitler invaded Poland just as Pyramid was putting the finishing touches on their first Technicolor super-production, *Say It With Stukas*. A musical about love, laughter and civilian casualties in which smiling bomber pilots gaily obliterate a fictional country called Angle-Land. The big premiere was picketed by a stunning array of Hollywood stars, notably those who were British or Jewish. Unlike the major studios, Pyramid didn't own its own chain of theatres – the Old Man hadn't let Junior buy that part of the train set. When exhibitors across the country refused to book *all* Pyramid pictures – not just the dive bomber musical – the studio faced ruin. Vultures gathered over the Home Estate. Dry Bone Mullins and Trooper broke their contracts and signed with Republic. A comedy remake of *The Fiend of Fog Lane*, set to introduce two new Sparx Brothers, Bongo and Flatbush, was abandoned unfinished.

The Lamia Munro Clinic had struggled since the disappearance of its respected founder. Dr Lionel R. Vaudois was never officially connected with the crazed horror film fan who got shot at the Karloff residence a few years back, mostly because that incident didn't get written up at all. The rumour was that the quack had embezzled as much as he could and skipped to Haiti to continue his experiments on the living dead. Norman F. Quin might actually have gone to the island. Or else was still in the basement of Home House, tinkering away. He hadn't shown his Frankenstein Monster face in public since that night.

If what happened was the Victory of the Overman, you'd hate to see what Defeat was like.

Junior could detonate all the vases he liked and review his robot troops every day of the week and twice on Sundays. But he was bankrupt, disinherited and under investigation by the FBI as a Nazi spy. A rare thing Franklin D. Roosevelt and J. Edgar Hoover agreed on was that Ward Home Junior was a pathetic, dangerous dope who ought to be locked up.

Just the sort to send killers after his enemies.

Bongo and Flatbush? That wired shotgun trick was a remake of the Murder of Dan Ysidro. Or was it one of the smarter Bims? Vengeance-crazed Munros?

It wasn't as if we were responsible for Junior's fall. He'd scared us off… even Joh, who scared less easily than me or Billy. What happened with Beata Sol was a persuasive argument that we should stick to writing or starring in mysteries and quit playing detective. But spiteful boys never blame themselves and bullies don't pick fights with people who can really hurt them. Looking around for people he could take revenge on and get away with it, he might easily seize on us. Joh had killed his pet mad doctor – and, probably less upsetting to him, one of his maternal relatives. If he now had a Death Touch, we were the sorts he'd want to use it on.

The three of us stood there, longer than we needed to.

I realised why Stephen Swift lingered.

She needed a lift back to Los Angeles – the ride she'd taken out to Malibu wasn't available. We both offered, but she picked Billy over me. He called her 'Steps' with something like familiarity.

Their voices were alike. Those strange pauses inside words. She wasn't mimicking him. She just came from a place near where he did. And I don't mean Potters Bar. A spiritual place. Imaginary England.

Billy asked me to call on him in Coldwater Canyon as soon as I could get away. I understood his thinking. Or at least, I thought I did. I'm a writer, not a seer.

We needed to protect ourselves. And we needed to do something for Joh.

Probably the thing he'd wanted us to do all along.

Slay Junior and burn down his house.

In this story, we weren't monsters. Not even Boris Karloff and Witch-Eye. We were peasants. It was time we lit our torches and marched on the castle.

32

I hadn't been out to Billy's home since the night he gave up the gifts forced on him at the Lamia Munro Clinic. The night Joh killed Dr Vaudois and Hector Munro. The night Beata Sol died – and came back.

Cissy and I had moved farther away, several times. Out of the city, to a cabin near Big Bear Lake, even. We still changed addresses every few months. I was stuck on a new Philip Marlowe I wasn't very satisfied with. Knopf wanted a title 'like *The Maltese Falcon*' so I pitched *The Brasher Doubloon*. Someone's niece said 'Brasher' sounded too much like 'brassiere' so I proposed the dullest, flattest title I could think of, *The High Window*. Knopf professed to be delighted. I'll change it – or maybe not. It might suit a dull, flat book. Mr Marlowe, I admitted to myself, was close to fagged out. I should crack on with *English Summer*… which, if done properly, would get me in a different weight class. Cornell Woolrich lives in hotel rooms. Somerset Maugham owns several villas.

Billy, too, had thrown himself into other pursuits. Even without the something extra of the Vaudois-Quin Process, he had a remarkable surge of middle-aged pep. Besides submitting to Jack Pierce's torture chair so he could lumber forth in *Son of Frankenstein*, he fathered his very own Daughter of Frankenstein. He did a lot of work for the British War Effort, determined to do his bit – even if in charity cricket matches rather than combat. He'd more than earned his red badge in battle with Bims and Munros and as unarmed rear-gunner in R.T. Chandler's Flying Horror Show. He played a Chinese detective in a series for the cheapie outfit,

Monogram. The films were throwaways, but I saw more of Billy in James Lee Wong than in most of his horror roles. He picked pieces of Joh I hadn't used for Marlowe, making Mr Wong more than an ersatz Charlie Chan. Mannerisms, a way of thinking aloud and watchful pauses before springing a trap on a culprit. The Monster was becoming a sleuth. But he was also in pain, all the time. Sometimes he had to wear braces on his legs. No one who wasn't there understood how much he had given up.

I might also have stayed away because Coldwater Canyon was the Scene of the Crime. I didn't like to count the number of laws broken that night or consider the extent of my own culpability and complicity. For anxious weeks, I was convinced the cops had only pretended to look the other way. A calculating big brain in homicide had us marked. When they had enough evidence to make charges stick, they would pounce.

That axe never fell.

The world of Mystery and Imagination went quiet for us. No more Ape Ricottes or Prospero Princes. No nocturnal depredations by the Catalina Cat Man. No need to impersonate Howard Hughes.

Ariadne must have been disappointed with the Heims. That Madonna in the church indicated she'd made a long-term investment in the family – and it wasn't paying off the way she liked. She had moved on and was playing with other toys.

Orson Welles terrified America with his *War of the Worlds* broadcast, then said it was a joke. In a photograph of his fractious press conference, there she was – white hair under a turban – seated three chairs away from the Boy Wonder. Why did a radio programme need a costume designer? The country was angry with Welles because he'd showed people things about fear – and about themselves – few wanted to own up to. I didn't envy him his sudden fame, which primed him for eventual comeuppance. Boy Wonders seldom make old bones.

If Billy and I saw each other less, Joh remained the tie between us – though, after the killings (one outright murder, one arguably self-defence), I kept raking over memories of our association as if it were a puzzle with missing pieces. I felt I wasn't seeing the picture on the box. I didn't grieve for Lionel Vaudois or Hector Munro – I'd shot Hector myself and only my rusty aim stopped me killing him – but Joh's executions struck me as a cynical shortcut. Pulp magazine private eyes dished gun justice like that. Grown-ups worked harder, made cases, got convictions.

In *The Big Sleep*, Marlowe kills a killer without qualm. He hadn't fully emerged from the chrysalis in which my *Black Mask-Dime Detective* bloodhounds – Mallory, Dalmas, Carmady – developed into him. My detective changed after I saw Joh shoot Hector Munro the way Marlowe shot Lash Canino.

The gunshots rang in my ears for a week. That'll happen when shooting starts indoors. I worried the tinnitus would be permanent, though it went away. I must use that clue. A suspect claims they weren't in the room when the shootee got shot, but Marlowe notices he has to repeat the questions because they're hearing something he can't. That wouldn't fit into *English Summer*, so Marlowe had some rope to play yet. Whenever I thought I'd got past him, ideas came up that only work with him on the case.

As a private detective, Joh pocketed more money than my gumshoe ever saw. 'Twenty-five dollars a day and expenses' sounds affordable till the itemised bill arrives and the penny drops that the term 'expenses' covers a multitude of the pricier sins. Whenever we got together, Joh tossed off four or five golden mystery ideas. I was never too tipsy to jot down items of interest. Joh clued me to the use of dental materials in the rare coin forgery racket. That's where the *Brassiere Doubloon* came from. He gave me one of Pinky Sparx's old ice-picks, along with instructions for its lethal use. Marlowe will eventually stumble over a corpse with an ice-pick in the back of the neck. If Knopf have their way, more than one. It takes three killings at least to hold the attention of a mystery fan.

Joh had quit even the marginally respectable magazine writing racket and turned to dashing off film stories for a fast payout. Not scripts – stories. Three-or-four-page synopses brought in as fat a fee as typing out a whole screenplay. Few of his skeleton yarns became A pictures. He came up with *The Man They Could Not Hang* for Billy. Twisted in mind and body after his execution, a scientist is brought back to life with a yen to electrocute the jurors who sent him to the gallows. Joh had gone back to 'write what you know'.

Privately, Billy told me playing too many Men They Could Not Hang made him seriously consider a return – aching back and all – to the legitimate theatre. The juvenile barnstormer of the Frozen North might be heading for Broadway. The farce on offer had only three jokes and too many murders. It was getting rewritten by everybody involved except the original playwright. It sounded like a close-out-of-town prospect to me, so I didn't invest. Guess how that turned out.

Two days after Joh's Studebaker was hauled onto a barge, I drove up to Coldwater Canyon.

I parked in Billy's drive and sat in the Packard for a minute or so, wondering whether I had the stomach to get out and go on. It was early afternoon. I could turn round and be in a bar in Santa Monica in twenty minutes, starting early on my next hangover. Lieutenant Corder could solve the case. Or not. Joh had got away with killing at least two people, so there would be a rough, *Black Mask* justice in someone getting away with killing him. Only I didn't believe that and neither did Billy. Philip Marlowe and James Lee Wong wouldn't quit.

Cissy hadn't asked about my trip up the coast. She hadn't passed comment when I followed our usual gimlets, sipped during the evening concert on the radio, with refills of straight gin, quaffed without the alibi of Rose's lime juice cordial. I told her Philip Marlowe was giving me gyp. The best, most sadistic detective in this story – Taki – knew exactly what I'd been up to and made her feelings known by mutilating cushions and swiping *animaux* from their shelf. Cissy said she had one of her heads coming.

It could not be put off. I got out of the car.

Joh was our friend. I didn't want to get in the habit of letting people who murder my friends waltz off free and clear. The rigged-up shotgun had *beheaded* Joh Devlin. We couldn't leave it at that.

The front door was open and, as I'd always done before, I walked through the house into the garden. I noticed child-related alterations – a basket of soft toys, carpeting over tile floor, that sweet formula-and-sick smell. The bullet-holes in the ceiling beams were plugged and creosoted over. A new mirror stood on the mantel.

I had the impression the garden had grown wilder. In the hills and canyons, you only have to look away for a minute and nature reasserts itself. All the oil and motion picture folk evaporate and you worry that behind every incense cedar is a Chumash Indian or a Mission Jesuit.

A low-fenced pen, half-filled with sand, was constructed well away from the pool. The Daughter of Frankenstein sat inside, holding the bars as if counting days till her time was served. A girl stood by the pen, watching the child, alert to the dangers of this garden. She was playing cat's cradle solitaire. Tight configurations of silk thread passed from one hand to the other.

Beata Sol was coming up to twelve. Tall and quiet, with a lightning streak through her long dark hair. Apparently, she didn't recall being dead. She was much changed, but at that age, who wasn't? She was grown out of her Lone Ranger mask and anticipating lipstick. When I asked Joh or Billy about her, they joshed me, as if I were worried she'd sprout fangs. She slept longer than most girls her age – which wasn't laziness. Beata said she needed more time to dream.

She had developed a talent. She could find lost things. Lockets fallen behind dressing tables. A half-read book left on a bench. An adventurous pet tortoise off on an odyssey in the long grass. If Beata thought about a lost thing, she knew where it was and – unlike any bogus psychic you could name – could give precise, practical directions to where it was. Joh had said that when she graduated from high school he'd take her into the investigations business. Her dowsing could mean big money.

Beata saw me step out of the house and shaded her eyes with her hands, stretching the cradle thread like a veil. She shrugged a greeting without saying words. She might have recognised or remembered me but, equally, might not. I was of little interest. She'd only think about me if I went missing.

The Karloff daughter eyed me as if I were bringing bad news from the parole board.

I looked at the widest and stoutest of the garden chairs. The one Joh used after flimsier lawn furniture let him down. I imagined him sat there, stubbing a cigar out in a cranium ashtray. Grinning. The sticking-up points of his moustache like little devil horns. Then I saw him without a head, a ring of blood-seepage marring his collar. I still wasn't getting the whole picture. Should I ask Beata where the missing pieces had fallen?

Billy appeared from behind the willow, clacking secateurs like a lobster claw. He wore cricket whites and a sombrero, a sportsmanlike border bandit.

'Monkey's under the back seat of Mrs Karloff's car,' said Beata.

Billy nodded sagely. 'An essential toy,' he explained to me, 'tragically lost and the cause of many tears. Now returned to his mistress.'

'Mrs Karloff's taken the car out,' said Beata.

'But Monkey is safe. There will be a joyous reunion.'

I looked at the kid and wasn't sure. Marlowe would have taken those tears another way and suspected tiny hands of shoving Monkey as far into shadow as possible, until the glass button eyes stopped glittering. The toy might be essential because the child was too terrified to risk – before now – trying to get rid of it. When it was restored, there would be recriminations. Monkey knew how to break things so the Daughter of Frankenstein took the blame.

'Let's go into the study, R.T.,' said Billy.

Billy had an office. A bright, airy room. His desk was next to a wicker basket into which he tossed no-hope scripts. Like a Muscle Beach Tarzan showing off with a telephone directory, he'd ripped *Ghost of Frankenstein* in half before consigning it to the oblivion bin. He'd had his fill of Jack Pierce and the flat head and neck-bolts. Let someone else be the New Lon Chaney – the New Boris Karloff, now. Universal could go hang. He was Broadway bound.

Billy's other guest was settled on a nap couch, perusing a book – *Creeps By Night: an Anthology of Modern Horror Stories selected by Dashiell Hammett*. She noticed our arrival and read aloud the blurb beneath the title…

'"A collection of spine-chilling stories by modern authors, wherein things that *can't* happen and ought not to happen *do* happen." I daresay we all know the feeling. Mr Chandler, hello again. I didn't get to mention it when we met, but I've read your books. I adore Moose Malloy and Little Velma.'

Stephen Swift wore black slacks and a jacket cut like a matador's. It was the sort of casual ensemble that takes a woman six hours to select and get into, and is best worn by someone hiding behind a curtain making sure the pointed toes of her pumps don't peep out.

Being fond of Little Velma scarcely suggested a wholesome personality. Still, I thanked her.

'Steps will be joining us,' said Billy.

'You're not worried about what happened to our previous associate?' I asked.

'Something closely related happened to me and is liable to happen again if a stop is not put to it,' she said. 'Recovering from fatal injuries is less gay and amusing than you might imagine. I've decided not sustaining fatal injuries is the way forward. How say you?'

I conceded she was talking sense.

'Besides,' she went on, 'there have been developments. All is not as it seems.'

'It rarely is,' I said.

Billy opened a desk drawer and took out something the size of an ashtray. It was wrapped in a handkerchief.

'I had a notion that a crucial piece of evidence was misinterpreted,' said Billy, holding up his finger like Mr Wong. 'I'm ashamed to admit I was the first to jump to a conclusion, which I suspect is precisely what I was supposed to do. The other team know us well. I suggested Steps appropriate the item from the Sheriff's Station so we could take a closer look.'

Billy had sent Witch-Eye on a mission. He'd married women on briefer acquaintance, so it shouldn't have surprised me they'd hit it off. Our introduction to her had been suitably dramatic.

'The lad from the coroner's office, Chet, was easily distracted,' said the secret agent, gesturing hypnotically. 'Doors can be opened. And locked boxes, though that's fiddly. Then, it was a simple matter of abstracting the contraband and spiriting it out of the clutches of the law.'

'Handily, you come from a long line of smugglers,' I said.

She was surprised. 'Joh told you that,' she said. 'It's a joke I made to him. I'm not used to people telling the truth about me. Or accurately reporting the lies I tell them. I really come from a very good, rather dull family. Not so much as a great-great uncle who ran off to sea to be a pirate. I'm the first Swift to disgrace the name with my antics. And the first with my talents.'

She tapped her temple – almost showing her witch-eye.

Steps didn't fidget or seem nervous but was never still. Her thoughts raced ahead. She might be two bright ideas away from speaking in tongues. Joh told us she worried about her brain bursting. Now, I saw why.

Billy put the mystery object on the desk.

'We've drawn our own conclusions,' he said, 'but won't force them on you.'

He encouraged me to sit and make an examination. He offered me an overlarge magnifying glass, which I waved away. I am always nagged by publicists who deem it a shining new idea that an author of mysteries poses with a magnifying glass rather than the usual pipe, typewriter and cocktail.

I unfolded the handkerchief and found a misshapen metal wedge.

I did not want to touch it.

'It's been washed,' said Steps.

'I'd say "I don't know where it's been" but, horribly, I do,' I said.

'Are you sure?' said Billy.

Sometimes – with the simplest, briefest statements – Billy gives the chills. It's that *voice*. The reminder that Billy Pratt is also Boris Ka-a-arloff.

Like a deducing nitwit I picked up the glass and peered at the silver cranial plate. It was irregularly shaped. The edges were ragged, as if torn or nicked. A silversmith's hieroglyphs were scratched through.

'Is this a serial number?' I asked. 'Or a manufacturer's mark?'

I made out part of a name. *Johan Devl…*

'Nice to know that if you mislay your skull it's nametagged so a passing kind stranger can return it to you,' I said.

I was disgusted by this ghoulishness.

A thing that ought not to happen was happening.

'There's more, R.T.,' said Billy. 'Look closer…'

I made out a few other letters, but the plate had been ill-treated... presumably when a shotgun blasted it free of its cosy spot close to Joh Devlin's brain.

... nt... artm... fle C... 93...

The letters were puzzle pieces.

I saw the picture on the box.

Second Place. Interdepartmental Rifle Contest. 1931.

This wasn't surgical silver. This was a shield, prised off a plaque.

I swore. Steps laughed in shock at my gutter language. My face burned with embarrassment.

It *was* that kind of case. A green-jacket job.

Cakes of ice. Blowdart venom. Curare in the fish tank. A body who was not who he seemed.

'Joh's alive,' I said. 'The bastard.'

33

'I didn't think I'd see Blood Bath Bungalow again,' said Steps.

'I assumed I'd never see it at all,' I said. 'Joh drove me all over Laurel Canyon one afternoon, looking for this place. He thought you'd scrambled his brain to make him forget where it was.'

'Nothing to do with me,' she declared. 'But I'm not surprised he said that, it's come up before. Show you can do *some* things most people think are impossible, then people believe you can do *anything*. Such, sadly, is not the case. Or else I'd find a bright new gold coin under my pillow every morning.'

We looked around the yard. The bungalow's concrete foundation was bitter poison. Nothing natural grew within fifty feet of it.

A sheet of wood had recently been tacked up to replace a broken window. Its orange newness emphasised the place's general white-grey tinge. The walls were the same no-colour as the sand.

Billy stood at the edge of the property, back to us, peering into scrub. He turned and I saw how much that simple movement hurt him. His hair was more silver than anything else. He rearranged his wince into a lack of expression. He kept so much to himself.

The bungalow didn't feel haunted. Just neglected.

I knew that was deceptive. In this coal mine, Steps was our canary – she was a wrong thing herself so she knew a wrong place when she came back to it. She made an effort to rein in her jitters. I worried what would happen if she shrieked.

I worried more about moments when her hair fell aside and I could almost see her red eye. If I ever looked into its bloody depth, I'd know too many answers. It'd be my brain erupting. That's how Stephen Swift made me feel. Afraid. Billy was of a different opinion. They had the understanding he had with most women and all cats − a shimmer of trust and delight that would always be a mystery to me. My envy did me no credit.

'I did what Joh and you did,' Steps went on. 'After a year or so, I got idly curious. I'd left a pile of corpses which isn't here now…'

She pointed to a stretch of sand.

'Coyotes,' suggested Billy.

'Nothing came out in the papers. To want to come back here was a ridiculous, foolish thing. A return to the scene of the crime, you know. But I couldn't not try. I started at the drug store. I thought I could get here from there. It's a ten-minute walk, if the place lets you find it. I annoyed local biddies by poking around driveways. I made friends with hermits and their dogs. I went high up and looked down. Nothing. I wondered if the plot was claimed and built over. Can you imagine the consequences of raising a dream home over the unmarked graves of evil clowns? But no, Dear Old BBB just went into hiding.'

With my shoe tip, I kicked something out of the sand − the mouthpiece of a brass instrument, white and crumbling as if it were the knucklebone of a wildcatter who tumbled down the hillside, head cracked open by a business partner, fifty years ago and was never found.

My Packard convertible − the one bought to replace the one Cissy took against − had left fresh tracks over recent tyre marks. I love automobiles, not for themselves but for where they take you. I can't identify a vehicle from tyre treads and paint flakes scraped off when criminals in books drive carelessly.

What was Joh driving in his afterlife? Another Studebaker?

I haven't memorised identification marks of tyre and car companies. That's not Marlowe's method, though many a sleuth is usefully up on such dull subjects for plot convenience. As you know, Watson, I have just completed a monograph on one hundred and fifty distinct types of truss.

Cops keep boring folders of things like tyre treads. No one wants to read about policemen matching car tracks.

Billy rattled the front doorknob.

'Allow me,' said Steps. 'This door and I know each other of old.'

Billy stood aside. She put her hand flat against the lock and nodded so her hair flicked away from her witch-eye for an instant. I went utterly cold, but it passed. Tumblers clicked and she pushed the door open, smirking like a little girl who has delighted Uncle Boris with a newly learned card trick. Billy smiled back at her like Santa Claus with a wood-axe hidden behind his back.

We filed into the bungalow – which was dingy, musty and dark. Boarding up the window hadn't done anything for the atmosphere.

No one was home, but someone had been recently. Supplies in the kitchen. Empty cans and coffee grounds in a garbage pail. Books laid out on a low table like a hand of solitaire. The thick nineteenth-century kind, suitable for long spells holed up away from the world. Anthony Trollope, Henry James, *Middlemarch*. Not a Spicy Mystery or Green Penguin in sight.

'We've missed him,' I said.

Billy picked up *The Princess Casamassima* and flicked the protruding end of a leather bookmark.

'He'll be back to finish this. If Joh had more than an errand to run, he'd have taken his book with him.'

'"First rule of detective work",' I quoted Joh. '"Take a book to read. If you sit doing nothing, people notice. If you're reading, they don't even see you. And you need something to pass the time. Besides, books are cheap and exercise the mind and don't give you a hangover."'

'That only works for men,' said Steps. 'If I sit outside with my nose in *Diana of the Crossways*, it's an open invitation to every clot in town. "Watcha readin', dollface?"'

It didn't take long to search the bungalow and attached garage.

'What is it about here?' I said. 'It's quiet, but so's everywhere in this city – if it even is a city – compared to London or Chicago. You can't see the neighbours and they can't see you.'

'Joh said it's not on maps,' said Steps. 'I went through a newspaper morgue and found a packet of unsolveds in this area. I could tell things were left out of the files. Or removed. I've been to other places like this. A church and a wood in England. A lodge in the Zemplén Mountains. Places not on maps. They have a magnetic pull for people like me. And people like you too – and Joh. You've seen behind the curtain. These places look after us, provisionally. We had to put down breadcrumbs to lead the Sparx Brothers here. Otherwise, we could have stayed hidden indefinitely or until one of us tried to kill the other…'

'… which did eventually happen,' I said.

'I don't know Joh tried to kill me when he put me in the trunk and fixed the car to crash off the pier. If he'd done it to you, it'd have been murder. He knew I might not die.'

'He also knew you *might*.'

She was disposed to be more forgiving than me.

I was coldly furious with my friend. And wounded. I wasn't here for revenge. I was here for an explanation.

'Places like this welcome people like me,' she went on. 'But they're not good for me. They don't save us, they save us for later. It wasn't coyotes, Boris. It was the sand and rocks. This place feeds on carrion. Not just meat. It ate the ghosts too. That's the quiet that rubs you the wrong way. The absence of ghosts. Everywhere in this country is haunted – except places like this, where ghosts don't last long. It's worse than no birds singing.'

We got out of the bungalow. It was cramped for three. We had all banged our shins against the too-low, too-heavy, too-wide table. Steps said it was an evil piece of furniture.

We didn't have long to wait.

A Ford Dodge rolled silently down the driveway. The man at the wheel didn't have Joh's face, exactly. The moustache was gone and his hair was combed forward. He winced as he got out of the car, as if nursing an ulcer. He was sweating through his new suit, no longer comfortable in his own skin. Fair enough – he had made a ghost of himself. And here he was, where ghosts didn't last long.

'How did you find the bungalow?' he asked.

'The same way you did,' said Billy.

'Little Beata,' he said. 'If I were a real murderer, I'd have killed her to cover my tracks.'

'You might not be able to,' said Billy.

'You're too ready to think the best of me, Boris. I've killed more people than you know about.'

'He doesn't mean it like that,' said Steps. 'You could convince yourself to murder an eleven-year-old girl and Boris knows it. What he means is that Beata Sol might not be killable. After the first time, some develop an immunity. Not that you knew that in my case. You went on with your test, thank you very much.'

He grinned and it was Joh's grin on that new face.

With the moustache gone, he showed more teeth – more Lon Chaney than Clark Gable. It was the spectre of Joh's smile.

'I am glad you came through, Witch-Eye,' he said.

'Why her, Joh?' Billy asked. 'Quin, I understand, but why Steps?'

He shrugged and didn't deny the man in the car was Norman Quin.

'What was it Jimmy Whale said? "Part of the ritual". A woman in the water. Every mystery should have one. Ray will tell you about that. He likes a lady in a lake. Besides, she's *wrong* and you know it.'

Steps held her breath and made tight little fists, aligning her thumbs with the seams of her slacks. She concentrated…

Joh felt her invisible touch and looked as if he might be sick.

Steps let her breath go and released him. She pressed a hand to her eye.

'I'm not worth the headache,' said Joh. 'That figures.'

From a purse-sized suede sheath clipped under her jacket in the small of her back, she drew a pearl-gripped Colt .25 automatic – tiny even in her small hand. She walked up to Joh and stuck it against his eye.

'I could shoot you,' she said. 'Just a lead bullet. Thruppence a pop, if that. No worries about my bleeding brain. Here's a footnote you'll appreciate: it wouldn't even be against the law. Because you're already dead.'

Now Joh *was* sick. He'd been through a lot.

Steps didn't shoot him. She stood out of the way as he heaved.

'I could be charged with mutilating a corpse,' she admitted.

Joh finished vomiting and wiped his mouth with a handkerchief.

'You're probably wondering why I've asked you all to meet in the library,' he said. 'You all had a motive to kill Lord Arbuthnot… except you, Reggie, and you *are* Lord Arbuthnot.'

He was the only one who laughed at his joke.

'Did you finish what you set out to?' asked Billy. 'I assume you've come from Home House.'

'Yes, Boris. You're the real detective here. What did I set out to do?'

'Punish Home. The villain in the story, providing we cast you as the hero.'

'You see all, Swami Karloff.'

Joh sat down on a large rock. Being sick put him out of breath. He might not be dead, but he wasn't well either. He pulled himself together and went on.

'Quin had to be stopped,' he said. 'So much of this is his fault. He made the machine that makes the monsters. The world had monsters before the little lightbulb went on over his head. You, Witch-Eye, are a prime example of the breed, conceived well before automation and the production line. Quin removed the accident of birth. With his magic, he could make a freak of anyone. All he needed was funding. Who pays Frankenstein's utilities, eh? Copper wiring isn't cheap. Quin needed a backer with deep pockets, and that meant giving up any say in what was done with his work. Not that he wanted it anyway. He was a particular type of mad. And a big guy. We could wear the same suits. Swap clothes. His hat-size was different, what with his flattened head and all – but that didn't matter. Roughing up my silver shield for rifle shooting and jamming it under his scalp was not among the most pleasant jobs I've ever done, but he was dead at the time. I got a grip on his head with a set of ice-tongs. You'll never guess why I had them…'

'We didn't guess,' I said. 'A clever policeman did. Wedge of ice. On the pedal.'

Joh laughed, then coughed, then got words out. 'I knew you'd *hate* that, Ray.'

'Is that why you did it?'

'And to see whether it'd work. Rigging up the shotgun was a risk too. What if it only took off the top of his head and you saw he didn't have my teeth? I packed his mouth with a little extra powder and shot in a tied-off condom, to give the effect more oomph. How was it?'

'How did you get to Quin?' asked Billy. 'He's not been seen in two years.'

'He was the one that got away that night,' admitted Joh. 'I don't know why I let him leave. We had what we wanted – Beata alive – so I suppose I was in a generous mood. And you wanted to be cured, remember? Only Quin could turn you back into a person. It didn't really hit me until later that he was the perfect puzzle piece. He fit two different pictures... the Home House horror and my homage to *The Big Sleep*. I took him out of one and slotted him into the other. As for finding him, well – I'm a detective, remember. I didn't even need Junior Miss White-Streak or whatever Beata calls herself. Quin was still using his basement workshop at Home House, refining his hellish process. Without Dr Voodoo, he was free to dream up all sorts of new madness. I took a part-time job at the leading supplier of custom electrical equipment in Hollywood and waited for the inevitable call. This would have happened six months ago if he'd run out of vacuum tubes earlier. I delivered a box of tubes and stifled the mad scientist. Killing him once wasn't enough. His eyes opened while I was inserting the silver shield. I banked on his self-improvements stopping short of the ability to grow a new head. He's dead now and the world's a better place.'

'And Junior?' I asked.

Joh looked almost apologetic. And very tired.

'There's a different story. You should see the state of the shrimp. The Pyramid lot is a ghost town. You said he had an army of robot people and a clan of killer hillbillies backing him up... well, they're fighting a war for territory inside the Home Estate now, Bims vee Munros. The Old Man is dying and the banks have put a stop to the oil money. If anyone's in charge, it's Lamia. Junior has lost control of everything, including his own body. All the things he wanted, he took. Height, mental radio waves, immunity to most forms of death. Chick Chang was that extra baked potato – the one he should have left on the plate. He got Chang's flexibility, but it galloped out of control. For all practical purposes, Junior doesn't have any long bones. He's strapped into braces and corsets, but can't stand up. Quin was working on yet more science to fix him, but that hope is gone. I went there today to finish him off. Being dead, I have the perfect alibi. I went over a speech in my head. He was going to die knowing how low he was and how I'd fooled him and everybody else. He would die knowing my name. I had more prepared, but that's the gist of it. I used the elevator behind the picture of Bismarck to get up to the floor of Home House where Junior is kept these days. I crept into his room, the perfect assassin… and saw the mess he'd made of himself. He's not a monster. He's a puddle. With a big red angry eye. I left him to it. How's that for a disappointing finish? The hero finds the villain has defeated himself, and wanders off… a tall, wide ghost. Oh, on the way out, somebody stuck me in the side. They used a sword. Imagine that, Ray. In this day and age. A bloody fucking sword. A Munro took me for a Bim. Or the other way around.'

We could have left him at Blood Bath Bungalow, where sand would slowly pull him under and scrape skin and flesh from his bones. But we didn't.

On the drive to Good Samaritan – the hospital where stars come to die, according to the late Jean Harlow – Joh drifted in and out of consciousness and told us many more things we had no business knowing. He gave solutions to mysteries, mixing up stories from books and films with cases he'd worked or had inside dope on. Solutions out of any context are just mysteries from another angle – if anything, more maddening. Steps sat next to Joh in the back seat, her small hand pressed to his side wound. She was still annoyed with him, but kept up the pressure. It wasn't enough. We took him to the Emergency Room, but they redirected the stretcher to the morgue. Steps went to a restroom to wash her hand.

A tired doctor wanted to question us.

'Who was he, Mr Karloff?' he asked Billy.

'I really don't know,' he said.

'We found him like this, in a garden,' I said. 'He wasn't making a hell of a lot of sense.'

'You did all you could,' said the doctor.

'Yes,' said Billy. 'I believe we did.'

34

The Daughter of Frankenstein and Monkey eyed each other across the sand-pen. Monkey was a strange animal. Only a Karloff would think it suitable for a child. Its arms were too long, its eyes too big. A cowboy hat was sewed to its head. A gift from a fairy godmother. Of course.

Billy and I sat, watching the child. Lamps came on in the garden and lights reflected in the dark water of the pool.

Beata Sol and Stephen Swift were playing cat's cradle.

Steps turned out to be a demon at the game, from school. She had advantages, which she didn't take.

My back hurt as much as I imagined Billy's did. But the gimlet would help with that.

Billy, a martini man, waited till nightfall to drink. I suspected the garden lights were rigged to come on early so he could cheat.

We sat, not together but near each other.

We were too tired and hurt to reflect on the friend we had lost – if we'd ever had him – or the lessons we'd learned – if learning was even possible.

I tasted the gin and lime juice and thought of the picture on the puzzle box. Horror is Mystery with the last chapter torn out. No solution. I'm tempted to forsake Mystery for Horror, but I'm not sure I could bear it. Despite everything I've said, I want to gather in the library and have an explanation laid out. Even if it doesn't make anyone feel better.

Billy, nut-brown in the shade, was inside himself too. That might be a thing to worry about. Monsters lived inside Billy. In his eyes, his voice, his bones that didn't knit the right way. He needed more than a Broadway hit. He needed work… or he needed to work. Billy needed to be Boris and Boris needed to be other people: the Monster, the Mummy, Professor Death Touch, the Man They Could Not Hang. More and more people. With browner skin and whiter hair. He'd stagger on, then act from a wheelchair… death hadn't stopped him and I'd have taken even money death wouldn't prevail in their eventual rematch.

I heard Steps and Beata talking, but couldn't make out their words.

A witch and a wonder. All along, in secret, the heroes of this story. They kept talking, exchanging thread patterns, sharing, and walked out of our sight, into the shadows beyond the willow and the pool and the house. They would make mischief, I was sure. They were beyond me.

Billy and I, two English public school men, drank cocktails. And it got dark.

Afterword and Acknowledgements

William Henry Pratt was born in London in 1887; Raymond Chandler was born in Chicago in 1888. The contemporaries lived close to each other in Dulwich in the early 1900s and Los Angeles from the 1920s to the 1950s… but if they ever met, no one took notes.

There are phantom connections between my imaginary comrades. One book has it that Boris Karloff was a classmate of Chandler's at Dulwich College (the Pratt family lived in Dulwich, but sent Billy away to school – or else he'd have been a day boy like Chandler). The IMDb states that 'The White Carnation' (1954), an episode of the television anthology drama *Climax!* in which Karloff stars, is a Chandler story. It's actually based on a novella by Dorothee Carousso; the confusion seems to stem from the fact that an unrelated episode of the radio series *The Adventures of Philip Marlowe* has the same title (*Climax!* did present a live adaptation of *The Long Good-Bye*, with Dick Powell, a few weeks earlier).

Like any two people in overlapping professions, Karloff and Chandler have many links. Leslie T. White, who had a few of the credits (and some of the biography) I give Joh Devlin, was one of Chandler's models for Philip Marlowe. His involvement as investigator for the DA's office in a 1929 murder-suicide ('the Doheny Case') is the source of Marlowe's backstory of losing a job for insubordination (and explicitly discussed, as 'the Cassidy Case', in *The High Window*). White turned to pulp writing (*The Arson Dick*) and then to screen stories – providing the source for the 1939 Boris Karloff vehicle *The Man They Could Not Hang*.

Among many projects Chandler considered as an alternative to writing more Philip Marlowe books was a collection of fantasy stories; in the event, he only wrote two ('The Bronze Door' was placed in the influential pulp *Unknown*) and they aren't among his best work. Some of the unlikely elements of *Something More Than Night* are from life. A child really did drown in Karloff's swimming pool. Chandler really did train as a fighter pilot. The British Board of Film Censors managed to persuade Hollywood to stop making horror films for a few years in the 1930s. However, this is a work of fiction, not biography. I've taken considerable liberties with Los Angeles history and geography.

Among the books I've consulted are: John Paul Athanasourelis' *Raymond Chandler's Philip Marlowe: The Hard-Boiled Detective Transformed*; Richard Bojarski's *The Films of Bela Lugosi*; Richard Bojarski and Kenneth Beals' *The Films of Boris Karloff*; John Buntin's *L.A. Noir*; Raymond Chandler's *The Notebooks of Raymond Chandler/English Summer: A Gothic Romance* and *The Simple Art of Murder* (and the novels, of course); Raymond Chandler, Owen Hill, Pamela Jackson and Anthony Dean Rizzuto's *The Annotated Big Sleep*; Al Clark's *Raymond Chandler in Hollywood*; Robert Cremer's *Lugosi: The Man Behind the Cape*; James Curtis' *James Whale: A New World of Gods and Monsters*; Barry Day's *The World of Raymond Chandler: In His Own Words*; William K. Everson's *The Detective in Film*, *Classics of the Horror Film* and *More Classics of the Horror Film*; Judith Freeman's *The Long Embrace: Raymond Chandler and the Woman He Loved*; Otto Friedrich's *City of Nets: A Portrait of Hollywood in the 1940s*; Neal Gabler's *An Empire of Their Own*; Mark Gatiss' *James Whale*; Denis Gifford's *Karloff: The Man, the Monster, the Movies*; Miriam Gross' *The World of Raymond Chandler*; Woody Haut's *Heartbreak and Vine: The Fate of Hardboiled Writers in Hollywood*; Charles Higham and Joel Greenberg's *Hollywood in the Forties*; Tom Hiney's *Raymond Chandler*; Tom Hiney and Frank MacShane's *The Raymond Chandler Papers: Selected Letters and Non-Fiction 1909–1959*; Stephen Jacobs' *Boris Karloff: More Than a Monster*; Paul M. Jensen's *Boris Karloff and His Films*; Tom Johnson's *Censored Screams: The British Ban on Hollywood Horror in the Thirties*; Arthur Lennig's *The Immortal Count: The Life and Films of Bela Lugosi*; Herb Lester Associates' *The Raymond Chandler Map of Los Angeles*; Cynthia Lindsay's

Dear Boris: The Life of William Henry Pratt a.k.a. Boris Karloff; William Luhr's *Raymond Chandler and Film*; Frank MacShane's *The Life of Raymond Chandler*; Gregory William Mank's *Bela Lugosi and Boris Karloff: The Expanded Story of a Haunting Collaboration, Hollywood Cauldron: Thirteen Horror Films from the Genre's Golden Age, The Very Witching Time of Night: Dark Alleys of Classic Horror Cinema, Hollywood's Hellfire Club: The Misadventures of John Barrymore, W.C. Fields, Errol Flynn and 'the Bundy Drive Boys'* and *It's Alive!: The Classic Cinema Saga of Frankenstein*; Sean McCann's *Gumshoe America: Hard-Boiled Crime Fiction and the Rise and Fall of New Deal Liberalism*; Sheridan Morley's *Tales from the Hollywood Raj: The British Film Colony On Screen and Off*; Robert F. Moss' *Raymond Chandler: A Literary Reference*; Francis M. Nevins Jr's *Cornell Woolrich: First You Dream, Then You Die*; William F. Nolan's *The Black Mask Boys: Masters in the Hard-Boiled School of Detective Fiction* and *Dashiell Hammett: A Life at the Edge*; Scott Allen Nollen's *Boris Karloff: A Critical Account of His Screen, Stage, Radio, Television and Recording Work* and *Boris Karloff: A Gentleman's Life*; Scott Allen Nollen and Yuyun Yuningsih Nollen's *Karloff and the East: Asian, Indian, Middle Eastern and Oceanian Characters and Subjects in His Screen Career*; Richard Rayner's *A Bright and Guilty Place*; Gary D. Rhodes and Richard Sheffield's *Bela Lugosi: Dreams and Nightmares*; Elias Savada and David J. Skal's *Dark Carnival: The Secret World of Tod Browning, Hollywood's Master of the Macabre*; Gordon B. Shriver's *Boris Karloff: The Man Remembered*; Alain Silver and Elizabeth Ward's *Film Noir: An Encyclopedic Reference to the American Style*; David J. Skal's *Hollywood Gothic: The Tangled Web of* Dracula *from Novel to Stage to Screen* and *The Monster Show: A Cultural History of Horror*; Jerry Speir's *Raymond Chandler* (the only critical analysis that doesn't skate over the simply astonishing supernatural element of Chapter 30 of *The Little Sister*); Jean Stein's *West of Eden*; Gary J. and Susan Svehla's *Midnight Marquee Actors Series: Boris Karloff*; Jon Tuska's *In Manors and Alleys: A Casebook on the American Detective Film*; Peter Underwood's *Karloff*; Elizabeth Ward and Alain Silver's *Raymond Chandler's Los Angeles*; Tom Weaver, Michael and John Brunas' *Universal Horrors: The Studio's Classic Films, 1931–1946*; Toby Widdicombe's *A Reader's Guide to Raymond Chandler*; Tom Williams' *A Mysterious Something in the Light: Raymond Chandler: A Life*; Donald C. Willis' *Chronology of Classic Horror Films: The 1930s*; Peter Wolfe's *Something More*

Than Night: The Case of Raymond Chandler (which I came across after I'd settled on my title). If I listed all the films and TV shows that have fed into this book, we'd be here for several months.

This is a standalone – where many of my recent books have been part of series or interconnected to a great degree. However, Ariadne appears in *Bad Dreams* (Titan Books) and 'Cold Snap' (in *The Man From the Diogenes Club*, Titan Books) and Stephen Swift/Miss Steps is an alumna of *The Haunting of Drearcliff Grange School* (Titan Books). Later periods in the history of Pyramid Pictures are covered in *The Quorum* (Titan Books) and *Where the Bodies Are Buried* (Alchemy Press).

Personal thanks are due to Peter Atkins, Prano Bailey-Bond, Nicolas Barbano, David Barraclough, Anne Billson, Randy and Sara Broecker, Simret Cheema-Innis, Dave and Lou Elsey, Dennis Etchison, Jo Fletcher, Barry Forshaw, Christopher Fowler, Christopher Frayling, Neil Gaiman, Lydia Gittins, Charles L. Grant, Antony Harwood, Sean Hogan, Kevin Jackson, Alan Jones, Stephen Jones, Grace Ker, Mark Kermode, Yung Kha, Leslie Klinger, Rachel Knightley, Paul McAuley, Maura McHugh, Marc Morris, Helen Mullane, Jerome Newman, Sasha Newman, Sarah Pinborough, Jon Robertson, Russell Schechter, David J. Schow, Mari Scimemi, Robert Shearman, William Sheehan, Adam Simon, Emily Smith, Peter Straub, Cath Trechman and all at Titan, Matt Turner, Stephen Volk, Karl Edward Wagner, Chris Wicking, Douglas E. Winter and my parents.

Kim Newman, London, 2021

ABOUT THE AUTHOR

Kim Newman is an award-winning writer, critic, journalist and broadcaster who lives in London. He is a contributing editor to the UK film magazine *Empire*, and writes its popular monthly segment, 'Kim Newman's Video Dungeon'. He also writes for assorted publications including *Video Watchdog* ('The Perfectionist's Guide to Fantastic Video'), *The Guardian* and *Sight & Sound*. He makes frequent appearances on radio and TV, and is the chief writer of the BBC TV series *Mark Kermode's Secrets of Cinema*.

He has won many awards, including the Bram Stoker, International Horror Guild, Prix Ozone, British Fantasy and British Science Fiction Awards, and been nominated for the Hugo, World Fantasy and James Herbert Awards. Kim also writes non-fiction books focused on popular culture, film and television, including a comprehensive overview of the horror film industry, *Nightmare Movies: Forty Years of Fear* (Bloomsbury).

You can keep up-to-date with Kim's events and writing via his website johnnyalucard.com. Find him on Twitter @annodracula.

For more fantastic fiction, author events,
exclusive excerpts, competitions, limited editions and more

VISIT OUR WEBSITE
titanbooks.com

LIKE US ON FACEBOOK
facebook.com/titanbooks

FOLLOW US ON TWITTER AND INSTAGRAM
@TitanBooks

EMAIL US
readerfeedback@titanemail.com